Share Me
Touch Me
Tie Me

One Night with Sole Regret
Anthology
Volume Two

Olivia Cunning

CONTENTS

Other books by Olivia Cunning

Sinners on Tour Series

Backstage Pass
Rock Hard
Hot Ticket
Wicked Beat
Double Time

One Night with Sole Regret Series

Try Me
Tempt Me
Take Me
Share Me
Touch Me
Tie Me
Tell Me

Coming Soon:
Tease Me

SHARE ME

One Night with Sole Regret 0.5
A Prequel

OLIVIA
CUNNING

Share Me
One Night with Sole Regret #0

Dear reader,

Before you cozy up with Sole Regret on a cold Christmas Eve night, remember that this is a prequel which takes place six months before the rest of the series. The men are not yet in relationships. No hearts were broken in the making of this erotic tale.

With ♥,
Olivia Cunning

CHAPTER ONE

The heavy bass guitar line that rumbled from the auditorium's loud speakers caused Lindsey's entire body to throb. She'd been to several Sole Regret concerts at stadiums, so was painfully aware that their local auditorium didn't do Owen Mitchell's skill with four-strings any justice. The intimacy of the small venue made up for the inferior sound system, however. She'd never managed to get this close to the stage before. The anticipation of seeing the five members of Sole Regret from the second row had her rocketing out of her worn velveteen theater seat and leaning against the curved wooden chair back in front of her. She didn't even care that the move earned her several annoyed looks and a loudly hissed, "Sit down!" from someone behind her.

Sit down? At a Sole Regret concert? Was it even possible to remain seated when they were on stage?

Lindsey's best friend, Vanessa, grabbed her wrist and forced her to sit in her seat again. "Your boss is here," she whispered harshly. "Try to control yourself."

That was easier said than done. Lindsey squirmed on the edge of her seat. Hearing Owen play, but not yet being able to see him was hell on her girly bits.

When Lindsey caught her first glimpse of the bassist as he strolled casually across the creaky wooden stage, fingering thick strings with a steady cadence, she almost swallowed her tongue. The man was devastatingly gorgeous. His light brown hair was styled into a playful sweep that brushed his forehead. She couldn't see the color of his eyes from this distance, but knew from staring at his pictures for hours on end that they were a hypnotic, brilliant blue. Her gaze moved from his perfect profile, down his neck to his body. Her hands clenched as she fought her need to launch herself on stage, tackle him to the ground, and explore every inch of his hard physique. Tonight Owen wore a tight navy blue T-shirt that clung to his nicely muscled chest and shoulders. A set of silver dog tags swayed between his cut pectoral muscles. As he continued his intro, she became fascinated with the masterful movement of his fingers over the thick strings of his bass guitar. Why were guitarists so fucking hot? It simply wasn't fair.

Lindsey groaned aloud as she imagined all the things that those strong, skillful fingers could do to her body. What she wouldn't give to be that man's fret board.

"Girl," Vanessa said, "you're seriously crackin' a moisty right now, aren't you?"

Lindsey's panties were decidedly wet. She couldn't deny it. "He's just so..." Her entire body shuddered as she couldn't find words sensual enough to describe the man.

Vanessa rolled her eyes. "Puh-lease. He's cute and all, but I don't think the mere sight of a man can inspire a big O."

Lindsey released a breathless chuckle. "You'd be wrong, Nessi. I'm halfway there already."

Vanessa turned her head in the opposite direction. "T. M. I," she said under her breath.

When the drummer, Gabe Banner, entered the song with a heavy, building progression of bass drum thuds, Lindsey's heart thumped to match his rhythm. She could just make out the red tips of Gabe's mohawk behind the drum kit and the occasional flailing drumstick as he pounded out a wicked progression of beats on the skins. As the tempo built, Owen turned at center stage and rushed forward, halting at the front edge as the rest of the band came into view and joined the song. Adrenaline surged through Lindsey's body. She was such a groupie for these guys. If her prudish boss, who was seated several seats to Lindsey's left, hadn't been sending her disapproving looks from behind her thick rimmed glasses, Lindsey would have already shed her bra and tossed it on stage. Fortunately, Lindsey still had enough self-control to keep herself from flashing her bare breasts at the band. Maybe.

Owen held a special appeal for Lindsey, but there was something about the band's vocalist, Shade Silverton, that demanded attention. He knew how to work a crowd. Shade encouraged the audience to its feet by holding one hand at waist level and lifting it up and down. Lindsey knew they wouldn't be able to keep to their seats long. Even the stodgiest of attendees—who normally wouldn't conceive of attending a metal concert—obediently rose from their chairs. It was easier for Lindsey to enjoy herself when the two rather large men beside her blocked her from Mrs. Weston's ever critical glare of death. She was grateful to Mrs. Weston for hiring her to work at her investment firm, but the woman seemed to think she was in charge of every aspect of Lindsey's life—both inside and outside the confines of the office. It was a good thing Mrs. Weston wasn't a mind reader. She'd have been utterly scandalized by the X-rated thoughts racing through Lindsey's mind as she watched Shade sing the chorus of Sole Regret's hit song, "Darker". Tall, dark and mysterious behind his pair of aviator sunglasses, Shade Silverton gave off an energy of raw, sexual power. What was it about the man that made her want to drop to her knees and suck his cock down her throat?

"Now that man makes my pussy quake," Vanessa said, her eyes glued to Shade, who completely dominated the stage in his unquestionable self-confidence. "I just want to…"

"Suck him off?"

Vanessa laughed. "Oh yeah. I'm on my knees already."

The rhythm guitarist, Kellen Jamison, was whispering into Owen's ear. They were both laughing at their lead singer and lead guitarist who seemed to be competing for crowd adulation. Lindsey worshipped the entire band. They didn't need to fight for her attention. But those two—Owen and Kellen—made her entire body hum with pent up desire.

Where Owen had light eyes and hair, Kellen was a bronze god with shoulder length black hair and almost black eyes that could stare a person into a coma. She praised all deities that the man never wore a shirt on stage. His long, lean body was filled out perfectly with tight muscles beneath taut, tanned skin. Tattoos decorated both arms in colorful sleeves. There was an intensity about Kellen Jamison that she couldn't ignore. She doubted any woman could ignore it. And when he and Owen stood side-by-side, there was nothing more inspiring on the planet. That's why the pair of them were at the top of her fuck-it list. She and Vanessa had constructed their fuck-it lists a few months before when complaining about their concurrent lack of boyfriends.

The list was comprised of the three men on the planet she most wanted to fuck and if given the opportunity she was given a free pass to slut it up. It didn't matter if she was currently involved in a relationship, married, eight months pregnant, or had become a cloistered nun. If the man in question was on her fuck-it list, it didn't count against her. Vanessa said so and her friend had never steered her wrong. *Much.*

Number one on Lindsey's list was Owen Mitchell, and number two was standing right beside him vying for the top position, Kellen Jamison. Luckily, Lindsey wasn't in a relationship or pregnant. And her current sexual dry spell might make her feel like a nun some days, but she hadn't taken vows of chastity. If only she could get close to them. Gain their attention. Offer her body willingly. Then maybe she could have at least one of the three men who made her drool like a recent root-canal-recipient.

In the middle of the song, the lead guitarist of the band, Adam Taylor, moved to the front of the stage to play the solo. His dark hair was thick and cut in a shaggy style that drew attention to his face. He had the most sensual lips Lindsey had ever seen on a man. And a collection of chains around his neck and at his hip that she wouldn't mind getting tangled up in. Adam's lightning-fast fingers flew over electric guitar strings, churning up images of fingertips brushing against Lindsey's highly attentive body parts. He was about to kick David Beckham from the number three spot of her fuck-it list. Unless Shade wanted the honor.

"God, I'm so horny," Lindsey growled under her breath.

"I can help you out with that," Joe, who worked at her office, said in her ear.

It was like a cold bucket of water over her head. He hadn't been sitting beside her at the start of the concert. He must have weaseled his way through the standing crowd when she hadn't been paying attention. Lindsey shoved him out of her personal space and changed places with Vanessa so she'd have a best friend buffer that no man was likely to cross. The look Vanessa gave Joe—her dark eyes wide, eyebrows threatening her hair line, lips pursed in a harsh line—had him staring at his shoes and running a finger under his collar.

"That's what I thought," Vanessa said and churned her neck for added affect. "Lindsey done told you she wasn't interested. Bye now."

Lindsey had told him. Many times. She'd thought he'd finally given up. Joe hadn't bothered her in weeks. She must be flinging out pheromones like a bitch a heat or something. It wasn't as if she could help it. The members of Sole Regret lit her on fire, but she'd rather sate her lust with her battery operated boyfriend than with Joseph Bainbridge. She was so not attracted to him and never would be. There was nothing wrong with him, but there was nothing *right* about him either.

Joe sidled away and Lindsey returned her attention to the stage. The song came to an end and the crowd cheered, the riotous noise echoing through the auditorium like waves of an angry sea. Shade moved to the center of the stage and spoke to the audience.

"Thanks for coming to our benefit concert on this cold Christmas eve."

The crowd cheered.

"Ellie Carlisle wanted to be here tonight to thank you for helping her family out with her medical expenses. Unfortunately, after a strong dose of radiation therapy yesterday, they wouldn't clear her to leave the hospital. So tonight she's getting a lot of rest so she can wake up tomorrow and see what Santa brings a perfect angel for Christmas."

It might have been the sound system, but Shade's voice sounded a little raw as he talked about the Ellie, a five-year-old girl who was fighting for her life in a local hospital. The town had come together several times to try to help her family out, but pancake breakfasts and silent auctions for afghans only raised so much money. A Sole Regret concert, on the other hand, brought in folks and their money for hundreds of miles.

"Her father is a big fan of ours," Shade continued, "so when he asked us to come out and help them raise some money to help his little girl fight for her life, we couldn't say no."

"Be sure to buy a T-shirt on your way out," Kellen Jamison said in the deepest, sexiest voice Lindsey had ever heard. How could she possibly think about anything but the sound of that voice in her ear when it echoed around her from every direction? "All of the profits from merch sales go to helping the Carlisle family too."

Owen stepped up to his microphone. "You know what? *Fuck* cancer," he bellowed, thrusting a fist in the air.

He soon had the entire auditorium chanting, "fuck cancer, fuck cancer, fuck cancer" over and over again. Even stick-up-her-ass Mrs. Weston was yelling it along with the others.

When the crowd settled again, Shade said, "Thanks for coming out tonight and supporting Ellie's cause. Now we're going to rock your faces off."

Shade started the next song with a battle cry that caused a thrill to streak down Lindsey's spine. Hard to believe this group of bad ass men would be willing to give up their Christmas Eve to help out a little girl they didn't even know. Lindsey was surprised that tears were prickling at the backs of her eyes as she thought of their selfless act. Suddenly, the members of Sole Regret seemed more substantial to her than walking aphrodisiacs. She wondered what kind of men they were. Maybe she could find a way to get to know them. And not just so she could check two tasks off her fuck-it list. She had a powerful need to thank them for being awesome.

CHAPTER TWO

Owen glanced around the tour bus, looking from one grim face to another. You'd think his band mates had just come from a funeral, not from a kick-ass benefit concert that would likely save a little girl's life. Owen shifted his Santa hat to the cocked and ready position and reached for the black garbage bag of decorations his mom had sent along with him when she'd learned he wouldn't be able to attend their family's annual Christmas Eve celebration. His brother wouldn't be attending either—Chad had been deployed to Afghanistan in August—so Owen was somewhat glad that he wouldn't have to sit across the table from an empty chair and wonder if his brother was dodging bullets while he was dodging Grandma Ginny's questions about when he was going to settle down and make pretty babies for her to spoil. Though he missed his family as much as the next guy—yes, even Grandma Ginny—Owen wasn't going to lounge here on the bus and sulk all the way from Wherever-the-hell-they-were, Idaho to Wherever-the-hell-they-were-going, Montana. He was going to make the best of their situation and not let his bummed out band mates ruin his perpetual good time.

Owen's prime target was Kelly. Not because the rhythm guitarist was the most depressed—that honor went to their vocalist, Shade—but because Owen needed a partner in Christmas cheer and Kelly always had his back. He didn't even have to ask Kelly for his assistance. They'd formed a pact of mutual mischief long ago.

Owen dug the snot-green, artificial Christmas tree out of the sack and set it on the end table between the pair of recliners where the band's drummer, Gabe, sat reading of all things and Shade sat glowering at nothing.

Straightening the branches of the tree into something slightly more pine shaped, Owen hummed under his breath and then broke out into song. *"O Christmas tree, O Christmas tree, how plastic are thy branches.*"

Shade lifted his head and one dark eyebrow rose above the frame of his aviator sunglasses. "Do you have to be obnoxious right now?"

"Why," Owen said, "is it interrupting your sulking?"

"As a matter of fact, it is." Shade reached for one branch of the hideously fake tree and bent it into a wider angle.

"And why are you sulking? It's Christmas Eve. Are you afraid you'll get nothing but lumps of coal in your stocking?" Owen dove into the sack of decorations and pulled out several strands of lights. His family was of the opinion that it was not possible to have too many lights on a holiday tree. When fully lit, the Mitchell Family Christmas Tree could probably be seen from Mars.

"Julie only has one third Christmas," Shade said. Arranging another branch, and then dropping his hand when Gabe turned his attention from his book to watch him try to perfect the unperfectable.

"But she doesn't have to," Owen said. "You can give her another Christmas when we get home next week. She'd love that. I'll even wear my Santa hat and shimmy down the chimney to put a smile on her face."

Shade crossed his arms over his chest, his scowl deepening. "It's not the same."

"At least it isn't my fault he's sulking this time," Adam said. The lead guitarist had his acoustic guitar out and was quietly strumming some riff he was working on for the next Sole Regret album.

"I'm not sulking," Shade said.

"Looks like sulking to me," Kelly said. He rose from the sofa to stand beside Owen. He inserted a long, tattooed arm into the sack and dug out a red rope garland. He lifted his eyebrows at Owen, before flicking his eyes at Shade pointedly.

Owen tried not to grin and give their silently exchanged plan away, but it wasn't easy. He nodded ever-so-slightly.

"You're the one who signed us up to play a benefit concert on Christmas Eve in the first place," Adam said to Shade. "You don't even know that kid."

Owen winced. Did the two of them really need to pick a fight tonight? Surely they could find it in themselves to put aside their differences on Christmas Eve.

"I didn't have to fucking *know* the kid, Adam. She has leukemia.

Her family has no insurance, no jobs, no money to pay for her chemotherapy. A few hours out of our busy schedules gives her a chance to see her sixth birthday. Do you always have to be such a selfish prick?"

"I had absolutely no problem with doing the benefit concert. It's not like I have better plans for Christmas anyway and believe it or fucking not, I do care. But you sitting there looking like your dog just died after you made the decision to do the concert in the first place is pissing me off. I'm not gonna lie," Adam said.

"There's a first time for everything," Shade grumbled.

"All I want for Christmas is a pair of ball gags to shut you both up," Gabe said and lifted his book until all that was visible of his head was his foot-high red and black mohawk. "I'm trying to concentrate over here."

"Ball gags?" Kelly nodded. "I can probably fulfill that wish." He started to wrap the rope garland in long loops from hand to elbow. Owen knew Kelly could produce two ball gags in a matter of minutes. He also knew exactly where Kelly kept his secret stash of kinky implements if he ever felt the need to borrow something. Recently Kelly had taken up a new hobby—tying knots. It was a perfectly innocent hobby for most people, but not so much for Kelly.

Carefully untangling a strand of lights, Owen pretended to be intensely interested in their drummer, Gabe, to keep attention off Kelly, who was fashioning a loose noose out of one end of the garland. The dragon tattoos on the shaven parts of Gabe's scalp stood in complete contradiction to the colossal, decidedly boring, book in his hands. "What are you reading about?" Owen asked, as if he didn't already know he didn't give a shit.

Gabe pushed his reading glasses up his nose and grinned deviously. "Friction."

"And how to reduce it with proper lubrication?" Owen asked. Gabe was the only person he knew who tried to apply the laws of physics to sex.

"You don't want to reduce the friction too much," Gabe said. "You want it slick and wet, but not too juicy."

"I disagree," Shade said with a grin. "The juicier, the better." At least his sulking had diminished.

"Yeah," Kelly agreed. "I like it dripping wet so I can lick it clean."

"The conversation on this bus always turns to pussy," Adam said.

"There's nothing better to talk about, is there?" Owen asked.

"No," his band mates said in unison. They all laughed at the one thing they *always* agreed on.

"And there's definitely nothing better to think about," Gabe said, "so you all need to shut up. I'm *thinking*."

"Who needs this worse, Owen?" Kelly said. "Shade or Gabe?" He was now prepared to act on his plan.

"Personally, I think they both need it," Owen said.

"Need what?" Shade asked.

"Looks like Shade volunteered to be first."

"First at what?"

Kelly moved fast—*like ninja*—and Owen stepped back out of his way, awaiting his opening to assist him.

Shade was bigger than Kelly, but Kelly had the element of surprise on his side. Before Shade could even react to Kelly jumping on him, Kelly had the garland of red rope around Shade's forearms, binding them together from wrists to elbows. Shade might have been able to break free of the garland given time, but the instant Kelly stepped away, Owen went after him with strands of lights, wrapping several strands around Shade's upper arms and chest, crisscrossed in a web of unbreakable art. Kelly had taught Owen all he knew about shibari and Owen had taught Kelly all he knew about calf-roping. Their combination of skill, teamwork and speed ensured that Shade wasn't going anywhere until they decided to free his arms.

As was common for Shade, once he got over his recent, perpetual dour mood—his divorce was to blame—he was happy to join in on their fun and play along. He laughed as a second strand of lights was used to secure him to the chair around the waist. He was in danger of hyperventilating with laughter when Kelly found some sparkly tinsel in the sack and wrapped it around his neck several times.

"Now you have no choice but to be in the Christmas spirit," Owen said. "No more bah humbug out of you."

Chuckling at the spectacle the coolest member of the band made trussed up like an abomination of a Christmas tree, Adam added to the festivities by strumming Christmas carols on his guitar. "*On the first day of Christmas my buddies gave to me, decorations on a Shade tree.*"

"Shut up," Shade yelled, but he was snickering too intermittently for anyone to take him seriously.

Kelly found a gaudy tree topper in the sack. Before he could add it to their *tree*, Gabe snatched the tinsel-trimmed star out of Kelly's hand and set it on the pinnacle of their Shade tree. Gabe wrapped the light cord under Shade's chin and then around the star to hold it somewhat upright atop Shade's head. Apparently, Gabe had given up on reading his *The Physics of Fucking and Friction* book or whatever it was called. None of them could resist messing with Shade. He worked so hard at being cool onstage and in public. Sometimes they had to remind him that he could still act like a kid and have some stupid fun when there wasn't anyone important watching.

Gabe found a package of blue glass bulbs in Owen's sack of Christmas cheer and dangled them from the strand of lights near Shade's crotch.

"You did not just give me blue balls, Force," Shade said with the deep, commanding voice that made their road crew scramble for their lives.

Owen laughed.

Adam added to his song, *"On the second day of Christmas my buddies gave to me, two blue balls and decorations on a Shade tree."*

"I will give you blue balls when I punch you in them," Shade said.

"You shouldn't threaten people when you can't fight back," Adam said.

"Plug him in," Owen said, hoping Shade and Adam didn't get into more than a pissing contest.

Kelly located the power cord and plugged it into the outlet behind his chair. Gabe plugged the star into the end of one of the light strands.

When the multicolored lights began to flash and cast brilliant specks of lights all over their tattooed, buffed-out, sunglasses-wearing lead singer, they all burst out laughing. Owen grabbed his cellphone out of his pocket. "Okay, this is going on Facebook."

"Don't you dare," Shade said, his smile fading and mouth opening in exasperation.

Oh, Owen dared. He even gave the candid picture a caption—*All Dressed for Christmas with No Place to Go.*

"Hey, guys?" their driver, Tex, called from the front of the bus. "We're going to have to pull over soon. The snow is coming down so heavily I can't see the road. We better park until it lets up or a snowplow blows through."

Snow! Oh yes. A perfect addition to Shade's festive attire.

"Sweet," Owen said, grinning at Kelly who quickly caught on to his newest nefarious plan.

"Shade tied down," Kelly said.

"Plus snow," Owen said.

"Equals projectile fun," Gabe said.

"You guys wouldn't fucking dare," Shade said, trying to lean out of the chair, but finding that while he'd been tethered mostly by complacency at first, he now had no choice but to stay put.

Owen grinned and straightened his Santa hat. "Wouldn't we?"

CHAPTER THREE

Lindsey squinted at the dark road ahead. The wipers scraped rhythmically across her field of vision to keep the thick snow at bay, but she was fixated on the glowing red taillights of her favorite band's tour bus. Storm or no storm, she wasn't giving up now. It had been a stroke of luck that Sole Regret's bus had turned out in front of her car as she pulled out of the auditorium after the benefit concert. Instead of taking the proper road toward home, she had continued following them eastward out of town, through the wilderness and up into the mountains. It was pitch black out here in the middle of nowhere and what had started out as a few flurries was now becoming a blizzard.

"It's getting really bad out," Vanessa said from the passenger seat. "We should have gone home instead of following their bus. The farther we go, the worse this shit gets. Can you even see the road?"

"Yeah, I'm used to driving in the snow. And they have to stop sometime," Lindsey said. "I want to meet them and thank them for helping out the Carlisle family."

Vanessa chuckled. "Bullshit, girl. You want to bone them."

Lindsey bit her lip. "Yeah, I do—all five of them—but just meeting them will be orgasmic enough."

Her engine roared as her front tires lost their grip and spun in the slick, wet snow. The car skidded slightly, before finding a better patch of pavement and righting itself.

Vanessa was clinging to the dashboard with long red nails. "Girl, you and your horny vagina are gonna get us both killed."

"It's fine," Lindsey said and laughed. "Well the car is fine. The vagina is still horny. God, those guys were hot on stage." She shuddered at the mere memory of their blatant sexuality. Just watching them perform made her wet and achy between her legs.

"That ain't no lie," Vanessa said. "Too bad they's all white boys."

"Once you go white, you think it's all right." She shrugged.

Vanessa laughed. "Girl, you are too much."

"You know you love me," Lindsey said. They'd been best friends since elementary school and twenty years later, still did everything together. Well, almost everything.

"You're lucky I don't jack your car and get us off this damned mountain," Vanessa said.

"You are all talk, Nessi. You know you want to meet them too."

"Maybe a little." Lindsey could hear the smile in Vanessa's voice. They liked to tease each other and pretend they were as different in attitude as they were in looks, but they really did have almost everything in common—including their taste in music and men.

The right blinker on the bus ahead began to flash. Lindsey saw the sign for a scenic turn out and turned on her blinker to follow them. Finally, her chance. Assuming they didn't think she was bat shit crazy for following them over seventy miles through a blizzard and falling at their feet to dry hump their legs.

The bus pulled to a stop and Lindsey parked behind it. She left the car running, the wipers working extra hard to keep the fluffy white flakes off the windshield. Lindsey's heart thudded faster and faster at the thought of getting out of her car, knocking on the tour bus door, and offering her body to anyone who would have it.

"You're going to chicken out, aren't you?" Vanessa said.

"No, I'm just thinking about how to approach them."

She could barely make out Vanessa's rolling eyes in glow of the dash lights. "Whatever. You say *I'm* all talk. You might *think* you've got the guts to raid their tour bus for cock, but sweetie, I know you. You ain't a ho."

"I'm three times the ho you are, beotch."

Vanessa sniggered. "So what you're saying is you're a ho ho ho?"

Lindsey laughed. "Yeah, when it comes to any member of Sole Regret I'm a ho ho ho." Once she got tickled she couldn't stop laughing for several minutes. She had to wipe tears out of her eyes with her thumbs. "God, we're corny. No wonder we can't snag decent boyfriends."

"What are they doing?" Vanessa asked, her attention now outside the car.

Lindsey's head swiveled and her heart almost stopped. The band's bassist, Owen had just launched himself out of the open bus door and onto the back of rhythm guitarist, Kellen. Kellen, who was inexplicably shirtless in a snow storm, flipped him into a snow bank and scooped up a handful of snow. He began to pack the fluffy flakes into a large ball. Owen retrieved his Santa hat from the snow and dove for cover behind the front of the bus. A battery of snow balls flew from Owen's hiding place and pummeled Kellen in the chest.

She caught a glimpse of a red and black mohawk just above Owen's hat.

"Gabe too?"

"Adam is sneaking around back," Vanessa said, pointing at the dark shadow at the rear corner of the bus. "The only one missing is the hottest of the bunch."

"Shade?"

"I'm sure he's too cool for this childish bullshit." Vanessa opened her car door. "All right, chicken shit, you brought us all the way up here to make complete asses out of ourselves, we might as well go talk to them."

"What? Wait! We don't have to. Let's just go home."

But Vanessa had already climbed out of the car and had closed the door. Lindsey took a deep breath, shut off her car, pocketed the keys and then surged into the uncharted snowstorm. Vanessa always gave her courage. With Vanessa at her side, Lindsey could have slain dragons, swam the Mediterranean Sea, or even talked to a rock star.

Vanessa was already shaking hands with the lead guitarist of the band, Adam. He'd been the closest target, but Lindsey really wanted Owen. Or Kellen. Or Owen *and* Kellen. So she headed into the epic snowball battle. Heart thundering in her chest, stomach a bit queasy, knees quaking, Lindsey stepped up behind Kellen and was about to tap him on the shoulder which was decorated with an amazingly realistic tattoo of a rearing black stallion, when he suddenly ducked. Fast—*like ninja.*

A barrage of snow balls walloped Lindsey in the face, neck and chest, catching her so off-guard that she just stood there and took every last one of them at full force.

"Oh shit," someone said. "Why did you duck, Kelly?"

A very large, wonderfully strong hand began to brush snow out of her face. "Are you okay?"

She was suddenly looking up into the gorgeous, strong-featured face of Kellen Jamison. "I am now," she whispered.

CHAPTER FOUR

Kellen winced at the welt under the attractive young woman's right eye. "That had to hurt," he said, gently rubbing the mark with his thumb.

"Um," she said.

He smiled. He could tell she knew who he was. She had that star-struck look on her face he knew so well. "I'm Kellen," he said.

"Yes."

"And you would be?" She had the biggest blue eyes he'd ever encountered. He was a sucker for that wide-eyed innocent look and if her eyes got any wider, they'd likely fall right out of her head.

"Um." She blinked and then scowled as if suffering from amnesia.

"Lindsey!" another woman ran over and began to fling snow from Lindsey's sweater. It hit Kellen in the chest, but she didn't seem to notice. "Oh my God, girl, what were you thinking? You could have been killed."

"I don't think snowballs are lethal," Kellen said. The look Lindsey's friend gave him could have melted the snow off the entire mountain.

"What kind of crazy person pelts a poor, defenseless woman with snowballs?" the woman said, flinging snow from Lindsey's chest like a weapon now.

Defenseless? The only thing that got Kellen's blood pumping hotter than that big-eyed innocent look was a defenseless woman. Tied down. Spread wide. Pussy open and exposed for him to feast upon. Kellen's mouth went dry as images of their guest spread across the tour bus bed entered his thoughts. Would her eyes get wider when she came or would she squeeze them closed? Damn, he hadn't been the least bit horny two minutes ago and now his cock was fully erect and straining against his zipper.

It couldn't be helped. Lindsey was exactly his type.

Merry Christmas to me.

Owen jogged over and assisted Lindsey's hot-tempered friend in cleaning the snow off of his accidental target. Rather than this helping Lindsey, Owen's hands on her made her shake uncontrollably.

"You must be freezing," he said. "Do you want to come inside and get dried off? We have towels. And I think we have hot chocolate." Owen turned toward the open bus door. "Tex! Make some fucking hot chocolate!"

Lindsey's friend nodded toward the car behind the bus. "We should probably get—" Her words were halted when Lindsey covered the woman's mouth with one hand.

"Yes, thank you," Lindsey said. "I'm liable to freeze to death if I don't get out of this wet sweater." Lindsey glanced back at the small car. Besides the spot of emerald green on the hood over the hot engine, the entire car was already white with a coating of snow. "And I don't think it's safe to drive in this weather."

She blinked up at Kellen, snowflakes clinging to her long lashes and Kellen decided he would have ripped the engine out of her car and tossed it off a cliff to keep her from leaving. And if she wanted Owen, well, he never had a problem with sharing. As long as he got to eat out the juicy delight between her thighs before Owen got down to business, Kellen would be satisfied. He just wanted to taste her. Every woman tasted different and he was a connoisseur of pussy. He couldn't get enough. He could lick it and suck it and kiss it and nibble on it for hours. Or until she begged for mercy.

Owen took Lindsey by the hand and yanked her toward the bus, breaking the spell she had over Kellen. "Let's go get you warmed up," Owen said.

"Yes," Kellen murmured to himself. "Let's do that."

CHAPTER FIVE

Oh God. Oh God. Oh God. Oh God. Those were the only words that were capable of echoing through Lindsey's mind at the moment. She was really here. *Oh God.* And Kellen really had touched her cheek and looked at her as if he wanted to fuck her brains out. *Oh God.* And Owen really was holding her hand and leading her up the stairs of Sole Regret's tour bus. *Oh God.* And Shade really was tied to a recliner, flashing with multicolored lights, and looking out of sorts. "Oh God!" she yelled and burst out laughing. Lindsey covered her mouth with one hand as she tried to comprehend what she was seeing. Well, whoever had turned Shade Silverton into a Shibari bondage tree was one hundred percent hilarious. And the pair of blue Christmas balls hanging at crotch level? Priceless.

"We have guests," Owen said to Shade as he led Lindsey past him. "Make yourself presentable."

"Fucking untie me," Shade demanded, straining bulging muscles against the intricately crisscrossed strands of lights. A garland rope bound his arms together from wrist to elbow.

"Don't you dare untie him," some man she didn't recognize said from the kitchen area. He was scooping hot chocolate mix into over half-a-dozen mugs. "He needs to get his sense of humor back. That bitch, Tina, sure did a number on him."

"Un-fucking-tie me," Shade growled between clenched teeth.

"Oh my," Vanessa said from the bus entryway. "Heavens."

She probably thought seeing Shade tied to a chair was hot regardless of the flashing multicolored lights and the slightly askew star on his head.

Owen paused at the end of the corridor and opened an oddly narrow door. He pulled out a towel and handed it to Lindsey. She patted at the snow around her neck. It was starting to melt and trickle down between her breasts, but the chill had nothing to do with how hard her nipples were. The musky, sweet scent of Owen's cologne and the ornery look in his blue eyes was one hundred percent responsible for that.

A hand settled at the base of her spine and she didn't have to look over her shoulder to know Kellen was standing directly behind her. That gentle, but commanding touch was one hundred percent responsible for the pulsating throb in her panties.

"Would you like to change your sweater?" Kellen's deep, quiet voice made Lindsey's eyelids flutter.

She'd like to rip her sweater off and light it on fire was what she'd like to do. That would ensure she'd have a good excuse to be half naked in the presence of strangers. Except they didn't feel like strangers. She felt as if she knew the entire band. And she definitely wanted to get to know them better. Especially the man directly in front of her and the one behind her, who made her feel like the giddiest piece of cheese to be melted between two hot pieces of toasted bread.

"Lindsey?" Kellen's voice brought her out of her fantasy.

And he knew her name. Squeeee! "Um, yeah," she said, hoping her voice didn't belay her enthusiasm to get naked. "Do you have something I can change into?" *Nothing, for example.*

Owen opened a door at the end of the corridor and entered a bedroom. Lindsey followed him without hesitation. When the door closed behind her, she didn't need to turn around to know Kellen had entered the room too. She could feel his presence behind her.

"You were following us, weren't you?" Owen asked.

Her face flamed. She supposed it was pretty obvious. "My friend Vanessa and I were at the benefit concert and we ended up behind your bus. When we saw you pull over we thought maybe we could meet you." It wasn't a lie.

"And how did you imagine that meeting would go?" Kellen asked. Dear lord, the man had a delicious voice. He was nice to look at too, but the mere timber of his voice was enough to separate her from her panties. She just wanted to obey him, even though he hadn't asked her to do anything.

"Well I didn't think I was going to get attacked with snowballs," she said and laughed. Her laughter died when Kellen's hard body brushed against her from behind. Her breath stalled in her throat and her eyelids fluttered closed. Her body naturally leaned against his. He was so solid. Hard. His skin cool. And she felt the huge ridge of his arousal against her ass. Oh dear God.

"Kelly has a thing for your type," Owen said.

"Yes, I do," Kellen's warm breath stirred a few damp strands of hair against her ear and her knees went weak.

One of Kellen's strong hands splayed over her belly to keep her from sliding to the floor.

"What do you want to do to her, Kelly?"

"I want to tie her down and eat her pussy. After I'm finished and she doesn't think it's possible to come another time, I want to watch you fuck her, Owen, and prove her wrong." His hand slid up her ribcage, stopping just short of cupping her breast. "Is that what you had in mind when you followed us up the mountain, Lindsey?"

She tried to draw air, but she was so lightheaded, her brain wasn't functioning correctly. Did he just say that? Or was she suffering from hypothermia in her car and hallucinating? That bulge against her ass felt real enough.

Kellen nipped her ear and her entire body jerked. "Answer my question."

She opened her eyes. Owen was gnawing on his bottom lip awaiting her answer.

"No," she whispered, her voice trembling.

Owen scrunched his face in disappointment and then glanced over her head to look at Kellen. Kellen took a step back and Lindsey reached behind her to tug him against her again.

"That's far more than I bargained for," she said, "but I want you. Both of you. To do exactly that. And more."

"You're sure?" Kellen said, his deep voice doing all sorts of tingly things to her spine.

"Yes."

"Once I have you tied, you won't be able to escape."

Her heart thundered in her chest. What would they do to her while she was utterly defenseless? She couldn't wait to find out. "I understand."

"Kellen knows what he's doing. He'll stop if you're in distress," Owen said.

"You'll be at my mercy," Kellen whispered. "I'll be able to do whatever I want to do to you."

She groaned.

"Does knowing that make you afraid?" Kellen asked. "Are you trembling because you're scared that we'll hurt you?"

"No," she whispered. "I'm trembling because I'm so turned on that I'm about to come."

Kellen's cool hands slid under her sweater and lifted it to expose her belly. "Make her quiver, Owen."

Owen bent forward to kiss and suckle and nibble on her belly. Sparks of pleasure danced across her skin. She was instantly reduced to quivering. The man had an amazing mouth.

Lindsey's sweater passed over her head and then Kellen's strong hands covered her breasts. She cursed her bra, wanting his cool palms against her bare nipples. They strained against the cups of her undergarment, seeking the pleasure offered by his hands.

A knock sounded on the door. Lindsey's entire body jerked.

"Hey, Kellen," a voice with a strong Texan accent said on the opposite side of the closed door.

"We'll take a rain check on that hot chocolate, Tex," Kellen said.

"That's not the problem. This chick out here is trying to *help* Shade by untying him and I think she's somehow managed to cut off the circulation to his dick and one of his spare legs."

Kellen released a heavy sigh and dropped his hands. Lindsey stifled a sob of protest as his warmth faded from her back. "I'll be back in a minute," he said. "Owen, I want her ready for me when I get back."

"She'll be ready."

Lindsey wasn't sure what either of them meant, but hoped making her ready involved more of Owen's mouth on her skin.

The door closed as Kellen left the room.

Owen grinned at her and she couldn't help but smile back. The man was cute and sexy and evoked a feeling of joy whenever she looked at him. She was pretty sure it wasn't due to the Santa hat he still wore, but she was definitely feeling some Christmas cheer.

"So what did Kellen mean about getting me ready?" Because she was already horny—her sex hot and swollen and seeping. She'd been horny since Owen had entered the stage back in the auditorium a few hours earlier. And as each member of Sole Regret had entered the stage on cue, the intensity of her desire had increased exponentially.

"Once Kellen has a game plan, he doesn't fuck around. He wants you naked, wet and limbered up."

Her jaw dropped and he laughed.

"How flexible are you, Lindsey?" he asked.

Kellen might be the one who seemed to be in control, but she was starting to believe that Owen was the truly wicked one.

CHAPTER SIX

Kellen cringed when he saw what Shade's little helper had done to the intricate weave of knots he and Owen had made to bind their band's vocalist. It had been enough of a challenge to make the pattern work with the little lights getting in the way, but if a person didn't know what they were doing when restraining or releasing a person, a lot of damage could be done to a person's soft tissues. Luckily, Shade was more hard than soft, but there was no way Kellen would be able to undo this mess. The art of untying was almost as practiced as the precise sequence required to bind someone properly.

"Did you make this mess?" Kellen asked the lovely black girl who was ringing her hands together and almost in tears.

"Don't take time to lay blame, just get me out of this," Shade said.

Kellen disconnected the plug from the wall. "Gabe, get me a knife. We're going to have to cut him—"

Before Kellen could finish the thought, the young woman launched herself across Shade's lap and was practically hissing at Kellen to back off. He would have laughed at her attempts to protect such a big, muscular guy, if Shade wasn't in danger of blood clots and tissue damage from lack of blood flow.

"I'll help him," the woman insisted. "Don't cut him."

"He's not going to cut Shade," Gabe said, with an exasperated shake of his head. "He's going to cut the wires. Now get back, Kellen needs to see what he's doing."

Gabe placed a knife in Kellen's hand and as soon as Shade's female savior moved out of the way, Kellen looked for the snag in Owen's original design. He severed one cord near Shade's left shoulder and another just beneath his sternum. The wires loosened and Shade took a relieved breath. Kellen handed the knife back to Gabe. "You could have cut him free."

"How was I supposed to know that?" Gabe said.

"Aren't you the brains of this operation?"

"Not about stuff like that."

"Well, see if you can get his arms loose," Kellen said to Gabe. He didn't want to waste any more time out here with these guys when he had exactly what he wanted in the tour bus's bedroom. And she was alone with his charmer of a best friend "Just start at the last knot and work your way backwards. Think of it as a puzzle."

"I'm not untying him," Gabe said. "You untie him."

"I'll do it," Lindsey's friend offered.

"What's your name?" Kellen asked her.

"Vanessa."

"Vanessa, do you promise you'll be patient and not jerk on the ropes as you untie them?"

"I promise not to jerk any ropes," she said, "but there is something in his pants I'd like to jerk." She burst out laughing when Kellen's eyes opened wide in astonishment.

"I'll leave you to that then," Kellen said. "He has been really cranky. Maybe blowing his load in front of a crowd will cheer him up."

Vanessa's jaw dropped. Kellen decided she wasn't used to men countering her outlandish statements with outlandish statements of their own.

Her dark-eyed gaze flittered to the bedroom door. "You be good to my Lindsey," she said.

"Oh, I'll be good to her," Kellen promised, "but don't be alarmed when she screams."

CHAPTER SEVEN

As soon as Kellen had left to save Shade from his rescuer, Owen shut the door and turned toward Lindsey. He knew Kellen could be a bit intimidating if one didn't know him. Owen was sort of glad he'd been drawn away for a moment so he could speak to Lindsey on a more personal level. He wanted her to be able to relax. Her elevated breathing rate led him to believe she was far more nervous than she was letting on. He knew from experience how exciting it could be to no-holds-barred fuck a stranger, but it could also be awkward and a little frightening. Especially in a situation where one woman mixed with two rowdy guys.

"I don't want you to feel like you have to do anything you don't want to do," Owen said, scraping the Santa hat off his head and trying to smooth his hair into place. He'd forgotten he was still wearing the festive accessory. And there was nothing Santa-like about the gifts he was about to bestow on sweet Lindsey.

"Are you kidding?" she said, with a laugh. "You have no ideas what sort of dirty thoughts I was having while watching you on stage."

"Yeah, well, were just a bunch of regular guys, who happen to make music that a lot of people enjoy."

"You're also all fuck-hot."

Owen smiled. He never tired of the ego boosts. Sometimes he wondered how he'd ever lived without them before fame had knocked at his door. "You're fuck-hot too, Lindsey."

She inched closer, until she was standing directly in front of him. Her succulent breasts were inches from brushing his chest. He was well aware that Kellen had instructed him to get her ready and was probably anticipating her to be naked and massaged into submission by the time he got back, but Owen needed a few minutes to get to know a girl before he stripped her of her clothes and got down to business. Just a minute. "So, Lindsey, what do you do for a living?"

"Investment banker. Well I just started, actually. First job out of college. I kind of suck at it so far. I don't have good instincts when it comes to picking stocks."

"I figured with a body like that you'd be a model."

She lifted an eyebrow at him. So she wasn't buying his lines. Moving on to plan B. "Why did you follow the tour bus tonight?"

"I have a fuck-it list. You've always been at the very top of it."

"A fuck-it list?"

"Yeah, my friend, Vanessa, and I made a list of the top three guys we'd most want to fuck. There's you and Kellen, and some soccer player who I can't recall the name of at the moment."

"I'm ahead of Kelly on your list? I know how much he drives the girls wild."

Her cheeks went pink. "He's a close second. Almost a tie."

"Well, just so you know what to expect, Kellen won't fuck you," Owen said.

Lindsey's brows drew together. "Isn't that why he invited me here?"

Owen shook his head. "No. I'm not saying he won't touch you, but when it comes to the actual act, he never goes that far." Or he hadn't since Sara had gone. All these girls who got Kelly's blood pumping at first sight had Sara's same blue-eyed, innocent look about them. Owen wondered if Kelly realized how transparent he was.

Lindsey's jaw dropped. "He's a virgin?"

Owen laughed. "Well, I wouldn't call him a virgin. He's very discriminate with where he puts his cock." He grinned at her. "But not his tongue."

Lindsey shuddered.

"I, on the other hand, will totally fuck you."

"Thank God." She giggled. "So are we going to do this now or wait for Kellen?"

"It's a long ritual for him, you know. I thought maybe you'd like to talk for a bit. He gets rather intense."

"It's a ritual?" She glanced at the door. "Like, what do you mean? I'm not a virgin if he's thinking I'd make a good sacrifice to the gods."

Owen shook his head. "No, nothing like that. He thinks sex is some sort of spiritual connection with the earth. That the body is the gateway to a person's soul. That the right connection between two people during sex can become a religious experience. That's why he only goes so far. It's far more personal for him than most guys." Which was partially the truth and partially a way to protect his friend's still wounded heart from questions Lindsey might ask. "Do you think it's weird?" Because if this woman was critical of Kelly in any way, Owen would show her to her snow-covered car in an instant.

"Not weird," she said. "Interesting. So if a woman was to get him to fuck her..."

"I think he'd love her forever." Owen chuckled. "Don't get your hopes up, doll. He's not ready for love just yet. We will make you feel wonderful though."

Lindsey placed her palms flat on his chest and looked up at him. "I'm ready for whatever you have in store for me."

He circled her back with both arms and tugged her forward to hold her loosely against his chest. Her entire body was quaking. As he'd suspected, she was far more confident in words than in actions. Owen stroked her back gently and brushed gentle kisses against her hairline. When Kellen returned there would be no time for tenderness and while what he did with Kellen made his balls throb just thinking about it, he liked a little connection with his bed partners before he got naked. Lindsey rubbed her face against his neck, her lips finding the pulse point in his throat. She placed a wet, tugging kiss on that sensitive spot and the sensation shot straight to his balls. Okay, he admitted it. It really didn't take much to seduce him.

Lindsey's soft breasts warmed against his chest.

"Can I take your shirt off?" she asked. "I want to feel your bare skin against mine." She didn't take her eyes off his as she reached for the hem of his T-shirt. "Owen," she whispered. She removed his shirt and released an excited breath as her gaze roamed his inked chest and the barbells in each nipple. "Your body is even hotter than I imagined."

Owen grinned. Unlike Kellen, he wore a shirt most of the time, but he worked out just as hard as his friend to keep his muscles tone and cut for the ladies.

Lindsey plastered herself to his chest. The heat of her skin permeated his thoughts until all he could think about was warm, soft, female flesh and being buried balls-deep inside it. He flattened both palms over her back and tugged her against him so that her full breasts pressed into his chest. Kellen was going to flip out when he saw how endowed she was. He would have turned her body into a work of art no matter her shape or size, but they both liked the way ropes looked when they dug into a full pair of tits.

What was taking Kellen so long anyway?

Owen began to massage Lindsey's back, kneading her muscles until she melted like butter against him. "I think Kellen wants to help me with this part," Owen said.

"With what part?" Lindsey lifted her head to look at him. She looked tranquil. She wouldn't be looking that way for much longer.

"Preparing your body."

"Oh my body has been prepared since the moment you walked out on stage tonight, Owen."

He chuckled low in his throat. "I honestly doubt that."

The door handle turned and Owen took a step back, drawing Lindsey deeper into the room with him. Kellen smiled when he closed the door behind him.

CHAPTER EIGHT

Lindsey had surely died and gone to heaven. Not only was she half naked in the arms of one Owen Mitchell, Kellen Jamison had just entered the room and was looking at her as if she was his Thanksgiving feast. It was sweet of Owen to try to make her feel comfortable with whatever was about to happen between them, but he honestly didn't have to. She had been serious about him being at the top of her fuck-it list. And Kellen really had always been second, but now that they were all together in the bedroom of their tour bus, she realized how shortsighted she'd been. Both of them at once. That was the true pinnacle of sexual delight. Would she survive the mere thought of being with them both? Even if Kellen did have an unusual way of thinking about sex, she was more than willing to see what his ritual entailed.

"I thought you'd be farther along by now," Kellen said. He moved to stand behind Lindsey. When the cool skin of his hard chest pressed against her bare back, she didn't bother stifling her moan of bliss. Sandwiched between the two hottest men she'd ever dared fantasize about, Lindsey was sure she really had died and gone to heaven.

Kellen's hands moved between Lindsey's belly and Owen's. He stroked her skin with long, strong fingers. The same fingers he used to make six-strings sing made her skin tingle with excitement. Owen's hands slid over her back with equal care.

Kellen's hands cupped her breasts and she shuddered. "Beautiful," he whispered. "I can't wait to create art with your body."

"Hmm?" she murmured.

Kellen and Owen moved away at the same instant and she had to take a step to keep from sliding to the floor.

"Take your pants off for us, Lindsey," Kellen said.

Without the slightest hesitation, she unfastened her jeans and slid them off. Struggling to remove her boots and socks while standing, she decided she must be quite a turn-off at the moment as she gracelessly got naked.

"She has the perfect shape for this," Owen said.

"I could tell from the start," Kellen said.

She stood before them in her bra and panties and fought the urge to cover herself. They were both assessing her with keen scrutiny.

"Diamond weave?" Owen asked Kellen.

"Except for her breasts and her ass. We're going to cage them."

"What are you talking about?" Lindsey asked.

"You said you were okay with being tied," Kellen said. "You haven't changed your mind have you?"

She glanced at Owen, who was smiling at her warmly, and then turned to look at Kellen, who was far more intense. He was almost animalistic in the way he looked at her. "No, I haven't changed my mind."

"It won't hurt," Owen said.

"I'm not afraid." A bit confused, yes. Hornier than a desert toad, yes. But not afraid. "Should I take off my underwear?" she asked. Though her thighs were quaking at the thought of being entirely naked, entirely exposed before two men she idolized, her voice was surprisingly steady.

"Owen will take care of that for you," Kellen said. "Get the oil," he said to Owen.

"Which one?"

Kellen surprised her by surrounding her in and embrace, which was now quite warm. He inhaled deeply. "Honeysuckle," he said. "You smell amazing," he whispered to her as Owen started rattling around in a cabinet on the other side of the room. "I can't wait to taste your cum."

Lindsey shuddered at the thought of this man with his head between her thighs. She wanted to fist his long, silky hair in both hands and rock her pussy against his face. And she wanted Owen to thrust into her mouth so she could suck him while Kellen ate her out. She wasn't sure if they were up for suggestions, so she just clung to the thought and Kellen's hard chest until Owen returned and unfastened her bra with a practiced flick.

Lindsey moaned as Owen's hands reached around her and began to rub oil into the skin of her belly. He started the sensitive flesh just above the waistband of her panties and worked his way up, fingers rubbing in small circles, thumbs massaging more deeply into her flesh. An instant later Kellen dumped some of the sweet smelling oil on his hands and standing before her reached around her to rub the oil into the flesh of her lower back. They worked their way upward—both thorough, both meticulous, both gentle in their muscle-loosening technique. Owen took two more handfuls of oil and covered her breasts, massaging them in slow circles. She was tempted to lean back against his chest, but Kellen's hands were working her back just beneath her shoulder blades and she didn't want to interrupt the dual assault on her senses. She couldn't even open her eyes to look at the magnificent specimen of a man before her. She could only concentrate on the sensation of their hands turning her muscles into delighted pools of relaxation.

"She has beautiful breasts," Owen whispered. His breath stirred her hair and though his body wasn't pressed against her back, she could feel the warmth of his skin behind her.

"They are beautiful," Kellen said. "Every inch of her is beautiful."

Lindsey wanted to deny it. She'd been carrying around a few extra pounds recently and felt decidedly plump most days.

"The give of her flesh will look beautiful in your ropes," Owen said.

So they had noticed she wasn't rail thin.

"I'm getting hard just thinking about it."

Owen's hands slipped under the curves of her breasts and lifted them. "We're going to have to devise a way to keep these pretty pink nipples hard."

Something warm and wet slid over the surface of one straining tip of her breast. Lindsey's eyes flipped open and her mouth dropped open in wonder. She glanced down to find Kellen licking her nipple as if trying to capture the last bit of pudding at the bottom of a parfait glass.

Owen caressed her breast.

Kellen rubbed his lips over its tip.

Oh God.

She lifted her arms and threaded her fingers through Kellen's shoulder length hair. It felt like silk against her fingers.

He tilted his head so he could look up at her while his tongue laved her tender nipple. His eyes were so dark, they were almost black in this lighting. His stare drew her in until she couldn't tear her gaze away.

"We definitely need to keep them hard," Kellen said. "So pretty when they're hard." He flicked her other nipple with his tongue and her entire body jerked. "We'll have to set up the rings."

She had no idea what he meant, but rings, ropes, whatever. She wanted every experience these two could offer her body.

Kellen gave her nipple a sharp nip with his teeth before kneeling before her on the floor. After collecting more oil from the bottle on the dresser, he began to massage it into her thighs. His forehead rested against her lower belly and he inhaled deeply through his nose. "God, baby, I can already smell your excitement." He nudged her thighs farther apart, hands working oil into the insides of her legs.

"Do you want me?" Kellen asked.

"Yes."

"And Owen?"

"Yes. Both of you."

"Are you wet?"

"Oh yes," she whispered, her pussy quaking with excitement.

"I bet you're sweet," he whispered. "Are you sweet, Lindsey? Have you ever tasted yourself?"

"You can't taste her until she's ready," Owen interrupted.

"That's why I asked you to prepare her for me, Owen," he said. "What were you doing while I was out untying Shade."

"Talking."

Kellen snorted. "Figures."

"I'm ready," Lindsey insisted. Staring down at the top of Kellen's head, his breath hot against her lower belly, his shoulders broad and bronzed and decorated with colorful tattoos that extended down both arms in beautiful sleeves, Lindsey was more than ready. Her juices had already saturated her panties and were wetting her thighs.

"Not even," Kellen said. "But we'll work quickly."

Owen massaged oil into her neck and shoulders. She wasn't sure how she was still standing. He shifted her back to rest against him while he massaged her arms and as Kellen, who was kneeling at her feet, rubbed oil into her lower legs. He continued to inhale deeply and released hot gasping breaths that penetrated her panties. Lord, just that sensation was enough to send her spiraling into nirvana.

"Maybe I should work the bottom half, bro. I think you're about to lose control."

"Lindsey," Kellen said calmly. "Go lie on the bed."

Owen released the hand he was massaging so thoroughly and stepped away. Lindsey didn't even consider questioning Kellen, much less disobeying.

"Remove all the bedding except the fitted sheet," Kellen added. "Wait for us."

She did what he instructed, tossing the powder blue covers on the floor. She spread out on the bed and watched Kellen and Owen explore a tall stack of drawers that were built into one wall. "Blue?" Kellen said as he pulled open a drawer. "Like her eyes?"

Owen pushed the drawer shut. "It's Christmas Eve. Let's do something more festive tonight."

"Red and green?"

He nodded. "And gold."

Kellen glanced over his shoulder at Lindsey. "She'll look spectacular in gold."

She didn't know if she should thank them for the complement, since she wasn't sure why they were discussing colors. Kellen pulled out several lengths of green and red colored rope and dropped them on the mattress next to Lindsey.

"This is your last opportunity to back out, Lindsey," Kellen said.

Her heart skipped a beat. She glanced at Owen who was rolling his eyes at Kellen. She was pretty sure he mouthed, *Mr. Drama*. She remembered Owen telling her that Kellen would stop if she asked. He was just trying to add a certain edge to her experience.

"I don't want to back out," she said. "I can't wait to find out what you're going to do to me."

They got to work. They started by forming a mesh out of the red ropes, tying knots to form a circular pattern that very much reminded Lindsey of a dream catcher, with quarter-sized hole at the center. She had no idea what they planned to do with it until Kellen fit it over her left breast and carefully tightened it so that she'd never been more conscious of her own flesh. Her skin was divided into diamond shaped sections by the ropes. Her nipple protruded through the hole in the center of the design. Owen lowered his head to flick his tongue over the small bud. It pebbled beneath his attention as pleasure radiated out in all directions. Kellen cinched the ropes tighter.

Her breath exploded from her lungs as her breast experienced a million simultaneous sensations, centered on the tongue flicking against its tip.

"Owen," she groaned.

He lifted his head and grinned at her. "There's more."

Soon Kellen had both of her breasts bound in the ropes and Owen had both of her nipples straining for attention.

They paused to admire her body. "Lovely," Kellen said breathlessly. "Arms to sides. I don't want them to block my view of her gorgeous tits."

Lindsey was eased into sitting position. Her arms were soon securely fastened from shoulder to elbow against her sides. The tension of the rope was all concentrated at the center of her lower back as another length of rope was stretched across her shoulders. They'd tied golden rings into the rope every few inches along both sides. She glanced up at the ceiling looking for hooks. "What are the rings for?"

"We aren't going to use them to suspend you," Kellen said. "You'll see what they're for soon."

They eased her onto her back again and even though her hands and legs were free, she wouldn't have been able to fight them off if she needed to. Something about being so utterly defenseless was exciting and terrifying at the same time. Her heart rate had doubled and she couldn't seem to find enough air. She fought the sensation of suffocation as the room seemed to shrink and the ceiling closed in on her.

"Are you okay?" Owen asked. He leaned into her line of sight and brushed her hair from her hot cheeks. The walls receded again as her attention diverted to Owen's concerned eyes. "If you have a panic attack we can cut you free in an instant."

"And mess up all the beautiful knots you've tied?" She smiled, forcing herself not to pant too excessively. She honestly didn't want them to stop. She liked the way the ropes pressed into her skin. They made her aware of her body. She loved it. Being confined was sort of a head trip, but she would endure.

Kellen's hands on the top elastic of her panties caused her legs to reflexively close.

"If you close your thighs to me, I'm going to spank you," Kellen said.

She was tempted to push him and squeeze her thighs together so that he would spank her, but her thighs had other ideas and immediately went slack. He slowly tugged her panties down her thighs and tossed them aside. Kellen worked on her left leg, and Owen carefully mirrored Kellen's collection of knots on her right. They bound her legs so that they were bent at the knee and hip—slightly more severe than fetal position. They worked hard to stretch her into a position she didn't know she was capable of attaining. They massaged her muscles and flexed and straightened her joints until it didn't pull painfully to have her legs bound with her heels against the backs of her thighs and her legs wide open. She did feel incredibly exposed as there was no way she could possibly close her legs even an inch.

The pair of gorgeous men stepped away and she struggled to keep her trembling muscles from collapsing.

"Let the ropes hold you, Lindsey," Kellen said gently. "Don't fight them."

"Think of it like a hammock," Owen suggested.

She didn't fight the ropes for long because she didn't have the strength to do so. As soon as she went slack, the ropes supported her weight entirely and she suddenly wished all those rings they had worked into their design would be used to suspend her. She also wished there was a mirror on the ceiling so she could see how she appeared from their vantage point. Lindsey had never felt more beautiful—as if her body was a cherished work of art. She wanted to be put on display. Her limbs felt wonderfully supported by the ropes as if they were holding her in a comforting embrace. In a cocoon of pleasure and pressure, her muscles had been stretched to their limits as if she were doing some rope-assisted yoga. There was only the slightest hint of ache in her muscles.

"I feel..." She sucked a rapturous breath into her lungs. "Amazing."

Kellen smiled. She wasn't sure if she'd seen him smile before. Owen constantly smiled, but Kellen seemed to reserve them for special occasions.

"We're going to turn you over. Owen won't let you fall." With her face in Owen's lap, her knees in the mattress and her rear end pointing up to the ceiling, she was treated to the most sensual massage of her life. Kellen's huge hands squeezed the globes of her ass until her back entrance was quivering and she was whimpering to be entered.

"Oh," she whispered desperately.

"Try something from Gabe's stash," Owen said.

She rubbed her face over his lap, wishing he'd removed his pants so she could take him into her mouth. She hadn't known what to expect when tied, but being rendered helpless made her want to please this man. And that man. Both men. Yet she couldn't. She just had to wait until they did with her as they wanted.

Kellen moved from the bed.

"Owen," she whispered. "Let me suck your cock."

He stroked her hair. "I can't let it out yet. I have a long while to wait before I get my turn."

"You don't have to wait," she assured him.

Something cold and slippery popped into her ass. Her core clenched at the unexpected intrusion and she shuddered in ecstasy. "Oh!"

She couldn't see what Kellen was doing, but she felt the ropes slide and press against the skin of her rump. Whatever he'd put inside her ass was driving her crazy with need.

"Are you almost finished?" she whispered. "I'm on fire."

"God, your ass looks amazing," Owen said. He released his hold on her upper body and she struggled not to tip to the side. He grabbed her ass in both hands and rubbed her cheeks together, making her acutely aware of all the ropes pressing into her skin and pulling at that amazing object in her ass. It only penetrated her an inch, but the shape of it aroused her like nothing in her experience. The way it teased her tight hole made her pussy spasm with unfulfilled need.

"Now for Kelly's added touch," Owen whispered. He sounded oddly proud of his friend.

They turned Lindsey onto her back again and Owen slid away since the ropes easily held her body in a stable position when she was face up. Kellen took a rope of gold satin and tied a knot in it. He then slid one end of the rope through the collection of rings that were projecting upward around the periphery of her torso. He centered the knot directly over her nipple and continued to thread the rope's end through more loops. When the rope passed over her other nipple, he tied a second knot and continued threading rope through rings on the opposite side of her body. When he was finished, a bit of knotted rope rubbed against each nipple. It drove her nuts. He moved to kneel between her thighs and took one end of each rope in either hand and tugged them back and forth. The rope slid easily through the rings and rubbed those distracting knots against Lindsey's straining nipples until her back arched involuntarily. She pulled against her bindings for a moment before going slack. The pleasure radiating out from her nipples coursed in all directions, following the paths of the ropes, blossoming between them. She was near orgasm already.

"Do you like anal pleasure, Lindsey?" Kellen asked. "Would you like a little tug on that plug I put in your ass? It has a loop I can thread the rope through."

The only word that really registered was pleasure. And she wanted more of it. Her body begged for more. "Yes," she gasped.

She couldn't see what the hell Kellen was doing between her thighs, but she felt a tug at her ass as he threaded a rope through something down there too. Her pussy was swollen and achy and dripping. Her clit was so excited it was driving her mad. The tug inside her ass had her shuddering in unfulfilled spasms. They waited until she'd settled again before tugging each end of the rope near her hips, which pulled the plug inside her puckered hole just enough to drive her insane. Her pussy clenched with a less than satisfying orgasm.

"Oh please," she begged. She needed to come much harder than that to be satisfied.

"Almost, Lindsey," Kellen promised gently. "You're almost ready."

He carefully tied the free ends of the knotted ropes to each of her wrists, and then secured those at her hips as well.

"You're in charge of pleasuring your nipples and ass," Kellen told her. He showed her that the slightest movement of her lower arms simultaneously rubbed the knotted ropes against her tender nipples and tugged at the plug inside her quivering hole. She couldn't stimulate one without pleasing the other, and she was perfectly okay with pleasing herself.

"Oh God," she gasped, getting the hang of the movement and moving her wrists in an alternating pattern to stimulate herself until another orgasm was teasing her pussy. Oh God, she was going to explode. She needed fucked and badly. "Please fuck me. Please. Please."

"I think you've outdone yourself this time, Kelly," Owen said.

They joined her on the bed. Owen at her head. Kellen down there. She lifted her head to look at Kellen. He was gazing down at her fully exposed pussy with hunger in his dark eyes. Oh God. She rubbed the knots against her nipples and tugged at her ass faster. She needed to come. Needed to come. Needed. Needed. Now. Oh. Could she come from this kind of stimulation? She was close. So close.

"I'm going to kiss your mouth to try to keep you from getting too loud," Owen said. "Okay?"

She nodded. *Do whatever you want to me*, she thought. *Anything. Just do something.* Owen leaned over her head to take her lips upside down in a long, leisurely kiss. He pulled away gently and whispered, "Kelly's going to make you come real soon. Don't work so hard. Relax, honey."

She watched Kellen tie his long hair back with a leather tie. He stretched out on his belly between her wide open thighs, and then Owen blocked her view by kissing her again. Lord the man had a strong and sensual mouth. She wouldn't mind him taking all that hot, achy flesh between her thighs in a kiss like this.

Warm breath stole across her swollen pussy. She shuddered and called out against Owen's persistent lips. He kissed her more deeply, his tongue teasing hers. His fingers began to trace patterns on the bare flesh of her upper arms between the braids of rope.

A warm, soft tongue traced the empty opening between her thighs and she almost shoot straight off the mattress.

Owen trailed open mouthed kisses along her jaw. "Easy," he whispered. "He'll take your edge off soon."

She whimpered when Kellen began to slowly and methodically trace her entrance with gentle swirls of his tongue. Her hips buckled. She fought the ropes holding her legs open, wanting so badly to press her heels into Kellen's back and writhe her sex against his face, but she was helpless to move.

"I need fucked," she said. "I need fucked." She couldn't believe the words were escaping her lips, nor how much she meant them.

"Kelly, have mercy on her," Owen said.

Kellen's little evil chuckle did nothing to ease her mind. His tongue brushed her clit and her entire body strained for release. She could feel his breath against her, but damned if he didn't touch her to send her flying over the edge. He waited until her body relaxed before he tongued her clenching pussy—in and out—with a slow, maddening rhythm. It made her want to be filled with a big, thick cock, but kept orgasm just out of reach.

Owen claimed her mouth again. "Concentrate on me," he said against her mouth. "I'll fuck you when he's finished. It's what you want isn't it?"

"Y-yes. Please. Owen, I need it."

"Shh, let him taste you. Do you feel good?"

She nodded, feeling as if she might burst into tears. She did feel good. Every inch of her flesh was aware. It was overwhelming for her to be so aware of her body. Not just her sensitive lips, clinging desperately to Owen's as he continued to kiss her. Not just her nipples and ass which she continued to stimulate intermittently with tugs of the silken ropes in each hand. Not just the maddening things Kellen was doing to her pussy. Every inch of her was either aware of the ropes or lack of ropes. The braided cords were exerting enough pressure that she couldn't ignore them. The sensation never went away.

Kellen suckled her clit and she went taut, straining to come. God, she needed release, but he pulled away and waited until she went limp before lapping at her center again.

Okay, she was going to die if she didn't have an orgasm soon. But she didn't die. Kellen just continued to pull her closer to the edge and she was sure she'd breech it the next time. He showed her just how wrong she was. Owen kissed her leisurely until she became so distraught that she couldn't catch her breath. He lifted his head to glare at his friend.

"For fuck's sake, Kelly, give her one," Owen said as he stroked her heated cheeks with cool fingertips. "Shit, dude, I think she's having another panic attack."

She heard Kellen's deep voice from down below. "I'll let her fly if you're willing to wait until I can bring her up again before you fuck her."

"I'll wait. I'm fine."

Kellen's mouth latched onto Lindsey's clit and he sucked, working his tongue against the sensitive bud until she sobbed, expecting him to pull away at the last moment. But he didn't. This time. This time, he let her shatter.

Lindsey screamed as her body quaked with release. Her ass clenched at something small and solid; her pussy clenched at devastating emptiness. Oh how she wanted filled. Wanted it even more than the intense orgasm turning her into a writhing, bucking creature of instinct. Perhaps the build-up and withhold orgasm pattern Kellen had been using on her had been for the best. Even after the waves of release dissipated, her body continued to quake uncontrollably.

"Don't cry," Owen whispered to her, kissing the dampness on her cheeks.

She wasn't sure why she was crying. It wasn't sadness or fear or anger or frustration. It wasn't even relief.

"I'm sorry," she sobbed brokenly. "I don't know what's wrong with me."

"We can cut you loose if it's too much," he said, stroking her hair gently.

"Please don't. I want to continue. I'm just…"

"Feeling things you never felt before," Kellen said. "It's okay. Sex is a deeply personal experience." He grinned wickedly. "Even when it's with a stranger it touches part of your spirit."

Kellen massaged the insteps of her feet while she pulled herself together. She gulped for air and reminded herself to relax into the ropes. Fighting them only served to exhaust her, but they did cut into her flesh in a most delicious manner if she pulled against them just right.

Still above her head, Owen kept his face buried against her neck, holding her loosely just under her breasts.

"Okay," she said, when she returned to Earth. "I'm good now."

Kellen licked his lips. "I'm ready for more too. How are you, Owen?"

He groaned into Lindsey's neck. "Hard as a fucking rock."

"Hey, you said you were okay," Kellen reminded him.

"I was until she came. Her facial expression totally did me in."

Lindsey's face flamed. Had she made a stupid O-face? In front of Owen Mitchell? How embarrassing.

"Take her high again," Owen murmured against her neck. "Just, please hurry this time."

Kellen released Lindsey's feet and stretched out on his belly between her wide open thighs again. "You're just going to have to suffer a while, buddy. This is the sweetest pussy I've ever tasted and I'm going to take my time making it cream for me again."

"If you don't hurry," Owen growled, "I'm going to kick your ass. I've waited long enough."

Kellen chuckled at his misery.

"If you suck on my nipples, it will really get my juices flowing,"

Lindsey whispered to Owen. She had no idea if it was true. She just really wanted that luscious mouth of his against her tender nipples. The knot on the rope just wasn't cutting it any longer. Even though it flicked over them in a most distracting fashion, she was ready for a different sensation.

Owen inched lower. As his chest came into view, she couldn't help but pull against her bindings so she could kiss the hard-muscled flesh before her. He nudged the knotted rope out of his way with his nose and latched onto her nipple, sucking hard. She caught the glinting barbell in his nipple between her teeth and tugged. He groaned.

"I shouldn't have moved," he said.

The glorious motion of Kellen's tongue against Lindsey's flesh halted as he lifted his head. "That's not part of our ritual, Owen."

"*Your* ritual," Owen said. He sounded a tad testy.

Lindsey tilted her head back and gazed longingly at the hard ridge in Owen's jeans. She could almost feel him inside her, rubbing her inner walls. Stretching her. Filling her.

She squirmed excitedly. Kellen latched onto her clit and sucked in rhythmic pulses. Was he intentionally matching the pull of Owen's mouth on her nipple? The two were in perfect synchrony.

Lindsey was building again. She gasped and shuddered, fighting release this time. Not wanting to come when she was empty inside.

Kellen lifted his head. "She needs you to do your part now," he said.

Owen moved in a flash. He bounded off the bed, shucked his jeans and was tearing open a condom before Lindsey could comprehend what was happening. Something metallic glinted just beneath the rim of Owen's swollen cockhead. He carefully unrolled the condom down his length and moved to the end of the bed behind Kellen, who was still feasting down below.

Lindsey lifted her head to try to track their motions, but it pulled a rope at her back uncomfortably so she closed her eyes and relished in the sensation pulled from her quivering flesh by Kellen's skilled mouth. Without Owen to divide her attention, she was quickly overwhelmed with sensation, mewing in pleasure as another orgasm teased her with promise.

"Yes," she whispered. "I'm coming again. I'm…"

Kellen moved aside and Owen took his place. He found her and slid deep with one hard thrust. Her eyes widened in surprise when she felt there was something inside her other than just flesh. Whatever that metallic bead near his cockhead had been felt amazing.

"What is that?" she asked.

"It's pierced," he said simply and then he slowly withdrew.

His modification rubbed down her front inner wall. He found a particularly sensitive spot a few inches inside her and she gasped brokenly as the piercing rubbed against it. A devilish smile lit Owen's devastatingly handsome face and he thrust quick and shallow, rubbing that little spot inside her until she thought she'd go mad. When the first throes of another orgasm gripped her, he thrust deep and held. She stared up at him unable to comprehend what he was doing. When her breathing stilled somewhat, he pulled back to that special spot again and took her with rapid shallow strokes. Rubbing. Rubbing. Rubbing against that perfect spot.

"Oh God, that feels good."

Owen grinned at her and thrust deep again. She realized he was just as bad as his friend, Kellen. Teasing her within an inch of a mind-blowing orgasm, yet withholding it from her at the last instant. She didn't know rather to curse them or sing their praises.

The mattress beside her sagged as Kellen moved to kneel at her side. He was naked now, having shed his jeans. She watched him, in total awe of his masculine beauty. He seemed so at ease with his nudity. Even with his enormous, engorged cock fully exposed and standing proud and rigid before him. She'd never seen a man so perfectly put together. So silently powerful. So...

She groaned as Owen shifted his hips and the metal ball in his cock stroked her inside as he thrust into her slow and deep.

Lindsey cried out as an orgasm unfurled within her again. She hadn't thought she was capable of coming three times in one night, but dear Lord, she was coming and having Owen's thrusting cock inside her brought her the full satisfaction she craved at last.

"She's getting off hard with you," Kellen said as if commenting on something far less amazing than the pulsing pleasure shattering Lindsey with bliss.

"She's not screaming the way she did with you," Owen said, shifting his hips and grabbing the ropes at her shoulders so he could fuck her harder.

Lindsey was too incoherent to scream. She could scarcely breathe. He had to stop. She couldn't take it. "Please, stop. No more. No."

"I think she's had enough," Kellen said, his fingers tracing the ropes that were digging into her upper arms. "Take it easy on her."

"S-sorry," she whispered. She wanted Owen to finish. Wanted him to take his pleasure while buried deep inside her, but she had reached her limit.

Owen slowed his thrusts and when she stopped shaking, he pulled free with a wet sound. As soon as he was free of her, she wanted him back. But he had already moved to kneel across from Kellen on her opposite side.

Kneeling across from each other on opposite sides of Lindsey's body, the pair of men stared straight ahead, locked in each other's gazes. Kellen's eyes were dark brown and intense, Owen's brilliant blue and glazed. She wasn't sure what they were doing, but it was as if she was no longer in the room, much less bound between them.

Kellen's hand moved to encircle his cock. He stroked himself slowly from base to tip, working slick oil down his length. Owen stripped the condom off his cock and mimicked Kellen's motions on himself. His body tensed and his mouth fell open to emit gasps of pleasure. Lindsey watched them, partially puzzled, partially turned on by the perfect synchronicity they displayed as they stroked their cocks over her lower belly.

Owen's eyes drifted closed after a moment. Kellen smiled that wicked little smile of his and reached forward to take Owen's cock in his hand. Lindsey's gaze darted from their faces, to the action below, back to their faces. Owen shuddered in pleasure and shifted his hand from his cock to Kellen's.

They tugged at each other in unison. Eyes closed, Owen was twitching uncontrollably at Kellen's hand. Kellen watched him gauging his reaction. His hand moved faster. Faster. Skimming over Owen's flesh with practiced eased.

Owen fell forward and Kellen caught him against his shoulder still stroking him, his long strong fingers rubbing over the piercing in Owen's cock with each tug.

Lindsey had never seen two guys stroke each other's cocks before. She wasn't sure why it had her so hot and bothered. She was lying to herself. Watching them got off on each other was the hottest fucking thing she'd ever seen in her life, even if she did feel like an intruder in her own threesome.

"Kelly," Owen whispered. "Can I come? Let me come. Kelly?"

"I'm not ready yet."

Owen began to stroke Kellen more persistently, paying extra attention to the head of Kellen's cock.

"I can't, oh God, I can't," Owen panted. "Please hurry."

Lindsey's eyes widened as Owen rubbed his open mouth across Kellen's shoulder, his eyes squeezed shut. She felt the first pulse of hot cum strike her belly. It wasn't Owen's, it was Kellen's.

She couldn't see Kellen's expression, but she could see Owen's and as he let go, his face contorted in bliss, she was seriously cursing herself for encouraging him to stop fucking her because she was certainly in need of more now.

Owen rubbed his open mouth over Kellen's shoulder in absolute rapture. He was the sexiest thing she'd ever witnessed in her life. After a moment, Owen lifted his head and gazed up at Kellen with questioning eyes. "Was that okay?" he asked.

Kellen lifted both hands to cup Owen's face. "That was perfect. Thank you." He dropped a gentle kiss at the corner of Owen's mouth and again they stared at each other as if Lindsey had left the planet.

"Let's bring her down slowly."

Owen smiled and nodded.

Was she supposed to believe they'd just jacked each other off all over her belly for *her* benefit?

Kellen's strong fingers played over the flesh on one side of her body, while Owen worked the other. They started by massaging their combined fluids into her skin. She'd watched them, trembling, wondering what part she had really played in the act that was obviously something more between them and less about her. She wasn't sure how she felt about being included in something like this. Oh, sure, she'd had an amazing sexual experience, but if the two of them were attracted to each other, why bother bringing a woman into the mix at all?

"I didn't realize you two were lovers when I agreed to this," Lindsey said as Kellen released one of her legs and slowly unwound the rope from around her thigh. He paused and looked at her as if she was a raving lunatic.

"What do you mean?"

"You and Owen. You obviously have a thing for each other."

Both men laughed. "It's not like that," Owen said. "It's part of Kelly's ritual."

It's Kellen's way of taking advantage of you, Lindsey thought. She winced as her left leg was slowly extended and Kellen's deft fingers began to massage its length. She hadn't realized that an uncomfortable ache had built in her hips until both legs were straightened and both men were kneading her muscles until she began to relax.

"It's cool," Lindsey said. "Watching you get each other off was hot and all. I just wasn't expecting it."

Kellen didn't comment, but Owen seemed a bit disturbed. His handsome face twisted in confusion and he glanced up at Kellen. "When did we start touching each other in the ritual? We didn't used to do that."

Kellen grinned. "A few months ago. It feels better that way, doesn't it?"

"Yeah, but she's right. It's kind of gay."

Kellen laughed. "What are you talking about? We both know we're not sexually attracted to each other," Kellen said. When Owen was looking the other way he sneaked a glance at him as if he wondered if Owen was buying it.

"You do know how to get me off hard," Owen said. "I completely forget where I am and lose track of what's going on. It's almost like really intense masturbation, since I have a cock in my hand. It's just not my own."

Lindsey chuckled. The guy was so cute. No wonder Kellen manipulated him into being his unsuspecting toy.

"I don't think I can find my connection without you anymore, Owen." Kellen stared at him reflectively and Owen grinned.

"Don't worry," Owen said. "I'll help you out until you find your perfect woman."

Kellen's smile was genuine this time. None of that usual wickedness in him backed it. "Thanks."

"I'll be your perfect woman," Lindsey offered.

"You were great Lindsey," Owen said, "but he has this crazy idea that he'll know his soul mate the instant he meets her. Ridiculous idea, huh?"

"Kind of romantic," Lindsey said.

"You're not supposed to share that with people, remember?" Kellen said.

They were unwinding the ropes around her torso now. Every inch of her body was massaged as they released her bounds one at a time.

Owen shrugged. "She's seen you stroke your best friend's cock until he came so hard he saw stars. I don't think much of what you share with her at this point is going to phase her."

"You came that hard, did you?" Kellen said, his lips twisted in that wicked grin of his again.

"Can't help it. You have strong hands."

"Kellen came way harder than you did, Owen," Lindsey said. "I think he bruised my belly with the force behind his load."

Owen chuckled. "I did my best to help him get off."

"We rushed it a bit," Kellen commented. "You were over-excited." He caressed Lindsey's breasts gently as they were freed from their bounds. "Which got me overexcited. I'm not sure if she was completely satisfied."

She couldn't lie, even if it did mean she might have more in store for her. "I was more than satisfied. And it feels absolutely amazing to be touched like this after having been confined," she said quietly. She liked it almost as much as the mind blowing orgasm she was still relishing.

"You'll sleep very well," Kellen promised.

"I am sleepy now," she admitted.

She felt the weariness to her very bones.

And despite her best intentions, her eyes drifted closed.

CHAPTER NINE

Kellen continued to unwind ropes and massage flesh long after Lindsey had fallen asleep. He could feel Owen's troubled gaze on him, but he pretended he was still working through his ritual. When had it become a way to be closer to his best friend? And why were the best orgasms of his life always at Owen's hand? He wasn't attracted to Owen. He didn't get aroused when he was around him or anything. It had to be a completely tactile response of his body. Nothing emotional behind it. Should he tell Owen that or just keep those thoughts to himself?

"I want some hot chocolate," Owen said. "Can you finish this on your own?"

Kellen forced himself to look up at Owen. He hoped his smile didn't appear as forced as it felt. "Yeah, I'm fine. Almost finished. Unless you want to retrieve her anal plug for me."

Owen grinned and Kellen took an unlabored breath. He hadn't realized how constricted his chest had become until Owen's easy smile had lifted some of the emotional burden.

"Sounds like a job for Adam," Owen said. "He's the one who loves ass."

Kellen really didn't want to make things weird between himself and Owen. So what if his orgasms were less intense when he finished himself at his own hand. Kellen had to stop encouraging Owen to touch him. Had to stop touching Owen in return. That's all there was too it.

"You can call Adam in here if you want," Kellen said.

Owen shook his head. "You aren't attracted to me. Are you?"

Leave it to Owen to throw it all out there in the open. Kellen shook his head. "No. I honestly never think of you in a sexual capacity."

Owen released a deep breath. "Thank God. I don't think of you that way either. Why then... Why do we both get off so hard that way? I come so hard when you jerk me off."

"Strong hands?"

"I guess," Owen said and nodded. "The other guys don't know about this, do they?"

"Not unless you told them."

"I can keep a secret if you can."

"Yeah, but can she?"

They both paused in their massage to gaze down at the sleeping girl. She looked so innocent in sleep. So exhausted. Kellen felt a renewed stirring in his groin. One he absolutely did *not* feel when he thought of Owen. It was a relief, yet he felt a little weird about it. Kellen would have probably felt less weird about getting off at his best friend's hand if he *were* attracted to him. At least then it would make sense.

He just couldn't bring himself to let a woman get him off. Not yet. He should probably move on with his life. Find someone to love. Sara would have wanted that for him. She'd told him as much the last time they'd made love. The last time he'd made love, period. He wasn't sure why the promises he'd made to her before she gotten sick—all those *forever* promises of their naïve, young love— were the ones that stuck with him the most.

"You're thinking about her again," Owen said.

Kellen swallowed the lump in his throat and returned his attention to massaging Lindsey's hand. She sighed in her sleep and his heart warmed. He wished he could love someone like her. He wished he could love anyone. Five years was long enough to grieve for Sara. It was much longer than the time he'd had with her.

"I think she'll always be there," Kellen said. "Sara."

"I'm pretty sure that's why you can't bring yourself to, you know." Owen's eyes flicked towards Lindsey's shaven mound. "Dam the beaver with your stick."

Kellen's brow crumpled. "That doesn't even make sense, Owen. You don't dam beavers."

Owen chuckled. "I do."

Kellen could still taste Lindsey's sweet pussy and yeah, things were definitely stirring down below at the thought, but he didn't want enter her shapely body. He didn't want to be wrapped in her arms. He didn't want to move inside her and stare down into her big blue eyes, because even though Lindsey resembled Sara, she wouldn't be Sara. She could never be Sara. Sara was dead.

"I'm all sorts of fucked up in the head," Kellen murmured.

"Hey, it's alright. No one knows, but me," Owen said.

Kellen chuckled. "I guess that's some consolation."

"Maybe if you tried again, you could do it this time. Instead of thinking of Sara while you bang the chick, you could think about my hand." Owen lifted his eyebrows suggestively and wriggled his fingers at him. "I know how much it turns you on."

Kellen might have taken offense if he hadn't known Owen was fucking with him. He laughed harder. "What? Are you tired of having to get me off, Owen?"

"Not as long as you reciprocate." Owen's face split into a wide grin. "We are a couple of fucking perverts, aren't we?"

"Hey, whatever feels good and God knows I need the release."

"I'm really ready for some hot chocolate now. Do you want some?"

Kellen shook his head. "I'll be out later. I need a few minutes to get my head on straight."

Owen climbed from the bed and slipped into his jeans. "I'm going to hold you to that. No lying back here, staring at some girl you don't know, feeling all depressed and lonely."

Kellen chuckled. The man knew him too well. He didn't know what he would do with himself without Owen in his life, reminding him to keep living. Or try to.

CHAPTER TEN

Owen left Kelly with Lindsey and entered the main corridor of the bus. Tex was near the driver's seat, cussing at his cell phone for having no service. With a candy cane dangling from his mouth, Gabe was back to reading his physics book, his attention drifting intermittently to Shade-and-company in the chair beside him. Adam was picking at his guitar strings with a distant look on his face. Shade was still seated in the recliner with the red rope still binding his forearms together. The main difference between now and when Owen had last saw him was that Shade's fly was wide open and his stiff cock was down the throat of Lindsey's friend.

When Owen closed the door behind himself, the girl looked up from her task and let Shade's cock pop free from her lush lips. "Are you all done with the bed? I'm all sorts of horny right now. I don't think this guy is ever gonna come."

"Not if you stop sucking it, I won't," Shade said.

She glared up at him from her kneeling position on the floor. "If you don't shut your mouth, I'm gonna knock your ass to the floor and sit on your face."

Owen laughed. He loved this chick's attitude. He found several cups of cold cocoa on the counter and popped one in the microwave.

"Is Lindsey okay?" the girl asked.

"She's resting. Kellen's giving her a massage."

"She sure didn't sound like she was getting no massage twenty minutes ago."

"That must have been when I was fucking her," Owen said. "I think she liked my cock piercing. She has a really sensitive G-spot." He grinned. The microwave beeped and he removed his cup. He grabbed a spoon out of the drawer and stirred the contents of his mug before taking a cautious sip of the scalding liquid.

"Vanessa?" Shade murmured.

Vanessa tore her interested gaze from Owen's crotch and looked up at Shade.

"Are you going to finish what you started or talk to Owen?"

She pouted. "My jaw is tired."

"Then mount up and ride it."

She eyed Shade's huge erection with concern. "You don't expect me to take off my pants and do you out here in front of everyone, do you?"

"You didn't seem to have a problem with our presence when you were trying to suck him off," Gabe said without looking up from his book.

"If you untie me, I'll help you out of those pants," Shade said.

"I like you tied," Vanessa said. "That's what got me so hot and bothered in the first place."

"Yeah, well it's keeping me from yanking your pants down around your knees, shoving your face into the sofa and fucking you doggie style," Shade said, his voice tense, almost agonized.

Still sipping his hot chocolate, which was sweet and absolutely delicious, Owen sat on the sofa in question. "You can bury your face in my lap while he fucks you," Owen said. "I won't mind." He patted his thigh with his free hand and took another sip of his cocoa. He was just trying to get a rise out of her. She didn't disappoint him.

"You want my face in your lap after you just did my best friend? Don't even go there." Her eyes flicked to his lap. "Is your cock really pierced?"

Owen nodded and reached for the top button of his fly.

"Don't take it out and show her," Gabe complained. "One cock out in the main cabin is more than enough."

"I'll just put Shade's away then," Vanessa said. Owen saw the teasing grin on her face as she turned to try to force Shade's rock hard cock back into his pants. Owen liked this girl. Anyone who messed with Shade was okay in his book. "Why won't this thing go down?" she complained and licked it from base to tip. "Maybe if I suck your balls..." If her goal was to get Shade to groan and twitch and rock his hips in excitement, then sucking his balls had been the right solution.

Kellen came out of the bedroom. Owen offered him a wave, but he didn't notice because he was gaping at Shade and the woman with Shade's balls between her lush lips.

"Fuck, Shade. Don't you have any shame?" Kellen said, raking a hand through his long, black hair, which now hung loose around his shoulders. He only tied it back when he was going down on a lady.

"No," Shade gasped. "No shame. But the bedroom's free now, Vanessa. Since you seem to have at least a little shame."

"Just a little," she said and laughed. She climbed to her feet and grabbed the rope between Shade's wrists, hauling him to feet.

His loosened pants got caught on his thighs as he shuffled down the corridor to bedroom. Well, the bedroom was *mostly* free. Lindsey was still in there. She might sleep through the commotion however.

Kellen rolled his eyes as Shade passed him. "I thought Gabe was going to untie you."

"I wouldn't let him," Vanessa said. "I like Shade helpless."

"I'll show you helpless in a minute," Shade said in a low growl.

"Yeah, *you*," she said, "helpless and flat on your back while I take that huge cock for a ride. And you aren't allowed to come until I say you can."

Owen laughed. Yep, he really liked that woman's spunk. He wasn't sure how Shade felt about it however. He was sort of a control freak.

"Untie me," Shade insisted again.

She hauled him into the bedroom, slapped his ass, and then shut the door.

Kellen took one of the spare cups of hot chocolate on the counter and carried it toward the lounge area.

"You gonna heat that up?" Owen asked him.

He shook his head and took a sip. "I like it cool."

"I swear," Tex said, "you five are the only guys I know who can find willing pussy in a deserted mountain pass during a blizzard." Tex sat on the arm of the sofa with his cellphone clutched in one hand. "Still no service. I hope the equipment truck didn't start up the mountain pass after they finished loading it. I tried to call and warn them to stay in the valley."

"They'll close the pass if the roads are treacherous," Gabe said. "They crew is probably more worried about us."

"We're fine," Owen said. "We have hot chocolate, a fake tree and the sounds of Shade fucking in the bedroom. What more could we ask for on Christmas Eve?"

"Presents?" Adam said, setting his guitar aside, and rubbing his face with both hands. It was always tense when Shade and Adam were in the same room, but now that Shade had sojourned to the bedroom, some of the strain had left Adam's body.

Owen wished the two of them would have it out once and for all. But not tonight. Tonight was for celebrating family and love. And he might be stuck in a mountain pass with his band instead of visiting his parents, siblings, grandparents, aunts, uncles and dozens of cousins, but these guys were just as important to him as any blood relative.

"Santa might leave some presents for you douchebags," Owen said. Which reminded him that his Santa hat was trapped in the bedroom with Shade and the woman who was currently screaming, "tear that pussy up, tear it up, baby, tear it up," and poor Lindsey. She couldn't possibly still be sleeping through all that swearing Shade was doing.

"There'll be a world-wide coal shortage if Santa visits y'all," Tex said and laughed like a demented Canadian goose until Owen shoved him off the arm of the sofa onto the floor.

"I know for a fact that Santa won't bring anyone coal," Owen said. "But good little boys have to get to bed and fall asleep before midnight or Santa might bypass a certain stranded tour bus."

"*Good* little boys," Tex said, rolling around on the floor laughing his ass off. Owen didn't realize people actually did that.

"Owen, did you get us presents?" Gabe asked. "We said we weren't going to exchange gifts this year."

"I didn't get you guys shit," Owen said.

"Good," Adam said, "because we didn't get you shit either."

"But I still believe in Santa," Owen said. "Don't you?"

"I don't know about Santa," Kellen said, "but Shade sure is praising Jesus at the moment."

CHAPTER ELEVEN

Lindsey's eyes snapped open. Was there an earthquake? Why was the bed rocking so hard? And what were all of those rhythmic, wet noises coming from beside her? She turned her head and her breath immediately stalled in her throat. A pair of chocolate brown thighs belonging to her best friend straddled the hips of some pelvis she didn't recognize. Vanessa was rising and falling over a thick, veined cock as if she were riding bareback broncos in a rodeo. Lindsey was completely engrossed with watching Vanessa's flesh ebb and flow each time she took him deep inside and lifted her hips to slide up his shaft.

"Did we wake you?" a deep voice said beside her.

Shade? She lifted up onto one arm and looked down at his sardonic grin. She couldn't see his eyes, because apparently he wore sunglasses even when he fucked. The Christmas lights were gone, but his arms were still bound before him with a red rope in a crisscrossing pattern from wrists to elbow. Lindsey immediately recognized Kellen's handiwork and began to tremble at the memories of what glorious things he and Owen had done to her body earlier.

"Sorry, girl," Vanessa said. "I had to get a piece of this. Damn, this man is fine."

"I understand," Lindsey said wearily and dropped back down on the mattress. Her body was so exhausted, so relaxed, so completely satisfied that she didn't want to move and lose the feeling of tranquility that suffused every inch of her. Unfortunately, she couldn't seem to stop watching Vanessa's pussy working Shade's cock, so the flesh between Lindsey's thighs started to swell and pulsate with renewed need.

"Your friend has a fantastic pussy," Shade said conversationally.

"Is that so?" Lindsey said.

"Soft and lush. Like her sexy lips."

"You ever been with a black girl before?" Vanessa asked him.

"A few," he said. "I've found that fantastic pussy comes in all colors. Speaking of coming, can I come now?"

"Not yet. I'm not finished." For which Lindsey was oddly thankful. She was completely mesmerized by what was going on beside her.

"You know what would be really hot," Shade whispered into Lindsey's ear.

"Hmm?" she murmured lethargically.

"If you moved up behind Vanessa, wrapped your arms around her and held her tits while she rides me."

Lindsey's eyes travelled up Vanessa's naked body to her breasts. Lindsey had seen Vanessa nude numerous times in the past, but she'd never thought of her friend's body as erotic. Or arousing. She also never thought she'd be so easily swayed by a man to obey his suggestion.

Vanessa glanced over her shoulder as Lindsey moved to kneel behind her. "Do you want a turn?" Vanessa asked.

Lindsey shook her head and kissed the warm, smooth skin of Vanessa's shoulder. Vanessa's back brushed Lindsey's suddenly hard nipples as she continued to rise and fall over Shade. With trembling hands, Lindsey cupped Vanessa's breasts. They were smaller than her own, their pointed tips pressed into her palms as Vanessa's back arched and her head dropped back on Lindsey's shoulder.

"Is this okay?" she whispered to Vanessa.

"It's okay," Vanessa said.

Lindsey massaged Vanessa's perky breasts, fascinated by the way the soft globes of flesh moved in her hands, how easy it was to make Vanessa moan by stroking her large nipples, how erotic the contrast of their flesh tones looked as she gave pleasure to her friend. Lindsey shifted so that Vanessa's soft ass rubbed against her shaven mound each time she rose and fell over Shade. This was definitely getting her hot and bothered again. Lindsey churned her hips to rub her mound more firmly over Vanessa and her hands began to wander—down Vanessa's slightly rounded tummy, over her hips, her thighs. *What am I doing?* Was she really going to touch her best friend *there?*

Vanessa began to move faster over Shade. Faster. Seeking her climax. Lindsey wanted to help her find it.

Lindsey's fingers slipped between Vanessa's swollen folds. She found Vanessa's clit with two fingertips and rubbed it fast and hard, the way she rubbed herself when she masturbated. Within seconds, Vanessa's body went taut before her, and Vanessa shuddered hard as she screamed through her orgasm.

"This is not okay," Lindsey said and yanked her hand away.

Vanessa grabbed her wrist and buried her hand between her thighs. "Yes, Lindsey. It's okay. It's perfect. Feel him inside me."

Lightheaded with shock, but for some reason unable to pull away, Lindsey held Vanessa's mound cupped in her palm while Shade's cock brushed rhythmically against her fingertips.

"That was beautiful," Shade said. "Can I come now?"

Vanessa chuckled. "No, stud. Lindsey needs a turn." She lifted her hips until Shade's cock slipped from her body and then took Lindsey's hand and placed it over the very slippery condom covering his shaft. "Have fun, girl. I need a nap."

Lindsey looked up at Shade, wishing she could see his eyes, wondering what he thought of her behavior. Was he as shocked by what she'd just done as she was?

"If you untie me," he said, "I'll make this easy on you."

"What do you mean?" Lindsey asked.

"You know you want to fuck, but you think you shouldn't."

"And how will untying you change those feelings?"

"You can blame your surrender on me, instead of taking what you want."

"I took what I wanted," Vanessa said.

"But she won't," Shade said. "Even though she does want it."

She did want it, but he was right. She'd already had sex with two strangers tonight. She sure wasn't going to go at it with another one. Unless he... forced her to.

"Are you going to force me?" she asked, her heart thudding with excitement.

"Do you want me to force you?"

"It's not really force if she *wants* you to force her." Vanessa rolled her eyes at him.

"I wouldn't really force her if she didn't want me to. That would be called rape, but it's different if she wants to be held down and fucked while she struggles."

"I do," Lindsey blurted.

Her hands moved to the first knot binding his arms together— his strong, very muscular arms. She had a hard time untying the rope as she thought about those strong muscular arms holding her down while he fucked her. Her fingers weren't trembling because she was afraid. They were trembling because she was excited.

"Should I leave?" Vanessa said.

"No, you're going to watch and not interfere. But I would appreciate it if you got me a fresh condom out of the drawer over there." Lindsey was floored by the gentle smile he offered Vanessa. Surely this big hunk of sardonic muscle didn't have a gentle bone in his body. She was actually hoping that he didn't. She especially hoped that the bone he was about to thrust into her throbbing cunt wasn't the least bit gentle.

Once his arms were free, he rubbed them for a moment and flexed his fingers. She watched the movement of his muscles contracting beneath his skin. He was so big. So powerful. So strong.

"I think you'd better run," he said in a deep voice.

Her heart slammed into her ribcage as she leaped from the bed. He pursued her and quickly trapped her against the inside of the bedroom door. She grabbed the doorknob, but his fingers were like steel bands around her wrists and she couldn't turn the knob.

"Let me go," she whispered, "Please."

"Do you know what I do to girls who make me want them as much as I want you?" He fisted a hand in her hair and tugged her head back. And it hurt. It hurt real good. She forced herself not to purr in surrender.

"I don't know," she said. "Just don't hurt me." *Much*...

Hand still clutching her hair, Shade jerked her back against his hard chest and grabbed her breast with his free hand. He pinched her nipple and she gasped in pain.

"I'm not going to hurt you," he said, his teeth scraping against the edge of her ear, "but I am going to fuck you. Spread your legs."

"No," she said breathlessly. Her blood was jetting through her vessels. She was so amped up on adrenaline, she doubted she'd ever come down.

"Spread your legs or I'll spread them for you."

His cock prodded her in the lower back as he forced a knee between her legs from behind.

"No," she said. "I'll never spread them willingly."

There was a knock at the door. "Are you really raping someone in there?" someone said on the other side of the thin piece of wood before Lindsey's face. "Do I need to geld someone with a rusty knife?"

"Go away, Gabe, you're fucking up our scenario," Shade growled at the door.

"I'm not going away until I'm sure it *is* a scenario."

"It is," Lindsey yelled, her face flaming with embarrassment. What must Kellen and Owen be thinking of her? When had she turned into a ho for real? And why wasn't she thinking that the best way to prevent her further mortification was to stop this? She didn't want to stop. Not at all. So what if this made her a ho ho ho. She was having a very merry Christmas Eve.

"It totally is a scenario, drummer boy," Vanessa yelled. "And damn, Shade," she said, "watching this is totally turning me on again."

"If you're sure," Gabe said, still in the corridor outside.

"We're sure," the three in the bedroom yelled in unison.

"Then you kids have fun, but keep it down. We're going to bed." There was a short pause. "*Alone* un-fucking-fortunately. Let's hope the generator holds out so we don't all freeze to death."

"Way to spoil the mood," Shade grumbled.

Lindsey grabbed Shade's wrist and yanked, trying to dislodge his fist from her hair. "I said let me go," she said and ground her ass into his cock as she tried to twist out of his grasp.

Shade groaned into her ear. "I am not going to last much longer," he whispered. "Vanessa got me too worked up."

Lindsey bumped her heel into his shin and, caught off-guard, Shade actually loosened his grip. She managed one step, before his fist tightened in her hair again.

"You'll pay for that, darlin'," he said.

Oh yes, make me pay.

In an instant he had her face down on the edge of bed, his big, strong hand pressing down in the center of her back so she couldn't rise. And it wasn't as if she wasn't legitimately trying, but he was so much stronger than her and no amount of trying to push upward with her spaghetti noodle arms could dislodge him. Breathing hard, she turned her head so she could draw air. As soon as she stopped struggling to rise, his free hand delved between her legs from behind, no doubt discovering how hot and wet she was down there.

Shade removed his hand from her back and she launched forward, trying to scramble away. He grabbed her by the thighs, yanking them apart and pulling her towards him until she felt his cockhead against her opening. Her core clenched with the tease of an orgasm.

"You want it, don't you?"

Yes, yes, I want it.

"No," she forced herself to say. She shook her head vigorously.

"Then why are you so wet?"

"I'm not," she denied.

He thrust into her, sliding to the hilt in one hard motion.

She cried out. Lord, he was huge. She couldn't help but rock back to meet his deep, punishing penetration stroke for stroke.

"Do you like that?"

"No," she forced herself to say.

"She does like it, doesn't she, Vanessa?"

"I think she does," Vanessa said.

"Do you know what else she likes?"

"Your finger in her ass?"

"I didn't think of that," he said. His firm grip released from one thigh and before she could use that advantage to pretend to fight him, his finger slipped in her ass and she exploded with a earth shattering orgasm. He didn't give her time to recover. He spread her legs wider and fucked her harder.

"Oh please," she begged as rubbed her face over the bedclothes in blinding ecstasy.

"What were you thinking Lindsey likes?" Vanessa asked.

"I think she likes to eat pussy."

"I hope so. My fingers aren't doing the trick over here."

Lindsey lifted her head and it took a moment for her eyes to focus on her friend, who was indeed trying to get off at her own hand.

"You want to lick Vanessa's cum, don't you, Lindsey?"

"N- no." She swallowed hard. He wouldn't make her, would he?

"I saw how turned on you were when you made her come. She was turned on by you too, Lindsey. I doubt she's ever come that hard before in her life. Her pussy gripped my cock so hard, I almost lost it. She came for you. You want to taste it."

"No, I don't." She honestly didn't want to taste anyone's cum, but would they believe her while she was playing this game of false denial with them?

"Come here, Vanessa," he demanded. "Let her taste you."

"Wait," Lindsey whispered.

Shade grabbed a fistful of Lindsey's hair and lifted her face off the mattress so Vanessa could position herself in front of Lindsey with her legs spread wide. Lindsey hadn't been this up close and personal to a vagina since birth. Shade released Lindsey's hair, but she didn't lower her head to do what they wanted her to do. She closed her eyes concentrated on the feel of Shade's powerful thrusts. Damn, the man was a good fuck.

Lindsey could smell Vanessa's excitement now and eventually had to admit it was enticing. Her mouth watered. She wanted to taste it. She did. But she'd never done anything like this before. She was afraid of where her own desire might take her.

Vanessa placed a gentle hand on the back of her head. "It's okay, Lindsey," she whispered, stroking her hair tenderly while Shade continued to pound into her.

"Are you sure, Nessi?" she asked.

"I'm sure, baby."

Lindsey lowered her head and drew her tongue oh-so-slowly over Vanessa's quivering clit. Vanessa collapsed back onto the bed with a startled outrush of breath. Lindsey licked Vanessa's inner folds, using the orgasmic, teasing technique Kellen had used on her earlier that night. Vanessa's cum was sweet and tangy and Lindsey couldn't get enough of it. She licked Vanessa's opening until her tongue got tired and then she sucked her clit until her friend came. Lindsey was scarcely aware of Shade thrusting deep one last time or his shouting and shuddering as he took his release. When he let go of her thighs and pulled out, she shifted her arm between Vanessa's legs so she could slide two fingers into Vanessa's sweet, silky pussy. Lindsey loved making her friend moan and writhe in ecstasy. When Vanessa found another orgasm minutes later, Lindsey gasped at the sensation of Vanessa's flesh clenching in hard spasms around her exploring fingers. When her friend had settled, Lindsey kissed Vanessa's shaven mound affectionately and slid her fingers free.

She lifted her head to find that Shade had left the room while she'd been otherwise occupied eating out her best friend. What. The. Fuck?

Vanessa grabbed Lindsey and drew her against her in a warm embrace. "Damn, girl, where did you learn to do that with your tongue?"

"Um." Lindsey flushed. "Kellen Jamison?"

Vanessa laughed. "That man just landed himself at number one on my fuck-it list."

Lindsey lifted her head to look down into the familiar face of her best friend. She loved this woman, she did, but she didn't *ever* want to eat her pussy again. "Nessi?"

"Yeah, sugar."

"Does this mean I'm gay?"

"Naw, baby. We was just caught up in the moment and got a little bicurious."

"Okay," she said and laid her head on Vanessa's shoulder.

"I don't know what it is about rock stars that makes us act all crazy."

Lindsey knew. "They're walking aphrodisiacs."

Vanessa chuckled and gave her an affectionate squeeze. "You said it, girlfriend. You said it."

Lindsey's mind soon wandered to the remaining two rock stars in on the tour bus.

"Hmm, I wonder if Gabe and Adam are cold and lonely."

"We could go check," Vanessa said.

CHAPTER TWELVE

Owen hopped out of his bunk and winced when his barefoot landed on a used condom. He was pretty sure it wasn't his, but who the hell knew after the orgy that had gone down the night before.

He peeled the sticky prophylactic off the bottom of his foot and tossed it into the garbage can under the sink. He was always the first to wake up, but this morning, it was important, because *Santa* had been too busy screwing the night before to dig his presents out of their hiding place.

Owen stepped over Tex, who was sprawled in the aisle wearing nothing but his cowboy boots, and for some inexplicable reason, his belt and prized rodeo buckle. Owen's toe connected with an empty whiskey bottle and it rolled across the floor to get lost under the dining room table, which had been used for a different kind of feast the night before. It had been fun while it lasted, but now his tongue would never work properly again and his lower back and hips were calling his insatiable cock every sort of a son-of-a-bitch.

Or maybe he'd dreamt it all. His band members were all stark naked and passed out in various uncomfortable positions around the cabin, but there wasn't a woman in sight.

He found the pair of female friends curled up together on the bed in the back of the bus. When the generous ladies had come out of the bedroom the night before, the only one who hadn't taken a turn at one or the other of them—or *both* of them in Owen's case—had been Kelly. He was still saving his love for a dead girl. Owen hoped his gift helped him get over her a little. If for no other reason, Kelly seriously needed to find something better than Owen's hand to get him off.

Owen donned a pair of discarded jeans he found on the bedroom floor—which turned out not to be his because they were several sizes too big—and his Santa hat. He flopped down on the floor, rolled onto his back, and shimmied his shoulders under the bed. He tugged out the velvet sack he'd stuffed way back under the headboard a few nights before.

A foot stomped right in the middle of his stomach.

"Umph!"

"Oh my God," Lindsey said as she pulled her foot back. "I'm so sorry. Are you okay?"

"You don't need a spleen to live," he said breathlessly and after some scooting around, rose into sitting position.

"Did we really have a sex orgy last night?" she whispered, her innocent-looking blue eyes wide in disbelief.

"Nope. What happens on the Sole Regret tour bus, stays on the Sole Regret tour bus." He winked at her and rose to his feet.

Owen slung his sack of presents over one shoulder and grinned at Lindsey. "Santa already gave you your present last night. You are now permanently on his naughty list."

She flushed and lowered her eyes to her clenched hands.

He leaned over and kissed her temple. "I meant what I said about every sinfully delicious thing that happens on this bus, doesn't leave it."

"Okay," she said breathlessly, but didn't look at him.

She really was a doll. He might have considered calling her if she hadn't slept with every last one of his band mates. Oh, and his bus driver.

"You had fun, right?" Owen asked.

She nodded earnestly and then her eyes rolled up in her head at whatever erotic memories were teasing her thoughts.

"Then don't let it bother you."

He tripped over what had to be Gabe's overlong pant legs as he left her to mull over her misdeeds. He should probably find his own jeans, before he started waking people. He found them in the shower and had no idea how they'd gotten there. He took the time to use the john before changing into his own pants.

"Merry Christmas," he bellowed from the end of the corridor.

Tex sat bolt upright in the middle of the aisle. "What the fuck?" He covered his head with both hands and winced in pain. He then noticed his state of undress and shifted his hands to cover his crotch. "Who gave me whiskey?"

Owen chuckled. He wouldn't remember a thing from the night before. He never did when he drank too much whiskey.

"Ah God." He tried to stand but ended up crawling to the

bathroom and locking himself inside.

"I said, Merry Christmas, assholes," Owen yelled. "It's time to wake up. Santa came."

"I remember him coming at least four times," Adam's said from his bunk. Well, he was mostly in his bunk. One hand and foot were dragging the floor. "I can't feel my arm."

"That sucks for a lead guitarist, doesn't it?" Shade grumbled from the sofa. He had a pair of pink panties stuck to his forehead. Owen grinned, wondering how long it would take him to notice.

Adam rolled onto his back and used his functional arm to try to rub the circulation back into his temporarily frozen one. "I'd flip you off if you were worth the trouble."

"Here's what Santa brought you, Adam."

"Let me guess. Another chain."

Owen laughed. "How did you know?"

"You buy me a chain every year. That's why I have like ten of them."

"Well now you have eleven. You're welcome."

Adam smiled at him—he really didn't do that enough these days. "Thanks, man. It's exactly what I wanted. And I really didn't get you shit."

"That's not from me, it's from Santa."

"Yeah okay. What are you—five years old?"

"On Christmas I am."

Gabe hadn't stirred from his upside down sprawl in the recliner. His mohawked head was on the extended foot rest, legs spread and draped over each chair arm. After seeing where Gabe's balls were currently situated, Owen vowed to never sit in that chair again.

"Gabe, are you awake? It's Christmas."

"I just wanna sleep," he said in a slurred voice.

"I guess you don't want this boring ass book that Santa brought you." Owen dropped the heavy book on Gabe's chest, which definitely got his attention. Clutching the book in both hands, he lifted his head and glanced around in confusion. "Um," he said. "How in the fuck did I wind up sleeping like this? It defies all logic."

"Sort of like your hairstyle."

Gabe lift the book and blinked his eyes until they focused well enough to read the title. "Theories in Antigravity? Now there's a thought. Imagine sex in space."

"Enjoy," Owen said.

He handed Shade a long flat box. "Sunglasses? For me? Good thing. Vanessa broke my last pair when she sat on my face."

"Nope, sorry. Had he known you would be without your precious sunglasses on Christmas morning, Santa would have gone with the usual, but he was a little more creative this year."

Shade opened the box and lifted the flat cross that dangled from a silver chain. He lifted an eyebrow at him. "Trying to keep me out of trouble?"

"Wear it over your heart," Owen said. "And read the inscription on the back while you're at it."

"Your angel," Shade read haltingly. "...is always." He scowled at the words.

"Close to your heart," Owen finished for him, knowing how the guy struggled with written language.

Shade bit his lip. "I wonder if she's awake yet. I need to call her. Do we have phone service yet?" He slipped the chain over his head and patted it into his chest, before peeling the panties off of his forehead and seeking clothes to make himself decent before he talked to his three-year-old daughter on Christmas morning.

"Yeah, we have service," Tex yelled from the back of the bus. "I just called the crew. The equipment truck didn't attempt the pass, so they're all fine. A snow plow is trying to clear the roads and they're sending up a tow truck to help stranded vehicles."

Not quite a Christmas miracle, but definitely good news.

Owen found Kelly in the driver's seat. He was wide awake, wrapped in a red plaid flannel blanket staring out at the bleak white landscape outside the bus. The snow had stopped during the night, but the wind had piled it into huge drifts. The sky was gray with dense clouds making the sunlight dim. Like Kelly's mood. Owen couldn't stand to see him depressed. Especially on Christmas. He stood beside his chair and stared at Kelly's reflection in the windshield for a long moment. Kelly had that familiar far-off pained look in his eyes. He didn't seem to realize that Owen was standing at his side.

"You're thinking about her again," Owen said.

Kelly sucked a startled breath through his nose and then released it slowly. "Christmas is tough," he said quietly, though his gaze never moved from whatever point in the distance held his attention. He was seeing the past. Still living in the past.

"Why's that?" Owen asked.

"She said she wanted me to take her to see the Christmas tree in Times Square before she died."

Owen knew Sara had died in January, so the opportunity had been there. "Did you go?"

He shook his head almost unperceptively. "I refused to take her. I wanted her to stay in bed. All those little things she wanted to do before she went, I wouldn't let her do them. I was so afraid of her dying that I didn't let her live."

"Are you going to let yourself start living soon?" Owen asked.

Kelly turned his head to look up at him. "You can't help but stick your nose in other people's business, can you?"

"Nope."

"And you can't let people wallow in their misery."

"Nope."

"You know why?"

"Nope."

"Nothing truly horrible has ever happened to you."

Owen smiled. "And I plan to keep it that way." He pulled the last gift from his bag and tossed it on Kelly's lap. "Santa got you something. When you wear it, Sara will know you're still bound to her. When you take it off, it's because you're finally ready to do what she wanted you to do and move on."

Owen hoped Kelly didn't wear the leather wrist cuff for too awfully long. He wanted it to be a constant reminder to him that Sara would want him to find someone to love. Or at least someone to screw properly.

He patted Kelly's shoulder and turned to go. Kelly grabbed Owen's wrist and stuffed a small box in his hand. "Santa got you something too."

Excitement flowing through him, Owen opened the box and found an engraved set of dog tags on a chain. He ran his fingers over his brother's name—Chad—and then donned him. He'd worn dog tags for years—even before his brother had joined the military—to symbolize how he loved his country. These tags meant something even more to him. He clutched the flat pieces of metal in one hand and sent a silent prayer to keep his brother safe in Afghanistan. He hoped Chad was able to have some sort of celebration. Maybe Owen could talk the guys into visiting the troops and putting on a concert for them someday. Or maybe he could fool Shade into thinking that he'd come up with the idea and he'd insist the band go overseas.

"Thanks," Owen said, "but don't you think it's kind of lame to give your buddy jewelry for Christmas?" He knew damned well he'd given three out of four of his band mates some sort of jewelry, but couldn't help but mess with Kellen. He was entirely too gloomy this morning.

"That's from Santa," Kelly said. "Don't tell me you stopped believing."

"Of course I haven't. It's Christmas."

He turned to find Shade talking on his cell phone and grinning like a loon. "Did you open all your presents already?" Shade laughed at whatever his daughter said on the other end of the line. "What did Santa a bring you?" He interjected a "wow!" and a "that's awesome!" every now and then, but otherwise just listened to her rattle on about her apparently huge pile of gifts. After several minutes, his smile faltered. "No, angel, I can't come see you today." He put on a pair of horribly bent sunglass to hide his suddenly watery eyes, but he couldn't disguise the breathless quality of his voice as he spoke to her. "I'm stuck in the snow." He chuckled. "Yes, I know it doesn't snow lots in Texas, but I'm in Idaho. It snows lots in Idaho." He bit his lip. "You'd make a perfect snow angel."

Owen pointed at his Santa hat to remind him that they were going to give little Julie a second Christmas this year.

"When daddy gets home…" He paused as she interrupted him again. "Eight more sleeps. I know that's a long time, honey. When daddy gets home in eight more sleeps, we'll have another Christmas with just you and me."

Owen crossed his arms over his chest and cleared his throat pointedly. He totally wanted in on the fun. He loved Christmas just as much as any three-year-old did.

"And Owen is going to get himself stuck in the chimney just for you." Shade laughed. "Yep, he does have a flying reindeer as a matter of fact." And then apparently his ex-wife got on the phone because his expression changed from his "melted daddy" look to his "oh my god what does this bitch want now" look. "Maybe he does have a fucking flying reindeer," Shade shouted.

Really? She was going to yell at him about *that*? Owen normally didn't interfere in Shade's drama with his ex-wife, but he wasn't letting Tina ruin Shade's entire day. He was miserable enough about not getting to see his daughter today.

He snatched Shade's phone out of his hand and lifted it to his ear, not really paying attention to Tina's caterwauling. "Tina," Owen said, "he'll be there to pick Julie up a week from tomorrow. Have a Merry Christmas."

He hung up and handed the phone back to Shade.

"Thanks," Shade said, "I can't seem to control my temper when I have to interact with her."

"No problem," Owen said. "I love hanging up on her."

"How about a nice Christmas breakfast?" Shade said.

"Are you cooking?" Owen asked.

"Yep."

"Pancakes?"

"What else?"

"I'm in."

"Me too," Gabe said, setting his new book aside.

"Me three," Adam said.

"Kelly?" Owen called. "You want breakfast?"

"Does Gabe have pants on yet?"

"I'm on it," Gabe promised.

"Then yeah." Kelly shed his blanket, his new leather cuff on his wrist.

It brought Owen no joy to see Kellen wearing the gift he'd given him. He looked forward to the day that Kelly took it off permanently.

Lindsey and Vanessa slinked out of the bedroom at the back of the bus.

"Can we join you?" Vanessa asked.

"Shade tugged a pair of panties out of his pocket and passed them discretely to Owen.

"Did you ever find your panties, Vanessa?" Shade asked.

"No," she said, crossing her arms over her chest. "I think some fool stole them."

Owen tucked her panties into his back pocket.

"I hope they turn up," Shade said. "We have a no panties-no breakfast policy on this tour bus."

"Whatever," Vanessa said.

"It's true," Gabe said. "Why do you think I decided to get dressed?"

"You wear panties?" Vanessa asked.

"Only on special occasions."

Lindsey grinned. "I found my panties. What's for breakfast?"

"Shade's famous melt-in-your-mouth pancakes."

"Sounds great." She moved to sit in the booth at the dining table.

When Vanessa tried to follow her, Adam reached out of his bunk with his now fully functional arm and grabbed her leg. "Panty inspection required."

"I said some fool done *stole* my panties."

"Then no breakfast for you."

Vanessa looked to her friend for assistance. "Girl, you aren't going to desert me, are you?"

"Sorry, Nessi, but I'm starving."

"Some friend you are." Vanessa eventually resorted to wearing a pair of Adam's boxer shorts so she could join them at breakfast.

It wasn't exactly the kind of Christmas morning Owen was accustomed to, but everyone was smiling and happy. That's all that really mattered to him.

CHAPTER THIRTEEN

It was a few hours before the snow plow and a tow truck made it up the mountain pass to clear the road and pull Lindsey's car out of a snow drift. She'd had one hell of a crazy night with the boys in the band, but was surprised by how normal they were as they had breakfast and joked around with each other and played a game of hide Vanessa's panties. Owen especially like to get Vanessa riled up. Lindsey was pretty sure Vanessa was overstating her exasperation with the five of them, but it was difficult to tell with Vanessa.

Lindsey almost didn't want to say good-bye to them when her car was deemed drivable and was ready to make the journey back home.

"Later, guys," Vanessa said. "Thanks for the multiple orgasms!"

The tow truck driver literally fell on his ass at this proclamation. He somehow managed to scrape himself off the pavement and climb into the cab of his truck.

Lindsey wasn't quite so bawdy in her farewell, though she was equally thankful for the multiple orgasms. She smiled and waved at them, knowing she'd never see any of them in person again, wondering why that made her a little sad. What they'd shared had just been sex—a hell of a lot of mind-blowingly awesome sex—but it hadn't meant anything.

Lindsey climbed in the car and watched the tour bus pull away, heading in the opposite direction from her boring hometown.

"That was fun," Vanessa said as Lindsey maneuvered her car cautiously down the steep grade.

"Yeah," Lindsey agreed. "Great guys."

"I can't remember ever having a better Christmas."

Lindsey chuckled. "That was very memorable."

Vanessa examined her fingernails. "You know, if you turned around right now and followed them, I bet we could have a very happy New Year as well."

"Vanessa! Damn girl, you and your horny vagina are gonna get us both killed." She said that, but it didn't stop her from contemplating a highly illegal U-turn.

"I'm about to jack this car and take off after them."

Vanessa pursed her lips together to try to stifle a laugh. She lasted almost three seconds before she bust a gut. Lindsey couldn't help but get caught up in the hilarity of their situation.

When the two of them stopped laughing, they exchanged a look of longing, but ultimately continued toward home.

"Merry Christmas, Lindsey," Vanessa said.

"Merry Christmas, Nessi."

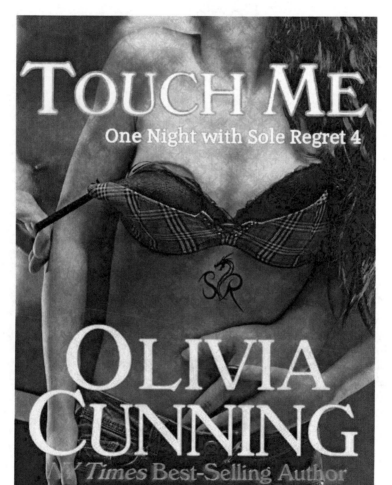

TOUCH ME

One Night with Sole Regret 4

OLIVIA CUNNING

NY Times Best-Selling Author

Touch Me
One Night with Sole Regret #4

CHAPTER ONE

Tonight, Owen's band, Sole Regret, would perform in San Antonio. Tomorrow night? Houston, maybe. And then New Orleans. Or was it Beaumont? Owen wasn't sure. The tour dates were starting to run together. He just got on the tour bus after the show and went wherever it took him. At least he knew they were still in his home state of Texas. He'd seen his family in Austin the night before, so some of his homesickness had abated. He loved touring with the guys, but his family had always been a tight-knit bunch, so he missed them when they weren't tousling his hair as if he were a four-year-old and insisting he have another biscuit with his fried chicken.

Owen stood behind the main stage, watching the crew make last-minute adjustments to the fire fountains and spark cannons. The fans had no idea how much work went into setting up the stage so Sole Regret could play for a mere hour. No one ever cheered for the stagehands, but their crew's hard work had paid off—the band would be live in less than five minutes. Owen appreciated all they did. He'd climbed out of bed that morning ready to hit the stage and without the crew, there wouldn't be a stage.

While he waited, Owen wrapped his hand around the dog tags dangling from a chain around his neck, closed his eyes, and sent a silent prayer to his older brother, Chad, currently serving in Afghanistan. *Be safe. Come home soon, soldier. Be safe.*

Owen prayed the same words before every concert. His routine. As if the powers that be were more likely to hear his prayers right before he went onstage. As if the energy of Sole Regret's fans made his pleas more noteworthy to Chad's guardian angel. Owen imagined that particular angel wore combat boots and camouflage. And carried a big fucking gun. Chad's angel of no mercy would keep him safe. Owen had faith.

Someone leaned against Owen's arm, and Owen knew it was Kelly before he even opened his eyes.

Kelly's mouth was set in a grim line, and his dark brown eyes held concern. If Owen hadn't known Kelly as well as he knew himself, he'd have thought he was always serious and stern. Kelly did loosen up on occasion, but only around people he knew well.

The leather strap supporting Kelly's cobalt-blue Les Paul guitar cut into his bare chest when he lifted a hand to give Owen's shoulder a comforting squeeze.

"Heard from Chad lately?" Kelly asked.

Owen sometimes wondered if his best friend could read his mind.

"He's supposed to Skype me tomorrow morning. Well, it will be night where he is."

"Tell him I said hey," Kelly said.

"Tell him yourself. I'm not your messenger boy."

Owen knew Chad liked to see familiar faces. Not just family or his girlfriend or all the friends who were waiting for him in Austin, but Kelly too. Chad had been a big brother to both of them, mostly knocking their heads together when they were being insufferable idiots, but he'd also stepped into a protective role more than once. Kelly had done his part to lessen the bullying Owen had endured in high school, but occasionally Chad's older, bigger fists had been necessary to get the point across.

Owen had plenty of friends now, but there had been a time when Kelly had been his only one. He was still Owen's best friend. Always would be. As members of the same band, he and Kelly spent more time together than should be allowable by law. That hadn't changed. Probably never would. But other things between them had changed in the past six months.

An uncomfortable tension had surfaced when Owen had given Kelly a wrist cuff for Christmas to remind him of Sara. Owen and Kelly had had a lot more fun before Owen had made Kelly's grief even more pronounced. *Smooth move, Owen. Fucked that one up majorly, you did.* He kicked himself on a daily basis for that overly thoughtful gift. Should have bought the guy a shirt instead, since Kelly didn't seem to own one. Owen had taken to plotting to steal the damned cuff in the middle of the night and setting it ablaze. Unfortunately, Kelly was a light sleeper.

"Are you ready for tonight's excursion?" Owen asked, shifting his hand from the dog tags to rest it on the solid gray body of his favorite bass guitar.

"I guess so. I can't believe the rest of the guys bailed on us." Kelly glanced at the other three members of the band and shook his head at their disgrace. "What about our pact?"

Yeah, what about their pact? They were supposed to keep each other from getting entangled in serious romantic relationships while on tour, but the guys were falling like dominoes. Kelly didn't have to worry about Owen falling into the same trap, however. Owen had no interest in romantic relationships. He was having far too much fun being wealthy and single. He highly recommended it.

"They must be getting old," Owen said with a grin. "Don't ever get old on me, Kelly."

"I don't have time to get old."

"We could invite Tex and Jack to come with us." Owen was sure the roadies would be up for a little late-night entertainment. The sex club they were going to was exclusive—invitation only. Owen couldn't believe there was a man alive who would turn down the opportunity to get inside. And Gabe, Shade, and Adam had all turned up their noses, as if guaranteed sex with a stranger wasn't good enough for them anymore. It had been good enough for them a week ago. It was still good enough for Owen.

"Nah, the crew has work to do. Tonight it's me and you, bro." Kelly lifted a fist, and Owen fist-bumped him.

"And don't forget the ladies," Owen said with a smirk. "They're the best part. You are going to actually do something with them tonight, aren't you?"

Kelly shrugged. "If I feel like it."

"I think you're getting old too."

Kelly's eyes dropped to the cuff on his wrist, and he traced it with one finger. "Maybe."

Whoever came up with that "it's better to have loved and lost" saying was the biggest fucking dolt who'd ever initiated a cliché.

Kelly had loved and lost, and the loss had all but destroyed him. Owen wasn't sure if he would ever be the same. Kelly would've been better off if he'd never met Sara. The year he'd dated her, he'd all but disappeared from Owen's life. He'd been so wrapped up in the woman, it had been hard to distinguish them as separate entities. And when she'd died, she'd taken his heart with her. Five years later, Kelly still hadn't recovered the battered organ from Sara's clutches.

Owen had suffered his share of heartache, but nothing in comparison to Kelly. Where Owen had lost love in quantity—an embarrassing amount of quantity—Kelly had lost in quality. Owen had long since concluded that romance was for suckers. There would be no more heartache in his future. He was through with trying to find someone to love him for who he was, not what he'd become. If a guy was burned enough times, he eventually learned to stop putting his hand in the fire.

"I could sample a few choice pies for you and let you know which tastes best," Owen offered, only half joking. He enjoyed pleasuring a woman with his mouth, and he knew how much Kelly got off on the act. Or he had. Until last Christmas.

Fuck. Owen vowed to never give anyone a thoughtful gift ever again. It would be tube socks and neckties all around this year.

One corner of Kelly's mouth rose. "I'm not sure we have the same discriminating palate, dude."

"If you need me to—" Owen glanced pointedly at Kelly's crotch. Owen longed for the days when they'd pleasured women together. Especially the part when they'd given each other amazing hand jobs. But ever since Owen had given Kelly that cuff, Kelly had remained distant. He no longer helped Owen entertain women, and he wouldn't touch him anymore. At all. The truly confusing part of this shift in their relationship was that Owen couldn't stop thinking about his best friend's hand. Before Kelly had backed away, their brief sexual contact hadn't meant anything to Owen. He hadn't even considered it sexual contact. It wasn't as if he was attracted to Kelly or anything. He just liked the way Kelly tugged his cock just right. But now that they no longer touched each other—at Kelly's insistence—Owen couldn't get the feel of the man's perfect grip out of his head.

Owen absently stroked the thick strings of his bass guitar. Those orgasms couldn't have been as great as Owen's memory served. His mind had a way of making the things he couldn't have seem so much better than they actually were. He knew how his head worked, but the truth didn't stop him from fixating on something best left in the past. He had to get over his bizarre obsession. Kelly certainly had. Whenever Owen brought up their brief brushes with intimacy, Kelly looked uncomfortable and hedged his way out of the conversation. But maybe if they had just one more go at it, Owen could move on. He could stop thinking about how much fun they had pleasing a woman in tandem and how those interludes had culminated.

Kelly had turned off like a light switch six months before and hadn't turned back on since. Owen glanced at him again. It wasn't healthy for a man to be so, well... *celibate*.

"I told you we aren't doing that anymore," Kelly said.

"Oh, I know. It's not like it's a big deal. You just look a little tense." If an over-tightened guitar string was considered a little tense.

"I am tense, but I'll take care of it. Unlike you, I don't need a different girl every other night to get off."

Of course. Why would Kelly seek the company of a woman when he had a perfectly good hand at his disposal? If Owen had that particular hand at his disposal, he might not be so anxious to hook up with some stranger either.

Memories of Sara had done this to Kelly; Owen just didn't understand why his friend was faithful to a dead girl. After Sara had passed, it had taken Kelly a couple of years to even touch another woman. Then he'd progressed to eating them out as long as they were restrained and Owen had been there with him. Now Kelly wouldn't do anything sexual with anyone, no matter how many times Owen agreed to give him a hand or any other body part he wanted to utilize.

When Owen had given Kelly the cuff, he'd hoped it would be another step forward. He'd wanted the bracelet to remind Kelly of how stupid he was being—that no matter how much he wanted Sara back, it was impossible. She was gone. But the constant reminder of her on Kelly's wrist had only managed to solidify his dedication to abstinence. He hadn't merely taken a step back; he'd fallen off the ladder. Sure, Kelly went to Tony's sex clubs with the rest of them, but he never did anything. Comparatively speaking.

"Don't you think it's time to take off that cuff?"

"Not yet," Kelly said. "But I am a little horny."

"A little? Dude, your balls are so blue, you should start your own Blue Man Group."

Kelly laughed. "And you know that how?"

"Gabe was checking you out in the shower. He told me you're suffering from a colorful condition."

Owen had noticed their drummer standing in the shadows—you couldn't miss that foot-high, red and black mohawk of his—but didn't know if Gabe was listening in or not. Hard to tell with Gabe—the dude was often lost in thought. A person could carry on an entire one-sided conversation with him, and he didn't hear a word. He was, however, paying attention tonight.

"They were a little blue," Gabe said. "I don't think they're quite up to Blue Man standards. Better luck next time, Kellen."

"Hopes, dreams, and aspirations dashed again," Kelly said. "One day they'll be blue enough, you wait and see."

Gabe chuckled and shook his head.

"Hey," Owen said, grabbing Kelly's arm and leaning close, trying to look earnest, "you're not allowed to leave the band for the Vegas spotlight. I don't care how blue they get."

"I thought you, of all people, would be supportive of my desire to attain permanent blue balls. Surely you recognize my need to find others of my kind." Kelly said this with such conviction that anyone who didn't know him would have thought he was serious and offered him a cash donation for his cause.

Owen tried to keep a straight face, but snorted as a laugh escaped him.

"God, will you two knock it off?" Adam said. His ever-expanding collection of chains rattled in the semi-darkness to Owen's left. "You act like a couple of prepubescent boys when you're together. If I wanted kids, I wouldn't have made an appointment to get a vasectomy."

"As much as I joke about my balls," Kelly said, "I'd never let anyone come at 'em with a scalpel. Ever."

"And that's why you'll end up paying child support someday." Adam crossed his arms to rest on the body of his guitar and lifted a dark eyebrow at Kelly. "Some gold-digger will poke pinholes in your condoms and whoops, there's a two-million-dollar mistake."

"Does your girlfriend know you're getting snipped?" Owen asked. "She seems like the type who'd want kids."

"That's why I'm getting them snipped."

"You don't trust her?"

"Of course I trust her. I just lose my head around her. She'd say the word and I'd be doing my damnedest to knock her up. I don't have any business fathering a child. Look at the example I had to follow."

Adam's father was the poster child for bad parenting, but that didn't mean Adam would follow in the old man's footsteps. Still, Owen understood his hesitation over kids. Just the thought of having a kid made him break out in hives. He might consider it in twenty or thirty years. Or never.

"Kelly's not getting any, so he doesn't have to worry about it." Owen said. "But I strictly adhere to the BYOC rule. No kids for me."

"With that monstrosity in your junk, you probably poke holes in your own condoms by accident," Adam said.

Another reason Owen always brought his own; certain brands were more durable than others. A man had to be careful to use the right protection if he had adornments in certain body parts.

"You guys don't know what you're missing," Shade said. "Kids are awesome." The band's lead singer had sported a stupid grin of one degree or another all day. Sure, Shade smiled now, but if his ex-wife ever found out why he looked like he'd been huffing nitrous oxide, he wouldn't be smiling then. Tina would rip his lips right off his face. His ex wouldn't take kindly to Shade dating her sister. Tina hated Shade's fucking guts and wanted him miserable for all eternity. So far, fate had been working in her favor.

"Not all kids are awesome," Adam said. "Some are the spawn of Satan. But yeah, Jules is pretty awesome. Even if she is related to you."

Shade laughed and punched Adam in the arm.

Owen exchanged glances with Kelly. They both stiffened in preparation for an inevitable fight—Shade and Adam had gotten into one in the limo after their last concert—but it seemed the two over-inflated egos really were just goofing off and no one was at risk for an ER visit. Good thing. Adam would have been pissed if he'd had to room with his father. Apparently, his dear old dad had gotten his hands on bad drugs and landed himself in the emergency room the night before. Owen had been surprised that Adam had even taken him to the hospital. Adam resented the old man, whether they shared DNA or not. Owen couldn't quite wrap his head around the idea of hating one's own father, no matter what he'd done. Owen would be devastated if anything happened to any member of his family—including any of his seventy-one third cousins.

"Have you heard from your dad?" Owen asked Adam.

"Yeah. He bitched me out on the phone less than an hour ago."

"Still in the hospital?"

Adam nodded. "And apparently they don't subscribe to his favorite TV channel."

"Well, fuck, Adam, you don't expect him to watch the Disney Channel, do you?" Owen said.

"That's the channel he was bitching about. Can't miss Hannah Montana."

Owen jerked back in surprise. "No shit?"

"Shit no," Adam said. "I swear, Owen Mitchell is a synonym for gullible."

"Adam Taylor is a synonym for asshole," Owen countered.

"Gabriel Banner is a synonym for let's get the fuck on the stage," Gabe said. "Isn't it already after nine?"

Owen turned to watch the crew standing around a bank of amplifiers on the stage. The head of their road crew, Jack, was squeezed behind the sound equipment, wiggling wires and garbling swear words around the penlight he held between his teeth. Owen moved closer and waved down one of the onlookers.

"What's the hold-up?" he asked.

"One of the new guys caught a cord with his foot and loosened some cables. Jack is fixing it."

"And he needs an audience? None of you has anything better to do five minutes *after* the show was supposed to start?"

The group scattered. In his earpiece, Owen heard Cash, their soundboard operator, say, "That's got it, Jack. Owen, we're ready when you are."

Owen was always ready to be on stage. He loved that he got to start every show—a few precious seconds to have twelve thousand screaming fans all to himself. Not many bassists got to stand in the limelight.

He gave the rest of the band the thumbs-up to let them know he was starting and took the steps up to the edge of the stage. In the near darkness, Gabe hurried to settle behind his massive drum kit, careful not to make a sound by bumping a cymbal with those long limbs of his. As soon as he collected his sticks, Owen began his bass riff. The crowd roared and whistled as the first sound thrummed. The curtain dropped and a blinding white light lit Owen from above as he sauntered across the stage playing the repetitive bass line of "Darker." He gave no indication that a surge of adrenaline had his heart galloping a mile a minute as he slowly made his way toward center stage. Owen lived for this shit. He couldn't believe this was his job. For the rest of his life, Owen would worship at the altar of rock god Kellen Jamison for sending him down the path of wickedness. Kelly had been the one who'd forced Owen to learn to play guitar in an effort to get him laid in high school. It hadn't worked then—chubby bassists didn't get the girls—but it worked like a charm now.

The crowd got louder and louder as Owen pretended to ignore them. When he reached his target—a white X taped at the exact center of the stage floor—Gabe entered the song with a wickedly rapid drum progression. Owen pivoted, beamed a smile at the crowd, and dashed toward the audience as the rest of the band entered the stage and the song.

The entire band was pumped tonight, which guaranteed an amazing performance. Shade was in a great mood and joked around with the audience and with Adam. The pair had talked out some of their problems that morning, but Owen had had no idea that a simple conversation would make such a noticeable difference in the feel of the show. Owen and Kelly always had a great time onstage; they were completely relaxed in each other's company and loved hamming it up for the crowd. Shade and Adam, on the other hand, had spent the last couple of years acting as if they were at war with one another both onstage and off. Owen couldn't believe how much the atmosphere had changed overnight.

Between "Going Down" and "Heaven to Pay," Owen slipped into the wings and grabbed a bottle of water from a roadie. He chugged the cool fluid while Shade told the crowd a story about their lead guitarist falling off the stage in New Jersey.

"Face-planted right on the cement," Shade said, slapping one palm against the other. "Wham!"

"It wasn't funny," Adam said. "I almost broke my neck." But he didn't sound angry about Shade's teasing.

Owen was grateful Adam had regained his sense of humor. His short fuse was a liability.

"Luckily, I was drunk enough that I didn't feel a thing," Adam said.

"Until the next morning," Shade said.

"I can't believe how well they're getting along," Kelly said to Owen as he sipped from his water bottle. "Calm before the storm?"

"Maybe. I keep waiting for one or the other to explode."

"Shade's been acting happy all day," Jack said. "It's just not right." He took the empty water bottles from Owen and Kelly.

"You can blame that on his bedmate last night," Owen said, grinning. "She must have a magic vagina."

"I don't care if it shoots glitter and rainbows," Kelly said. "That relationship can only end in disaster. We'd better enjoy this while it lasts."

As the pair returned to the front of the stage, Shade asked, "Did you have a nice break?"

"No," Owen said. Shade's microphone was close enough that it picked up his words and they were broadcast through the stadium. "I was hoping the clear stuff in my bottle was vodka, but it was only water."

"Mine had vodka," Kelly said. "The crew has seen you drunk, Tags. Not something they want to see again."

"I'm a fun drunk," Owen said. "Everyone loves to hang around when I'm drunk."

"Yeah," Kelly said, "everyone who wears a skirt and wants it up around their waist while you go down loves to hang around when you're drunk." He rolled his eyes.

Feminine approval roared from the crowd.

"If it bothers you so much, stop wearing skirts, Cuff," Owen said.

The crowd's laughter egged them on.

"It's called a kilt. And how else am I supposed to show off my legs?" Kelly asked.

"Kilts don't come in floral patterns."

"Okay," Shade said, "that's enough out of you two. This isn't open mic night."

"These people came to hear music, not your lame jokes," Adam said.

Since Gabe didn't have a live mic, he played a mini drum solo to enter his opinion on the matter. Owen and Kelly kept their jokes to themselves for the remainder of the show, but they still managed to have fun.

And the crowd responded, stomping on the floor and thrusting their fists into the air.

"I'm heading for the shower," Owen said after the encore. He handed off his bass to one of the road crew and looked at Kelly expectantly.

"I'll join you," Kelly said. "I'm drenched."

"Last chance for you pussy-whipped disgraces to join us tonight at Tony's new club," Owen said, looking to his other three band mates.

"Not happening, Owen," Shade said. "Have a good time."

"I'll have a good enough time for the three of you," Owen said. He glanced at Kelly, knowing he probably wouldn't utilize the club to its fullest capabilities. "For all five of us," he said under his breath. He vowed never to fall hard for a woman. Monogamy. Where was the fun in that?

A pair of hands appeared over Shade's sunglasses. "Guess who," a soft, sultry voice said from behind him.

Shade's hands reached back and began to explore the feminine body at his back. "I know these tits," he said, a huge smile stretching across his face.

"Are you sure?"

Owen cocked his head to the side, and his suspicions were validated. What in the fuck was *she* doing here? Amanda made Shade happy—hell, that was obvious. But she was trouble for him. Big trouble.

"Yeah," Shade said. "It's been ages, Pamela. Are you ready for another musician to rock your bed?"

Amanda grabbed his nose and twisted.

"Ow! Amanda, I was only joking."

"You knew it was me?"

"Of course I knew it was you. Pamela's tits are enormous, and yours are massive, at best."

She scowled at her ample bust. "Maybe I'll get them enlarged," she said.

"Don't go messing with perfection, babe."

She looked up at him. "You're not surprised I came?"

"You came already? Geez, all I did was fondle your tits a little."

Owen chuckled. God, he'd missed this Shade—the guy who smiled and joked and didn't look as if a perpetual doom cloud was tailing him.

Amanda slapped Shade, but was unable to hide her grin. This sister was so much easier to get along with than the one Shade had married the first go round. But, yep, still trouble.

"Or," Shade said, "do you mean I'm not surprised that you couldn't wait until Saturday to see me again? Or that you'd drive almost five hours just to get in my pants? Nope. Not surprised."

"Ugh," she groaned. "I forgot how big your ego gets after a show."

"It's not the only thing that gets big."

She wiggled her eyebrows at him. "I hope you're planning to show me that other big thing."

Shade turned and grabbed her, hauling her against his body. He whispered something in her ear, and she nodded eagerly.

"Owen." Kelly snapped his fingers in Owen's face. "The limo is waiting for us. If you want a shower, you'd better stop gawking at the happy couple and get your ass to the dressing room."

He couldn't help but gawk. Train wrecks waiting to happen were mesmerizing.

Owen hurried through his shower, keeping his eyes diverted from Kelly's naked body. Especially when Kelly placed one hand on the shower wall and used his free hand to thoroughly lather his cock. Lucky cock. Owen stuck his head under the shower head, shut his eyes, and let the water flood his face. Worrying about Kelly's neglected dick was bizarre—Owen knew that. He should concentrate more on his own fifth appendage, which was half hard in anticipation of seeking a new conquest at the club tonight. Or something.

"Remember when we used to see who could jerk one out the fastest?" Owen said, soaping his own cock now.

Kelly chuckled. "God, we were immature," he said.

"Um, yeah, immature."

Owen hurried to rinse the soap from his body. He then shut off the water and found his clothes. Before he slid into his boxer briefs, he switched out the metallic balls in his centered dydoe piercing to a larger, mismatched set. He found the . . . what had Adam called it— the monstrosity in his junk—gave both himself and his partner the greatest thrill if the balls were of different sizes. He absolutely loved the reaction that little piece of jewelry got from the ladies the first time they saw it. And loved it even more the first time they experienced it inside them.

Grinning in anticipation, Owen dressed in all black, but not the typical jeans and T-shirt he usually wore. He slipped into a pair of tailored slacks and a button-down shirt. He did wear his Converse though, because they were the only shoes he ever wore. His tattoos all concealed beneath his clothes, he decided to play down his rocker image. He removed his lip piercing and the barbells in his nipples, but left the half-inch black plugs in his ears since when he went without jewelry, the holes were even more noticeable. He fingered the hoop in his eyebrow and decided to leave it in as well. The piercing had never healed right, so he had a hard time getting the ring back in the hole if he took it out.

"All black tonight? If you had a cape, you could be a vampire," Kelly said, using his towel to dry his long hair instead of using it to conceal his body.

"Black is slimming."

"You're not fat any more, Owen."

"I know." Owen ran a hand over his flat belly, making sure those rock hard abs he worked so hard to maintain hadn't suddenly disappeared. Still there.

He added a touch of product to the ends of his damp hair, arranging the dark blond locks into disarray. "Hurry up, Kelly," he said, suddenly eager to get to the club and fuck any woman who would have him.

"Keep your pants on," Kelly said as drew a brush through his longish black hair.

"Hopefully, I won't have to for long."

CHAPTER TWO

Caitlyn was going to screw every man in this club. That would show the insufferable bastard. She had trusted him, loved him, and picked his damned dirty underwear off the floor for twelve years. How could he do this to her? Her no-good, lying, son-of-a-bitch ex-husband had cheated on her with a freshman in his introductory English class. A nineteen-year-old. A *baby*. Then he'd had the audacity to file for divorce stating irreconcilable differences. Yeah, he wanted to put his dick in someone, and Caitlyn had an irreconcilable difference of opinion that it should be only his *wife*. The worst part was that because she made more money than the asshole, she had to pay *alimony* to buy off his financial interest in *her* corporation—the one he'd never believed in or supported and had resented until he'd found out he could line his pockets with all of Caitlyn's sacrifice and hard work. And where was her support currently going? To fund his summer in Italy with that fucking little tramp. How was that fair? How was that even legal?

Caitlyn was going to screw every man in this club *twice*. That's what she'd told herself while she was purchasing sexy lingerie in the shop downstairs. What she'd told herself when she'd been changing into her new white lace nightie, thigh-high stockings, and four-inch heels. That's what she told herself when she'd marched into the club and strutted—the best she could in these ridiculous shoes—across what might have been a dance floor if anyone had been dancing. But the other patrons were occupied with activities that made Caitlyn alternately gawk and avert her eyes. They were involved in things she hadn't done in the privacy of her own bedroom, much less in public.

Yeah, she was about to go do some of that stuff herself. Lots of that stuff. And she would mentally give Charles the middle finger the entire time another man was stuffing her with his cock.

So why was she hiding in a secluded corner avoiding eye

contact? And why were her knees knocking together?

She'd asked Jenna to bring her to the club. Asked Jenna to *leave* her here. By herself. Because Caitlyn had been afraid that she wouldn't be able to open her thighs to a stranger and at the first sign of masculine interest, would have begged Jenna to take her home. That wouldn't have done anything to hurt Charles. Not that she cared if she hurt him as much as he had hurt her—she doubted it was possible anyway. Word would get back to him that she'd come here, and she'd make damn sure he thought she'd participated in the orgy of her life. And that she'd loved every minute of it. Without him.

At least that had been her plan when she'd arrived.

But instead of participating in the overt sexual acts going on around her, Caitlyn observed. And tried not to feel like a coward and a loser and the most unattractive, undesirable, *oldest* woman in the place. Tried to pretend she was alone because she wanted to be, not because no one wanted her. Being here was not making her feel better about herself or empowered or even sexy. Why had she come?

Caitlyn had only ever slept with one man. Charles couldn't claim he'd slept with only one woman. He couldn't even claim he'd slept with only one woman when he'd been *married*. Would removing Charles's claim over her body help her heart mend? She'd thought so at first, but now she wasn't so sure.

Caitlyn watched yet another couple leave the main parlor to go to one of the private rooms in the back and then lowered her eyes to stare at her thumbs. The man had held the woman's breast in his hand and had his other hand down her panties—teasing her, stroking her, making her moan—as if he couldn't wait to take her, to touch her.

Caitlyn wanted someone to take her. To touch her.

God, how she wanted someone to touch her.

How long had it been since a man had found her irresistible?

Had a man *ever* found her irresistible? Yeah, Charles had once. When she'd been a freshman in his introductory English class. An innocent, trusting virgin. It seemed he didn't find women over thirty attractive at all. Did anyone?

What did she have to do to feel sexy again? To feel wanted? Sitting in a frilly white negligée in the corner of a sex club staring at her thumbs wasn't working so well for her. Not the way she'd thought it would. She'd thought braving this place would make her feel confident. Attractive. Desirable. Instead she felt out of place and uncomfortable.

"Do you know what your problem is, beautiful?" a deep voice asked from the chair across the table from her.

She hadn't realized anyone had sat down. "What?" she snapped.

"You're much too pretty to give off such incredible men-suck vibes."

She caught herself before she said, *Men do suck. They suck shit-encrusted balls.* But she'd have been lying. Not all men sucked. *Charles* sucked. But not all men did. She liked men. Most of the time. Most of her colleagues were men, and she got along just fine with them.

Caitlyn stared at a pair of dog tags resting against a black button-down shirt covering a man's chest. Her heart thudded too fast for her to find the courage to actually meet his eyes. He'd called her beautiful. Pretty. Was this that masculine attention she'd both coveted and dreaded? She was pretty sure he was hitting on her. Wasn't he? She'd never dated much before she'd gotten married. She wasn't sure how this worked.

Oh God, what was she doing here? If she made eye contact would he expect her to have sex with him? Could she go through with this? "You're very perceptive," she managed to say.

"I was wondering why the most attractive woman in the room was sitting by herself in a corner. I thought maybe the possessive, hot-tempered, black-belt martial artist you were with was in the bathroom or something, but I watched you for a while and figured out why you're not surrounded by admirers. It's those men-suck vibes you're giving off."

"So why didn't they scare you away?" She lifted her eyes, and her breath caught. Not only was he the most gorgeous man she'd ever laid eyes on, he was young—in his midtwenties. His dark blond hair was lightly gelled into a devil-may-care style that matched the twinkle in his blue eyes. Those eyes were a mesmerizing contrast to the warm tanned hue of his skin. A small hoop pierced one eyebrow, and he wore round cylinders in both earlobes—plugs or whatever they were called. She'd have thought he was an actor or a model if not for those accessories marring his otherwise perfect features.

"I don't scare easy when I see something I want." He grinned at her, flashing even white teeth and self-confidence that made her believe he didn't want for long. No, this one attained. "What's your name, beautiful?"

He'd called her beautiful again. She'd never needed a man's praise to make her feel good about herself before she'd caught Charles with his pants around his knees while he thrust his pathetic cock into that nubile nineteen-year-old vagina on his desk. Sure, that vagina had been part of a person, but watching it engulf her husband's cock was an image Caitlyn would never be able to scrub from her memory. With all the long hours she'd been working, their sex life had gotten a little stale, so she'd thought to surprise him in his office. Oh, she'd surprised him all right. And gotten the shock of her life as well.

The attractive man's fingertips lightly brushed the back of her wrist and drew her away from her thoughts. That slight contact had emotions warring within her. She was flattered yet skeptical. Tense and uncomfortable, yet relieved that someone had noticed her. Grateful that he had called her beautiful. Thankful that he was either a great actor or actually was attracted to her.

Shoot, maybe he just pitied her for being alone.

"I'm Caitlyn," she said, remembering that he'd asked her name.

"Why did you come here, Caitlyn?"

Because I'm lonely. Because my husband left me for a younger woman and I feel ugly. Old. Oh God, it's been so long since someone has made me feel attractive that I don't even know what to say to you.

"I was curious," she said.

That was partially true. She *had* wondered what went on in places like these. Jenna's husband was friends with the club's owner and when Jenna had jokingly said Caitlyn needed to go there to get laid and work Charles out of her system, Caitlyn had surprised even herself by insisting she did. But she wasn't going to start spilling her guts to strangers. She scarcely spilled them to her closest friends. She'd come to visit Jenna, her college roommate, in San Antonio on a whim. Mostly because she couldn't stand to sit alone in her big house on the bay for another night. A house she'd once dreamed of filling with a loving family. Back when Charles had led her to believe that he wanted that too.

Stop thinking about him. Stop thinking about him. Just stop. Caitlyn squeezed her eyes shut and gave her head a hard shake. She then opened her eyes and shared her most dazzling smile with the hottie in black sitting across the bistro table from her.

"What's your name, gorgeous?" she said, doing her damnedest to keep her men-suck vibes under control, because wouldn't it be spit in Charles's eye if she hooked up with this good-looking man— this *young* man—and fucked him all night.

"Owen."

"Why did you come here, Owen?"

"I thought that was obvious," he said.

She crinkled her brow in puzzlement.

"I was looking for you."

She laughed. "I'm pretty sure the only reason you came to talk to me is because all the good ones were already taken."

"Good ones?"

"The *young*, pretty ones."

"She was younger than you, wasn't she?"

He stroked the back of her hand gently and held her gaze. Caitlyn quickly found herself lost in his startlingly blue eyes.

"Caitlyn?"

She blinked and took a deep breath, trying to remember what he'd asked. "*Who* was younger than me?"

"The one he cheated with."

"How do you know he cheated?"

"Men-suck vibes. They're usually caused by a cheating asshole."

She wondered how many women he'd seduced this way. He was very good at it. She especially liked that he called Charles an asshole, even though he had no idea who Charles was.

"She was younger. Twenty-five years younger than him. I think what hurts the most is that I was just like her when I met him. I was her age when he left his first wife for me. Took my virginity on the exact same desk he plowed her on. I'm going to send his first wife flowers. What an awful, awful wretch I was to her. I even called her old."

Caitlyn cringed. When Caitlyn had married Charles, Gladys had been a year younger than Caitlyn was now. That made Caitlyn *really* old. She wondered if the poor girl he'd seduced was as proud of stealing him away as Caitlyn had been when she'd been in the same position. Had his little co-ed been a virgin? Had Charles told her she made him feel alive and that his dried up old wife had lost her spark? Caitlyn had been referring to Charles's latest ego booster as "that little tramp" for months. Caitlyn needed to direct all her anger at the truly guilty party. *Charles Theodore Mattock, you're a fucking, lecherous bastard.*

"So you seduced a married man? I guess you're not as sweet as you look in that sexy white lace." Owen winked at her.

"Well, no. I didn't realize he was married at the time. And for the record, *he* seduced me."

"Perhaps he could offer me a few pointers."

"You're doing fine so far." He smiled again, and her heart flopped down into the pit of her stomach.

"Would you like a drink?"

She was a *tad* overheated but said, "I think I'd better keep my wits about me."

"Now where's the fun in that?"

"I'm not going to send you away if that's what you're worried about. I came here to get laid, just like everyone else."

His eyes widened, and he laughed. "I guess that is why everyone is here, and everyone knows that's why we're all here, but we don't really discuss it. It's more fun to pretend there's a challenge."

She felt like a fool because she didn't know the rules. Didn't know the rules because she'd never played the game. "Oh. I didn't mean to offend you."

"I'm not offended. Just a little surprised by your straight-forwardness."

"Why?" No one she knew was surprised by it, but then she wasn't exactly dressed for her usual role as CEO and head engineer of Starpower Industries. *There* she was unequivocally confident and master of her domain. *Here* she was nervous, out of place, and utterly attracted to this guy. Maybe he didn't like strong women? She hoped she didn't intimidate him. Perhaps she should pretend to be meek, timid, and afraid, because she was feeling all those things at the moment and it rattled her to her core.

Owen stared at her for a long moment and just when she thought he was going to get up and leave her, he said, "Would you like to meet my friend Kellen? He's over in the corner booth waiting for me."

Caitlyn looked in the direction Owen indicated with a nod of his head. She could see silky black hair on the crown of Kellen's head, but the rest of him was concealed by the high-backed booths. Caitlyn immediately realized what this was about. The good-looking one, Owen, captured unsuspecting women for his homely friend Kellen. It explained perfectly why he was coming on to her in the first place. Wouldn't they be surprised when she turned the tables on them and rejected them both? She didn't like to be taken for a fool.

"Sure."

Owen rose from his seat, and she couldn't help but notice the hard cut of his body and how his perfectly pressed shirt clung to his shoulders and chest. How it tapered down to be tucked into a pair of well-made slacks that accentuated his narrow hips. A leather belt drew her attention to his trim waist. She'd seen pictures of guys built like this, but wasn't sure if she'd ever encountered one in real life. It took her a moment to realize he was holding his hand out in her direction. She slid her palm into his, finding it warm, strong and, apart from the calluses on his fingertips, smooth. She couldn't help but wonder what those fingers would feel like against her skin.

She slipped from her chair and stood on the spindly high heels she'd purchased at the club's basement shop. They were white patent leather and made her pretty white negligée seem a little less innocent. She'd chosen the piece of lace lingerie because they wouldn't let her in the club wearing her tweed and denim and it was the least trashy of the items they offered. Plus, the short teddy came with a thigh-length gauzy robe which, though transparent, gave her the illusion that she wasn't showing so much bare skin to strangers. She wondered why the one man she wanted to see naked had been allowed to bypass the no-street-clothes rule. Owen was dressed all in black, except he was barefoot. Every other person in the room was at least partially undressed, and a few were entirely naked.

Clutching her transparent robe at the waist, she took a hesitant step. While she didn't wear heels in the lab, she wore them in the boardroom, but she'd never worn a pair four inches high until tonight. She was so busy concentrating on not breaking her neck that she didn't realize Owen had stopped until his hand touched her arm. She froze in midstep and looked at him in question. What had she done wrong this time? She was so not used to this scene.

Owen's eyes raked down her body. "Mmm. You must realize I asked you to stand so I could get a better look at you," he said.

Anywhere else in the world, she'd have been pissed by his blatant come-on and told him to go fuck himself, but here, she was expecting it. In a strange way, hoping for it. She was going to let this happen tonight. Tonight, but probably never again.

"And?"

"Even better than I'd fantasized. Stunning. Now walk that way so I can check out your ass without you noticing." He winked at her, and she burst out laughing.

"You're bad," she said.

"You have no idea." The devilish grin left his face and his expression warmed, leaving him looking sweet and gentle. "I can be good, if that turns you on. What turns you on, Caitlyn?"

"You," she blurted, and heat rose up her cheeks. She couldn't believe she'd actually said that, even if it was true.

"Then I'll improvise," he said.

He placed a hand on the small of her back to urge her toward the booth where his homely friend was waiting to make his move after Mr. Smooth Operator took his leave. Caitlyn focused on keeping her ankles from twisting as she stalked in that direction. It was impossible for her to walk in heels without taking confident steps. She forced herself not to look behind her to see if Owen really was checking out her ass. She hoped he enjoyed the view. The white thong she wore couldn't be hidden, even with the gauzy robe in place.

She paused at the table, eyes going wide when Owen's presumably ugly friend looked up from his beer. Kellen was on par with his gorgeous friend, even though they looked nothing alike. Where Owen had blue eyes, dirty-blond hair, and even features, Kellen was rugged and dark. Dark hair, dark eyes, dark mood. He was shirtless, which allowed her to scan the tattoos that decorated the hard muscles of his broad chest. His black hair was straight and just long enough to brush his collarbones. He looked untamed, like a Plains warrior. She could easily picture him astride a Paint Horse, hair flying out behind him as he aimed his bow at some animal he hunted. This guy was ruthless and hard. At least that was her impression until he smiled and his features softened. Her heart thudded so hard, she thought it might explode in her chest. Okay, if these two planned a bait and switch, she wouldn't mind at all. Her goal to have sex with a hot, young stranger would be fulfilled by either of them.

"Is Owen making an ass out of himself again?" Kellen asked as his gaze shifted above her shoulder to his friend.

"Can't help it," Owen said. "I had to corral her before some other jerk found enough confidence to approach her."

He moved close behind her, and she was promptly engulfed by

his warmth. An instant later she caught the scent of his clean-smelling aftershave. Her eyelids fluttered.

"Would you like to sit?" Kellen asked her.

Yeah, on Owen's naked lap. Or yours. Yours would work. Because now she didn't feel the need to screw *every* man in the club to help her get over her ex. Just one. Or maybe two.

"You'd better do it soon," Owen whispered close to her ear, "or I'm going to bend you over that table and break the club's no-penetration-in-the-lounge rule."

She gasped, her nether regions clenching with a surge of lust. So those parts were still functional. She had been starting to worry.

Kellen chuckled and shook his head. "Easy, stud. Do you even know her name?"

"Caitlyn," Owen said.

"Sit, Caitlyn," Kellen said, "before he whips out his dick and gets himself kicked out of here."

Caitlyn sat and crossed her legs. She wriggled slightly to give the unbearably swollen and achy flesh between her thighs some relief. No good. She'd never had anyone say such things to her in her life. She wasn't sure why it was such a turn-on. Thanks to Owen's outlandish behavior and her response to it, she had no doubt that she could have sex with a stranger. She might regret it in the morning, but she wouldn't tonight. Tonight she was tossing propriety aside and giving herself permission to get as dirty as she wanted.

Owen sat beside her and she scooted around the semi-circular, fairly private booth to give him more room. He moved closer so that their hips touched, and she scooted a bit more. He placed a hand on her knee and moved up against her again. That's when she realized he wanted to be touching her. She smiled and relaxed as much as she could. It was a challenge to remain calm with the profusion of butterflies fluttering about in her belly.

"So, Caitlyn," Kellen said, "what brings you to a place like this?"

"Curiosity."

"You're sure it wasn't horniness?" Owen asked. "Because I was really hoping for horniness."

She laughed. "Well, a little," she admitted.

Owen's fingers slid along the side of her knee, and her pussy gave an attention-shattering throb of need. Okay, so he was making horniness her prime focus.

"Do you guys do this often?" Caitlyn asked.

"This is our first time here," Owen said.

Kellen chuckled. "I guess that's true, but yeah, we do this often. Tony has clubs like this all across the U.S. We've been to most of them. How do you know Tony? Entry into his clubs is by invitation only. Keeps him out of jail."

"I don't know him personally," Caitlyn said. "My best friend's husband knows him."

"I see. So is it what you expected? Are you enjoying yourself?" Kellen asked.

"Truth be told, I'm terrified," she admitted.

"Of me?" Owen asked, giving her a sad little smile that made her laugh.

"No, but I probably should be."

"He's harmless," Kellen said. "Mostly."

"How long have you two been friends?" Caitlyn asked.

"A long time," Kellen said.

"No personal questions," Owen said.

Caitlyn turned her head to look at him in surprise. "None?"

"That's how anonymous sex works; it's anonymous. That's what you had in mind, isn't it? Hot, dirty, walk-bowlegged-for-the-next-two-days, anonymous sex?"

"Of course." She didn't point out that by exchanging names this wouldn't be entirely anonymous. Unless Owen wasn't his real name. Should she have used a fake name? She probably should have. Crap! She really was a novice at this.

Owen's arm moved to rest behind her. His fingers brushed her cover-up from her shoulder and toyed with the satin strap of her negligee. In response to Owen's gentle touch, Caitlyn's nipples hardened. She wasn't the only one who noticed. Eyes riveted to her chest, Kellen sucked in a sharp breath. Caitlyn squirmed at the sight of Kellen biting his lip as if in pain. Owen stroked her arm with the back of his hand, drawing the sleeve of her robe lower and bringing goose bumps to the surface of her skin.

"Don't you miss this, Kelly?" Owen's nose brushed against her ear, and his warm breath bathed the side of her neck. "Touching a woman."

Caitlyn shivered.

Owen's lips brushed her skin just beneath her ear. When his soft, wet tongue flicked out to delight her throat, her eyelids fluttered and her mouth dropped open.

"Tasting a woman."

"Don't torment me, Owen," Kellen said. "I'm not in the fucking mood tonight."

"She'd look beautiful restrained. Wouldn't she? Ropes pressing into her supple flesh." Owen nibbled her earlobe and whispered, "Would you let us tie you up, Caitlyn?"

"*Both* of you?" Caitlyn sputtered. Okay, now she understood why Owen had brought her here—so they could do wicked things to her. Things she was not okay with. Make her helpless. Their victim. The thought both thrilled her and scared her. Fear won over in the end. There was no way she would agree to being restrained while two strangers did any perverted thing that occurred to them. "I'd rather tie *you* up," she said.

Kellen chuckled. "I think that's a great idea. Good call, Caitlyn. I'll help."

"I'm game for anything you want to try," Owen said.

Caitlyn hesitated before turning her head to look at him. "*Anything?*"

"Yes, anything," Owen said. "Do you have a dirty fantasy, Caitlyn? Something you've always wanted to do but never dared?"

"I have plenty of fantasies," she said. "I really would like to tie you up. Dare to do things to you."

"What kinds of things?"

She tried to think of the most outlandish sexual act she could imagine, wanting to call him on his bluff. She was pretty sure he was full of it and saying things he didn't mean just for effect. True, her kink-o-meter was fairly mild, but he didn't know that. He had to be as scared as she was by the idea of being rendered helpless and at the mercy of a stranger. Caitlyn imagined him tied to a bed, his cock rigid and proud. She could touch him any way she liked. Kiss every inch of him. Suck him. Ride him. Torment him. Tease him. Delay his gratification until he begged. But that didn't seem really all that outlandish. What man wouldn't agree to that? At least for a while. Then she pictured him tied face down, on his knees, ass exposed to the air, and a that naughty devil she kept buried inside her subconscious spread a slow grin across her face.

"I think I'd like to screw you," she said. "From behind."

She glanced up at him, expecting shock. He just looked confused.

"I'm not sure if my dick will bend that way, but we can try it."

Kellen laughed so hard, Caitlyn was concerned he'd rupture his spleen. She managed to keep a straight face, however, and shook her head. "That's not what I meant." Could she really say the next words? She was an excellent public speaker, but she usually talked about alternative energy sources, not about claiming a guy's ass. "I want to do things to your... ass." She said the final word so quietly, she was surprised he heard her.

Owen's jaw dropped and for the first time, Caitlyn saw the smooth operator take a hike off a cliff and fall fast and hard.

"Um," Owen said, "I've never done anything like that."

"They have strap-ons in the gift shop," Kellen said helpfully. "Big, thick ones, so be sure to use plenty of lube."

"Is that what you meant?" Owen said. "You want to tie me down and fuck me in the ass?"

Her face felt like it was on fire, but she said, "Yeah, that's what I meant." There was no way he was going to go for it. She was going catch him in a lie. All men were lying bastards. They only managed to get her hopes up, say they were going to do something, but never followed through.

"Well, okay then," he said, "but promise you'll be gentle. I'm a virgin back there."

And now Caitlyn was the one whose jaw was on the floor.

Kellen slid out of the booth. "Let's get going. I don't want to sit around here all night waiting for him to get his rocks off. I'm tired of being a slave to his libido."

"You didn't have to accompany me," Owen said. "I could have come alone."

"Then you wouldn't have come at all," Kellen returned, "and I'd have had to listen to you bitch about how much fun you would have had if you'd gone out. And how I'm no fun anymore. And how you should think about getting yourself a new best friend. One who is as insatiably perverted as you are."

"I don't bitch. And I don't want a new best friend, even an insatiably perverted one. You used to be insatiably perverted. Remember?"

"Nope. Don't recollect that," Kellen said. "Get out of the booth, Owen. I haven't tied anyone up in months, you know."

"Why are you so anxious to tie me up?"

"Because you're being an incredible pain in my ass, so maybe if you experience a little pain in yours, you'll stop tormenting me all the time. Now move. If you annoy me, I might find myself out of practice and pull certain ropes too tight. If I were you, I wouldn't drag my feet too much."

"I'm not dragging my feet. And you wouldn't be in such a bad mood if you'd—" He cut himself off and tore his gaze from his friend to look at Caitlyn.

"Are you really going to go through with this?" Caitlyn asked when she was finally able to retrieve her mandible from the floor.

"I said I'm game for anything. I meant that." His tone was surprisingly calm.

"Owen doesn't fuck around," Kellen said. "Well, yeah, he always fucks around, but when it comes to kink, he's all in. Trust me, he's been subjected to far kinkier things than what you're proposing."

No shit? Based on her limited exposure to what went on outside her own bedroom walls, she couldn't think of anything kinkier than screwing a man. To let him know what it felt like to be invaded. Overpowered. Taken. Not because she didn't enjoy being on the receiving end. She loved being filled. Overwhelmed. Fucked. But she had always wondered what it would be like if the roles were reversed. Caitlyn hadn't ever mentioned her fantasy to her ex-husband because she'd known he'd never try something so daring. His favorite kinky act was fucking on his desk during office hours. And he didn't seem to discriminate when it came to his partner. Caitlyn scowled at her thoughts.

"We'd better hurry," Owen said to Kellen. "She's giving off those men-suck vibes again."

"I'm glad it's not my ass she's about to take them out on," Kellen said and started walking toward the stairs that led to the basement.

Owen slid out of the booth and offered Caitlyn his hand. As she stared up at him, she was taken by how attractive he was. She really shouldn't take out her anger toward Charles on him. "I'm sorry, Owen. You don't have to go through with this."

"Baby, I want to go through with it," he said. "I love experimenting in the bedroom, and though I thought I'd tried just about every sex act, I've never done that. You have my complete attention, beautiful." He smiled reassuringly.

She took his hand and slipped from the booth. "I can't believe I'm about to do this," she said under her breath. And she really couldn't believe how much she wanted to.

· CHAPTER THREE

Out of the corner of his eye, Owen watched Caitlyn examine strap-on dildos. He wasn't going to interfere with her selection, but he was silently praying that she chose something small. Very small. As in so small it was invisible.

Kelly was purchasing rope and sniggering every time his gaze landed on Owen. Bastard. Would a true friend find this situation *that* fucking hilarious? Owen grinned. Yeah, totally. If Kelly had been the one about to be taken by a complete novice, Owen would laugh at him until he puked.

"Anything here you want me to try out on *you*?" Owen asked Caitlyn, sidling toward a collection of vibrators and clit stimulators.

"Maybe later," she said. She took the biggest, blackest dildo down from the shelf and tested its firmness by bending it slightly. "Midnight Power Hammer," she said. "I like it. It has some meat to it."

Owen winced.

"Since you're a virgin," Caitlyn said, "I think we should go with something huge and hard. What do you think?" She glanced up at him, her soft brown eyes inquisitive.

Owen felt the blood drain out of his face before he noticed the corner of her mouth quirk as she tried to maintain her composure. She had an ornery streak. He enjoyed that about her immensely. There was no arguing that she was a stunning woman. That had been what had attracted him at first. He loved her thick, long dark hair that fell in gentle waves almost to her waist. Her inquisitive brown eyes scrutinized her surroundings, which gave him the impression that she was intelligent. He appreciated a woman with a strong mind. He also appreciated a woman with a strong body, and Caitlyn had a body that wouldn't quit. The fact that she was a bit older than he was and yet maintained a youthful wit had him over the moon with excitement. This woman was *exactly* his type. So what if she was a little kinky. He liked kinky. Especially when it took him out of his comfort zone.

Plus, he couldn't resist a woman who gave as much bullshit as he did. But two could play at her game.

"Yeah," he said breathlessly. "Why settle for one cock? You should get two of them and shove them both up there at the same time."

She grabbed a second dildo off the shelf. This one was wide at the tip, flesh-toned and covered with tortuous veins. Owen forced himself not to gag at the sight of it. She held both phalluses to her crotch and simulated thrusting. "I don't know," she said. "I'm new to this. Do you think I can control two at once?"

"I can't control the one I've got. I'm not sure how anyone could control two of them."

She laughed and put both giant dicks back on the shelf. The one she selected to purchase was blissfully small, but not quite invisible.

"For beginners," she read from the package as they headed for the counter. "Suitable for anal play. Maybe if you like it, we can move up to the Midnight Power Hammer model on our next attempt."

He smiled. He'd let her have her way the first time but was confident he wouldn't be the one on the receiving end the rest of the night. Or ever again. He'd try anything once, but that didn't mean he'd try it twice.

The clerk offered them some complimentary lube at check-out, and then the three of them made their way upstairs to the back of the place, where private rooms were available for rent.

"You could join us, Kelly," Owen said. "We used to have a great time when we worked together."

"I'm just here to help her tie you properly. I wouldn't want her to injure anything permanently."

"Just temporarily," Owen said.

"Exactly."

Caitlyn clutched her paper bag in both fists, her brown eyes wide as they made their way through the rooms to one near the very end of a labyrinth of hallways. Hopefully it would be a little more private back here; Owen didn't want anyone to hear him yelling in agony if it came to that. He was pretty sure this was going to hurt like a son of a bitch. Not that he was against a little pain. Not as long as it was followed by plenty of pleasure. He regretted removing the barbells from his nipples earlier; they could give him pain and pleasure simultaneously.

Kelly unlocked the door and it swung open to reveal a small room. It held a full-sized bed with sterile-looking white bedding, a functional sink, and a basket full of condoms on a side table, but little else. Tony was a stickler for cleanliness and safety in all his clubs. Owen would, however, be using his own condoms. Call him paranoid, but he didn't trust anyone but himself with the health of his dick.

"I'm going to borrow a pommel," Kelly said. "Caitlyn, make him naked while I'm gone."

She saluted him. "I'm on it."

A pommel? Wow, Kelly was serious about doing this properly.

Kelly closed the door, leaving Owen alone with Caitlyn. Every time he started to feel nervous about what was about to happen, he just had to look at her and the lust he felt chased his concerns away. It was as if he'd found a magic take-out menu and checked off everything he found attractive in a woman, which had resulted in Caitlyn being delivered to his door hot and ready in thirty minutes or less. This woman could do anything she wanted to him and he was not going to protest.

She approached him cautiously. He swallowed hard, forcing himself not to grab her and tumble her to the bed. All his instincts told him to make his move, but he forced himself to remain civilized and not attack her like a wild creature. For now.

"Can I make you naked now?" she asked as her hands slid over the fabric of his shirt.

His chest muscles flexed of their own volition. "Yeah."

"Are you as nice to look at under those clothes as I imagine you are?"

"Only one way to find out."

He held very still as she slowly unbuttoned his shirt. Her fingers started at his collar and made their way down, slowly, slowly, toward his waist. He was always self-conscious about his body. It didn't help that she stared up into his eyes while she worked at the buttons, as if she wasn't sure if she wanted to see him naked or not. But soon he didn't care. He was too lost in her gaze to feel anything but desire.

Owen fought his urge to drag her body against his. To kiss her. He fought other urges as well—like talking. He wanted to ask her about herself. To get to know her. He legitimately enjoyed women. He could talk to them for hours. Unfortunately, he'd learned long ago that anonymous sex worked better when he kept a certain distance from his lover. He couldn't get attached to Caitlyn and so he needed to be careful not to give her the wrong idea. It would be an easy mistake to make. He already liked this woman—those few glimpses he'd seen of her true personality—and he would love to know what made her tick. Maybe he could even convince her that getting to know each other was a good idea.

But it wasn't a good idea. It was never a good idea. He'd learned from past entanglements that unless he enjoyed getting his heart broken, he shouldn't throw it into the equation. Ever. And he didn't enjoy getting his heart broken. He'd allowed it to happen far too many times in his youth. And it always hurt. He was sure a mangled heart hurt far worse than getting it up the ass by a woman with no thrusting experience.

Caitlyn opened his shirt and pushed it off his shoulders. It fell to the floor at his feet. She glanced at his body and drew her tongue over her sensual lips. She made a little sound of pleasure in the back of her throat and then held up a hand to shield her eyes.

"My God, Owen, you're so gorgeous it hurts my eyes to look at you," she said. "Do you have a pair of sunglasses I can borrow?"

He laughed. This was one of the main reasons why he found himself liking her more than he cared to admit; she made him laugh. "Fresh out. If my friend Jacob was handy, I'm sure he'd have a spare pair or three. He's never without his shades."

"Hmm," she murmured, looking reflective. "First you, then Kellen, now Jacob. Tell me, is Jacob as attractive as you are? Because you hotties seem to travel in packs."

"Most would argue he's better looking than I am," Owen said. "But I don't think he's your type."

"How do you know my type?"

"Well," he said, "when I touch you, you show signs of attraction. To me."

"I do?" she said, her mouth dropping open as if she were shocked by his claim.

He nodded and lifted his hands to her shoulders. He slipped the flimsy wrap from her body, and it fluttered to the floor. She shivered and the darkened tips of her breasts grew hard beneath the transparent white lace. God, even her nipples were perfect. He so wanted to nibble them and then suck them raw.

"You do," he said. "So either you're attracted to me or it's been so long since a man has touched you that your body would respond to anyone."

She frowned. "I don't think I'm that desperate."

"So that means you're attracted to me. And Jacob and I are very different. He's sort of a caveman type."

"A caveman in sunglasses?"

Owen chuckled as he imagined Shade Silverton in a loincloth and sunglasses. "Exactly."

Her gaze dropped to his chest, and she made that little sound of pleasure in the back of her throat again. The tone made shivers race down his spine. He couldn't wait to hear what she sounded like when she came. His cock twitched in anticipation making her call out in ecstasy.

"I like your tattoos," she said as her eyes explored his chest. "Do they mean anything special?"

"Some of them, but we're not discussing personal details, remember?"

Her finger traced the cross tattoo on his left pec. "You must work out constantly."

"I'm working out right now as a matter of fact." He flexed his pecs in an alternating pattern.

She giggled and tilted her face up at him, looking a bit more at ease. When they'd been walking to the room, he'd thought she was going to bolt.

"Are you less nervous now that we've shared a few laughs?" he asked.

She nodded. "How did you know I was nervous?"

"With those big brown eyes of yours, you look like a calf being dragged to slaughter."

"You're the one who should be nervous." She bent to pull the strap-on out of the bag she'd set on the floor. "I don't think they should let someone operate one of these things without a license."

"You'll do fine," he said. "Let me help you with that."

She stiffened when he moved to stand behind her. He lifted the hem of her negligee to expose her succulent ass. He took a moment to enjoy the view. The woman had a great butt. And something about seeing a thong disappear between the two plump globes of flesh did things to his self-control. Unable to just look—he had to feel—Owen tugged Caitlyn's body back against his. He stiffened when his cock brushed against her cheeks.

When he had her pressed securely against him, he looped both thumbs through the elastic of her panties and eased the tiny garment over her hips, shuddering when her thong's strap scraped the length of his cock through his pants.

Her entire body jerked when his fingertips brushed the bare skin along either hipbone as he lowered her panties.

"What," she said in a broken gasp, "what are you doing?"

"You have to take off your panties to put on the harness."

"How do you know?" she asked. "I thought you'd never done this before."

"I haven't. But I've played with a couple of girls who used one of these on each other. It never occurred to them to use it on me. I guess they weren't as kinky as you are."

"Do you really think I'm kinky?"

"Everything is kinky the first time you try it."

He slid her panties an inch lower, shifting his hands forward to rub his thumbs over her smooth-shaven mound.

"Oh!"

"I'd really like to sink my fingers into your heat," he said, "and then bring them to my mouth to taste your juices." She shuddered at his words. He ran one thumb along the apex of her cleft, pausing just before he brushed her buried clit. "But that will have to wait until later."

She groaned.

Owen slid down her back slowly, rubbing his bare belly and chest over the skin of her buttocks, pressing open-mouthed kisses along her spine through the lace of her teddy as he lowered her panties to the floor. Crouched at her feet, he lifted them one at a time to remove the scrap of fabric from around her ankles. He paused to admire her ass and sank his teeth into one cheek. She jerked, but didn't pull away, not even when he latched on to her flesh with a tight suction. He continued to suck as he took the harness from her trembling hands and helped her slip into it. He pulled his mouth free, grinning when he saw the reddened spot he'd left behind to mark what was his—all his—at least for tonight. Owen slowly tugged the harness up her thighs, drawing his entire body up her length as he went.

"Owen?" she said brokenly.

He wriggled his hips to nestle his now fully erect cock in the crack of her ass. Damn, he needed to lose these pants.

"Yeah, beautiful?"

"M-maybe we can just skip this fantasy of mine and you can, um, put yours inside me instead."

He grinned at the sweet way she'd just said, "Fuck me."

"Did that make you all hot and achy between your legs, Caitlyn?" he asked.

"Y-yes."

"Is your pussy wet for me now?"

"It's been wet since I first looked at you."

"Good. Do you want me to fuck you?"

She groaned. "Oh yes. Very much."

"I will," he promised. "But not until you're finished with me." He unbuckled his belt and removed his slacks and underwear with one downward jerk. He kicked them aside and then, blissfully naked, he moved up against her back again.

When the head of his cock prodded her in the lower back, she gasped. He took his shaft in his hand and rubbed the sensitive tip against her buttocks, introducing her to his piercing for the first time. She went completely still.

"What is that?" she asked.

He bit her earlobe and held it tightly between his teeth so she couldn't turn her head, but didn't answer her question. It felt amazing to rub himself against her skin. He let the fantasy of sinking unprotected into her wet, swollen heat tease his thoughts. He had to settle down or he would lose his head. He couldn't let that happen. He slowly slid his cock up the crack of her ass and tugged her back against him to hold it nestled between them.

"What was that little hard thing I felt?" she asked.

He released her earlobe. "I'll give you a proper introduction later."

He tightened the straps of the harness on her hips. Once it was securely in place, he gripped the base of the rubbery phallus. It felt very odd to be standing behind a woman holding a dick in his hand, but he was curious to see what it would feel like inside him. He slid his hand to cup her mound, the dildo nestled between his thumb and forefinger. She sucked a breath through her teeth, which prompted him to rock his hips forward.

"Now I'll show you proper technique," he whispered into her

ear. "Move with me, baby. Nice and easy. Find a rhythm."

He imagined sinking into her as they thrust together—a slow sensual dance that soon had him eyeing the bed in longing.

"Owen?"

"Mmm-hmm?" he murmured into her ear.

"I can't wait to try this out on you." She circled the phallus with one hand, thrusting into her loose fist. "Do you want me to take you slow and easy like this?"

"Whatever feels right. You'll know."

"I don't want to hurt you."

He bent his knees a bit so that the base of his cock brushed against her back entrance. Caitlyn moaned and squirmed against him.

"Have you ever been penetrated back here?" he asked.

"A few times," she said.

"So use that experience as a guide."

"Okay." Her hips rotated slightly as she practiced thrusting. Her ass rubbing against him drove him insane with need. The woman plain turned him on.

"I think you have the hang of it," he said, rocking his hips faster. He released his hold on her mound and slid his hands up the lace along her torso. She arched forward slightly, seeking his touch. The brush of her thick hair against his belly and chest drove him wild. It smelled so sweet and clean that he couldn't resist pressing his face to the side of her head and inhaling her intoxicating scent. When he cupped her breasts, she released a moan of bliss. Owen's thumbs rubbed her nipples in small circles.

"Oh God, Owen, just take me from behind. I can't take much more."

The door open and Kelly entered carrying a wooden pommel that had a thick, white satin pad on top.

"Damn it, Owen, you couldn't wait five minutes?"

"He's just showing me how to move my hips," Caitlyn said.

"And we're going to make it so he can't move at all." Kelly set the pommel in the center of the mattress and collected several lengths of rope from his sack of purchases.

"Come on, Owen," Kelly said. "Don't try to get away now."

As turned on as Owen was, there was no way in hell he would try to get away from Caitlyn, but he released her reluctantly and took a step back. She peered over her shoulder at him, her gaze going directly to his cock. "I knew it! It's pierced."

"Ever been with a man who had his cock pierced?" Owen asked.

She laughed hysterically. "Sorry," she said, gasping for air. "I can't imagine my ex getting his cock pierced. Ever. Ever. Ever." Her gaze slid up his body. "Or a tattoo, for that matter."

"What about the guys you had before him?" Owen asked. "Or after?"

"There were no others."

While this tidbit of information ricocheted about in Owen's brain, Caitlyn went to stand next to Kelly by the bed.

"I think you should have gone for the Midnight Power Hammer model," Kelly said, nodding toward the small attachment at her crotch. "Give him a night to remember."

"I guarantee he'll never forget this," Caitlyn said.

And why did that statement make Owen's heart kick in his chest?

"You ready, buddy?" Kelly asked him.

"Don't call me buddy when you're about to tie me down so I can be fucked up the ass," Owen said.

"You just showed her how to do it properly," Kelly said. "I'm sure you'll be fine. Knowing you, you'll probably even like it."

Owen wasn't so sure about that, but he climbed up on the bed and leaned his belly against the pommel.

Kelly tied two long ropes together. The knot landed in the center of Owen's back and his friend got to work. It didn't matter that Kelly had taken a several-month-long hiatus from his Shibari hobby. He still tied knots with the precision of a sailor and the care and attention of someone building a ship in a bottle. Just as he did with women, Kelly followed the contours of Owen's body with each length of rope and adjusted each knot so that it hit upon some pleasure point that Owen didn't even know he had. Owen wasn't sure if Kelly was aware of each caress against Owen's skin as he carefully arranged his masterpiece, but Owen felt every touch of Kelly's hand. It didn't help that Caitlyn had already tied him in knots before Kelly had even started. Owen tried to think about something else—anything else—other than what was happening to his body. He had never expected this to turn him on so much.

Caitlyn assisted Kelly occasionally, but mostly she just watched the master at work. Owen wondered what she must think of him. It was impossible to hide his arousal, seeing as he was buck naked.

Did she realize how excited he was?

"This really is an art form," Caitlyn said. "He has a gorgeous body as it is, but the way you tie the ropes... It's as if you're tracing his lines to draw attention to his beauty."

"Hear that, Owen? She thinks you're a beauty," Kelly said.

Owen couldn't move if he'd wanted to. His arms were tied to his sides. Ropes crisscrossed from his thighs, up his back and over his shoulders to another rope that formed a diamond pattern across his chest. He might have been able to curl into a tighter fetal position, but the pommel at his belly was in the way.

"Should we tie his—?" Caitlyn asked.

"Do you want him to be in pain?" Kelly asked.

"No."

"Tie my what?" Owen said. The pair of them were standing behind him, and he couldn't see what they were plotting.

"Your cock and balls," Kelly said.

"No," Owen said, though it might prevent him from making a fool of himself from blowing his load too soon. God, he was turned on. He'd never in his life been more aware of his body.

"Okay, then," Kelly said, moving back to admire his handiwork. "That should keep him where you want him."

Every inch of Owen's heated flesh was trembling. He'd said he was game for anything, but restrained the way he was, with his ass so exposed and vulnerable, he wasn't sure if he was up for this. Well, yes, actually he was up for this. He was painfully up.

"Have you restrained many men?" Caitlyn asked Kelly.

Owen's trembling stopped as he strained his ears for Kelly's answer. "Just as favors," he said.

Who? Owen wondered. Kelly had never mentioned tying up men to him. Maybe he'd done it during his training. He'd shown Owen the ropes only after he'd mastered the art himself, but surely he would have told Owen if he'd done things with a man. He told Owen everything. Didn't he?

"When you have your partner at your mercy like this, take it slow," Kelly instructed.

"Right," Caitlyn said, as if Kelly were telling her how to sweep a floor or program her DVR.

"Tease him."

Owen squirmed. Just them talking about it as if he wasn't present was enough of a tease for him.

"Right. I like the look of his balls and cock swinging freely. I'm glad we decided not to restrain them too. Do you have your cock pierced?"

Kelly chuckled. "No."

"God, I just want to rub those two little balls. Kiss them. Suck them in my mouth. What else would feel nice?"

"Licking," Kelly said.

Oh God, stop talking and touch me or something. I can't stand this for much longer.

"He doesn't seem hard enough to me," Kelly said. "Owen?"

"Yeah?"

"Are you hard enough?"

He was about to split, he was so hard, but he shook his head slightly. "I could be harder."

"I thought so. When you take his cock in your hand," Kelly said to Caitlyn, "don't stroke him vigorously enough to make him come. Delay his orgasm until you've had enough. He doesn't get to come until you say so."

Owen groaned. He was going to have to have a serious talk with Kelly about having his back in these situations. The jerk was making this unbearable. Owen got the sinking sensation that Kelly was getting back at him for making his stint of abstinence as unbearable as possible.

A warm hand circled Owen's cock, completely robbing him of rational thought. Instinctually, he rocked his hips forward, unable to curtail the urge to thrust. He couldn't move more than a couple inches, but God, the woman had great hands. Owen shuddered in bliss. Her grip was firm, yet gentle. Just enough friction to drive him wild.

"See how loose my fist is?" Kelly said. "I'm barely skimming the surface."

Owen's breath stalled in his throat. That was *Kelly's* hand stroking him with perfection? *Oh God. Don't let me come in his hand. Then he'll know how turned on I am by him.* Owen closed his eyes and focused all his attention on the palm lightly stroking his flesh. Every time Kelly's hand skimmed over the jewelry in his piercing, his cock jerked with excitement, his balls tightened, and his body strained toward him.

"I'm not sure I get your technique," Caitlyn said. "I think I need further demonstration. Please, continue." Owen could hear the amusement in her tone. And somewhere outside the room he could hear a stranger's laughter and a woman's startled cry. He was so glad they'd found a private room. Owen let his head drop forward. Most of his view was hindered by the pommel he was draped over, but he could see Kelly's hand come into view each time he slowly stroked Owen's length.

"Harder," Owen whispered and then sucked his lips into his mouth so Kelly wouldn't realize how incredibly turned on he was to have his hand on him. He knew Kelly wasn't attracted to him. They had helped each other attain orgasm multiple times but unlike Owen, Kelly didn't get overly excited and explode like a rocket when he came at Owen's strokes. And they hadn't touched each other in over six months. He was glad Caitlyn had asked for Kelly's assistance in tying him down, but he was in no way prepared to explain why with every kinky act he participated in, the most exciting thing he ever experienced was an unenthusiastic hand job from his best friend.

"I think you can take it from here." Kelly moved his hand away. Owen whimpered. "Have fun."

And then he was gone. The door slammed behind him, which was a blessing and like a knife to Owen's heart in the same beat.

"You okay?" Caitlyn asked.

"Never better," he said breathlessly. *Just let me get these emotions under control and everything will be fan-freaking-tastic.*

"If you've changed your mind…"

"Nope," he said. "I've always wanted to be fucked up the ass by a sarcastic brunette."

She laughed. "You're adorable."

"I get that a lot," he said. "But only because people can't read my thoughts."

Her warm, soft lips brushed his buttocks, and he jerked. Kelly had heightened his sensitivity such that he was ready to toss Caitlyn on her back and sink into the soft, wet heat between her thighs. Unfortunately, he was completely immobilized, so he had no choice but to keep his senses.

Her hand found his cock, and she stroked him so gently he began to twitch, needing rougher stimulation, needing… Hell, he didn't know. He needed something. He was missing something. He just didn't know what it was.

She continued to stroke him while she trailed kisses over his ass.

When her fingers brushed his hole, he swore under his breath. He wasn't sure if he'd like being fucked there, but he knew from past experience that he enjoyed the occasional finger inside. Her lips moved to his sac. She licked and suckled and kissed the loose flesh until he began to rock his hips to thrust into her hand as best he could. God, he was excited.

Caitlyn's sexy little finger dipped into his ass, and he shuddered, almost blowing his load right then.

"Does that feel good?" she asked, her warm breath teasing the moistened skin of his balls.

"Yes," he gasped.

"Do you want me to go deeper?"

"Please."

Her finger slipped into him as far as it could go. He squeezed his eyes shut. She moved her finger in slow circles while she sucked his balls and stroked his shaft gently with her other hand. He was so consumed with pleasure, he couldn't keep his eyes open. Her tongue traced the seam between his balls. Up, up toward the place where her finger penetrated him. Sensations streaked up his spine, drawing a moan from between his lips. Lord, the woman was going to kill him with pleasure.

"Do you want more?" she asked.

"Yes," he gasped. "More." More what, he had no idea. He just hoped she never stopped what she was doing.

Her finger slipped free of his body and something cool and wet dripped onto his hole. Two fingers slipped inside him. His eyes flew open and he tensed. A sound, half-gasp, half-moan, escaped him.

She trailed playful nips over his ass cheeks until he was distracted enough to relax. That's when she began to thrust her fingers in and out. She pressed down against his prostate, and his mouth dropped open. Dear lord. Was he actually drooling? He pressed his lips together and swallowed.

"Right there," he murmured. "Right there."

Her lips moved to his balls again, her one hand still stroked him, her other teased his ass. He was delirious with pleasure—experiencing gratification more intense than an orgasm. He didn't realize he was fighting his restraints until his shoulder pulled painfully.

"Too much?" she asked. "Don't hurt yourself."

"Oh God," he groaned. "More."

Her fingers stretched him to his limits as she added another digit.

"How's that?"

"Yes."

"Deeper?"

"Yes, deeper!"

He groaned when she pulled her fingers free. Her thighs brushed the backs of his, and he tensed. Was she really going to use that thing on him? He bit his lip when he felt the hard rounded tip of it against his ass. She rubbed it in circles over his hole until his belly began to quiver. He was about to plead with her to stop when she slipped inside and pressed forward.

Owen's eyes rolled into the back of his head.

"You okay?" she asked.

He shook his head. He wasn't going to be okay until he came. And damn, he was close.

"Do you want me to pull out?"

He chuckled. "No, Caitlyn. Can't you tell I'm about to explode? I want you to fuck me."

"Oh!" She took a deep breath. "Okay. Don't let me hurt you."

"Maybe I want you to hurt me. Maybe I want you to fuck me as hard as you can until my ass is so raw I beg you to stop."

She leaned over him and kissed the center of his back. The phallus slipped several inches deeper, and Owen bit his lip so he didn't yell and startle her.

"I don't want to hurt you," she whispered. "I can't believe you're doing this for me."

Doing this for *her*? Hell, he was doing this for himself. She rose again and leaned back, pressing deeper inside him still. Oh fuck, he wasn't going to last much longer. She held onto his hips with both hands as she slowly withdrew and then slowly pushed deep inside him again. She found a slow rhythm of insertion and withdrawal, obviously not wanting to hurt him as she slowly claimed his ass.

"Do you like it?" she asked with a tremulous voice.

"Yes. You can do it harder." *Please, do it harder.*

She worked up her courage and her speed. Filling him. Filling him. Oh God, filling him. What was wrong with him that he liked this so much? What would a real cock feel like inside him? What would a huge, hard cock like Kelly's feel like? Kelly's hand stroking him. Cock filling him. Hand stroking him. Owen's dick and balls hung freely beneath him, so his orgasm caught him completely by surprise. He cried out as he began to spurt. His load caught him in the chin.

Caitlyn abruptly stopped moving. "*Kelly*?" she said.

Still trembling, Owen lifted his head. Had Kelly returned? Had he seen how hard Owen had come while being fucked? He listened—no one had entered the room. "What?" Owen said.

"Why did you call Kelly's name when you came?"

Heat flooded Owen's face. "I didn't."

"Were you thinking of him while I was fucking you?"

"No!" Yes, he thought, God, yes. He squeezed his eyes shut against the emotions welling up inside him.

She pulled out and pressed her face against his back, dropping gentle kisses along his spine. "Does he know how you feel about him?" she asked.

No, he thought, God, no.

"I don't have feelings for him," Owen said with a snorted laugh. "I thought your name was Kelly. Sorry about that. I just have sex with so many women, I lose track of names. It was Caitlyn, right?"

"Yeah, it's Caitlyn. Don't worry, sweetie. I won't tell him," she said. "But you should."

No way ever in fucking hell would he tell Kelly that he'd started having fantasies about him when they'd stopped touching each other. No way. And he would definitely not tell him that he'd been fantasizing about him while being fucked. Or that the thought of Kelly fucking him had turned him on so much that he'd come without any stimulation to his cock at all.

"Well, that was fun," she said after a moment of his silence. "Do you want to continue?"

"I want you to untie me now," he said. Because he was going to fuck her brains out to show her that he was not infatuated with his friend. He was one hundred percent hot-blooded heterosexual male and when he was finished with her, she wouldn't ever be able to forget it.

CHAPTER FOUR

Caitlyn wasn't sure if she should untie Owen or not. He was obviously feeling very vulnerable. And it seemed he hadn't yet come to terms with what was in his heart. Caitlyn didn't have a problem with him not feeling a deep emotional connection with her. They'd just met; it wasn't as if she'd expected him to fall madly in love with her. She'd only wanted to have a little fun. To feel sexy. He'd given her both already. But damn he looked hot all tied and helpless. And God, she'd made him come hard, even if he had been thinking of someone else at the time.

Now that the sexual excitement had drained from his body, he looked like he needed someone to hold him and tell him everything was going to be all right. That instinct to care for him won out in the end. She removed the strap-on, tossed it in the sink, and then climbed up onto the bed beside him. She stroked his hair gently as she tried to gauge his emotions and he did his damnedest not to meet her eyes.

"Thanks for fulfilling my fantasy," she said. Her fingers moved to the ropes that bound him and she carefully untied the first knot. "I know it's weird, but I've always wanted to screw a man. I just wanted to see what it was like."

"I told you I was up to try anything. Do you have any other kinky fantasies you've never been able to play out?"

She chuckled. "Doesn't everyone?"

"You'll have to tell me about them."

Caitlyn released the ropes binding Owen one at a time. She wanted to get some answers from him and figured the best way to get them was to ask while he couldn't get away. She just had this feeling about him, as if he actually wanted to talk to her—to get to know her better—but something was preventing him from trusting her. She could blame inexperience on her desire to get to know him better, but what was his excuse? He did this kind of thing all the time. Sex didn't mean anything to him, did it?

"So," she asked as the second knot came free, "how long have you known Kelly?"

"He doesn't like to be called Kelly," Owen said.

"You call him that."

"And he complains about it constantly."

"Okay," she said, "how long have you known *Kellen*?"

"We aren't supposed to be getting personal. Remember?"

"If you won't talk to me, I guess I'll just come to my own conclusions about the two of you then," she said, working at a third knot, but taking her sweet time about loosening it.

Owen stiffened. "What kind of conclusions?"

"That you're in love with him and the only reason you go after women is to cover up your feelings for a man."

"That's one possible explanation," Owen said, surprising her yet again by not saying what she expected.

"Is it the correct one?" She didn't want it to be. She had no problem sleeping with Owen unless he was in love with someone already. If that was the case, then she felt in her heart that she was the other woman. Or maybe the only woman in this particular case.

"No," Owen said with such conviction that she believed him. "I'm not in love with him."

"In lust with him?"

"I'm not sure."

"Have you been in lust with a man before?"

"Never. And I'm not sure I'm in lust with Kelly either. I'm not sure about anything at the moment." He glanced over his shoulder at her. "Except that I'd really like to be untied now."

"I'm working on it." She released the knot she'd been fiddling with unnecessarily and moved on to another one. "Does he have feelings for you?"

"He doesn't have feelings for anyone anymore."

"And why's that?" She met his eyes, and he didn't look away. Were they starting to connect on a more personal level? She wouldn't mind. This sex for the sake of sex thing was new to her, and she wasn't sure if she could forget this guy that easily. Wasn't sure she wanted to forget him. So far, he was pretty terrific.

"He was in love with a woman. Planned to marry her."

"Was?"

"She died."

Empathy made Caitlyn's heart pang. She'd lost her sister a few years before, she still felt as if a gaping hole was eating its way through her heart whenever she thought about Morgan. The sad thing was, she thought about Morgan less and less as time went by. She couldn't seem to stop her from slipping farther away. "He's still grieving?"

"Yeah, I'm pretty sure he'll always grieve for her."

"Probably. But it will lessen with time." And then he'd probably feel guilty for moving on. Caitlyn did.

"It's already been five years."

"That's not so long, really."

"It is when you're twenty-seven."

Caitlyn paused. "Is that how old you are?"

"Maybe. Does it bother you?"

She chuckled and moved to the next knot in Kellen's intricate and beautiful design. "You're quite a bit older than my ex-husband's new fling," she said. "But then she can't legally drink in this country."

"Age doesn't matter."

"You don't think so? I think society would disagree."

"Fuck 'em. No one understands what's between two people except the two involved. Outsiders, they don't get it."

"I guess I am an outsider in my ex-husband's relationship. But I don't agree with it and yes, partly because of their age difference. I'm sure he took advantage of her innocence."

"I wasn't talking about them. I was talking about us."

"Oh, did I take advantage of your innocence?" Caitlyn paused and flexed her fingers. They were starting to ache from working the knots free. "And I didn't think there was an *us*."

"If there was."

"If." Caitlyn traced the outline of the tribal tattoo on Owen's shoulder. "*If* is a very big word, Owen."

"Are you almost finished?" he asked. "My muscles are starting to cramp."

"I'll hurry." She began to work faster, releasing knots in the reverse order that Kellen had tied them.

"You know," Owen said, "most people have a difficult time releasing the knots properly and we usually have to cut the rope."

She paused and looked up at him. There she went being weird again. "I… uh… watched him closely when he was tying them."

"And you memorized the entire sequence?"

As she'd been blessed with an amazing memory, she did remember the entire sequence, but she played down her unusually sharp memory. "It's not too hard really. You just follow the rope from one end to the other. It's getting more difficult now that the free end is so long."

"It would be faster to cut them."

"But then I wouldn't get to admire your body for a long, long time."

He grinned. "You can admire my body for as long as you like."

"What if I want to gaze at you for days?"

"I'll send you a picture."

She laughed and swatted his ass playfully. His arm was loose enough now that he could get a hold on her. He wrapped a strong hand around her wrist and tugged her down to the mattress.

"God, I want to kiss you so bad I can hardly stand it," he said. "Hurry up and untie me."

"You want to kiss me?"

"Yes, and so much more."

"I thought you wanted to be untied so you can leave."

"What? No way in hell. We haven't even begun yet."

His certainty made her smile. She couldn't help it. "We haven't?"

"No, that sweet pussy of yours must need some relief. Untie me and I'll fuck you senseless," he said. When she did nothing but stare up at him as if she'd just won the sex lottery, he glared at her. "Untie me, Caitlyn."

"I will, but I need to kiss you first," she said, lost in his gorgeous blue eyes. They reminded her of the waters of the Caribbean. Warm. Inviting. Deep. "I think my lips have waited long enough."

She scooted her body so her face was beneath his. He tried to stretch his neck to claim her mouth, but she remained just out of reach. She loved the look of anticipation in his eyes. He really seemed to want her. Badly. And she wanted to make him crazy with need.

Why hadn't she thought to do it until now? He was already half untied. She could have been teasing and tormenting him—as Kellen had suggested—for the past ten minutes.

"I want to kiss you too," she said. "Our first kiss."

He chuckled. "I guess that's true. You've fucked me and haven't even kissed me yet. My God, I'm a total slut."

OLIVIA CUNNING

She chuckled. "I kissed you," she said. "Just not on the lips."

She lifted her head and gently brushed her lips against his. That small contact had her heart racing and her sex swelling with unfulfilled desire. She was so glad he wasn't through with her. He might have already enjoyed an explosive orgasm, but she hadn't, and she was very interested in finding out what being "fucked senseless" entailed.

Owen strained to try to deepen his kiss, but she dropped her head back onto the mattress and continued her new favorite hobby, staring at him.

"There are other things I want to do to you, Owen."

"There are plenty of things I want to do to you too. Finish untying me."

"Not yet," she whispered.

He groaned and dropped his chin to his chest. His soft hair tickled the tip of her nose. She lifted a hand to brush it back and then kissed his forehead.

"It's unfortunate that the pommel blocks most of your chest and belly. I'd really like to touch every inch of your skin."

"You can as soon as you untie me," he said.

Her attention focused on his beautiful cock. "But I do see one part of you is fully exposed. I could start there. I really want to get a closer look at that piercing."

His head jerked up. "Kelly put you up to this, didn't he?"

"He might have planted a seed of thought," she said. "You can thank him later."

Caitlyn shifted to the opposite side of the pommel. It pressed against the middle of his chest and his upper abdomen, but lying on her back beneath him, she could see his lower belly, the delightful V of his hipbones, and his suddenly attentive cock. He liked her idea. She could tell by how quickly he was getting hard again. She ran her fingertips down his lower belly and he shuddered, his partially freed arm lowering so he could fist his hand in a tangle of bed sheet. She took her time exploring his flesh—stroking, nibbling and licking his belly and hips, forcing herself not to go for the decorated and engorged prize at the center. She wanted him hard and fully excited before she pleasured him, but she couldn't take her eyes of his cock. There was something about those two little metallic balls decorating the rim that fascinated her. What would that feel like inside her?

"Touch me," Owen whispered. "I can't stand it, Caitlyn. Touch

120

me."

"Touch you where?"

"Where do you think?"

She cradled his balls in one hand, ever so gently massaging. He sucked a breath through his teeth.

"Here?" She didn't wait for his answer. She lifted her head and licked the wrinkled skin of his sac, swirling her tongue in chaotic patterns that caused his breathing to skitter and shake.

"I want to fuck you so bad right now," he said in a growl of a voice.

She crossed her legs and squeezed them together, pretending his words didn't make her throb with excitement.

"More than you wanted to kiss me?" she asked.

"Mmm," he murmured. "Please."

She wanted to touch him, direct his thick hard cock into her mouth and suck him down her throat, but those little metallic balls gave her pause. Would they get stuck in her throat? There was one trip to the emergency room she'd never live down.

"Are you finished driving me insane?" he asked.

"Not yet. I like playing with you."

"I want to play too."

Caitlyn stared up at his cock; its tip was mere inches from her lips. She licked her lips and gnawed on the bottom one, trying to decide if she dared to show him one bedroom skill she was really good at. Her eyes focused on the tattoo that decorated one hip and curved around the top of his thigh.

"What's with the snake?" she asked. She'd never seen a more realistic tattoo.

"Are you afraid of it? Is that why you're taking your sweet time untying me?"

Caitlyn traced the bit of art with her fingertips.

"Oh, you mean my tattoo," he said. "I thought you were talking about the spitting cobra in the center."

She laughed. "This one?" She lifted her head slightly and flicked her tongue out to tease the sensitive flesh of his cock head. She worked her way around the tip until her tongue encountered something hard and metallic. She hesitated before squelching her inhibition and suckling his head.

"Damn, woman," he said breathlessly. "Don't you want any pleasure for yourself?"

"I like this," she said. "I can explore your body at my leisure. Do whatever I want to you. But if you really want me to stop…"

"I don't want you to stop. I want to fucking reciprocate."

She grinned. "You'll get your chance." She rubbed her thumb over the barbell in his piercing and he sucked a sharp breath through his teeth.

"Did it hurt when you got this pierced? Aren't there a lot of nerve-endings in this area?"

"Fuck yeah, there are, and you're exciting every one of them."

She rubbed her tongue over the smaller ball which was situated just above his rim in his sensitive glans. Even though she wasn't a guy, she imagined having that particular location pierced would be agonizing. She moved her attention to the larger ball just behind his rim. The tang of metal was foreign against her tongue, but she liked it. It reminded her that this wasn't Charles's cock. This cock belonged to someone new and exciting. While she toyed with Owen's bit of jewelry, she wondered if the two balls were different sizes for a reason other than aesthetics.

He sucked another breath through his teeth when she sucked a kiss over both ends of the barbell and flicked it with her tongue. "The pain wasn't too bad," he said shakily. "Took a while to heal. I decided on the dydoe because other cock piercings make you piss weird. I have a hard enough time aiming for the toilet without an extra exit hole."

He slipped free of her mouth as Caitlyn chuckled. She absolutely adored how he said anything that popped into his head. Being with him was fun, and when was the last time she'd had fun? The last time she'd laughed this much? The last time she'd enjoyed anyone's company so much? She couldn't recall.

"So this type of piercing doesn't make you pee weird?" she asked.

"No, it doesn't go through the urethra. Just the rim. If you'll untie me, I'll show you the reason I got it done. It's fun for me and even more fun for you."

She was eager to experience all that piece of jewelry had to offer, but she wasn't yet ready to let him get away. She was afraid that once the sex was over, he'd be gone. That had been their arrangement, after all.

"Why are the balls different sizes?"

"I'm not telling you."

"Why?"

"It's better if you feel it for yourself."

"Maybe I should try it out with my lips first," she said. "A practice run."

"Or you could untie me and we could skip practice entirely."

His protest turned to sighs of pleasure as she worked the head of his cock with her lips and tongue. The piercing felt foreign against her lips as she drew him in and out of her mouth. Foreign and sexy and exciting. She was afraid to take him too deep into her throat, but she didn't have the same concerns for the swollen, achy flesh between her legs. She wanted him inside her. Okay, she couldn't wait any longer. She had to have him.

Owen's breathing had become labored while she'd pleasured him with her mouth. She reached for the next knot.

"Wait," he said. "You're going to have to put a rubber on me before you release me. I'm not sure I'll be able to do the responsible thing once I'm free."

She grinned, delighted that she had such an effect on him. She rose from the bed and went to the basket on the side table to collect a condom.

"Use one of the ones in my pants pocket," he said. "But please hurry."

She dropped the complimentary condom back in the basket and picked up his pants. "Your wallet's in here," she said.

"Are you going to rob me?"

"I'm more interested in snooping for your address. In case I decide to become your stalker."

"I didn't think of that."

She chuckled at the concerned look on his face. "Don't worry. I won't invade your privacy. But you are worth stalking. I do need to ask why you insist on wearing a condom you brought yourself. Are they special?"

"Because I know it's safe. It's kind of like when they ask you if you've had your luggage with you at all times when you're going through airport security."

"Ah, so you don't trust anyone with your protection."

"Surprisingly, I trust you with it. Or maybe I just don't trust myself at the moment."

She found a little square package in his back pocket and carried it with her to the bed. Kneeling behind him, she rested her breasts against his lower back and leaned forward to stroke his cock with both hands. She barely skimmed the surface, teasing him the way Kellen had shown her. While she increased his excitement to the breaking point again, she trailed gentle kisses over his back between the few ropes that were still in place.

"Caitlyn, *please*."

She smiled to herself and opened the condom wrapper. Still leaning against him from behind, she reached around and slowly unrolled it down his length.

Owen drew a breath through his teeth. "Mercy. You should probably put three or four of them on me. I'm so over-sensitized, I—"

"If you think it's necessary."

She started to move away.

"No, I was kidding. Just kidding. Untie me."

Deciding he was finally excited enough to be free of his bonds, she hurried to untie the last of the knots holding him.

The instant the last rope came free, Owen shoved the pommel off the bed with a loud thud. He grabbed Caitlyn by one arm and tossed her onto her back in the center of the mattress.

"Fuck, I want you," he said in a low growl. "Are you trying to drive me insane?"

His fingers tangled in the straps of her negligée. The straps ripped from the delicate lace as he yanked the garment down to expose her breasts. Heat spread across her chest, up her neck and her cheeks. Owen's mouth latched on to one taut nipple and he sucked so hard, she felt it in her womb. Her clit throbbed with excitement.

"Oh!"

Was it possible to come solely due to the stimulation of one nipple? As the first spasm of release gripped her pussy, she cried out in surprise.

"Owen!"

"So I'm not the only one who's turned on enough to come without penetration," he said in a teasing tone. He pulled on the sides of her negligée until the fragile lace split down the front. "God, you're gorgeous."

He bit into her nipple with just enough pressure to send her flying over the edge. She was still caught in the throes of her miniature orgasm when he slid down her body, plunged two fingers deep into her clenching pussy, and latched onto her clit with his mouth. She cried out as her ecstasy escalated into pleasure so intense she forgot how to breathe.

"Give me more, Caitlyn."

More what? Her fingers stole into his hair and clung to his scalp. Her back arched off the mattress. He slammed his fingers into her and worked her clit with his tongue until the spasms wracking through her pelvis subsided and she took a startled gasp of air.

"Oh my God," she moaned.

"I think you can do better next time," he said. His lips brushed the inside of her thigh and her belly clenched, making her entire body jerk. Every nerve-ending was over-sensitized and seeking pleasure for itself.

"Do what better next time?" she whispered.

"Come," he said matter-of-factly. "With me inside you."

"Oh," she said breathlessly. "Sounds good."

He chuckled. His warm breath danced across the wet flesh between her thighs.

Owen slowly crawled up her body, kissing and biting her skin until she dug her nails into his shoulders and encouraged him to move faster.

"Caitlyn," he whispered, "you just found my trigger."

She wasn't sure what he meant, but he surged forward and his cock bumped against her. She gasped and squirmed beneath him, trying to help him find her opening. She needed him inside her.

He shifted onto his side and used his hand to guide himself home. As he slid deep, she became very well acquainted with his piercing and his back became very well acquainted with her nails.

"God, yes, baby," he said, "scratch me. I love it."

Good thing, because it wasn't as if she could consciously control her clenching fingers. She was so caught up in the feel of him filling her and that little extra bit her rubbing her front wall so exquisitely that she couldn't do anything but hold on to him and call out in bliss. Every so often, he rubbed a spot that made her toes curl involuntarily and her mouth fall open in shock. She wasn't sure when the pleasure broke as quaking release, but she went mindless with it, gasping and crying out. Everything inside her was one hot mess of indecipherable bliss.

Owen's hands moved to grip her ass and the earth shifted. He dragged her across the bed and planted his feet on the floor.

Holding her hips tightly, he fucked her even harder.

Shuddering in ecstasy, Caitlyn forced her eyes open. Watching Owen gasp and strain with a pleasure that rivaled her own was easily the most beautiful thing she'd ever seen. His thrusts slowed unexpectedly and he took a deep breath, opening his eyes to look at her. His gentle smile warmed her heart. He touched cool knuckles to her flushed cheek.

"You okay?" he asked. "Am I hurting you?"

She shook her head vehemently.

"Some women can't take the piercing for more than a few minutes. It starts to hurt."

"I can take it," she assured him.

A smile teased his lips and he pulled out. "I'm glad, but my back can't take much more of your, um, *enthusiasm*."

She released her grip on his back and before she could apologize for tearing at his skin like a possessed demon, he flipped her over onto her belly.

"Let's try it this way for a while."

He sank into her. He possessed her with slow gentle strokes, and she wasn't sure how she could find it as exciting as when he'd taken her hard and fast, but it was. She closed her eyes and concentrated on all the sensations within her body, clinging to the sheets beneath her belly to keep herself grounded. Something that felt so amazing had to be capable of launching her into the stratosphere.

His hands reached under her to cup her breasts and lift her slightly from the bed. "Which position feels better?"

"Both feel so good," she said, "but there's this…" She lost her train of thought as his jewelry rubbed a particularly delightful spot inside her. She knotted her fingers in the sheet and rocked to meet his hips. "Oh God, Owen."

"There's this *what*, Caitlyn?"

"Sp-spot. In front."

"Mmm, yes, I know all about that spot."

She strained her neck to look back at him. To watch his face as he took pleasure in her body. He gnawed on his lower lip. His nostrils flared slightly with each labored breath. A film of sweat brought a sheen to his tanned skin. He was so gorgeous, she had a hard time comprehending that he wasn't a figment of her imagination. What she found even more baffling was that what was inside seemed to be as a beautiful as the outside. His eyelids fluttered open and he paused his thrusts. His eyes met hers and he took a calm moment to just stare at her, and she couldn't take her eyes off him.

"The spot," he said. "Right."

He'd misunderstood why she was staring.

He pulled out, and she only partially stifled her sob of protest.

"It's okay," he whispered. "I'll find it again."

He eased her onto her back and lifted her legs to rest on his shoulders. "I do love a woman in thigh-high stockings," he said, his hands splaying over one thigh at the margin where skin met silk. "So sexy. Everything about you is sexy, Caitlyn." He held her gaze, his blue eyes sincere and intense. "Everything."

He bent to kiss the inside of her thigh.

Caitlyn whimpered. She was never at a loss for words, but she couldn't form a coherent thought.

"If you hadn't tied me up and done dirty things to me, I would have taken my time with you."

She didn't need him to take his time, she needed him inside her again. She tried to sit up, to reach for his cock, but her hamstrings pulled painfully and she collapsed back on the bed. He straightened, smiling down at her with an ornery gleam in his eye. Why did she think this was about revenge?

"You know where else that piercing feels good?" he murmured.

She shook her head, her mind racing through possibilities.

Cock in hand, he rubbed the little metal ball against her clit. Shockwaves of pleasure streaked up her spine.

"Spread your legs wide for me, Caitlyn. Let me in."

She'd do an inverted Chinese split if it would get him inside her again. She slipped her ankles from his shoulders and bent her knees, grabbing her thighs to pull them as far apart as she could bear.

"Beautiful," he whispered.

He rubbed the head of his cock and that wondrous piercing against her clit. Teasing her. Delighting her. Driving her mad with pleasure. When he slipped inside her, she cried out in bliss. And then he was rubbing himself against her clit again.

"Almost," he whispered.

Caitlyn's body began to tremble uncontrollably. Her toes curled. Her thighs tried to close as the pleasure became unbearable, but she held them open with tense fingers. "Owen."

"Almost," he whispered again.

Her back arched off the bed as his persistence paid off, and she came so hard, her vision tunneled. And then he was inside her, riding her orgasm. Thrusting with a hard, consistent rhythm. Rubbing against that perfect spot with each inward thrust and withdrawal until Caitlyn was certain she'd found heaven. She'd had orgasms in the past, but she'd never felt them in every inch of her body. She would have screamed if she'd had the mental capacity to make her lungs work properly.

Owen's breath hitched and she pried her eyes open to watch him come. His gorgeous face twisted into a mask of unmistakable bliss as he thrust into her one last time and clung to her ass, shuddering hard as he let go.

"Fuck, yes," he said in a breathless growl.

Her sentiments exactly. Dear God, the man was amazing.

He collapsed on top of her, his skin hot and moist against hers, his breath hard and heavy in her ear. She released her thighs, but only so she could wrap her arms and legs around him. She wanted to tell him how wonderful he was, but her brain still wasn't online. So she clung to him and rubbed her mouth against his shoulder, hoping he understood that he'd blown her mind by making her experience things in her body she'd never known existed.

After a long moment, his breathing stilled and he lifted his head to look at her. "Well that was fun," he said.

She smiled and nodded, though fun was much too small a word for what she'd experienced.

He started to draw away, and she hung onto him feebly, her limbs like gelatin.

He kissed her lips and brushed her hair from her cheeks. "I'll be right back," he promised, standing beside the bed.

She realized that she wasn't in the most comfortable position and squirmed farther up on the mattress. She didn't take her eyes off of him as he removed the condom and disposed of it. With one eye closed and a curious look on his face, Owen took a moment to clean his backside and then wash his hands. Caitlyn gnawed on her lip, anticipating the disappointment of him putting on his clothes and leaving her lying there alone to sort through her suddenly jumbled emotions. Her heart skipped in delight as he returned to the bed and lay beside her. He really had come back.

Owen rested his head on Caitlyn's belly, one hand gently stroking the inside of her thigh as he took deep, calming breaths.

Caitlyn's body continued to shudder with aftershocks of pleasure as she slowly reconnected with earth. It was a long way down from nirvana.

"Wow," she said after a long moment. "Just... *wow*."

Owen chuckled softly and turned his head to place a suckling kiss just above Caitlyn's navel. Her flesh quivered. Goose bumps rose to the surface of her skin. It seemed every inch of her wanted to be physically closer to the man—even her damned hair follicles.

"I've never..." she whispered, unable to find the words to express the depths of her pleasure, but feeling the need to try. To let him know he'd been amazing, although amazing just didn't seem like a strong enough description. Nor did phenomenal, earth-shattering, or fantastic.

"You've never what?" The deep timber of his voice made her nipples pebble. He noticed—bless him—and rubbed his lips over the sensitive tip of her breast. She shuddered. Her body wanted more of him.

"I've never..."

His tongue flicked out, teasing her into wanting still more. She lifted a weary arm and ran her fingers through his hair, toying with the soft, slightly sweat-damp strands at his nape.

"You've never..." he prompted.

She took a deep breath, her body quivering as she exhaled. "Come so hard that I felt it in the soles of my feet. You're something special, Owen... uh... Owen... Um..." Dear God, she'd just had the most amazing sexual experience of her life, and she didn't even know his last name.

"Mitchell," he supplied, as if he were a mind-reader.

"Owen Mitchell," she said. "I've never done anything like this before."

"You're supposed to save your regrets for when we're awkwardly putting our clothes back on and avoiding each other's eyes."

"But I don't regret it," she said. "Not at all. I only regret that I didn't find you sooner." She flushed, realizing too late that it wasn't the kind of thing you said after having sex with someone you didn't know.

"Were you looking for me?" he asked, amusement in his tone. She knew he'd be smiling. Wasn't sure if he'd laugh at her or not, but what the hell? She liked him. And she wanted him to like her too. Would being frank scare him away? Or make her intentions clear? She wasn't sure. That's what she got for marrying the first man who ever paid her any attention.

"I must've been. If not, I should have been." She took another deep breath, her heart thudding with nervousness. "I'm sorry if I'm going about this all wrong. You probably do this kind of thing all the time."

"If I'm lucky."

She laughed and hugged him with as much strength as she could muster. "So what do we do now? Are we supposed to put our clothes back on and go our separate ways immediately? Or can I stay with you longer?"

"We do whatever we feel like."

"What do *you* feel like?" she asked.

He lifted up on his elbows and stared down at her with such intensity, it stole her breath. She hoped their night together wasn't about to end prematurely because she was such a novice when it came to one-night stands.

"Pastrami on rye," he said.

Having thought he was going to say something profound, she laughed. "Do they serve sandwiches here?"

"No," he said, "but I'm sure we can find one somewhere. Are you hungry?"

She wasn't really, but she did want to spend more time with him. Preferably in a horizontal position. The man had definitely earned himself a sandwich. And despite her best intentions to keep this as impersonal as possible, she wanted to know about him. Know everything about him. Beside the fact that he was a-*maz*-ing in bed. And might be sexually attracted to his best friend. She couldn't let herself dwell on that though. Owen obviously knew his way around the female anatomy. It would be a horrible tragedy if he switched teams.

"Yes," she said. "I could go for a sandwich."

"I like the bread lightly toasted and double pastrami. And don't forget the dill pickle spear on the side."

He wasn't really expecting her to get up and make him a sandwich was he? She lifted her head and caught the smirk on his lips, right before he kissed a trail along the bottom of her ribcage. The man was a consummate tease, she decided.

"Would you like a cold beer with that?" she asked.

"That sounds heavenly," he murmured against her skin. "And some waffle fries."

"With cheese?"

"Ketchup."

"Anything else with your order, sir?"

"Make yourself something real nice while you're up," he whispered, trailing soft kisses down her belly toward parts of her that could still feel the effects of that delightful cock piercing of his.

"No problem. I'll just make my way to the nearest kitchen. I should probably take off these stockings so I'm barefoot."

He lifted his head and grinned. His blue eyes twinkled with mischief. "I'd prefer if you wore those *and* those sexy as sin white high heels while you prepare my meal."

"And nothing else, I presume."

"That's a decent presumption," he said. His hands skimmed the skin along her sides.

"Glad you approve."

"You might as well put your clothes on. It will be at least an hour before my sexual appetite matches the hunger in my belly."

"So why are you still touching me?"

"Because you're beautiful," he told her, as if to say *duh*.

And he was doing a great job at making her feel that way when she had felt anything but beautiful for the past six months. "Thank you," she said, grateful that her voice didn't crack from the emotions welling in her throat.

"No, thank *you*." He slid up to gaze into her eyes before capturing her lips in a hungry kiss. After several toe-curling moments, he tore his lips from hers and scooted off the edge of the bed. "If I don't get up now, I'm going to end up getting up again." He glanced at his glorious cock to let her know which part of him would be up again. "And if that happens, we'll be at this place all night. I don't think I can stand to listen to the guy in the next room make those distracting sounds for much longer."

Caitlyn hadn't noticed until Owen mentioned it, but coming through the wall was some sound between grunting and yowling. She'd had almost forgotten where she was, why she'd come here, and that Owen was just some pick-up at a sex club.

"Oh yeah, little pussy cat," their wall-mate hollered, "reach under there and scratch my balls."

Caitlyn giggled.

"That's it, pussy cat." The words penetrated the wall. "Now *meow* for me."

Caitlyn couldn't hear the woman's meows, but the man's sudden and startling barks sent her into hysterics. She laughed until tears sprang to her eyes and her belly ached.

"Okay, yeah," Caitlyn said, forcing her body from the bed. "Let's get out of here. Find some place for me to make you a sandwich."

"I don't really want you to make me a sandwich, Caitlyn."

She grinned. "I know that. I can tell when you're teasing."

"And you were teasing me back?"

She nodded. Owen drew her into his arms and held her close. She smiled against his shoulder.

"Can't seem to keep my hands off you," he said.

"I don't mind," she assured him.

"Well, here, no, but in a restaurant? I might embarrass you."

"We could get room service in a hotel," she said. "Then you can put your hands anywhere you like."

"I sort of want everyone to see that you're with me," he said.

She crinkled her eyebrows. "Why?"

"Because you're a smokin' hot babe and I get off on the ego trip."

She stepped back, one step and then two. *What?* He'd taken his constant stream of compliments one step too far. No man said things like that unless… Caitlyn scowled and leveled him with her best glare of doom. "Okay, how much did Jenna pay you to make me feel like a million bucks?"

"Pay me?"

"You're a male escort, aren't you?" No wonder he was so good in bed. Women paid him to be good in bed. She slapped him in the chest with both hands, pretending not to notice his look of astonishment. "I should have realized it sooner. You're really smooth, Owen Mitchell, if that's even your real name."

She expected him to either admit he was paid to entertain women or indignantly deny it. She never expected him to cover his initial astonishment, real or put-on, with a hearty laugh.

"Do you think I could actually make money doing this?" he asked, pausing to catch his breath. "You know, in case the rock star thing doesn't work out for me."

"What?" Caitlyn stared up at him with her mouth agape. "You're not a rock star. You liar. Everything you've said to me has been a lie, hasn't it?"

The teasing light died from his eyes. "Caitlyn, I'll allow you to insinuate that I'm a male prostitute. I'm even okay with you struggling to believe I'm part of a famous rock band, but you don't get to blatantly call me a liar. I'm not a liar. I never lie. I might tease and exaggerate a bit, but I don't lie."

She wasn't sure if he was truly angry, but his body was tense and his expression had gone hard.

"You haven't been lying to me?"

He shook his head, and she concluded he was the best con man on the planet, an award-winning actor (both distinct possibilities), or he was telling the truth. She felt a mix of relief and concern. Relieved that he was legitimately attracted to her and her friends didn't have to pay a hot guy to sleep with her. Concerned that she liked that knowledge more than she should. She wasn't even over Charles yet, was she? This was just a revenge fuck or something, *wasn't* it?

"Wait," she said, "So you're *really* a rock star?" She giggled as soon as the words escaped her lips, because seriously, who claims such things and expects people to believe it without some proof? "A rock star?"

"Yep. We were the headlining band in the concert at the AT&T Center tonight."

"Oh yeah?" That was the most ridiculous thing she'd ever heard and maybe he didn't like being called a liar, but she was about to call him one again. "What instrument do you play?"

"What?" he said with a crooked grin. "You don't think I'm lead singer material?"

He wasn't lying? He really was a rock star? She took another look at him, unable to believe someone this attractive and apparently famous would want anything to do with her. He was definitely dynamic enough to be a lead singer. "Do you sing?"

"A little," he said, "but mostly I play bass guitar."

"What's the name of your band?" She realized that he was sharing personal information. This was a good sign, wasn't it? She had to keep him talking, because if he was her revenge fuck, she wanted to continue to seek her revenge for a lot longer.

A loud thumping on the wall broke the spell Owen had over Caitlyn. How did he do that, make her feel as if they were the only two people on earth?

"I'll tell you all about it over a sandwich," he said. "Do you have clothes in the outer dressing room?"

She nodded. "Yeah, I don't think what's left of that negligée legally counts as clothing."

He cringed at the discarded pile of torn lace on the floor. "Sorry about that. I don't usually get so worked up that I rip off a woman's clothes."

She smiled. "I liked it. It made me feel irresistible."

"You are irresistible."

She was starting to believe him. Starting to remember that she was sexy and desirable and beautiful, even if her husband hadn't been smart enough to see it. "You'd make a fortune," she said with a smile.

"Huh?"

"As a male escort. I'd definitely pay for this feeling."

He snorted. "You don't have to. But it's good to know I have something to fall back on, you know, if I get myself kicked out of the band or something."

He stepped away and retrieved his black dress shirt from the floor. He helped her shrug into it and slowly buttoned it from its hem—which hit her midthigh—to the very top button just under her chin.

"That should keep the hawks at bay," he said and tapped her nose with his index finger.

"The hawks?"

"Men circling to make their kill now that I've chased away those man-hater vibes you were giving off."

"I still hate men," she said. "Well, one man. But not you. I like you."

"You're making this way too easy for me," Owen said.

She tilted her head at him coyly. "Should I be playing hard to get? A little late for that, don't you think?"

He shook his head. "I hate players probably as much as you hate your ex-husband."

She lifted an eyebrow at him. "Aren't you a player?"

He scowled. "Not intentionally. I'm looking for something and just don't know exactly what it is yet."

"Do you honestly think you're going to find what you're looking for in a sex club?"

"Maybe I have." He winked at her. "You're going to call me,

right?"

"Depends," she said.

"On what?"

"Will you answer?"

He smiled. "Of course."

"Then I'll call you." Caitlyn found her shoes and put them on. He watched her with his devilish little grin firmly in place and only then reached for his own clothes.

"Then I'll give you my number," he said.

She watched him slip into his underwear and slacks. As he fastened his leather belt, naughty ideas began to filter through her thoughts. Ideas that involved belts. Would he let her try all those fantasies that she didn't want to admit she had? And did he really want her to call him or was he just getting her hopes up? She wasn't sure why she didn't trust him—he hadn't done anything to break her trust. In fact, he'd been absolutely wonderful. Too good to be true. She kept waiting for him to treat her badly, as if she deserved such treatment.

Damn, Charles sure had done a number on her. Maybe she should have given her heart time to mend before getting in this revenge fuck. What if this turned out to be something she wasn't ready for? She wasn't looking for a relationship, but she'd be an idiot not to see how far things could progress with Owen. He wasn't the kind of guy who came along every day.

"So you never answered me: what's the name of your band?" she asked as he settled a hand on her lower back and directed her out the door.

Heads turned as they passed through the main lounge. She was sure they were all looking at Owen. He had a gorgeous body and he happened to be shirtless.

"Sole Regret," he said close to her ear, as if it were a secret.

She caught the scent of his body and the spicy, slightly sweet fragrance of his cologne. When he leaned away again, she inhaled that same delectable scent from the fabric of his shirt at her shoulder. She wouldn't mind wearing his shirt for the rest of the night. Unfortunately, they had paused just outside the changing rooms and she was going to have to find her own clothes and relinquish the garment to him. There were, however, two problems with that. One: she would no longer be surrounded by his intoxicating scent. Two: the clothes she wore to the club were likely to send him packing. She didn't exactly have the sexiest wardrobe.

"I think I've heard of them," she said. She had never heard of a band called Sole Regret and figured he'd been playing up the star part of rock star.

He chuckled. "No you haven't. I can tell. If you had, you'd be impressed."

"I'm sorry, I was trying to be kind. What kind of music do you play?"

"Metal."

She winced. "I don't listen to that stuff."

"That's okay. So what do *you* do for a living?"

And now he was about to lose all interest in her. She decided to play down her geek-i-tude. If her wardrobe didn't send him fleeing for a sexier woman, her career most certainly would.

"I... uh... own a business."

"What kind of business?"

When she hesitated and tried to think of way to make herself sound less geeky, he grinned.

"I know," he said. "You're a madam for high-class prostitutes. It would explain why you're so good in bed."

She was good in bed? News to her. Caitlyn was most remembered for her complete lack of athletic prowess. Any activity that required her to move her body in a coordinated fashion ended in disaster. But perhaps she'd finally discovered her *sport*.

"A madam? Now that would be an interesting career," she said. "Especially if you were one of my wares."

"You're done with me already? Going to sell me off to the highest bidder, are you?"

"No," Caitlyn said. "Hopefully, I'm just getting started with you. I think we have a lot of pleasurable moments in our future."

He avoided her interested gaze, and her heart plummeted. She hoped he knew that she was teasing about the male prostitute thing. Had she insulted him? It was a pretty insulting topic to joke about. She opened her mouth to apologize, but he patted her on the butt and nudged her toward the dressing rooms.

"You go get dressed. I'm going to find Kelly and let him know we're leaving. Would you be overly upset if he caught a ride back to the hotel with us?"

"Of course not," she said, but her heart gave an unpleasant pang. This was it. The thing that made him too good to be true.

Kellen was her biggest competition for Owen's affection, and Owen didn't even realize it. "Should I wait for you outside?" she asked.

"Just wait here. I wouldn't want someone to pick you up off the street."

As if.

"Just so you know, I only have sex in sex clubs, so once we leave here, I won't want to have sex with you again tonight. I didn't want you to think it was anything personal if it came up."

Caitlyn blinked at him, her heart twanging with a strange ache. So she was good enough to screw in a sex club, but not after a sandwich? Of course she'd think that was personal. Fine. Even if he didn't want to screw her again, it didn't matter. She wasn't only interested in him for one thing. At least he'd been honest with her. It was something her husband had never been.

"I understand," she said. "I still want to spend time with you." Did that make her a desperate loser?

He smiled awfully bright for a man who didn't want to have sex with her. "You just made the honor roll, babe."

She had no idea what he meant by that, but apparently she'd said something right.

CHAPTER FIVE

Owen found Kelly sitting with a woman in a booth near the back of the club. So he might not want a ride back after all. Maybe he'd found someone to get busy with. Or maybe he was hoping that Owen would rescue him. It was difficult to read Kelly's face.

Owen paused near the corner of the table and caught a snippet of Kelly and the woman's conversation before either of them noticed him.

"Come on, baby," the woman purred, "you're hard as a rock. Let's go find a room and—"

"Of course I'm hard as a rock," Kelly said testily. "You keep shoving your hand down my pants."

Okay, it was rescue that Kelly needed.

Owen cleared his throat and grinned at his friend who, yeah, looked relieved to see him.

"Are you finally finished?" Kelly asked.

"Not really."

"Then what—"

"I'm taking Caitlyn out. She doesn't belong here. Or maybe I don't feel right with her here."

He wasn't sure what he meant exactly. There was just something about her that deserved better than this. Better than him. And for fuck's sake, she didn't seem to see it at all. He wanted to show her, but not here. *Here* was seedy, and being in this place made him want to take a shower. He'd never felt that way about one of Tony's clubs, but perhaps the entrepreneurial genius had just missed the mark with this one. Or maybe something in Owen's mindset had shifted and he was ready for more than a string of one-night stands. He honestly didn't know. But he meant to find out. Her reaction to his claim that he wouldn't want to have sex outside of the club had given him hope. He wasn't sure exactly what he was hoping for. *More.* But more what?

Kelly's eyes widened. "Wait! You're taking her home with you?"

It went against their rules and promises to each other, but Caitlyn was special. Kelly would recognize that soon enough.

"I don't know if it'll go that far, but maybe. We're going to grab a bite to eat and see if it goes anywhere from there. Are you ready to go?"

Kelly tugged his companion's hand out of his pants again. "I'm ready."

"Can I come with you?" the woman asked.

"No," Kelly said and slipped out of the booth.

Owen couldn't help but notice that Kelly was indeed hard as a rock. He had no explanation as to why he was rapidly getting that way himself. He'd assumed that after that fantastic pair of orgasms, his lust would be sated for a while.

"You should at least let that chick blow you or something," Owen said. "You have to be hurting right now."

Kelly shifted the crotch of his pants. "I'll take care of it back at the hotel."

Owen tried to stop memories of Kelly masturbating backstage in the communal shower from entering his thoughts, but it was impossible. They used to compete with each other to see who could get himself off the fastest, though they hadn't done it for several years. In a weird way, it had further cemented their friendship when Kelly was first trying to get over Sara. He still wasn't over her and he kept receding deeper into himself. It wasn't healthy. Owen supposed masturbating with your best friend in the shower was pretty fucked up as well, but at least Kelly hadn't been alone. He didn't like Kelly to be alone. Kelly had too much to give to be so bottled up inside.

Owen glanced at the girl who was sulking in the booth. Kelly deserved better than her. He deserved the best. Someone more like Caitlyn. Someone he was unlikely to meet in a seedy sex club. The kind of woman Owen had been purposely avoiding because he knew how easily he fell for them. Owen wasn't sure if he'd gotten lucky tonight or was setting himself up to get hurt again. He'd been avoiding that at all costs for years now. Maybe he was ready to put his heart on the line, but he'd be an idiot to not see how far this thing with Caitlyn might progress. She didn't seem like the type who'd rip his heart out just because she could.

Kelly headed for the exit, and Owen fell into step beside him.

"So you like this one, do ya?" Kelly asked.

Owen shrugged. "I guess so."

"Or are you just trying to get me to help you pleasure her?"

Owen stopped midstep. Because, yeah, if Kelly was up for it, Owen would love his assistance.

"That's it, isn't it?" Kelly said. "You're so predictable."

"No, that isn't it. Or it wasn't until you mentioned it. Do you want to join us?"

"Not at all."

Owen didn't understand the feeling of disappointment in his chest, so he slugged Kelly in the shoulder. "Then don't bring it up."

"You're the one who keeps bringing it up. I think you're more worried about *my* love life than your own," Kelly said.

"That's because there's more to worry about when it comes to your love life. Or complete lack of one."

Kelly chuckled. "You're as blind as you are predictable, Tags. Do you remember where you put your shoes?"

"In the locker room."

"And your shirt?"

"Caitlyn's borrowing it."

Kelly nodded in the direction of the front door. "I'll wait for you in the limo."

"What about your shirt?" Owen glanced pointedly at Kelly's bare chest.

"I didn't bring a shirt."

"You don't own a shirt."

"I own a shirt," Kelly said. "*A* shirt. One."

Owen grinned at him. "You're an odd duck, Cuff."

"That's why you get along with me so well."

A woman Owen didn't recognize paused beside them, more diamonds on display than a De Beers store.

"I'll pay you ten thousand dollars if you let me watch you two fuck," she said.

When Owen and Kelly just gaped at her, she looked from one to the other and said, "Cash."

"We were just leaving," Kelly said.

"We're not a couple," Owen sputtered. Did they look like a couple? True they were standing rather close and were both shirtless, but...

"Obviously you're not a couple," she said, rolling her eyes. She had a thick European accent, but Owen couldn't identify its origin. French, maybe. "Why would I pay ten thousand dollars to watch a gay couple fuck?" She laughed. "They'd probably let me watch for free."

"We don't need your money, lady," Kelly said and pushed Owen to uproot his bare feet from the floor.

"Do straight guys actually fuck each other for you?" Owen had to ask.

"Depends on how desperate they are for money," she said. She grinned slyly. "Or how much they've secretly wanted to fuck a man, but never had someone else to blame it on."

"Owen?" Caitlyn said from just behind him.

Heat flooded his face. He cringed and turned to find her dressed in a pair of blue jeans, a white blouse with an out-of-style flop of a bow at the throat, and a tweed blazer his grandmother would be ashamed to own. And why did her conservative attire turn him on as much as that negligée had? He was in trouble.

"Hey, Caitlyn. Are you ready to leave?"

"Are you whoring yourself out?" she asked.

"What? No, of course not."

"I'm not sure why you're even having a discussion with this woman," Kelly said, nodding toward the diamond queen. "As if you're considering this bullshit or something."

"I wasn't considering it. I just wondered if men actually went through with it. That's a lot of money."

Caitlyn's arm circled Owen's waist, and her hand slid over his bare belly. "You know I get half of every dime you make, baby. How much did she offer you?"

Owen laughed. Kelly gaped at her. Owen slapped Kelly on the chest. "Inside joke. I'll explain later. Let's go."

"How do you have inside jokes with someone you just met?" Kelly said as he started toward the exit again.

"Good luck finding your fantasy," Owen said to the woman in diamonds. Sex with another man was one of those sex acts he'd never tried. Probably never would. Letting Caitlyn have her way with him was as close as he was going to get to having a homosexual encounter. He didn't think reciprocal hand jobs counted.

As the three of them stepped onto the walkway outside, the cool cement registered in Owen's brain. "Shit, I forgot my shoes," he said. "I'll catch up with you in the limo."

"You sure you want to leave me alone with your girl?" Kelly asked.

"I expect you to take good care of her."

"Oh, I'll take real good care of her." He wrapped an arm around Caitlyn and tugged her against his side. Her eyes opened wide. Kelly was only teasing, but Caitlyn had no way of knowing that.

"I'll hurry," Owen said. Assuming he didn't get distracted between here and there by rich women with money to blow and fantasies to fulfill.

CHAPTER SIX

The limo pulled up just as Owen dashed back into the building. Caitlyn didn't feel right being plastered to Kellen's side. Not that it was a bad thing. She just felt as if she were cheating. On a guy she'd just met, barely knew, and who had no long-term interest in her. Boy, was she all mixed up inside.

"You're tense," Kellen said near her ear. "You don't have anything to worry about from me. I was just giving Owen a hard time."

"You don't find me attractive?"

"You're gorgeous," he said. "I just have a certain type."

"Big blue eyes?" *Like Owen's...*

"How'd you guess?"

"You and Owen need to have a talk."

Kellen's dark brows drew together. "About what? So Sara had blue eyes, what does that have to do with Owen?"

So maybe there wasn't any attraction on Kellen's end at all.

The driver opened the door, and Caitlyn hurried to climb inside. The relationship between Kellen and Owen wasn't any of her business. She wasn't sure why she was so fixated on it.

"Owen will be out in a couple minutes," Kellen said to the driver. "Just wait here."

"No problem, Mr. Jamison."

Kellen slipped into the seat beside Caitlyn. She stared at her hands, which were folded in her lap. She probably shouldn't have said anything to Kellen about Owen. They knew their feelings for each other far better than she did. She wasn't even sure if they actually *had* feelings for each other.

"Why do I need to have a talk with Owen? He already knows what type of woman I'm most attracted to. In fact, he said I'd have better luck getting over Sara if I dated someone who doesn't look anything like her. What do you think?"

"I couldn't say," Caitlyn said. "It must be hard to be reminded of someone you lost when you look at some other woman."

"I see pieces of her in everyone," he said. "In everything."

"Even in me?"

He grinned crookedly and released a huff of a laugh. "Yeah, you have soft lips like Sara's." Kellen reached over and touched a finger under her chin. He rubbed his thumb along her bottom lip, sending sparks of pleasure down her nerve-endings. "I still remember how she tasted."

"How did she die?" Caitlyn asked, hell-bent on sticking her foot in her mouth repeatedly tonight. "Was it sudden?"

"Owen told you just enough to encourage annoying questions, I see." Kellen dropped his hand. "Not sudden. It took her several months to die once they found the tumors in her lungs. But a thousand years with her wouldn't have been enough." A distant look stole across his chiseled features. "One was definitely not enough."

Caitlyn bit her lip and ducked her chin, swallowing around a lump in her throat. It didn't seem fair that a dead girl had the unwavering devotion and love of someone as vibrantly alive as Kellen Jamison.

"I shouldn't have asked. I apologize. And..." She looked up to find him staring off into space. Why did she hurt so badly for him? She didn't even know him, but she could practically feel the devastation seeping from his pores. "I'm truly sorry for your loss."

He nodded curtly, avoiding her eyes. She couldn't possibly ask him if he had any feelings for Owen. Not with him so obviously hurting over a woman. She sat awkwardly beside him trying to think of something, anything, to say.

"I lost my sister a couple of years ago."

"Cancer?" he murmured.

"No. There was an accident at work. She was training to be an astronaut and..." She couldn't continue. Morgan's loss was like a fresh wound every time Caitlyn had to tell someone what had happened to her. "The safety harness failed. They say she didn't suffer." Which is more than could be said about anyone who battled cancer.

"It hurts most when you speak of them, doesn't it?"

She nodded, drawing deep breaths through her nose to keep threatening tears at bay.

"So you find yourself avoiding talking about it," he said. "To anyone. Because it reminds you that it happened. It wasn't just a nightmare. It's reality."

She wasn't sure if he was really talking to her. He wasn't looking at her.

"Don't break his heart, Caitlyn," Kellen said unexpectedly. "He likes to pretend he's a player, but he's very sensitive when it comes to love. He's nice. Too nice at times. He only sees the good in people. So when you shred his heart, be it tonight, tomorrow, or years from now, take it easy on him. He doesn't take rejection well."

Kellen turned to her then, and she couldn't speak. Could only stare into his dark eyes. It was as if she were under some sort of spell. After a long moment, he looked away and she found her tongue.

"It's a bit soon to be talking about love," she said.

Kellen laughed softly. "I knew I would love Sara for the rest of my life the first time she smiled at me."

And what in the hell was she supposed to say to that?

Before she could think of a response, Owen slipped into the car beside Kellen. Relief flooded her. She wasn't sure why. Maybe it was because Owen was all light and wonder, while Kellen was all dark and practicality. Caitlyn needed Owen, because she was more like Kellen than she cared to admit. As soon as the door closed behind Owen, he climbed over his friend's lap and wriggled until he slipped between Kellen and Caitlyn's hips.

"You could have asked me to move," Kellen said, scooting closer to the door to give Owen breathing room.

"I wasn't expecting you to be sitting on top of her," Owen said.

"I wasn't."

"Not that I blame you," he said. "Are there any decent sandwich shops around here that are open this late?" he asked Caitlyn.

"I wouldn't know."

"Don't you live close by?"

She shook her head. "I'm from Houston. I'm just here visiting a friend." She smirked. "And enjoying the nightlife San Antonio has to offer."

"You know what?" Owen said. "Tony has a club in Houston. I'll take you sometime. We can try out some of your other kinky fantasies."

"As tempting as that sounds, I don't think I'll be visiting another of Tony's clubs," she said. "Not that I didn't enjoy my time there tonight, I did, but my curiosity is sated now. Maybe I'll try Internet dating next." Or maybe she'd take time for herself. To get over Charles. She hated him, yes, but she still wasn't over him. She wasn't ready to love again. Hot sex with Owen? Yeah, she'd been ready for that, had *needed* that. She was ready for hot sex with Owen again, truth be told. But if he was one of those guys who believed in love at first smile, like his excessively intense friend, then she should probably take her leave as soon as possible. Before she shredded his heart or something equally appalling.

"I'll see if I can find a place that's open," Kellen said as he tugged a cellphone out of his pocket. "What are you hungry for? Wait, I get one guess. Pastrami on rye?"

Caitlyn chuckled. "How did he know that?"

Kellen grinned as he tapped a search into his phone with one finger. "Owen always craves pastrami after sex."

"Not always," Owen said.

"Owen usually craves pastrami after sex," Kellen amended.

"Only when I sweat a lot," Owen said. "And Caitlyn definitely made me sweat a lot."

She stared up into his grinning face, fighting the urge to kiss him. Just looking at him made her feel good about herself. Made her *happy*. She didn't understand why, but didn't care overmuch at the moment. She wasn't supposed to like him this much. The attraction was supposed to fade after their tumble in bed. She was supposed to have sated her lust and lost interest—that's the way it worked. But she hadn't lost interest. She was more intrigued than ever.

She still wanted him. For sex. Yes, she understood that attraction, but she wanted more than that too. She wanted to get to know him. Figure out what made him tick. Determine how a guy as good looking as Owen ended up being nice and sensitive. Damn it. Maybe she should have turned down their sandwich excursion and gone back to Jenna's house. Every extra minute she spent with him made her like him a little more. This was definitely more than she bargained for.

Owen threaded his fingers through her hair, his eyes searching hers in the low light inside the back of the car. "I can't get over how beautiful you are. Isn't she beautiful, Kellen?"

Warmth spread across her face, and she ducked her chin to hide a pleased smile.

"Gorgeous," Kellen said. "There's a twenty-four-hour diner two blocks from here. No guarantees they serve pastrami."

"Alert the driver," Owen said.

Caitlyn looked up and found Owen still staring at her.

"Remember when I said that once we left the club, I wouldn't have sex with you again," he said.

She scowled. "How could I forget?" It was the only mean thing he'd said to her since they'd met, and she wasn't sure he'd meant it the way she'd taken it.

He touched a fingertip to her lips. "Apparently, I am a liar."

Caitlyn's heart skipped a beat.

Kellen released a long sigh of annoyance and shook his head. "Can you at least drop me off at the hotel before you start round two?"

"Round three," Owen corrected.

"Even worse."

"We'll drop you off after we eat," Owen said.

"I'm not hungry," Kellen said.

"If you're not careful, I'm going to think you don't want to hang out with me anymore."

"I don't want to hang around with you if you're going to flaunt your hot woman in front of me all night."

Was that what he was doing? Or was he trying to tempt Kellen into doing something he'd later regret? Caitlyn didn't know either of them well enough to have a good handle on their dynamic, but she didn't want to be involved in drawing out Kellen's pain. The guy had been through enough already.

"It's probably best if you tone it down a little in public," she said, not because she actually wanted Owen to tone it down, but because she felt bad for Kellen.

"Tone it down? You don't mean that. I haven't taken a woman out in over six months and you expect me to tone it down."

She nodded, even though she was incredibly flattered that he'd broken his rules for her. "I do mean it."

"Damn, I knew we should have ordered room service."

"I think you can keep your hands to yourself for an hour." Because that's about how long she thought she could keep her hands to herself.

Kellen chuckled. "If you knew him better, you wouldn't think that."

"I can be good," Owen said. "If you reward me for it later."

"I can probably handle that," she said. "But not until we're alone." She peeked around Owen's body to see if Kellen looked any less miserable. He was no longer staring into space. The slight smile on his lips led her to believe he was amused by her stipulation.

"I can be a perfect gentleman," Owen said.

Kellen chuckled and shook his head.

Owen glanced at Kellen and then smiled at Caitlyn. He seemed to realize that she was setting boundaries for Kellen's sake. She expected Owen to torment Kellen as he'd been doing all night, but instead he relaxed and folded his hands demurely in his lap.

"I'm going to be so well behaved, you're going to have to reward me until dawn."

She wasn't sure she could keep up with him until dawn but, by God, she would try.

The limo pulled up to a diner that had probably never had a limo parked in front of it in all its years. But the open sign was glowing orange, and that was all the motivation Owen needed to tug Caitlyn out of the car by one wrist.

"I'll just wait here," Kellen said.

"What is wrong with you tonight?" Owen asked. "If I didn't know better, I'd think you'd been possessed by grumpy ol' Adam."

Kellen glared at him from the interior of the limo.

"Pod person!" Owen yelled and pointed into the open car door.

"Oh, for fuck's sake," Kellen said, but Caitlyn caught his smile as he hefted himself out of the car. He eyed the No Shirt, No Shoes, No Service sign and after releasing a sigh of annoyance, pointed at the driver. "Trunk."

The driver hurried to open the trunk, and Kellen searched the compartment for something. He donned a plain white T-shirt and moved to stand next to Owen. Pity really. Kellen didn't look comfortable in a shirt and he'd have definitely been the most delicious-looking thing in the diner without it.

"Are you happy?" Kellen said.

"Getting there," Owen said.

Kellen smiled to himself, ducking his head so Owen didn't see it, but Caitlyn did. She wondered how much darker Kellen would be without Owen in his life.

Caitlyn felt a strange sense of pride as Owen walked her through the nearly deserted restaurant with his hand on her lower back. At this time of night, there weren't many people to witness that they were together, but she was pleasantly surprised that heads turned. Most of them were female heads checking out Owen and Kellen, but a few were men and she was pretty sure their eyes were on her. They were probably wondering what was good enough about her to gain Owen's attention. She always wondered that when she saw an average guy with a really hot woman, so she assumed men wondered how an average woman ended up with a really hot guy too.

"Sit wherever you like," a harried-looking waitress called from behind the counter. She seemed to be working the entire dining room alone.

They snagged a booth near the back, and Caitlyn found herself trapped against the wall beside Owen. Kellen sat wearily across from them. The menus were stuck behind the napkin holder, so Caitlyn took it upon herself to pass them around.

She was probably too anxious to eat. She really wanted to be alone with Owen now that she'd made it clear that she wasn't interested in being naughty in public and he'd made it clear that he was making a concession for her. Since he was breaking his own rules, she wouldn't mind it so much if he broke one of hers. Especially since he'd retracted his earlier statement about not sleeping with her outside of the sex club. She was ready for a little foreplay.

"Do they have anything that isn't swimming in grease?" Kellen asked as he perused the menu and wiped off the tell-tale grease spots.

The waitress chose that moment to arrive. "The water is low in fat," she said and smiled at Kellen.

"I'll have one of those," Kellen said. "Bottled."

"Okay."

"Do you have pastrami?" Owen asked hopefully.

"Sandwiches are on the back of the menu."

Owen flipped his menu over and ran a finger down the plastic. "Score! I'll have a pastrami on rye." He glanced at Caitlyn and winked. "Extra pastrami. Do you have waffle fries?"

"No, sorry. Just have the regular kind."

"Side of chips then."

"To drink?"

"Bottled water. What do you want, Caitlyn?"

"Is your pie any good?" Caitlyn asked.

Owen chuckled. "What do you think, Kellen? Is her pie any good?"

Caitlyn slapped Owen with her menu.

"Not in the mood for pie jokes, Owen," Kellen said.

The waitress flushed and crossed her arms. "My pie is excellent," she said, "but the diner's is mediocre. The cheesecake is good though."

"I'll have a piece of cheesecake then," Caitlyn said. After the workout she'd just had with Owen, a few extra calories wouldn't hurt. "Kellen, you're going to get more than water, aren't you?"

"I'd like to try the pie," Kellen said, grinning, "but I guess I'll go with cheesecake too."

"You can try the pie," the waitress said. She tossed her hair behind her shoulders. "You can try anything you see."

Caitlyn's eyes were on Owen. And he watched Kellen's reaction carefully. He really was fascinated with his best friend's sex life.

"Cheesecake for now. Maybe I'll be hungry for pie later."

Owen smiled. "Do you want something to drink, Caitlyn?" he said, turning his attention to her.

"Tea?"

"Sweet and iced?" the waitress asked.

"Yes, please," she said.

The waitress gave Kellen one more look of longing and then headed toward the counter with their order.

"She's into you, man," Owen said.

"Every woman in the room is into him," Caitlyn said.

"Including you?" Owen asked.

She shook her head and slid a hand over his thigh. "Not when I'm sitting next to you. But if I wasn't already in lust with you, yeah, I'd be into him too."

"This is why I make him hide when I try to pick up a girl," Owen said. "If they see him first…" Owen shrugged.

"Not buying it," Caitlyn said. "You're both gorgeous. Just depends on if you like your men dark and mysterious, or light and—"

"Annoying," Kellen supplied.

"I was going to say sweet," Caitlyn said.

"I'm not sweet."

He totally was. In the limo, Kellen had only validated what she'd already suspected. "I mean excellent in bed."

"Kellen's excellent in bed too," Owen said.

"I can only speak from personal experience."

"I think I'm better in bed than he is now." Owen's thigh tightened beneath Caitlyn's hand as he kicked Kellen under the table. "He's out of practice."

Kellen didn't seem to mind the taunt, though he didn't hesitate in returning Owen's kick.

"You're also a troublemaker," Caitlyn said.

"One of my most endearing qualities," Owen said.

"You get used to it," Kellen said. "He doesn't know how to stay out of trouble. It's like he was born for the sole purpose of getting into trouble."

"Kellen's just jealous because he's forgotten how to have fun."

"That's a shame," Caitlyn said. "I spent the last ten years of my life forgetting how to have fun. It's starting to come back to me, thanks to Owen here. And you have him around all the time."

"I think I'm all funned out," Kellen said.

"Speaking of fun… Wanna dance?" Owen asked her.

She gawked at him. "Dance? *Here?* But…" She rummaged through her brain for an excuse. "There's no music."

Owen pulled his smartphone out of his pocket and started his playlist. The tiny speaker sounded awful, but they had music. Very hard and heavy music. Caitlyn frowned. "Is that one of your songs?"

"Yeah," he said, "do you like it?"

"Not especially," she shouted. Even though the music wasn't loud, she felt compelled to yell when confronted by the sounds blaring from the speaker.

"What kind of music do you listen to?" he asked.

She hesitated, looking from one musician to the next. She couldn't lie about it. It would be much too easy to catch her at it. "I… uh… I don't listen to music."

Based on the look Owen gave her, she must have contracted a severe case of purple Chicken Pox.

"You're kidding," he said.

"No. I mostly listen to podcasts. And, well, I'm a fan of silence." She reached over and muted the song blasting from the speaker. Much better.

"Have you ever even been to a concert?"

"Oh, sure. Charles took me to the symphony once." She'd even bought a new dress for the occasion and had worn it exactly once.

"Symphony? That doesn't count. What about a rock concert?"

She bit her lip. She was about to lose her cool-card. "Never been."

Owen gaped at her. Her pox must have started seeping blueberry jelly.

"Inconceivable," Owen said. "That needs to change."

"I agree," Kellen said.

"Tomorrow night we play in Houston. You're going."

She might be able to handle a Journey or .38 Special concert, but Sole Regret? If the ten seconds of music from Owen's smartphone had made her ears bleed, what would an entire show do to her? Make her head explode?

"I couldn't possibly," she said.

"Do you have other plans?"

"Yes, actually. I came to San Antonio to visit Jenna, and I've hardly spent any time with her yet." Nice save.

"She can come with you."

"She has to work."

"So you can come with us—"

"On the tour bus?" Kellen interrupted.

"Yes, on the tour bus."

"I don't think that's a good idea."

Caitlyn wondered why. Considering the kind of clubs these guys frequented, she could only imagine the kind of debauchery that occurred on that tour bus.

"I didn't ask for your opinion," Owen said to Kellen. Then he turned his attention back to Caitlyn. "You can come with us, and I'll send you back to San Antonio—in a limo if you want—to return to visit your friend."

"I honestly don't think I'd like it."

"You have to try it at least once. I can't be seen in public with a woman who's never been to a rock concert before."

She chuckled. "Well I wouldn't want to ruin your reputation."

"It was ruined years ago," Kellen assured her.

"So is that a yes?" Owen pressed.

"I could save your reputation by asking you to take me someplace private," she said. "Then you wouldn't have to be seen with me in public."

"Damn, woman. You're killing me."

"Smart girls," Kellen said. "They pay attention to what you actually say and use it against you."

She hadn't meant to use anything Owen said against him. She just enjoyed their easy banter. "I'll go," she said decisively. Kellen's wink made her realize that she'd just been outsmarted by a rock star. Damn it!

"Awesome," Owen said. "I was trying to think up an excuse to get her to have sex with me on the tour bus. This played out perfectly." He glanced at Caitlyn when she gasped. "Did I just say that aloud?"

She laughed. "Unless I'm imagining things."

"I think she's onto me," he said to Kellen.

Kellen scratched his nose. "Since you tend to show all your cards, I'm not surprised."

"I don't show all my cards. I still have an ace or two up my sleeve. Did you know dancing with a woman is a great method of seduction? If you move to their liking, they subconsciously think you'll be compatible in bed."

"You made that up," Kellen said.

"Did I?" Owen took Caitlyn's hand in his and caught her gaze. As she stared into his eyes, her heart thudded faster and faster. Her palm became increasingly damp. "Caitlyn, may I have this dance?"

Her first instinct was to accept, but then the rattling of dishes in the diner's kitchen reminded her where she was.

"I'm not going to dance with you here," Caitlyn said in a loud whisper.

"Why not? We have music. I'll even download your favorite song if you'd like."

"This isn't the kind of place where you dance."

Owen looked at Kellen. "Name three places where I would never dance."

"Never?"

"Never."

Kellen shrugged. "Can't think of one."

"This is why he's my best friend. He always agrees with me."

"I didn't say it was normal."

Owen blocked his screen from view as he downloaded something to his phone. The waitress set two bottles of water and a glass of ice tea on the table. She smiled first at Owen and then at Kellen before blushing and rushing back toward the kitchen.

"Do you think she knows who we are?" Kellen asked.

"Did she rip off her shirt and ask you to sign her tits? No, she doesn't know. She just thinks you're hot."

Caitlyn reached for her tea, but before she could take a sip, Owen took her by the hand and pulled her from the booth.

"What are you doing?"

"Dancing."

From his phone, "The Chicken Dance Song" began to play. When Owen began to flap his arms and scratch and peck, Caitlyn gaped at him.

"Dance with me, Caitlyn."

She laughed—half mortified, half amused. "Oh my God, you are so embarrassing!"

"Dance, Caitlyn, or I'm following this with 'Play That Funky Music White Boy.' "

"You don't want him to go there, Caitlyn," Kellen said, opening his water and sipping it nonchalantly.

Every person in the restaurant was gawking, pointing, or laughing. And if Owen hadn't been so fucking cute, they probably would have called the cops on him for disorderly conduct.

"Dance, Caitlyn."

"I don't know how," she lied. She'd danced to this song as a child. Back when she'd known how to have fun.

He whirled her around and stepped up behind her, one hand on her belly and his groin pressed against her ass. She wasn't sure how he made The Chicken Dance sexy, but by God, she was completely turned on the instant he began to move with her. Especially when he made her shake her hips and rub up against him just right.

Her face was flushed with something other than embarrassment as she let loose and started to move.

"I thought you didn't know this dance," Owen said in her ear.

"I'm a fast learner."

Two young women in a booth several tables away climbed to their feet and joined in. It appeared that they'd had a few too many as they stumbled around more than they danced. When one of the girls spotted Kellen in the booth, looking amused rather than annoyed, she grabbed his wrist and tried to pull him to his feet.

"Come and dance with us," the tipsy girl said. "Come on. It's fun!"

"No, thanks." There was no room for argument in his tone, so with a scowl she released his wrist and settled for rubbing up against Owen from behind.

Owen laughed as he attempted to avoid hands not belonging to Caitlyn. "Three on one, no fair. Save me, Kellen."

"There isn't enough tequila in Mexico to make me dance The Chicken Dance in a diner at one o'clock in the morning."

Caitlyn turned to face Owen and wrapped both arms around his neck. She lifted an eyebrow at one of the eager young women behind him and the woman stepped back, tripping over her own feet. Her friend kept her from falling to the floor.

"Want to go party with us?" one of the girls asked Owen. "We love to party."

"Caitlyn's all the party I can handle right now," he said and kissed Caitlyn, as if to make his intentions clear.

She drew him closer, kissing him deeper, still sort of wiggling to the song. He squeezed her to stop her motion and tugged his mouth free. "Now that I have you loosened up," he said, "how about a slow song?"

"How about you hurry up and eat your sandwich so we can go to your room and be alone?"

Owen glanced at Kellen and lifted his eyebrow to accompany the I-told-you-so lift of his head. "Now do you believe that dancing is a great method of seduction?"

"I have less obnoxious methods," Kellen said.

"Yeah, sitting there looking cranky actually works well for you," Owen said.

Kellen gave him the finger.

"There's a bar that's open for another couple hours just down the street," one of the young women said, "if you want to have some fun. Come on, you don't want to hang around with *her* all night, do you?"

Caitlyn hoped it was the alcohol making the girl so impolite.

The girl tugged on Owen's arm, and he pulled his gaze from Caitlyn's to look at her. "I'm not interested. But my friend might be." He nodded toward Kellen and grinned at the look of horror on Kellen's face when both girls squeezed into the booth with him.

"If you don't stop torturing him, he's going to wind up hating you," Caitlyn said.

"Not possible."

But based on the look on Kellen's face as he tried to put some space between himself and the tipsy women now crowding into his booth, Caitlyn wasn't so sure.

"Are you ready for that slow song?" Owen whispered. "I need a good excuse to hold you close in public until my sandwich arrives."

"You really do show your cards," Caitlyn said.

"Did you think Kellen was joking?"

"I didn't think Kellen was joking, I've just never met anyone who throws it all out there in the open."

"Do you like it? I hope so, because I'm not sure if I can keep a lid on it now that I've let loose."

Caitlyn leaned back so she could look him in the eye. He scared the hell out of her, to be honest. She had no idea what to expect out of him next, and he had no problem alerting her to the fact that it would be something she was *not* expecting, but yeah, she did like it. "I like it when you're being yourself. Don't put a lid on it. Just be you. That's what I like."

His brilliant smile did things to her heart, and she definitely wanted to be pressed against him, swaying to a slow song in the middle of diner at one o'clock in the morning.

"Can I pick the song this time?" she said. "I wouldn't want to end up doing the chicken dance again or worse, dancing disco to some song better left in the past."

"Promise you'll pick something slow and sexy."

"I promise." Caitlyn found the song she wanted on his phone while Owen tried to talk the young ladies into leaving Kellen alone since Kellen was having no luck convincing them that he didn't want to get drunk with them. Even though they kept yelling, "Party!" intermittently, Kellen was obviously not the least bit interested in joining their brand of fun. The young ladies had no business drinking any more than they already had, anyway.

When Caitlyn found the song she had in mind, she had to hand the phone to Owen so he could enter his password and purchase it.

"Don't peek," she said. "I want it to be a surprise."

"I won't peek," he said.

"Strange as it sounds, Owen loves surprises," Kellen said.

"I do."

"He can't keep a secret though."

Caitlyn chuckled. "Why does that not surprise me?"

When the song began, Owen tugged Caitlyn against his chest and stole her breath by singing along in a low sultry voice. She wasn't sure how he knew "Unchained Melody," but he sang it as if he were a long lost Righteous brother. He had a pitch-perfect tone. He *should* be a lead singer. She'd pay to hear him sing.

Her body was entirely in tune with his. Her skin tingled in want of his touch. Her ears strained for more of the sensual words pouring from his lips. She'd never felt a song before, but she felt every word of this one. They swayed slowly as he led her into a leisurely turn around the floor between their booth and a small table. Caitlyn clung to him and let him lead. Allowed herself to enjoy their dance and not worry about what everyone else was thinking or whispering. She didn't much care at the moment. Owen gave her an odd measure of courage. Even though he was several years younger than she was, he was teaching her something she hadn't realized she'd been missing—how to have fun and not worry about what people thought. She tugged him closer and nuzzled her face into his neck.

"Most women don't make it past The Chicken Dance," he said as the music played without accompanying vocals.

"So you dance in diners on a regular basis, I take it," she said. She wished she could say that she had something special with him. And not the things she'd done to him back at the sex club. She hoped he didn't hold that against her. She'd been really hating on men when he'd approached her. And she should have never taken out her frustration on his ass. Even if he had seemed to like it.

"Not regularly," he said. "I've danced in a few. But it's been years."

Caitlyn caught sight of the waitress, standing with a large tray beside the table. She was watching them with a smile of longing on her face, waiting for their song to finish. Maybe all women wanted a man like Owen, a man who didn't care if the world thought he was a little crazy for making his own dance floor, just so long as he got to hold his woman close.

When the song came to an end, several people clapped. Owen released her. "There's only one thing I want right now more than you," he whispered to Caitlyn.

"Pastrami on rye."

He chuckled. "You're getting to know me already." He lifted her hand to his lips and kissed her knuckles. Of all the intimate things he'd done to her that night, that chaste gesture was the only one to make her belly quiver.

Owen helped her find her seat again. Across from them, both drunks smiled a greeting, but he ignored them, still giving Caitlyn his full attention. "You're still planning on rewarding me for good behavior, aren't you?" he asked. His hand found her leg beneath the table and slid from the inside of her knee to her upper thigh.

"We did agree on no public displays of affection." She caught his hand before it found its target.

"Dancing doesn't count."

"What about kissing?" she challenged.

"No?" It wasn't a statement. More a hopeful question.

As if she could tell this man no when he was looking at her like that. But she refused to let him off easily; teasing him was too much fun.

"I have to be honest: that public display felt rather affectionate."

"Can you please go back to your own table now?" Kellen said to the pair of young women who were still harassing him about going to a bar that would close in less than an hour.

The waitress looked apologetic as she set their food before them. "Should I get the manager to remove them from the premises?" she said quietly, as if the young women wouldn't be able to hear her.

"That won't be necessary," Owen said. "I'll take care of it."

The waitress nodded and took her leave again.

"So how are you ladies getting home tonight?" Owen asked them, selecting a potato chip from his plate and munching it.

"Lisa's car is parked across the street."

Owen nodded. "I see. How would you like to go for a ride in a limo?"

"What?" the one who wasn't Lisa said.

"We have a limo parked outside. Want to go for a ride?"

Caitlyn was too busy trying to figure out what Owen was thinking to touch her cheesecake.

"Owen, I don't think…" Kellen gave the girls pointed looks.

Owen ignored him. "You don't believe we have a limo, do you?"

"I'd have to see it to believe it."

"All right, I'll show you." Owen slid out of the booth and helped the two wobbly ladies to their feet. He leaned across the table and whispered, "I'll be right back," to Caitlyn.

Befuddled, she watched him escort the two women out of the diner.

She exchanged a confused look with Kellen. And then Kellen's scowl softened. "Wish I'd have thought of that," he said.

"Thought of what?"

"Hey, hey, hands off the merchandise," Owen shouted just before the diner door shut behind them.

"Is he leaving with them?"

"When he has you?"

"Then what?"

Before he could answer, Owen was headed back in their direction.

"What was that all about?" Caitlyn asked.

"Neither one of them had any business driving," Owen said, "so I had the driver take them home. They were too excited about riding in a limo to be upset that they weren't getting into Kelly's pants tonight."

"And how are we supposed to get back to the hotel?" Kellen asked.

"The driver will be back before I finish my sandwich. Their place is only a couple of miles from here. They told me so when they were trying to get me to go with them."

Caitlyn squeezed his knee under the table. "That was a really nice thing you did."

"What? Rescuing Kellen from two drunk girls?"

"Making sure they got home safely."

"Everyone is happy," he said, and took a huge bite of his sandwich. "Especially me," he added, talking with his mouth full. "Good stuff."

Kellen grinned as he used the edge of his fork to cut into his cheesecake and took a bite.

"Better than pie?" Owen asked.

Kellen shook his head. "Too sweet."

Owen devoured his sandwich while Kellen decided he'd rather steal the chips off Owen's plate than finish his cheesecake. It was indeed decadent—moist and creamy with cherries in thick, sweet syrup. After only three bites, Caitlyn was full, but there was no way she was going to let something that delicious go to waste.

"How far is it from Houston to Beaumont?" Kellen asked.

"That's a weird question," Owen said.

"Less than two hours," Caitlyn said, "depending on traffic."

"Why do you care?" Owen asked.

"I was thinking of spending tomorrow night in Galveston and

meeting up with the rest of you in Beaumont later."

"If you take the ferry from Galveston Island to Bolivar Peninsula, you can miss the Houston traffic," Caitlyn said.

"Thanks for the tip."

Owen shifted uneasily. "Don't go. It never makes you feel better."

Kellen shrugged. "I don't go there looking to feel better. I just like the ocean."

Caitlyn was missing something, but she didn't want to pry. Kellen's trip to Galveston probably had something to do with the lover Kellen had lost. Everything that caused tension between the two men seemed to have something to do with her.

Both men stared at the table in silence for several long, uncomfortable minutes. Caitlyn tried to think of something that would lighten the mood again.

"So you're in Owen's band too, right?" she finally asked.

"Owen's band?" Kellen lifted an eyebrow at his friend. "Did he tell you it was *his* band?"

"Where would the band be without me?" Owen said.

"Bassists are a dime a dozen."

Ouch! Caitlyn glanced at Owen, expecting him to look hurt or offended. He was grinning.

"You're over-paying, Kelly. I can easily get you a dozen bassists for a nickel."

"Bargain basement bassist."

"What instrument do you play?" Caitlyn asked Kellen. And because she'd learned her lesson with Owen, she added, "Or are you the singer?"

"I play guitar," Kellen said, still not out of his funk.

"You're so matter-of-fact about it."

"Why wouldn't I be?" Kellen said. "It's a fact."

"It seems so foreign to someone like me, that you can make a living playing music."

"Do you work?" Kellen asked.

"Yeah," she said. "Too much. But I'm doing what I love, so I don't mind the long hours."

"She has her own company," Owen said. "She's the boss."

He sounded proud of her.

She snorted on a laugh. "Yep, I'm the boss."

"What kind of company?" Kellen asked, sipping from his water as he waited for Owen to finish his sandwich.

"Alternative fuel sources. We started with solar panels and wind turbines, but recently started branching out into fuel cells. R and D is finally over, next is production and marketing. My two business partners are in charge of that stuff. I'm the main geek of the triad. So things have slowed down a bit for me while I wait for the next big idea to smack me upside the head. You can have a very fulfilling career discovering new technologies, but it sure won't make you rich. It's a good thing I have Peter and Lillian to find my markets."

Owen paused with his nearly finished sandwich halfway to his mouth. "So you're not only brilliant, good in bed, and hot, you're also rich?"

She flushed. "I'm sure I'm not as rich as you are."

"Your husband must be a complete tool," Owen said.

"You're married?" Kellen asked, looking scandalized for the first time that night.

"Divorced."

"Her husband—"

"Ex-husband," Caitlyn interrupted.

"Her *ex*-husband cheated on her."

"Maybe he was lonely," Kellen said.

"Kelly," Owen admonished.

"I'm sure he was," Caitlyn said. "I've been working eighty-hour weeks for several years now. Sometimes we didn't see each other for days."

"He could have made an effort," Owen said.

She leaned against him and squeezed his arm. "Then I wouldn't have had a reason to hook up with you."

"Thank God he's a thoughtless idiot."

She smiled and couldn't resist stealing a kiss. His lips tasted salty. They went well with the sweetness still on her tongue. When he licked her upper lip slowly, she moaned and curled her fingers into his shirt to tug him closer.

Kellen cleared his throat uncomfortably. She could have sworn he grunted, "P-D-A."

Caitlyn drew away regretfully. "We need to get to the hotel," she said.

Owen tossed the rest of his sandwich on his plate and signaled the waitress for their check.

The car was waiting for them when they left the diner. Kellen made Owen check the back seat for stowaways before he agreed to get in. Caitlyn did nothing to hide her laughter.

"Geez, Kelly, those girls weren't that bad."

Caitlyn and Kellen exchanged a look of agreement. Those girls had been pretty bad. Caitlyn wondered if Owen and Kellen had to deal with women like that on a regular basis. She supposed some guys would like that kind of girl; she suspected Owen might be one of them. If she hadn't been with him, she wondered if he would have gone off to join their party.

This time when they sat in the back of the limo, Kellen made sure to sit between them. "I'm in no mood to watch you two make out," he explained. "You can attack each other back at the hotel."

"Whose fault is it that you're in such a mood?" Owen said. "It's not our fault you didn't get laid. Again."

"I'm sure you could have picked up someone at the club," Caitlyn said.

Kellen ran a finger under his wrist cuff. "I went in there knowing I wasn't going to participate."

"So why do you go to sex clubs if you aren't planning to have sex?" Caitlyn asked. Seemed like a strange place to hang out just for the hell of it.

Kellen stared at her for a solid minute before answering. He had the most hypnotizing eyes she'd ever encountered.

"Because Owen needed someone to accompany him."

"Whatever, dude," Owen said. "You don't have to torture yourself for my benefit."

"Next time you can go alone."

Owen shifted in his seat. "Yeah, fine, whatever. You're a drag anyway." When Kellen didn't respond to his insult, Owen said, "Gabe will go with me."

"Gabe has a relationship thing he's trying right now. He won't go with you."

"Then Shade…" Owen scowled. "Why did he have to hook up with Amanda anyway?"

"You really wouldn't go by yourself?" Caitlyn asked.

"I could," Owen said. "But then I wouldn't be able to prove that I scored the hottest woman in the place."

She chuckled. "You have a competitive streak unlike any I've ever encountered. Why do you care who knows who hooks up with you?"

Owen's smile faded, and he stared at his knees. After a moment, he shrugged. "No reason."

There had to be a reason. Maybe he didn't want Kellen to know. Or more likely, maybe he didn't want *her* to know.

"You might as well tell her," Kellen said. "Why you are the way you are."

"What way am I, Kelly? You're twice as fucked up as I am."

"I'm not going to argue that point."

"You can tell me," Caitlyn said. "If you want to."

Owen glanced at her. "I had hoped that we could hook up again at the hotel."

"Yeah, me too," she said, still not accustomed to his bluntness.

"He's afraid you'll tell him to take a hike, because he still doesn't get that he's not the same man he used to be on the outside, though he's always been a bit strange on the inside."

"Don't tell her, Kelly."

"You're the one who brought her out of the club. That means you're interested in her, right?"

"Maybe, but don't tell her."

"Why? Are you afraid she's as shallow as you are?"

Owen shoved him. "I'm not shallow."

"You sure pretend to be," Kellen said. He caught Owen's wrist just before it connected with his shoulder. "He used to be fat," Kellen said to Caitlyn.

"I told you not to tell her."

"In high school they called him Piggie."

Owen flushed such a bright scarlet, the color was noticeable even in the dim interior of the limo. "You fucking asshole, why'd you tell her?"

Kellen didn't try to block Owen's next blow. Maybe because he felt he deserved it.

"That's cruel," Caitlyn said. She grabbed Owen's hand before he used it to punch Kellen again. Kellen pushed back against the seat, looking decidedly uncomfortable to be wedged between them. "Is that why you keep telling me I'm beautiful? Because no one ever made you feel that way?"

Owen scowled. "How the fuck should I know? I just like to make people happy."

"What about making yourself happy, Owen?" Caitlyn asked. He'd had her fooled into thinking all was right in his world, but now she wasn't so sure. "Are you happy?"

"Yeah, I have glitter shooting out of my ass, I'm so fucking happy," he yelled.

"I'm sorry," Kellen said, "You're right. I shouldn't have told her."

"Thank God you did so I can dump him before I start to like him too much," Caitlyn said. "I would never be interested in a guy who was called Piggie in high school due to a weight problem." She was joking, but Owen didn't laugh. He seemed to expect her rejection.

"Should we take you back to your friend's house then?" Owen asked quietly.

Kellen huffed out a breath and shook his head. "Still clueless. She's kidding, fucktard."

"Shut up," Owen said, but some of the tension had eased from his body, and he glanced at her from under his lashes.

This really was his issue. Kellen understood his friend well. So why had he felt the need to share something so personal about Owen? She was missing something here. Something major. Either Kellen was trying to scare her away—which didn't seem likely—or entice her into staying so he didn't have to accompany Owen to sex clubs any more. Of course it was possible he had no motivation at all and was just striking up conversation, but she took Kellen for the kind of person who calculated his every move. Why had Kellen risked Owen's obvious animosity by sharing something that personal about Owen's past?

At least she understood why Owen was so adamant about making her feel beautiful and why he was so nice to everyone even though he was easily the best-looking man she'd met in person. Though he had to own a mirror, he didn't see himself as mind-bogglingly gorgeous. Did he go to sex clubs because he thought he required a sure bet? She was just speculating, of course, because she didn't live in his skin. She didn't know what the world looked like through his eyes. But she wanted to. She wanted him to feel as good about himself as he made her feel about herself. And lord she was thankful that he was as attractive on the inside as he was on the outside. His personality sparkled even more than the twinkle in his pretty blue eyes.

"I don't want to go back to Jenna's house," Caitlyn said. "I do wish I'd met you somewhere other than a sex club. I guess I should be glad I met someone like you at all."

"Someone like me? What's that supposed to mean?"

"Guys like you don't usually talk to girls like me. Girls like me don't get invited to prom. Guys don't make fools of themselves for girls like me. Girls like me are ignored. Invisible. But I'm not a girl anymore. I'm a woman. Thanks for reminding me."

"You are definitely a woman. I like women so much more than I like girls."

"Uhhh…" Caitlyn wasn't sure what he meant by that.

"He prefers older women," Kellen said. "When he first saw you in the club, I thought he was going to eject himself out of his pants and directly onto your lap."

Caitlyn laughed. "Well, that definitely would have gotten my attention, but I doubt my reaction would have been positive." She wished Kellen wasn't sitting between them, because she suddenly wanted to draw Owen into her arms. "So I take it you were hurt by a younger woman."

"Young women, but they were the same age as I was."

Kellen released a deep sigh. "Most of it happened in high school and the year following graduation. This really hot girl broke his heart. He asked her out and she agreed. When she stood him up, her excuse was that she liked him as a friend."

"They all liked me as a friend."

"What's wrong with that?" Caitlyn asked.

"I didn't want her to like me as a friend. I wanted her to like me as a man. And so after high school, I lost a lot of weight. Got in good shape."

"I'll say," Caitlyn said appreciatively.

"And then he became a man whore," Kellen said with a laugh.

"I'm not a man whore. I don't get paid. Even though Caitlyn seems to think I'd be good at it," he said under his breath.

"You know I was kidding, right?" she said. "I value you as a person, not just for the hot body under those clothes."

"It's okay, Caitlyn. He likes to be treated like a piece of meat," Kellen said. "That's why I'm so surprised he invited you out after getting what he wanted. It's not his usual pattern. He won't let anyone get close because he's so afraid of getting hurt."

"I figured everyone else is breaking the band's no-relationships-while-we're-on-tour rule, so I might as well give it a shot. And I'm not afraid of getting hurt."

"You are," Kellen insisted.

Caitlyn's head was swimming. "Relationship?"

"Are you against that?" Owen asked.

"I don't think I'm ready for a relationship. The ink is barely dry on my divorce papers."

Owen laughed. "Good, because as soon as I said it, I got cold feet."

"So what ever happened to that girl in high school?" Caitlyn said.

Kellen rolled his eyes. "You wouldn't believe it if he told you."

"Try me."

"I went out with several of her friends," Owen said, "slept with them all and made sure I got the job done properly. And then when the girl who broke my heart asked me out, I turned her down. I said I only liked her as a friend."

"Sweet revenge?" she asked.

He shook his head. "I regret it now. It was an asshole move. The stupid things kids do."

"Twenty-year-old kids," Kellen said.

"Yeah, well, I'm immature. Get over it."

"So now you prowl sex clubs," Caitlyn said. "What are you looking for, Owen?"

"Nothing but a good time."

"He's still afraid to open up, so he seeks connections that aren't real," Kellen said. "He was hurt too many times when he was young. Becca was the first who ripped his heart out, but she wasn't the last."

"Yeah, see, I learned my lesson. It's better this way, isn't it? Avoid heartache, but still get your rocks off?"

Kellen touched his wristband and shook his head. "No."

Owen watched him for a moment and then turned his attention to Caitlyn. "So does it bother you? Knowing I used to be someone you wouldn't have even considered sleeping with?"

"How do you know that? Not everyone is superficial. Though I must admit that I was first attracted to you because you're so easy on the eyes and I thought having you would make my ex-husband seethe with envy."

"Shit," Owen said. "You want him back, don't you?"

"What? Of course not. Why would you think that?"

"Why else would you want to make him jealous?"

Caitlyn absorbed his words. Why *did* she want to make Charles jealous? It wasn't because she wanted him back. Maybe she wanted the life they'd once had, but after his betrayal of her trust, even if they'd made amends, their relationship would have never been the same.

"At first I thought I did, but I don't love him anymore. Not the way I once did. And I wasn't trying to make him jealous. I wanted him to see that the guy I was banging was better looking than his nineteen-year-old co-ed. Save face, you know?"

Owen laughed. "Well I don't mind being your trophy lover, baby."

Kellen groaned and sighed, sounding exasperated. "Bullshit, Owen. Will you just stop? Stop acting like this is all a game. Stop pretending you ooze self-confidence. Just stop. She knows, okay? You can drop the pretense and just be yourself, not the guy you present to women, to strangers, to get laid. Be the guy who still sees a miserable fat kid when he looks in the mirror." Kellen whacked him on the side of the head for good measure. "Be yourself. The person I'm lucky enough to know. She deserves to get to know him too."

Owen crossed his arms over his chest and glanced at the window. "I have no idea what you're talking about."

"Of course not." The car pulled to a stop. Both men silently fumed while they waited for the driver to open the door.

"She's not the kind of woman who would hurt you for being who you really are," Kellen said. "She might even love you for it. I'm sick of you always shortchanging yourself and thinking it's for the best. If I have to look at you for another minute, I'm going to strangle the life out of you."

Apparently too annoyed to wait for the driver, Kellen flung the door open and climbed out of the car. Caitlyn and Owen sat there in uncomfortable silence, avoiding each other's gazes.

Had Kellen really just said she might love Owen? And how could Caitlyn possibly hurt a guy she'd only known for a few hours? She glanced at Owen and caught the flash of panic in his eyes. Way to turn an evening of fun into something awkward and frightening, Mr. Kellen Whatever-Your-Last-Name-Is Guitarist Guy.

"I think he's a little freaked out because I brought you home," Owen said.

"Oh, is that all?"

Owen shook his head. "Don't worry about what he said. I just want to enjoy your company for the evening. I'm not going to let you hurt my feelings. I'm not as sensitive as I used to be."

She wasn't buying his denial for a minute, but she had no intention of hurting his feelings. So what if he was sensitive? She liked that about him. She scooted up against him and slid a hand over his hard-muscled thigh. He flexed beneath her palm. At least she understood why he did that now. He was still self-conscious about his body.

"Are we allowed to make out in the back of the limo now that Kellen is gone?" she asked.

"I'd say yes," he said with a grin.

His lips had barely brushed hers when her cellphone began to bleat in her purse.

"Who's calling you at two in the morning?" he murmured against her lips.

Caitlyn didn't know who'd call her this late, but it had better be an emergency. She finally had Owen alone again, and she wanted to exploit every second they had together. She fished her phone out of her handbag and saw Jenna's name on the caller ID.

"Hey, Jenna," Caitlyn said as she answered the phone. "What's up?"

"Where are you? You were supposed to call me to pick you up and the club is closed now. I've been worried sick."

"I'm fine. I decided to leave with someone."

Owen lifted her hand and kissed her fingertips one at a time. Her belly began to quiver on cue.

"You met someone?" Jenna asked. "Is he nice?"

"Naughty and nice."

Owen apparently liked that description. He was grinning ear to ear.

"So I won't be home tonight," she told Jenna.

Owen made a victory fist and Caitlyn smiled at him. She liked the feeling she got when she made him happy.

"Tell me all about him," Jenna insisted.

"I will when I see you tomorrow," Caitlyn said. "We were about to get busy when you so rudely interrupted."

Jenna laughed. "About time you had some fun."

"How irresponsible of me. But don't worry, okay? I'm perfectly fine."

"Okay."

"She's safe with me," Owen said near the phone. "Well, relatively speaking."

"Oh," Jenna said, "he sounds cute."

"On a scale of one to ten, he's an eleven." She winked at Owen. "We'll talk later."

"Okay, have a good time. Just be careful."

"Did you forget that you're talking to Ms. Responsibility?" Caitlyn said.

Jenna laughed. "Yeah, for a second I did forget."

Caitlyn ended the call and tucked her phone back into her purse.

"Who was that?" Owen asked. "Or is that not any of my business?"

"That was my friend Jenna. I was supposed to call her for a ride. She was worried."

"I thought maybe it was your ex-husband. He heard you were getting it on with an eleven in the back of a limo and decided he wanted you back."

"Screw him," Caitlyn said and wrapped her arms around Owen's neck.

"No, screw me."

"An even better idea."

CHAPTER SEVEN

Owen held Caitlyn's hand as they rode the elevator to the top floor. Kelly hadn't stuck around after he'd left the limo. Owen didn't like that they'd ended the evening with harsh words, but he never liked to be in disagreement with Kelly because if Kelly had a beef with something, there was usually a good reason.

Still, Owen wasn't sure why Kelly was so interested in his love life all of a sudden. It had never bothered him that Owen kept all interactions with women on a cursory level. He wasn't sure what was going on in Kelly's head, but it was a relief that Caitlyn knew the thing Owen hated most about himself and it hadn't turned her away.

Caitlyn covered her mouth and stifled a yawn. Owen wondered if they'd put some sort of sleeping powder in the cheesecake. Or maybe she wasn't used to being up so late.

"Are you tired?" he asked.

She nodded.

"Don't think I'm going to let you sleep when we get to my room."

"I'm sure you'll find a way to keep me awake," she said with a smile.

He loved her smile. It made her inquisitive brown eyes crinkle at the corners.

"That sounds like a challenge."

When the elevator stopped, Owen placed a hand on Caitlyn's lower back and directed her toward his room. He remembered a time when all five members of the band had to share one seedy hotel room. It had been years ago, but they'd been closer then somehow. Of course it was hard not to be close when five guys shared one bathroom, one bottle of whiskey, and a few groupies between them.

Owen opened the door and Caitlyn entered his hotel room

without hesitation. She was already comfortable in his presence, trusted him. He wondered how far he could take her tonight. Wondered if she'd stick around after the concert the next night and get to know him even better.

Standing behind her, Owen wrapped his arms around her and unbuttoned the three leather-covered buttons of her tweed jacket. He pulled the garment free and tossed it onto the sofa in the seating area just inside the door.

"Do you always wear suit jackets in the summer?" he asked before planting a gentle kiss on the side of her neck.

"I'm usually indoors, so yeah. Otherwise, I freeze in the AC."

He didn't plan on letting her freeze tonight.

She dropped her head to the side, allowing him to explore the silky flesh of her throat with his lips.

"Owen?" His name was like a soft caress on her lips.

"Yes?"

"I feel like I've known you for a long time. Has it really only been a few hours?"

"I know what you mean." He worked at the knot of fabric at her throat, wanting to sample more of her flesh. "Tell me about your business."

She hesitated and then lifted her hands to help him untie the bow at her neck. "Now? But what I do isn't sexy. I want to feel sexy when I'm with you."

He kissed her ear and lowered his hands to cup her breasts. He squeezed gently. "I always think you're sexy," he promised. "Especially when you're telling me about yourself."

"Like I said, we work on alternative forms of energy. I know it's hard to believe, but I'm sort of a geek." She giggled.

"Are you sharing something you thought I didn't already know?"

She slapped his thigh. "You think I'm a geek?"

"I know you're a geek. I *think* it's sexy."

She shook her head. "You're a weird guy, Owen Mitchell."

"Are you complaining that I think you're sexy?" He reached for the top button of her blouse and unfastened it.

"No. I'm not sure I believe you. What can possibly be sexy about a woman who is more interested in the flow of electrons than she is in her hair?"

"I love your hair." Thick, black, and lustrously wavy.

"That's because I actually combed it today."

"And I had a great time messing it up."

He unfastened another button on her blouse and then another. She seemed content to fall silent as he slowly unbuttoned her shirt and tugged it free of her jeans. He tossed it aside on the sofa as well. His hands moved to cup both breasts, and he kissed the side of her neck until some of the tension left her body. He rubbed his thickening cock against her sweet ass in case she didn't trust his words. He'd been with a lot of women, but this one pushed every one of his buttons, and he was ready to launch into orbit.

"Cute bra," he said, watching over her shoulder as his finger traced the lace that bordered a plaid pattern.

"It doesn't match my panties," she said. "I figured I should warn you."

"Warn me?"

"That it doesn't match."

He chuckled. "Why would I care if your bra matches your panties?"

"That's not sexy either. I didn't think about dressing appropriately for outside the club. I didn't bring a little black dress on the trip, or anything to wear but my business attire, because I don't own anything but what I wear to work. I simply don't remember how to be sexy for a man." She looked at him over her shoulder, her eyebrows furled in a most adorable way. "Or maybe I never knew how." She ducked her head, and he understood how she was feeling. He never felt confident in his sex appeal either. He was good at pretending, because women responded to a man with self-confidence, even if it was the biggest load of bullshit anyone ever laid on them.

"Caitlyn."

When she kept her eyes downcast, he circled her body to stand before her. After a moment, he tucked a finger under her chin to force her to look him in the eye. She flushed when their eyes met, but held his gaze.

"What's truly sexy about a woman isn't what she wears. It isn't how much time and attention she spends on her hair. It's not that her bra matches her panties. It's the way she thinks, moves, speaks. That's what's sexy about a woman."

He could tell by the look on her face that she wasn't buying his lines.

"And why did you pick me at the club?" she asked. "It wasn't because you knew I could think, you had seen how I move, and I hadn't spoken yet."

"Damn, woman, I'm not used to talking to women as smart as you are. You're supposed to be happy that I want you for more than your fantastic body."

"But I don't think you're being sincere."

"Why?"

She shook her head. "I don't know."

"What do I have to do to prove that I'm sincere? As soon as you stepped out of the dressing room at the club wearing that horrible jacket—"

"See, my jacket is horrible."

"Let me finish. When I saw you wearing it, I was instantly hard again. I insist that you wear that horrible jacket as much as possible."

She glanced at the discarded garment on the sofa. "Should I put it back on?"

He chuckled. "No. I like when you wear it in public, not when you're alone with me. What's so hot about it is that it completely conceals what's beneath. Yet I know what's there. Those guys looking for a woman in a short skirt and tight sweater, they're not giving you a second glance because they're too blind to see how smoking hot you are. I mean look at yourself, Caitlyn. You're a ten." His gaze traveled down her body, and he made a sound of desperation. "An eleven."

"Takes one to know one." She chuckled. "Though I think you're overstating your interest."

He shook his head at her. Words didn't seem to work with the woman—she'd apparently been lied to one too many times—so maybe actions would do the trick. She squeaked in surprise when he grabbed her around the waist and lifted her up over his shoulder. He took several long strides toward the bed and tossed her on the mattress.

"Show me that you want me," she said, her eyes riveted to his crotch.

"If I let it loose, I'm going to have to fuck you with it." He ran his hand over the hard ridge in his pants and sucked a pained breath through his teeth. "And I haven't tasted you yet."

He reached for the button of her jeans and unfastened it. He couldn't wait to see her naked again. To smell her. Taste her. Touch her. He unzipped her pants and then tugged them down her legs. Her sensible loafers caught in her pant legs and joined her pants on the floor.

He stopped to check her out. When she'd said her panties didn't match her bra, she hadn't been joking. Her bra was black with plaid sections at the bottom of each cup. Her panties were a lurid fuchsia and decorated with a fluffy sheep. He smiled, but didn't laugh. He doubted a man had ever seen her wear that sheep, and maybe she didn't believe the privilege of being with her turned him on, but his twitching cock demanded to be pressed against those sweet panties.

"Owen?"

He unfastened his slacks and tugged his cock free. He ran his hand down its rigid length, pausing when his thumb pressed against his piercing. He rubbed the hard ball against the rim of his cock head, twitching as the pleasure registered.

"I want to come all over your sweet, little panties, Caitlyn," Owen said. "I want to make them dirty. I want to make you dirty."

"Yes, Owen," she whispered. "Make me dirty."

He leaned over her, supporting his body weight with one hand on the mattress beside her. He used his other hand to rub himself against those ridiculous panties that had him all worked up.

"Your clothes need to go," she said. "I want to look at you."

When he didn't comply with her wishes immediately, she reached up and unbuttoned his shirt, shoving the fabric from his shoulders and caressing his chest with both palms.

"Every inch of you is perfect," she whispered, and then she looked down to where he was introducing his cock to her sheep— well, the one on her underwear. Her fingertip brushed his cock head, and ripples of pleasure coursed down his length and settled at the base of his spine. "Especially this inch."

"*Inch?*" he said defensively.

"Oh baby, your entire cock is massive and gorgeous, but that last inch, with this little treasure?" She flicked one end of his barbell stud. "That's the best inch of all."

He chuckled. She'd become enamored of his modification quickly, and it didn't seem to bother her at all. Owen did enjoy turning a good girl bad.

"On second thought, I'd rather get those pretty, pink panties dirty with your cum instead of mine," he said.

"Huh?"

He dropped to his knees on the floor, grabbed her by the hips and pulled her pussy to his face. He used his lips, tongue, and teeth to work her lips and clit through her panties. The taste of cotton overpowered her sweetness, but he'd be damned if the smell of her excitement seeping through wasn't completely worth the unusual mix of flavors.

"Owen!" she gasped. Her fingers twined in his hair, and she pulled him against her. "Yes, yes," she crooned as she approached her peak.

Her panties were completely drenched within seconds. Some was the moisture from his mouth, but most was her juices. He used his tongue to press the fabric against her opening.

"Oh God, take them off me," she gasped, still clinging to his hair. "I can't stand it."

"Can't stand what?" he asked. He shifted to caress her clit with his lips, massaging the swollen bit of flesh through cotton.

"I'm going to come. Owen. I'm…" She sucked in a ragged breath when he began to gently scrape the edge of his teeth against one swollen lip. "Wait! I didn't. So close…"

He smiled and blew a hot breath through her panties.

"Whoa. That's… That's…"

He loved that she was incoherent. There was something about blowing a smart girl's mind that totally rocked his world.

"Do you want me to take these off now?" He ran a finger under the elastic at her inner thigh and dragged it through the slick heat that promised him heaven.

"Yes," she whispered. "I want your tongue against my bare skin."

His cock jumped in response to her words, but he played it cool. "I don't think they're wet enough yet."

"I don't think they could possibly get any wetter."

He planned to prove her wrong. He shifted closer, so that his cock was lodged firmly in her cleft, and moved his hands to her breasts. She reached behind her back and unfastened her bra, yanking the garment from her body and tossing it to the floor.

He couldn't take his eyes off her luscious breasts. He loved the contrast of his tanned hands against the soft white globes of flesh cupped in them. Liked the way her nipples pebbled into hard buds against his thumbs as he caressed the tips of her breasts in repetitive circles. He began to churn his hips in time with his thumbs, rubbing his engorged cock against her.

"Oh!" she gasped when he managed to work her clit just right.

Staring in her glazed eyes, he massaged her breasts, stroked her nipples, and rubbed his cock against her swollen heat until her mouth fell open and her body convulsed with pleasure.

"Are you coming, Caitlyn?" he murmured.

"Oh God, I need you inside me," she said, her hands gripping his forearms and pulling at him. "Put it inside."

"Are you coming?"

"I was, but... I fought it back."

"Why?"

She shook her head. "Inside me, Owen, please."

He rather liked the feel of her wet panties against his bare cock, but he shifted away and reached for his pants to don a condom. It would be nice to be in a monogamous relationship so he could experience sex raw on occasion.

Condom in place, he returned to his previous position between Caitlyn's thighs. Breathless, she reached between her legs and slid her panties to one side. She sat upright on the edge of the bed, took his cock in both hands and rubbed the head against her opening.

"Oh, yes," she said. "I want it."

"Take what you want," he said, claiming her mouth in a deep kiss.

She rubbed his cock head against her clit, using the ball in his piercing to stimulate herself. It felt amazing for him as well. Not quite as wonderful as being buried balls deep within her heat, but he liked her sense of urgency and his sense of calm as she rubbed him against her clit faster and faster.

"Yes, oh," she gasped and pressed him into her opening as she shuddered with release. Her pussy clenched rhythmically around his cock head and he grabbed her ass so he could force himself deeper. He fucked her shallow and fast until her orgasm subsided and then pulled out. Her body went limp, and she gazed at him through half-closed eyes. "That felt amazing."

He slipped her panties back in place and caressed her through them. "I'd say they're wet enough now."

She chuckled and lifted her butt off the mattress so he could remove the garment.

"Are you too tired to be on top?" he asked her.

"I'm too tired to move," she said in a slurred tone.

"Then I probably shouldn't have held back that time."

"This is why you need to focus your attention on someone young and active, who's addicted to energy drinks"

"I feel like taking it slow now anyway," he said. "You look sleepy." He was being kind; she looked exhausted.

He pulled back the covers and joined her on the bed. "I hope you don't mind if I have my way with you while you sleep," he said.

He rolled on top of her, and she feebly wrapped her arms around him. "I won't fall asleep," she promised.

He kissed her skin tenderly, starting with her throat and working his way down her limp body. She sighed in sweet surrender. He liked that her urgency was gone and he could take his time with her, spend some quiet moments learning her body. He also liked when she got excited and demanding, so he hoped the calm that had settled over her was due to lack of energy and not waning interest.

He kissed her belly until she giggled, licked her pussy until she moaned, and then allowed himself to possess her. His thrusts were so slow, at times he wasn't moving at all. He relished the feel of her beneath him and around him. Allowed himself to experience her with more than his skin. It was probably a good thing that she was half asleep so she didn't recognize the emotions threatening to overwhelm him. Yeah, hard, quick fucks were much better for keeping those tender feelings at bay. Maybe this languid lovemaking was a mistake, but for tonight, he'd give in to the craving for a personal connection.

When urgency began to build in his groin, he hastened his strokes, deepened them. She wrapped her arms and legs around him, holding him close as he moaned in her ear and tried not to suffocate on the heart trying to force its way up his throat. Did she have any idea how affected he was by her? Did she want to know? It was too soon, he decided. He buried his face in her neck, churning his hips, wanting to be deeper, deeper inside her, so deep that he couldn't find himself as a separate entity from her. He'd been denying his need for this for far too long. He wasn't sure why he'd finally let go of his false desire for autonomy while in the arms of a woman, but letting her close felt so good. She would undoubtedly freak out if she knew what he was thinking. He groaned as his release finally found him, surprised when she came with him. Her fingertips dug into his back—not harshly as he'd asked of her earlier, but as if she were afraid of going under and he was the only thing she trusted to keep her head above water.

When his breath had calmed and his cock had softened, he lifted his head. She smiled drowsily.

"That was beautiful," she whispered.

He kissed her gently. "You're beautiful."

Reluctantly, he pulled free of her body. She winced. He probably should have removed his jewelry—she'd be sore in the morning. Hell, she was already sore, he could tell. He disposed of the spent condom and brought her a moist washcloth so she could clean up a bit and sleep more comfortably.

"Thank you," she said, a beguiling blush staining her cheeks.

When she'd settled into her pillow, he switched off the light and climbed into bed beside her. He lay in the darkness wondering if she'd think him strange for wanting to snuggle up against her while he slept. It had been so long since he'd used a bed for *sleeping* with a woman that he felt uncertain. He knew what he wanted to do—he wanted to hold her close all night—but he wasn't sure if she'd appreciate that level of intimacy.

He tensed when she rolled over, rested her head on his chest, and wrapped an arm around his waist. Then he smiled, breathed in the scent of her hair, and allowed himself to hold her close as he drifted to sleep.

CHAPTER EIGHT

The knock at the hotel door pulled Caitlyn from a deep sleep. She blinked several times and rubbed her eyes, surprised by the brightness in the room. The door opened, a set of squeaky wheels approached, and the door shut again. She smelled soap—as if someone had recently showered—and a moment later, bacon.

"This will do nicely," Owen said.

Caitlyn's eyes flew open, and she grabbed for the sheet which she found tucked securely around her nude body.

"Thank you, sir," an unfamiliar voice said. "If you need anything else, be sure to let us know."

Caitlyn peered over a pillow to watch a server leave the room. Her eyes then landed on Owen, who was dipping his pinkie in pancake syrup and sampling it on his tongue.

"Sorry to wake you," he said, "but I was starving." He looked over at her and offered her a smile. "Good morning, beautiful."

"Good morning," she croaked and then cleared her throat. "Good morning," she said again. Wow, he looked good in the early morning light. His damp hair was scattered in disarray, and he'd had the decency to leave his shirt off after his shower, thank you, God.

So last night had really happened? Holy smokes, she'd bedded a hottie. More than once. She couldn't help but flush and stare at him in complete awe and flush some more.

"Are you hungry?" he asked. "There's enough here for two. Or five."

"Um, yeah, I guess so." She attempted to sit up, and her muscles protested every motion.

Owen grinned knowingly. "Stay there. I'll bring it to you."

"I've never had breakfast in bed," she said.

"Never?"

She shook her head and watched him wheel the cart around the bed.

"No romantic breakfasts on your anniversary?"

"My ex-husband wasn't the romantic type."

"That's too bad. Your mother didn't feed you in bed when you were sick?"

"My mother isn't really the nurturing kind. Did you get breakfast in bed when you were sick?"

"Yep. My mom is so nurturing it borders on smothering."

"What's her name?"

"Joan," he said. "But I call her Mom for short. She's an amazing woman."

Caitlyn smiled and tilted her head. "Are you a mama's boy, Owen Mitchell?"

His blue eyes met hers, and he grinned. "I can't deny it. She requires it. My brother's a mama's boy too and he's a bad-ass Marine, so don't think I'm the only one."

"You have a brother?"

"He's currently stationed in Afghanistan. His name is Chad." Owen glanced at the clock on the nightstand. "He should be calling soon, actually. It's a call I can't miss, so you'll have to excuse me when I take it."

"Of course," she said. She wanted to ask about his brother, but wasn't sure if talking about him would upset Owen. With Chad being stationed in a war zone, Owen must be constantly worried.

"So which part of my breakfast would you like?" he asked, nodding at the collection of plates and bowls on the cart.

"You ordered all of that for you?" There was more than enough for half a football team.

"Hey, I like to eat. That's why I had to spend so much time at the gym this morning."

He'd already been to the gym? Was the sun even up yet? She searched the bedside table for a clock.

"Wait?" she said. "What time is it?"

"Almost noon."

Heat flooded her face. He really had worn her out.

"I got enough food for both of us. I never planned on eating everything. Tasting everything, yes, so whatever you pick, you have to share a little."

"Let's just share it all," she suggested.

"Now, that's a plan." He pushed the cart up against the edge of the bed and sat on the mattress near her feet.

She scooted into a sitting position, wincing as the tenderness between her thighs registered. Holy mother of too much sex in one night. She wasn't sure if her body would ever be the same.

"It's the piercing," he said. "I knew I should have taken it out that last time."

"Worth it," she said breathlessly. "Totally worth it."

"After you finish your breakfast in bed, I'll kiss it and make it better."

She gaped at him. It was one thing for him to say things like that to her at night when she was delirious with lust, but here in the light of day? She wasn't sure if she could handle such naughty suggestions.

He chuckled. "You look scandalized, baby."

She closed her mouth and ducked her head. "I think I came to my senses while I was asleep."

"Well, we can't have that now, can we? Coming to your senses is one kind of coming I don't want you to experience while you're with me."

At a complete loss for words, she bit her lip to stifle a nervous giggle. After the intimacy they'd shared the night before, she was surprised she felt shy in his presence.

"You aren't the only who will be walking funny today," he said.

Her gaze darted to his ass. "Are you sore back there?"

He chuckled. "Nah. You took it real easy on me. I'm just trying to make you blush some more."

Owen selected a strawberry from a bowl of fresh fruit and crawled up her body until their noses were inches apart.

"Taste," he said, and he rubbed the strawberry over her lower lip. Her mouth watered, but she was pretty sure it was from being so close to him, not the anticipation of food.

Caitlyn bit into the fruit and got lost in his eyes. Such blue, blue eyes. The dark rims around the irises made them look even more striking. She chewed slowly, her pulse thrumming in her throat. She swallowed, still unable to pull her gaze from his.

"Taste," he said, and leaned forward to kiss her.

His mouth tasted minty. Caitlyn's practical sense abandoned her once again as he deepened the kiss and reminded her why she'd not only had sex with him, but spent the entire night pressed against his hard, warm body. He drew away slightly, and her eyelids fluttered open. Transfixed, she gazed into his eyes.

"Do you have a preference?" he asked.

"Huh?"

"In taste?"

"Oh." Her face grew warm again. "It seems I've lost my senses again."

"Good." He fed her another bite of strawberry.

"And since you asked," she said around the piece of fruit in her mouth, "I much prefer your taste."

He reached for the food cart again and flicked something just under her nose. "Even more than bacon?"

She laughed and bit into the piece of crisp bacon. "Is there anything that tastes better than bacon?" she said with her mouth full. Her self-consciousness waned a bit with each passing moment. He had an uncanny ability to drive her to distraction in one breath and soothe her in the next.

He took a bite of bacon and winked at her. "I'm sure there's something in this bed that's more appetizing, but bacon hits the spot at the moment."

He fed her samples of everything he'd ordered from the menu—which appeared to be every item they offered—and he tasted each as well.

"So you have a brother," she said, deciding he might be more open to prying questions on a full stomach. "Do you have other siblings?"

He shook his head. "Nope, just the one brother. I have dozens of cousins though. What about you? Do you have siblings?"

A familiar knot formed in her throat. The problem with asking him prying questions was that he was likely to reciprocate. "I had a sister. She died in an accident."

"Oh," he said flatly. "Sorry. Were you close?"

"Not really," she admitted. "I'm not sure if that makes it easier or more difficult. I wish I'd spent more time with her."

"Regrets can eat you alive."

"Regret. Like your band," she said. "Why the name Sole Regret?"

"Kelly named the band. There's always one thing in your life you wish you could undo more than any other. Your sole regret. You know, Kelly is actually a very deep person."

"You admire him."

"If you start bringing up that little slip involving his name last night, I'm going to toss you out in the hallway. Naked."

Little slip? But if he didn't want to confront his issues with Kellen, she wasn't going to push him into it. She wasn't particularly keen on being ousted from Owen's place of admiration by his friend.

"You wouldn't dare," she said.

"You sure about that?"

The ornery twinkle in his eye kicked her heart rate up a notch because she was sure he would dare. Before she could respond, he leapt from the bed and lifted her off the mattress.

"Wait! What are you doing?" she asked as he started to carry her toward the door.

"I never back down from a dare. I probably should have mentioned that before you baited me."

"Owen, don't you dare." She realized she'd used the word again and wrapped her arms around his head. "Owen! Please."

"Please, what?"

"Please don't toss me into the hallway naked."

"What happened to your sense of adventure, Caitlyn?"

"That's not adventure, that's horror."

"Not from my end," he said. He lowered her to her feet near the door, and she backed up against the cool surface in case he got the bright idea to open it and try to push her through.

His gaze shifted over her body, and she flushed, fighting the urge to cover herself. He really did seem to like what he saw.

"Now that I think about it," he said, "I wouldn't want anyone else to see you naked; I'd like to keep this gorgeous view all to myself. I could look at you all day."

"Likewise."

A loud song blared from the far side of the room. Owen's face lit up with a wide smile. "My brother!"

He dashed across the room and reached for his phone. His ring tone was some loud song. Probably a Sole Regret one.

"Chad!" Owen greeted his caller with the biggest grin Caitlyn had ever witnessed. "What's up, bro?"

Caitlyn shuffled into the bathroom. She could use a potty break and a shower. And she would hate to intrude upon something as sacred as a conversation with his brother. She was, after all, just Owen's current one-night stand.

CHAPTER NINE

Owen's favorite older brother—his only one—smiled a greeting on the phone's screen. Chad looked a little dirty and a lot weary. Owen would never get used to him with a buzz cut. When he pictured Chad in his head, he was still the seventeen-year-old in his letterman jacket. The same blue eyes, but lots more thick, curly hair.

"Let me guess," Chad said. "You're bored, stuck in a cushy hotel room until tonight when you have to put up with thousands of girls—who all think you're hot for some unfathomable reason—screaming your name at the top of their lungs."

"Wrong," Owen said.

"Don't have a show tonight?"

"We perform in Houston tonight."

"Hotel not cushy enough?"

"No, it's one of the cushiest."

"Then why am I wrong? I know how predictable you are."

"I'm not bored."

"Is Kellen there with you?" Chad tilted his head as if he could see more of the room surrounding Owen.

"Nope. I brought a woman home last night. Well, not home exactly. Back to my room. She's in the shower now." He could hear the water running.

"You spent the night with a woman? What happened to your lame rule about not sleeping with the women you sleep with?"

"I made a concession for Josie. She's just so lonely with you overseas."

Chad's nostrils flared and his blue eyes narrowed dangerously. "Not funny, assmunch. First, I know Josie would never cheat on me, especially not with a twerp like you. Second, I talked to her ten minutes ago. And third, you can't keep a straight face when you lie. But I'm still going to hit you really hard the next time I see you, so consider wearing a mouth guard."

"Any idea when that will be?"

"Can you keep a secret?" he asked.

"Probably not."

"Well then, I'll just say sooner than we thought." Chad smiled.

"How soon?"

"I'm not telling you because you'll ruin the surprise for everyone."

"Six weeks?" Owen said hopefully.

"I'm not telling you."

"I can keep a secret."

"Yeah, like the time I told you not to tell Josephine Tulane that I had a crush on her."

"And now she wants to marry you, so that worked out horribly, didn't it?"

Chad grinned. "I told you because you're predictable and I knew you couldn't keep a secret."

Owen had always wondered if Chad had told him about his feelings for Josie so he would break the ice. Josie had been the new girl in Owen's senior class and Chad had already graduated, so Mr. Love-at-First-Sight didn't have the opportunity to interact with Josie much. "You suck."

"So who's the woman in your shower?"

"Some hot chick I picked up at a sex club."

"You're still going to those things?"

"Maybe I'll stop. If Caitlyn turns out to be someone special to me."

"For your sake, I hope she does. Sex with a woman you love is amazing."

"Better than sex with two women who take turns blowing you?"

Chad closed his eyes, tilted his head back, and laughed. "You'll have to tell me, little brother. I've never had two women take turns blowing me."

"It pretty much rocks."

"So are you going to get me a backstage pass to one of your shows when I come home?"

"That depends," Owen said.

"On what?"

"Our current tour ends in September. Should I reserve a pass for you before then?" Owen hoped his brother would fall for his attempt to milk him for information.

"Yeah, you probably should."

"A couple of months before then?"

"Probably."

"Yes! Are you just returning on leave or—"

"Don't you watch the news? They're starting to pull troops out of here."

"No, I don't watch the news. It's too depressing."

"Still living in your insular world. I'd think with as much as you travel around, you'd be a more well-rounded individual."

"Screw you."

Chad chuckled.

"I had dinner with Mom and Dad night before last and neither of them said anything about the possibility of you coming home soon."

"I don't want anyone to know. I want to show up unannounced and surprise them. So you keep your big mouth shut, got it?"

"Yeah. But I am going to tell Kelly."

Chad rolled his eyes. "That's a given. At least he can keep a secret. Unlike you."

The bathroom door opened and a puff of steam preceded the sexiest woman ever to wear a hotel towel.

"What are you looking at?" Chad asked. "Pick your jaw up off the floor, bro."

Owen switched cameras to the one on the back of his phone to give Chad a glimpse of what he was looking at and then switched back.

"Well, I see why you're not bored." Chad laughed. "I've got to go. I'm over my time limit already. Promise you won't say anything to the folks back home."

"I promise."

"Take care of yourself, Owen."

"Stay safe, Sergeant Mitchell."

Chad saluted with two fingers. The screen went dark. Damn, those calls always went fast.

Caitlyn crossed the room to sit on the arm of the sofa next to him. She propped one foot on the coffee table, and her towel shifted enough that the delights between her legs were barely concealed.

"Is your brother well?"

Owen grinned. "I'm not supposed to tell anyone, but they're

sending him home soon." He really couldn't keep a secret.

"That's great," she said. A smile widened across her face and her eyes lit up. "You must be excited. And relieved."

"I won't be completely relieved until he's home safe in his own bed, but yeah, it's the best news I've heard in months."

"I came out here with the intention of showing you my underdeveloped gag reflex, but I know for sure I can't top your brother's good news, so I guess…"

She started to rise from the sofa arm, but he grabbed her and tugged her onto his lap before she could get away.

"How come you haven't mentioned this limited gag reflex before? And please, God, is it what I think it is?"

She smiled coyly. "A lady can't reveal all her secrets in a single night."

"Which is why you'll be staying with me tonight as well."

"I will?"

"But just in case I do something to fuck this up before tonight, you'd better show me what you mean."

"On one condition," she said.

He was pretty sure that no matter what condition she made, he'd agree to it.

"Name it."

"Take out the barbell in your piercing. I wouldn't want it to get stuck in my throat."

He chuckled. "I don't think that'll happen, but if you're concerned, I'll take it out."

She squirmed off his lap, pushed the coffee table away from the sofa, and knelt on the floor before him. Her hands gripped his thighs just above his knees and tugged his legs apart. Then Caitlyn blessed him with the most devious smile he'd ever seen. His heart suddenly thudded a rapid beat. Heat and lust flooded his groin. Oh God, he was about to have the treat of his life.

Her hands slid up his thighs to his hips and then moved to unfasten the button of his jeans. She didn't take her eyes off his while she unbuttoned his pants and slowly lowered the zipper.

He'd gone for a workout in the hotel's gym while she'd been sleeping that morning, so his muscles were still tight. He appreciated every crunch he'd forced himself to do when her hands slid up his belly, bumping up over the six-pack he worked so hard to maintain. His chest, shoulders, and arms were treated to the same exploratory touch of her warm, soft hands.

"You're the most beautiful man I've ever touched," she said.

"Thanks," he said lamely.

"But what is really amazing about you is that your soul is even more beautiful than all these tight muscles and bronze skin." She grinned. "And that's saying something."

She lowered her head and kissed his belly. His muscles clenched involuntarily, and his cock began to rise with interest.

"You're beau—"

Her hand shot up and covered his mouth. "No talking. It's your turn to be flattered."

It made him uncomfortable to accept praise without reciprocating, but he nodded slightly and allowed her to continue.

"Even your belly button is sexy," she said.

She traced his navel with her tongue and then nipped the skin just beneath. His breath came out in an excited rush.

"I never really liked tattoos until I saw yours." Her hands slid up his ribs to his chest. She traced the lines of a tattoo. "I would have thought the ink would detract from your gorgeous body, but it actually adds something. They make you even more alluring." She crawled a bit closer and extended her tongue to lick his nipple.

He sucked a breath through his teeth. His cock throbbed with need.

"Are your nipples sensitive?" she asked, tracing the tiny bud with her tongue.

He nodded slightly. "They're both pierced, but I can't stand to wear jewelry in them very often." He did wish he had his barbells in at the moment, however.

She latched on to his right nipple, alternately sucking and rubbing it with the flat of her tongue. He clung to the sofa cushion beneath him so he didn't grab her head and direct her to give the same treatment to his fully engorged cock.

When she bit his chest, he gasped in surprise at how sexy he found the act. She moved to his other nipple and looked up at him as she traced it with the tip of her tongue.

"I love touching you," she whispered. Her hands slid down his torso. "I'm really going to love sucking you. I want to watch you erupt."

He gaped at her, his breath now coming in excited gasps. Occasionally she said something that he never expected her to say, and he wondered what went on in her head. Were these naughty thoughts of hers infrequent or just infrequently voiced?

"Will you come for me, Owen?" she whispered. "Let me see how much pleasure I give you."

Hell to the yeah. His mouth had gone dry, so speaking wasn't an option. He nodded instead.

Caitlyn gripped the top of his jeans and tugged them down his thighs. When he lifted his foot to help her remove them completely, she shook her head.

"I like them around your ankles," she said.

Fuck, who was he to upset her fantasy? She grabbed his cock in both hands and tilted her head back so he could watch her trace his rim with the tip of her tongue. He was already seeping pre-cum, and she avoided the little bead of moisture glistening at the tip. Did she not like the taste? When her tongue did flick over the opening to collect his small offering, it took every shred of his willpower not to grab the back of her head and shove his cock down her throat. Could she possibly realize how sexy she looked kneeling on the floor between his thighs, her thick lashes fanned over her porcelain-white cheeks as she sampled his cum? He could see his fluids glistening on the tip of her tongue before she flicked it into her mouth and then licked her lips. Lord, he wished he'd been born with more self-discipline. He was seconds from losing all control.

"Caitlyn," he groaned.

"I do prefer your taste over strawberries," she said, and she opened her brown eyes to gift him with another look of deviousness.

"Do you want me to take the stud out now?" he asked, because there was nothing he wanted more than to watch Caitlyn's mouth stretch around his thick shaft.

"I think I can figure it out. I do have master's degrees in physics and engineering."

"The balls unscrew," he said. A little assistance never hurt anyone. Not even a brainiac like Caitlyn.

"So I don't just yank it out?"

Even though her tone was teasing, Owen flinched. "God, woman. No, you don't just yank it out."

"I'd never hurt you," she said. "Unless you asked me to."

She bent to suckle the head of his cock. Her tongue flicked over the sensitive skin trapped inside her warm, moist mouth until his back arched involuntarily. She began to bob her head slightly—just enough for her plump lips to bump against one ball of his piercing each time she went down.

"God, you give good head," he thought. Or maybe he said it. He wasn't thinking clearly. All he could concentrate on was the pleasure she gave him with her brilliant mouth.

She paused, her tongue flicking the underside of his cock while her fingers unscrewed the ball to remove his barbell. When she pulled the piece of jewelry out of its hole, he almost yelled in triumph. The sound caught in his throat as a moan when she took him deep into her mouth. She pulled back and then took him even deeper. Pulled back and went deeper again. She sucked as her mouth retreated, and he groaned. She let him fall from her mouth, took a deep breath, and descended on him again. This time his cock head lodged in the back of her throat. Dear God, she hadn't been kidding about her suppressed gag reflex. She grabbed his hips and forced him an inch deeper into her throat. She swallowed, which tightened her throat around him, massaging him in a way he'd never experienced.

"Fuck," he growled.

His eyes widened when he felt her tongue slide down the last inch of his cock and brush against his balls. Dear God! His head dropped back onto the back of the sofa. It felt amazing. There was no way he could watch her do those things to him without blowing his load. And he wasn't ready to come yet. He wanted more. He'd like to remain buried in her throat, or sucked by her amazing mouth, for an eternity. Caitlyn pulled back. She licked the head of his cock as she caught her breath and then after a moment, she took him deep again.

"Caitlyn, Caitlyn," he chanted. Even with his eyes squeezed shut, he wasn't going to last much longer.

She found a rhythm of suck and swallow as she rose and fell over him. His pleasure quickly built to uncontainable levels.

"Gonna come," he warned.

She pulled back and wrapped both hands around his shaft, pumping him hard as he came.

"Come hard for me, Owen. I want to watch you explode."

Her thumbs stroked the ridge on the underside of his cock as she jerked him harder and faster. Harder and faster. Until he didn't have a choice but to let go.

"Oh God, Caitlyn," he groaned as hard spasms gripped the base of his cock and his fluids erupted—hot cum splattering over his belly.

He tried to open his eyes, to catch her reaction as he spent himself, but his entire body was locked in the throes of ecstasy, and he'd lost voluntary control of his eyelids.

"That's what I wanted," she whispered.

He shuddered as his orgasm subsided, and he panted, floating on pleasure. Eventually he was able to open his eyes again.

"You are the sexiest thing I've ever seen when you come," Caitlyn said. She dipped her fingers into the mess he'd made on his belly. "And you didn't call someone else's name that time."

So that was still on her mind? Hadn't he proven to her that he was interested in only her?

She lifted her hand to her mouth and licked his cum from her fingertips.

"I think it's time I make you come so hard you scream *my* name," he said. Just as soon as he could find the strength to move.

CHAPTER TEN

Caitlyn gasped in surprise when Owen moved suddenly. She'd thought he was completely spent, but apparently she'd underestimated his stamina. He yanked her towel free and tossed it aside. He knelt behind her and shoved her face into the sofa cushions before lifting her hips so that she was on her knees in front of him, her ass in the air. She raised her head to look at him, and a smack on her butt cheek caused her to gasp in surprise.

"Keep your face in that cushion," Owen commanded.

Normally she didn't like to be told what to do, but she was pretty sure she was going to like what he had in store for her if she obeyed. She dropped her face into the sofa cushion and allowed him to arrange her body as he wanted. He spread her legs a bit more and then drew his fingers through the wetness between her parted pussy lips. Sucking him off had really turned her on. She'd never done that to anyone but Charles, and her ex had never shown his appreciation for her skills the way Owen had. She'd never seen a guy come so much. Just thinking about how his milky fluids had erupted from his body in arching spurts made her twitch her hips to try to alleviate the throbbing between her thighs.

"Your pussy looks incredibly inviting, Caitlyn," Owen said. "It's so swollen, I know it'll grip my cock just right if I slide into you."

He was staring at it? She flushed and pressed her face more securely into the cushion.

"While I wait for my libido to catch up with my dirty thoughts, I'm going to teach you a lesson."

"A lesson?" she gasped, her words muffled by the cushion. Was he going to spank her? Yes, please.

"There are three exceptional characteristics that distinguish the fingers of a guitarist," he said.

She lifted her head to ask what, and he shoved her face back into the cushion.

"Keep your face in that cushion, Caitlyn, and just listen."

She nodded, rubbing her nose against the thick fabric.

"The first exceptional characteristic is the calluses that develop on their fingertips. They're thick and a little rough."

He rubbed his fingertips over her clit, and her body jerked.

"Do you feel them?"

He rubbed her repeatedly and yes, she felt them. They were so much more stimulating than the soft fingers of an academic. She groaned and opened her legs an inch wider, hoping to encourage him to continue.

"The second exceptional characteristic is the speed at which a guitarist can move his fingers."

The motion of his fingers against her clit became mind-bogglingly swift. Within seconds her pussy clenched and the spasms of a hard orgasm gripped her core. "Oh," she gasped. "Oh, oh, oh."

"Oh-*wen*," he supplied, still stroking her with maddening speed and precision.

"Owen," she echoed. "Owen, Owen. What's the third thing?" The anticipation was killing her.

"I'm glad you asked. A good guitarist often has exceptionally long fingers. It gives him a better range, especially when playing solos."

He did have long fingers, but did bass guitarists play solos?

Owen slid two fingers of his free hand deep inside her slick, clenching pussy. Her body gripped them tightly, drawing them deeper. And yes, they were long, but not quite as thick as she wanted them to be.

"Oh God," she sputtered, rocking back to fuck his hand.

Still stroking her clit with one hand, he rotated his fingers inside her, stretching her inner walls in wide circular motions. Pleasure continued to throb through her body even after her orgasm began to fade.

His warm breath teased her back entrance just before he drew his tongue over the tightly clenched hole. Shocked to the depths of her soul, Caitlyn bolted upright.

Owen chuckled. "Too much?" he asked. "Sorry. It just looked so clean and inviting, I felt compelled to lick it."

"I've never," she gasped.

"Well, maybe you should. And I thought I told you to keep your face in the sofa cushion."

He removed his hand from her clit and pushed the center of her back until she bent over again. "I do love to scandalize you, baby," he said. "Now stay where I put you."

He swatted her ass, and her pussy clenched around the fingers buried deep inside her.

This time when his tongue flicked over her ass, she was expecting it, but that still didn't prepare her for how intensely erotic she found the light caress. His free hand located her clit again and though she honestly didn't think it was possible to come more than once in the span of five minutes, Owen had a way of making the impossible inevitable.

She called out to him as her pleasure continued to spiral upward, taking her to heights she never knew existed. Her clit tingled from over-stimulation. Her pussy ached from clenching so hard around his rotating fingers. Her ass twitched in delighted spasms. God, she loved his tongue there. How could she love that? It was so dirty. So perverse. But it felt so fucking good. She wanted him to show her more kinky things. She wanted him to show her *all* kinky things.

When he backed away, she released a sob that was a mix of relief and remorse. He slowly slipped his fingers free of her body, and damn if she couldn't hear how sopping wet he'd made her.

His teeth sank into one ass cheek, and she shuddered. She'd never had anyone bite her ass before. It made her feel naughty. Made her think about him borrowing her strap-on and plunging it into her ass while his thick, pierced wonder claimed her greedy pussy. She wanted him to spank her ass raw while he fucked both holes. Maybe he could pull her hair while he was at it. She could feel the heat rise up her neck as the thoughts and images consumed her and made her crave more of the man behind her. Damn, she'd never been this interested in sex before. Not even on her honeymoon. She sure as hell had never craved hot, dirty pain with her pleasure.

"Are you about ready to meet up with the bus?" he asked. "We'll need to leave soon."

Did he really expect her to think rationally about anything after what she'd just experienced due to his exceptional, guitarist hands and naughty tongue?

"Huh?"

"Did you need to stop by your friend's house to pick up a change of clothes?"

Would she need clothes? She somehow hoped not, but the rest of the world might not agree.

"I think so," she said, her thoughts still thick from her release and overwhelmed with fantasy. "Maybe? I dunno."

Owen tugged her against his body, her breasts pressed into his bare chest. His hands moved to cup her ass. "Do you know how sexy you are when you're too delirious to think? You're making me all hard again."

He kissed her slowly, gently, and for the first time since they'd been together, she not only felt something for him in her body, she felt something for him in her heart.

Shit, that would never do.

Shaken by the direction of her emotions, she pushed him away and climbed to her feet.

"Yeah, I'd better pick up some clothes. My sweet little sheep panties are pretty dirty thanks to you."

He laughed and rose to stand beside her. "And I love that about them."

Riding in a limo was still novel, and Caitlyn checked out every nook and cranny in the back seat. She wondered if traveling in a limo ever became routine. Even Owen enjoyed playing with the stereo.

"You need to get used to loud music for tonight," he told her as he cranked up the tunes and then tugged her into his arms.

That was probably true, but she wasn't sure how deep, passionate kisses—the ones they were sharing—were necessary to acclimate her to metal. They did have her horny, however, and feeling brave. Brave enough to whisper her newest fantasy in Owen's ear. He groaned.

"You should have told me in the hotel, where I was in the position to do something about it."

"Next time," she murmured.

He grinned. "Next time," he agreed. And he sank his hands into her mass of hair so he could pull it, as she'd fantasized, while he suckled and kissed her neck.

The car pulled into Jenna's driveway, and Caitlyn jerked away from Owen to try to compose herself before she faced the limo driver. She was incredibly grateful that her tweed jacket concealed her aroused nipples, though it did nothing to hide her kiss-swollen lips or the tousled condition of her hair. But the driver didn't even spare her a glance as he opened the door. She decided he was used to averting his gaze when couples rode in his car.

Caitlyn left Owen to wait in the back seat while she hurried to collect a few things. He'd insisted that if they wanted to ride on the bus, she'd have to hurry. She was a bit nervous about that, actually. She'd prefer to take the limo to Houston, but assumed the expense would be astronomical. The car and driver had been leased for the band's use, but only for their stay in San Antonio.

Caitlyn let herself into the house using the key Jenna had given her.

"There you are," Jenna said. "Out all night getting laid. I'm surprised you can still walk."

Caitlyn whirled around, her hand over chest, her heart thudding against her palm. She took a deep breath. "You scared the shit out of me. I thought you would have left for work by now."

"I called in sick. I thought we could go to the salon and have a mani-pedi, grab some margaritas with a side of lunch while you tell me all about the cute guy you spent the night with, then we'll pick up some dumb romantic comedy that will make Daniel flee from the house in horror and have the place and a gallon of chocolate ice cream all to ourselves."

Caitlyn's face fell. "Oh, I sort of told…"

She glanced out at the driveway and at the limo waiting for her. As much as she liked Owen and wanted to spend the day and evening with him, her loyalties had to lie with Jenna. The woman had put up with her during her early college years and all the crazy angst she'd suffered while having an affair with one of her professors. One of her *married* professors. After trying to talk her out of marrying Charles, Jenna had served as her maid of honor because she'd said she would always be loyal to her friend, even if she didn't agree with the choices she made.

Caitlyn felt terrible that she even considered spending time with Owen over Jenna.

"I'll just tell him to go on without me," Caitlyn said. She couldn't very well turn down her friend when she'd taken a day off work and made plans to spend it with her.

"Wait," Jenna said. "He's *here*?"

"He's out waiting in the car. He wanted me to go to Houston with him. But I'd rather spend the day with you." Caitlyn almost believed her own lie. She would love to spend the day with Jenna, but Owen was new and exciting and as much as she loved Jenna, Jenna was… comfortable.

And suddenly Caitlyn was looking for anything but comfortable.

Jenna ran to the window beside the front door and peered out. "That's not a car, Caitlyn. It's a fucking limousine."

"Yeah, well…" Caitlyn shrugged.

"Who is this guy? Is he rich?"

"I don't know. He's some musician."

"Like a rapper or something?"

Caitlyn snorted on a laugh. "Not quite. He's in some metal band. They're called Sole Regret. He had convinced me to ride the tour bus and hang out with him backstage until his concert tonight, but I'd much rather have great nails and watch a dumb romantic comedy with you."

"I call bullshit, Caitlyn Marie. You're going." She smoothed her light brown hair that always looked sleek and salon-styled. "And while you're collecting your things, I'm going to introduce myself to your rock star. Is he really cute?"

"If you weren't madly in love with Daniel, I wouldn't let you within ten feet of Owen."

Jenna laughed. "It's not like I'm going to hump his leg or something."

"I wouldn't blame you if you did. Do you work tomorrow?"

"Nope."

"Can we do the girl thing then?"

"Of course." Jenna gave her a quick squeeze. "I'm just so glad to see you smiling again."

"Am I smiling?"

"Like you've been hitting the Prozac a little too hard, honey. Good for you. Why don't you borrow something from my closet?" Jenna suggested. "You dress like my grandmother."

"Owen likes the way I dress."

"I highly doubt that. Now I'm going out to meet the man who put that smile on your face, while you change into something a little less you. "

"Don't tell him any embarrassing stories about me!" Caitlyn called after her.

Jenna closed the door securely behind herself on her way out. She was totally going to tell Owen all sorts of embarrassing stories about her, Caitlyn just knew she would. Caitlyn rushed to collect her things.

In the guest room, she upended her overnight bag in the center of her borrowed bed and looked for something to wear to a rock concert. Jenna was totally right—she couldn't be seen someplace cool dressed in any of her clothes. She shoved a pair of twill weave slacks and a matching emerald-green sweater into the bottom of her bag and then helped herself to Jenna's closet. Most of Jenna's clothes would be too small for Caitlyn's rounder backside, but one of her flirty dresses should fit. Was she daring enough to wear red? Yesterday Caitlyn would have said no, but today she was feeling particularly daring. And sexy. All thanks to Owen.

She wasn't quite daring enough to wear the dress during the day, so she added it to her bag to change into later. Then she filched a pair of red heels from Jenna's massive shoe collection, but she refused to borrow Jenna's underwear. Caitlyn's cartoon cow panties would have to do. Why had she bought those novelty panties in the first place? Owen had seemed to like the fuchsia pair with the sheep; how would he feel about turquoise with a cross-eyed cow?

Would he insist on making her saturate them with her arousal?

Oh lord, she was going to embarrass herself for sure.

Next time she saw Owen, she promised herself that she'd wear sexy underwear for him.

If there was a next time. She was starting to believe there might be a lot of next times.

After tossing her toiletries and make-up into her overnight bag, Caitlyn yanked the zipper shut and went to rescue Owen—and her own reputation—from Jenna's clutches.

As expected, Jenna had Owen in stitches. They were standing next to the car, Owen leaning against the door so he didn't collapse in hysterics and Jenna talking in her typical animated fashion. Caitlyn could only guess what her friend had been telling him. Probably about the time she'd forced Caitlyn to go zip-lining and she'd gotten stuck over a canyon. Caitlyn had been fascinated by the physics of the exercise and had determined the effectiveness of hand-braking via experimentation. Her experiment had been a marvelous success—she'd stopped dead in the center of the line— and it had taken her nearly an hour to pull herself, hand over hand, to the nearest station, much to the displeasure of everyone waiting a turn to zoom across the canyon.

"When she fell, she grabbed the nearest guy—by the pants,

unfortunately—and we all soon discovered that he was a man who went commando."

Owen sniggered and rubbed his forehead.

Oh, this was her rollerblading fiasco story. What was next, the "stuck upside-down between two rocks in a kayak" story? Jenna had never gotten it into her head that Caitlyn had the athletic prowess of a common sea slug. While their exploits were adventures for Jenna, those excursions had been exercises in injury and humiliation for Caitlyn. But she went because she knew how much Jenna enjoyed the not-so-great outdoors. And Jenna sometimes accompanied Caitlyn to science fiction conventions because she knew how much Caitlyn enjoyed pretending she was from space. Caitlyn pinked at her thoughts. She hoped Jenna hadn't told Owen that she liked to dress up as Princess Leia on occasion. She kept the fake-braid earmuffs in the top drawer of her dresser at home.

Though she should be mortified, she wasn't really. It was stranger to see Owen laughing with Jenna than knowing he was laughing because Jenna was embarrassing her. Seeing him with her best friend made it seem possible that Owen could become a part of Caitlyn's regular life and not just be the guy who'd given her one night of thought-shattering sex.

Did she even want Owen as part of her regular life? That hadn't been what she'd been after when she went to the sex club.

Just because something was possible didn't mean she had to follow up. Maybe she could still blow him off and spend the day with Jenna. Jenna was… safe.

Owen smiled a greeting when he noticed Caitlyn approaching. Jenna turned and her face fell. *You didn't change?* Jenna mouthed without speaking.

"I put on clean panties," Caitlyn said defensively.

Jenna turned and said to Owen, "Can you give us just five more minutes?"

He turned to the driver, who stood next to the front fender. "When does the bus leave?"

The driver checked his watch. "We need to leave here in the next couple of minutes to make it."

"I guess you have time to put your dirty panties back on," Owen said.

Jenna burst out laughing and patted his chest playfully. "This one *is* naughty and nice," she said, tossing her hair in an obviously flirtatious way. "You were so right about him."

"He has his cock pierced too," Caitlyn blurted, and then she clamped her hand over her big mouth.

"Hurry, baby." Owen said. "We need to get going. I can't wait to introduce you to Force."

"What force?" Caitlyn asked.

"Our drummer. He's going to love you." Owen scratched the back of his neck. "On second thought, I should probably keep you away from him."

"We'll be right back," Jenna said, pulling Caitlyn back into the house. She slammed the door behind them and spun to confront Caitlyn. "Oh my God, Caitlyn, he's gorgeous. And funny. And sweet. And apparently rich and famous. How in the hell did you luck into *that*?"

"I dunno. He likes older geeky women who give off men-suck vibes in sex clubs."

"If you want to keep his attention, you're going to have to dress better. You look like you climbed out of a thrift store Dumpster."

"I'm telling you," Caitlyn said, "he *likes* this look. I don't get it either."

"He can't possibly like this look," Jenna said. "He likes you and, unfortunately, you come with this look."

"He likes me?" Caitlyn said breathlessly.

"Well, duh. What's not to like?"

In a semi-trance, Caitlyn allowed Jenna to strip her down to her bra and panties. After a deserved eye roll at Caitlyn's cow panties, Jenna stuck her in a pair of black capris that were tight in the rear and a soft pink T-shirt that stretched taut across her boobs.

"It's not me," Caitlyn said.

"You look cute."

"I look like you."

"Right," Jenna said. "You look cute. Now do me a favor."

"What?"

"Pretend to be cool."

"Jenna…"

"Just for today."

Caitlyn released an annoyed sigh. "Fine. I'll *pretend* to be cool. But I need to hurry." After being forced into sandals, she shoved her discarded clothes into her overnight bag and hurried out to the limo.

"What are you wearing?" Owen asked when she paused before him.

"Uh, Jenna thought…"

He shook his head slightly. "She thought wrong."

For a moment, Caitlyn believed he was going to tell her to get lost, but he opened the door to the back of the limo, and she slipped inside.

He climbed in beside her, and the driver shut the door.

"I told you I like the jacket. I like the bow at your throat that begs to be untied. I like that your bra doesn't match your panties."

"It still doesn't," she said. "So you're only attracted to me for my wardrobe, is that it?"

"No, you'd look hot in anything you wore—or nothing—but this outfit doesn't give me a permanent boner. I have to be honest."

"That's probably a good thing," she said and laughed. "My vagina needs a few hours to collect itself. It's not used to so much attention."

"Well, then, I'll try to contain my blinding lust." He grinned and took her hand, holding it gently in his. His thumb rubbed a lazy circle on her knuckles. "So," he said. "Tell me about your camping trip. Jenna said you'd kill her if she told me about the skunk that got stuck in your tent."

Caitlyn cringed. "She's right. I'd kill her for that."

"I didn't take you for the outdoorsy type."

"That's because I'm not. Jenna is, though, and I am weak to her charm. She can talk me into anything."

"It's great to have a best friend, someone who pushes you to try things you'd never consider on your own. Makes life interesting."

Caitlyn smiled, knowing he was thinking about Kellen again. Kellen was Owen's Jenna. She suddenly felt a lot more comfortable about Owen's relationship with Kellen. Caitlyn probably would never call Jenna's name during sex, but whatever. If Owen said there was no attraction between them, she believed him.

"*Interesting?* I guess that's one way to describe it."

They both laughed and somehow ended up kissing all the way to the tour bus. Maybe it wasn't her pathetic wardrobe that turned him on after all.

Their driver handed off their bags to some guy who stuffed them into a compartment under the bus.

"I'll need to change later," Caitlyn said.

"You can get your bag when we stop at the venue."

She nodded.

"Ready to meet the rest of the band?"

Her stomach flopped. She was scared out of her mind, to be honest. Who'd have ever thought she'd be riding on a tour bus with a bunch of heavy metal musicians? Not her.

"I guess," she said.

"You already met Kellen. He's not so scary, is he?"

A little, yeah, but she shook her head bravely.

"And I'm the worst one of the bunch, so if you can handle me, you can surely handle the rest."

"I highly doubt that you're the worst," she said. Because he was decidedly terrific. And it was hard to top perfection.

"Where have you been?" A muscle-bound hunk in aviator sunglasses spoke from the top of the bus steps. He had short dark hair and an abundance of bulges in all the right places. "If I'd have known you were going to be this late, I would have had Amanda stick around for one more quickie before I sent her home."

"Caitlyn needed to stop by her friend's house to pick up some clothes."

"Who is Caitlyn?"

"That would be me," Caitlyn said.

"Sorry, didn't see you there."

Which was the typical-man's reaction to her. That's why Owen's attention had her completely befuddled and Jenna's insistence that she was attractive didn't hold much cotton. As a rule, men tended to ignore her.

"This is our vocalist, Shade," Owen said. "He's pretty much an egotistical asshole, but he grows on you after a while."

Caitlyn couldn't believe Shade let the insult slide without a rebuttal. Instead he focused on her.

"You're not planning on her riding the bus, are you?" Shade said. "You know the rule: no chicks on the bus."

"Fuck the rule," Owen said. "She's riding with us to Houston." He took Caitlyn's hand and tugged her up the bus past a very confused-looking Shade.

At the top of the steps, she came face-to-chest with another band member. This one was long and lean. She tilted her head back to peer into the greenest pair of eyes she'd ever encountered.

Wow. While she did have a limited gag reflex, she thought

choking on her own tongue, as she was now doing, might be fatal. Especially considering the sudden overabundance of drool in her mouth.

"This is Force," Owen said.

"May the force be with me," Caitlyn mumbled, lost in Force's amazing green-eyed gaze.

"It seems we have a problem," she heard Kellen say from somewhere down the corridor. "She's been drawn in by the power of the Force. You'd better do something and quick, Tags."

Owen kissed her, which effectively broke Force's spell. She smiled at Owen. She wasn't used to being with a man who was so easy with affection in public, not that she minded.

"Who is this?" Force asked as he tugged his baseball cap lower on his forehead.

"That's Caitlyn," Kellen said. "Owen is breaking all his rules with her."

"All of them?" Force asked.

"Well, hopefully not the "BYOC" rule, but the "only one poke per bush" rule and the "never sleep with the women you sleep with" rule and the "never eat breakfast with a chick" rule and apparently the "no ladies on the bus" rule. Did you break the "never meet her friends" rule too, Owen?"

He cringed and pulled a hand through his hair. "Yeah, I broke that one too."

"Stupid rules anyway," Force said. "My name is Gabe, by the way. You don't have to call me Force."

"Do you like Star Wars?" Caitlyn blurted stupidly.

"Star Wars is for geeks," Gabe said, one slim eyebrow arched at her.

"Oh," she said, her face almost in flames it was burning so hot.

"I *love* Star Wars," Gabe said. "Which episode is your favorite?"

"*Return of the Jedi.*"

He shook his head at her. "*The Empire Strikes Back.*"

"Oh my God, who scheduled a geek convention on the tour bus?" another rock-star type asked.

This one was dressed in black from his biker jacket to his tight T-shirt to his jeans to his motorcycle boots. Even his hair was unnaturally black—probably died to match his shoes. His only non-black accessories were the collection of silver chains he wore around his neck and dangling from one belt loop.

"That's Adam," Owen said.

"So Shade is the vocalist, Kellen plays guitar, Owen plays bass, and Gabe is the drummer." Caitlyn did a quick mental inventory. "That must make you... the keyboardist?"

Adam did not look amused. More like offended. Was there something wrong with the keyboard? What other instruments were played in a rock band? She'd once heard a flute in a Led Zeppelin song. She was proud of herself for remembering.

"I know," she gushed, "you play the flute!"

Everyone burst out laughing, except Adam, who looked even more out of sorts than when she'd accused him of playing keyboard.

"No, I don't play the fucking flute," he said. "I'm *lead* guitar."

"But..." She pointed at Kellen. "I thought Kellen played guitar."

"He plays *rhythm* guitar."

She didn't know the difference. "You have two guitarists? Well, *three*, if you count Owen's bass?"

"That's right."

"Why do you need three? Isn't one good enough?"

"She doesn't listen to rock music," Owen explained.

"Then why is she here?" Adam countered.

"Hmm," Owen scratched his jaw. "Probably because she doesn't listen to rock music. I felt she needed an education."

And she'd very much enjoyed the education he'd given her about guitarists' fingers. Her gaze dropped to Adam's hands and then darted to Kellen's. Long fingers. All of them. She was sure they were callused and swift as well. Caitlyn really wished Owen would stop making her blush. She hadn't blushed this much when she'd been a bride and fallen off a pier in her wedding gown after having one too many to drink.

"Speaking of education," Owen said, turning his attention from Adam to Gabe.

Oh God, he wasn't going to mention her morning lesson was he? She'd die of mortification if he did.

"Guess what she has her degree in?" Owen said.

Caitlyn blew out a relieved breath.

"Based on the size of her rack, I'd say cheerleading," Gabe said.

Caitlyn glanced down at her chest, which was straining against Jenna's too-tight T-shirt. "Despite popular belief, big boobs are a liability for a cheerleader. They throw off your center of gravity, get in the way of your pom-poms, and jiggle around until you get one hell of a back ache." She hopped up and down to demonstrate.

All eyes settled on her chest. As far as breasts went, she wasn't overly well-endowed, but they did move when she did.

"Where's that jacket of yours, Caitlyn?" Owen asked. "It's a bit chilly here on the bus."

She glanced up at him, not sure why the sparks of jealousy in his eyes were so endearing.

"Everyone ready to go?" a man in a white Stetson said from the front of the bus. He settled behind the driver's seat and the door swung shut.

"Head on out," Shade said. He brushed past the group congregated in the seating area near the front of the bus. "I'm going to catch a nap. Amanda kept me up all night, so I'm beat."

Caitlyn assumed Amanda was his wife or girlfriend. She didn't want to pry, so she didn't ask. Shade disappeared behind a curtain that concealed his bunk near the back of the bus.

"So if you weren't a cheerleader, what was your major?" Gabe asked, his brilliant green eyes alive with interest.

"Don't make me say it," Caitlyn said. "I'm supposed to pretend that I'm cool today."

"If it makes you feel better," Owen said, "like you, Gabe went to college to be a career geek. But we kidnapped him and chained him to a drum kit."

"Were you a physics major?" Gabe asked, his eyes wide.

"With a chemistry minor. My master's is in mechanical engineering."

Gabe insisted she tell him all about her current projects in fuel cells. She didn't give him too many details since they were working on a new prototype and you never knew if your competition just happened to be a drummer in a rock band. But Gabe was apparently ravenous for cerebral stimulation, so she shared what she could. Owen seemed content to listen to them talk.

She and Gabe eventually got into a highly competitive game of backgammon. None of his band mates would play with him. With the exception of Shade, who was evidently a heavy sleeper, they all cheered her on to beat their drummer. Even Kellen, who seemed sullen today, and Adam, who was slow to warm up to Caitlyn, got in on the competition.

"Kick his ass, baby," Owen said. "He gloats for days every time he beats someone."

"Which would be every time I play," Gabe said, rolling the dice and getting a pair of sixes. Again.

"I think his dice are loaded," Caitlyn complained.

"I'm just lucky." Gabe winked at her. She lost her train of thought for a moment. The physics majors in her class hadn't looked like him. If they had, she wouldn't have been fooling around with her English professor.

Gabe hit another of her pieces and lifted it from the playing field to sit it on the bar in the center of the board.

"Damn it."

At this rate, she wasn't going to get a single piece into her home base. It was impossible to make it across the board when she was spending all her time re-entering her captured pieces.

"This is why no one ever beats him," Owen said. "He's an offensive player."

"I definitely find his playing offensive," Caitlyn said.

The guys laughed, and she flushed again.

By the time they reached Houston, she was completely at ease in the presence of Owen's band mates. And she'd even managed to beat Gabe in one out of their three games, which made her some sort of hero, especially in Adam's eyes.

The bus stopped behind an empty stadium. Caitlyn peered out a large tinted window, surprised by the controlled madness shown by the road crew as they moved equipment inside. The huge semi-truck was nearly empty. They'd obviously been at it for hours before the band's arrival.

As the other guys filtered off the bus, chatting, Owen pulled Caitlyn aside.

"Are you glad you came?" he asked.

"So far. I haven't been subjected to your eardrum-damaging music yet."

"You'll enjoy it," he said.

She wasn't so sure, but she knew the guys in the band, so like the dutiful aunt of a school kid, she'd go to their music performance and tell them they sounded great no matter how horrible they were.

When the last of the guys stepped off the bus, Owen leaned in to steal a kiss. "I've wanted to do that for hours," he said.

"Then why didn't you?"

"I have to live with these guys," he said. "And they can be pretty immature about teasing a guy about his girl."

"But you're not like that, right?"

He grinned, and she guessed he was the ringleader of the teasing. "Of course not."

He backed her into the square dining table where she and Gabe had been playing backgammon and lifted her to sit on its surface. His hands cupped her breasts, and he massaged them gently.

"I've wanted to do this for hours too."

She wrapped her legs around his hips and urged him into a tight hug. He melted into her.

"I liked having you here with me today," he said. "The guys didn't seem to mind either. I thought they'd give me hell for bringing you along, but they seemed to like the idea."

She turned her face into his neck and inhaled. Mmm. What was it about this man that drove her to distraction?

"I know we haven't known each other long," he said.

"That's true," she murmured.

"But you fit here somehow. You fit with me."

She went still, anticipating words she was not ready to hear.

"So anytime you want to come hang out with us, you're welcome."

Was that all? She snuggled closer to him again.

"Because I really like you and I'd hate to think we wouldn't get to see each other again."

"I'd hate that too," she admitted.

"You could come with us tonight to Beaumont," he said. "And then after that we're in New Orleans. I could take you to another sex club, if you like. There's an interesting one there."

Her lips brushed his throat. "Too soon, Owen," she said. She didn't want to say no, but she did need him to slow down. He was like a bullet train, and she was only prepared for freight.

"Oh," he said, the disappointment in his voice perceptible.

"I'm not saying I don't want to be with you," she whispered in his ear. "I just have a lot of responsibilities, and I need to take things slowly." She leaned back and cupped his face in both hands. "I'm not rejecting you." She knew that was what he really feared.

"Feels like it," he said.

Her heart gave a little pang for hurting him. She understood why he had rules for his entanglements with women, he got his feelings hurt much too easily to expose his heart. But he'd exposed it to her, so she was going to have to be careful with it.

"Why don't you try kissing me into oblivion, Owen?" she said huskily. "I seem to agree to your crazy plans when I'm not thinking straight."

He grinned and tugged her closer. "Now there's an idea."

She was halfway to oblivion when someone marched up the steps. Owen drew away and stared into her eyes for a long moment before turning his attention to the man waiting for him to finish his business. As far as Caitlyn was concerned, Owen's business wouldn't be finished until his cock was inside her and she was shattering in one of those fantastic orgasms he gave her, but apparently this guy had other ideas.

"Can I help you, Jordan?" Owen asked.

"Uh, sorry to interrupt," Jordan said, as if he was sorry he was no longer watching Owen make out with Caitlyn. "You're needed for sound check."

"I figured," he said. "I'll be there in a minute."

"Okay."

Jordan watched him expectantly until Owen said, "I don't need an escort, Jordan."

"Okay." Jordan stared at them for one more uncomfortable moment and then turned to leave the bus.

"Nice kid," Owen said, "but he's a little slow on the uptake."

"I think he's overwhelmed with idol worship," Caitlyn said. She rubbed her breasts against Owen's hard chest, in no way ready to release him to his job.

"I think he was dropped on his head as an infant."

Her hand moved between their bodies to cup his crotch. His cock jerked against her palm.

"Do we have time for a quickie?" she asked. "It's been several hours since my last orgasm, and I think I'm developing an addiction to the feel of you inside me."

He groaned. "That makes two of us." He kissed her deeply and then pulled away. "But we're going to have to wait until after sound check."

"I hope it's one of those things that only takes a few minutes."

"Doubtful. Do you want to come backstage and watch or stay here on the bus?"

If he had to ask, he didn't know how curious she was to learn how things worked. *All* things. But he'd learn that about her soon enough.

"I'd love to come backstage and watch you work."

"Okay," he said, "but it will cost you a blowjob."

She knew he was just trying to get a rise out of her, but she played along. "Great. I gave you one of those this morning, so I'm all set."

"Another blowjob," he hurriedly remedied.

"You can't change the rules after you state your condition," she said.

"Of course I can. I'm a rock star."

"It's a good thing I don't care about that. You'll have to find someone else to be in awe of your fame. I'm just in awe of your skill in bed."

"Well, that's something, I suppose," he said, and he helped her down from the table.

He took her hand and led her off the bus and into chaos.

CHAPTER ELEVEN

Caitlyn was overwhelmed by the amount of activity going on backstage. She could never do Owen's job; frayed nerves would be a constant for her.

"Once sound check is over, we can find someplace a bit calmer," Owen said in her ear. "Get in that quickie."

"So you can tell I'm out of my element?"

"You look just a little freaked out," Owen said.

"She looks entirely spooked," Gabe said.

Her eyes widened when she glanced at him. He'd been wearing a baseball cap all day, but he wasn't wearing one now. He had a mohawk spiked a full twelve inches in the air. It was black near his scalp and scarlet at the tips, but what really set her jaw on the floor were the dragon tattoos inked on his scalp.

"*You're* scaring her," Owen said, and covered her eyes with one hand. "Don't look directly at it or you'll turn to stone."

She laughed and elbowed Owen in the ribs. She was grateful he'd given her a moment to collect her wits. Gawking at Gabe's head was a pretty crappy thing to do to him, especially since she knew what a great guy he was. She adored his quick wit and intelligence, even if she couldn't stomach his ruthlessness on the opposite side of a backgammon board. And she didn't hold his ink-work against him; she'd just been stunned, was all. She'd had no idea he had dragons tattooed on both sides of his head.

"Sorry for staring," she said, forcing her eyes not to wander to the flames and the scaly hide inked on his scalp. "I just didn't realize…"

"If he didn't want people to stare, he wouldn't style his hair like that," Owen said.

"It's not the hair, it's the…" Caitlyn reached up and grabbed Gabe's head between her palms and forced him to bend over so she could inspect the tattoos. "Damn, Gabe, didn't that hurt? It looks damned painful!"

"Yeah, it hurt," he said. "I swear I saw God that day. But the tattoo artist assured me that the unexplained sparks and the tunneling in my vision were due to the pain, not a higher power."

"I bet it hurt worse than when Owen had his cock pier—" Caitlyn slapped a hand over her mouth. She couldn't believe what she'd almost said to Gabe.

Gabe snorted and burst out laughing. "You know what I like about you, Caitlyn?"

"My dashing smile?" She smiled so wide, her cheeks hurt.

"That is *special*," he said, "but no. You have a naughty mind. You might try to censor it, but I know it's there."

"I like that about her too." Owen pried her hands off Gabe's head. "Here, hold on to this."

Owen wrapped Caitlyn's arms around his waist and placed her hands on his ass.

"Oh yes," she said, giving Owen's firm ass cheeks a squeeze. "This is much more fun to hold on to than Gabe's head."

When it was time for Owen to work with his instrument, Caitlyn reluctantly released her hold on his firm backside. She noticed the bulge in his jeans before he shifted his bass guitar in front of it. So she wasn't the only one in need of a quickie. A long, drawn-out lovemaking session would work too. She was game for anything with Owen.

She did her best to stay out of the crew's way as she watched.

She was surprised by how well Owen played. For a moment, she thought he was showing off his skill for her benefit, and then it dawned on her that he was playing some of the band's songs.

When the low tones of his riff throbbed through her body, she was suddenly completely astounded by his musical skill. To her way of thinking, music was an auditory expression of mathematics, mostly fractions—flats and sharps changing tones by halves, the lengths of notes in quarters and thirds. She'd always admired anyone who could play piano, and she was starting to feel the same admiration for a certain bass player. A man who had that much skill in music was a genius in her book.

There was also something to be said about the way Owen's fingers moved on the strings, about knowing that's what caused those thick calluses to form on his fingertips. About remembering what they felt like against her swollen, achy clit.

She was suddenly on fire for the man—no touching required.

Caitlyn's original intention had been to watch the logistics of preparing equipment for a live show, but somehow all the machinery and technology—which usually fascinated her—was far less interesting than the man stroking four thick strings. The technicians were talking to Owen and he was nodding, but she couldn't hear what was being said over the din of hammers banging against steel pipes. After several minutes, Owen smiled at her and then lifted the strap of his guitar over his head and handed it off to one of the crew. Her heart thudded faster and faster as he approached her. He never took his eyes off her face.

"Are you finished?" she asked.

"I haven't even started," he said.

"Oh." She couldn't keep the disappointment out of her voice.

"But I'm done with sound check."

"That was quick."

"Technically, they could do the sound check without us, but Shade insists that we all play a part in it. If we sound like shit, it's not the technicians who get booed off the stage."

"I guess that's true," she said. "So what do you usually do to waste time before the concert starts?"

"Depends. Sometimes we hang out on the bus. Other times we hang out in the dressing room. Occasionally there are VIP groups that hang out with us backstage, and I have to pretend I'm charming for several consecutive hours. We might do a promotional signing here or there but no matter what's on the agenda, there's usually a sandwich involved. Are you hungry?"

Her stomach rumbled at the thought of food. She'd enjoyed a large breakfast but had turned down a tour bus lunch consisting of beef jerky and Spanish peanuts. "Yeah, I could use a sandwich."

"I think I need to earn mine first."

She was in perfect agreement.

"Are we going back to the bus? I need to change clothes before the concert."

"You're changing again?"

"Aren't you going to change for your performance?"

Owen looked down at his baggie, distressed jeans and smoothed both hands over the belly of his navy-blue T-shirt. "Nope. This will work fine."

She was surprised he didn't dress better onstage. He was wearing what most guys would wear to spend the day on the couch watching football and eating nachos. She wasn't sure what to expect from the show. Apparently the band didn't wear suits when they performed. Would the flirty red cocktail dress she'd borrowed from Jenna be appropriate attire?

"What should I wear, Owen? I've never been to a rock concert, remember? I don't want to make an ass out of myself."

"I have to admit I'm interested to know what you were planning on wearing."

"Why? So you can make fun of me?"

"I would never make fun of you."

She offered him a reproachful look.

"Not in a hurtful manner," he added. "So why don't you change into what you'd planned to wear and if I think it'll make an ass out of you, I'll let you know."

"It's not a tweed jacket," she said.

She laughed at the disappointed look on his face.

"Well, I still want to see it."

"Fine." She didn't much care if her wardrobe wasn't metal-concert appropriate. It wasn't like she was going to see any of these people in her real life. Though since they were in her home town, it was possible that someone would recognize her wearing a cocktail dress at a rock show.

They started toward the bus. Out of the corner of her eye, Caitlyn kept catching the profile of the same surly-looking stranger. She didn't think it was a coincidence.

"Owen," she whispered. "I think that shady-looking character is following us."

Owen glanced over his shoulder and laughed. "Hey, shady-looking character. Follow us out of her peripheral view. You're freaking her out."

"Will do," the man said and slowed his pursuit to allow them to walk farther ahead.

Caitlyn lifted a questioning eyebrow at Owen.

"That's Frank, one of our security team. He's making sure you don't attack me."

"You need security?"

"Obviously."

"You didn't have security following you around last night," she pointed out.

"That's because the chances I'll be recognized when I'm not at a venue are relatively small. No one is looking to see me. But here, if I'm recognized, almost everyone knows who I am and then it becomes a mob situation. Ask Adam about that. He about started a riot a couple nights ago because he was stupid enough to roll down the limousine window in front of the stadium."

"It's sort of weird to think of you as famous," she said. "Do people really try to attack you?"

"Just women trying to get in my pants," he said.

"Ha ha," she said before realizing he probably wasn't joking.

When they reached the bus, Frank didn't follow them inside. There was another guy standing just outside the bus door, who Caitlyn assumed was another member of the security team. She supposed his job was to keep groupies from stowing away on the bus when no one was paying attention.

Owen had someone retrieve her overnight bag from beneath the bus and when she had it clutched against her chest, she looked at Owen expectantly.

"You can change in the bathroom," he said. "I'd join you but unless I stand in the shower stall, there isn't room for two."

"I can dress myself."

"That's fine. As long as you allow me to undress you."

She hurried to the bathroom to change while Owen fiddled with his smartphone and checked his messages.

He was right about the bathroom being too small for two. She had to stand with one foot in the shower stall to get dressed. The dress was knee-length, with a flirty wide skirt and a halter top that she realized was much too revealing to wear in public. Cleavage wasn't the right word for what was showing. She half expected her belly button to be visible.

"Dear lord, Jenna, why do you even own a dress like this?" she asked the mirror. Noting that her bra was showing, she took it off and did her best to keep her boobs in her top while she slipped into the matching heels. The dress wasn't appropriate for a rock concert or anything but the privacy of her own bedroom. Sure, a movie star might get away with wearing something like this, but she was no movie star. She laughed at her reflection.

"What were you thinking, Caitlyn Marie Mattock?" Her eyes widened when she heard herself use her married name. She realized that unlike the past few months—when it seemed her every thought had been focused on how she'd been jilted—she hadn't thought of Charles all day. "Caitlyn Marie *Hanson*," she corrected. She'd taken back her maiden name in the divorce. It was time to claim it as her own again.

She stepped out of the bathroom, smoothing her hair with her palms and trying not to feel overly self-conscious about how much skin was showing. The back of the dress was cut so low, she wouldn't be surprised if she had plumber's crack going on back there. And to say the neckline plunged was an understatement.

Owen glanced up from his phone and froze with his finger hovering over the screen. His jaw dropped and eyes bulged. His phone hit the floor and he didn't even bother to pick it up before striding toward her.

"Good God, woman, you are *not* wearing that."

"Yeah, I realized how ridiculous I look the second I put it on."

He was staring at the inner and under curves of her breasts that were far too visible for her peace of mind. If she wasn't already used to him seeing her naked, she would have covered herself with her hands.

"Fuck hot," he said, and then he shook his head as if to clear his thoughts. "You look fuck hot, Caitlyn. Too fuck hot."

"Fuck hot?"

"That's way hotter than regular hot," he said. "On the hotness scale there's hot, really hot, and then fuck hot. I think we need to invent a new hot just for you."

She shook her head at his silliness, but she couldn't help it—she liked his over-the-top compliments. He made her feel good about herself. She'd always been confident about her intelligence and her creativity and her ability to lead a team, but physically? She was the woman who'd tripped over her own feet at an indoor football game and ended up with her face buried in the crotch of the team mascot. She wasn't used to being admired for her physical attributes.

Owen's finger traced a path along the inner curve of her breast. "Where did you get this dress?"

"I borrowed it from Jenna."

"I'll thank her next time I see her."

"You plan to see her again?" Caitlyn squeaked. Jenna had dated a lot of men in her day, but she was happily married now. Or did her friend have something she needed to talk to her about?

"She's a big part of your life, isn't she?"

"I wish she was more a part of my life," Caitlyn admitted.

"And I want to be a big part of your life."

"You do?"

He traced the inner curve of her other breast, and she shivered with delight. "Yes."

"Oh." She wasn't sure how to respond. Wasn't this just a long version of a one-night stand? But it didn't have to be. "Okay," she said. "I guess we can go out again."

He chuckled. "You *guess*?"

His hand slid into the front of her dress, and he palmed her breast.

"I'm not rejecting you, Owen," she said.

"Good, because I don't handle rejection well."

"Kellen sort of told me that in the limo outside the club."

"He's been quiet all day; I'm not sure what's wrong with him. He really shouldn't go to Galveston tonight. Surrounding himself with happy memories does not make him happy with the present."

"What's in Galveston?"

"The house he bought her after she died."

"Huh?"

He shook his head. "Don't worry about it. I shouldn't have brought it up."

"You can talk to me about it. I know you're concerned for him."

"I'm more concerned that someone other than me will see you in this dress and try to do this."

His thumb rubbed her nipple, and she moaned in pleasure. This dress had one thing going for it. It made getting to second base a breeze.

"I think Kellen's trying to let her go," she said, struggling to follow the thread of their conversation while her body awakened beneath his expert touch.

Owen shook his head. "I think seeing me and you together is really bothering him."

"Do you think he wants to hook up with you?"

His eyes widened, and he shook his head. "No. I think seeing me with a woman makes him miss her. You're still caught up on that thing that happened back at the club?"

"You called his name when I was screwing you, Owen. And he touched you. I saw him. And I think he rather enjoyed touching you. I know you enjoyed it. I didn't know your O-face at the time, but I know it now, and you were about to come in his hand."

"That's ridiculous."

"If you say so."

"I say so. Drop it, okay?" he said.

"I won't mention it again." She meant it.

"Now that you've dropped that, you need to drop this dress. There is no way I'll be able to perform with you standing in my corner of the stage looking this fuck hot. And if another man sees you in this, I'll be tempted to kick his ass."

She couldn't picture Owen getting into a fight. Like Kellen had said, Owen saw the good in people. In all people.

"Well I wouldn't want you to hurt your knuckles on some guy's face. I guess I'll go change."

She took a step back, but he grabbed her and pulled her against him, capturing her in a tight embrace. "I think you should wear it just a little while longer. There's no one here but you and me."

"And me," Kellen said from the living area.

Owen stiffened. He was probably wondering the same thing Caitlyn was wondering: how long had Kellen been there and had he overheard their conversation about him?

Owen immediately relaxed and stepped away from Caitlyn. "You're the only dude allowed to see her dressed like this. Doesn't she look fuck hot?"

"Fuck hot," Kellen agreed with a half-smile.

"Couldn't you just bend her over that table and fuck her for hours?" Owen said.

Caitlyn slapped at him for making her blush again.

"If you'd like to tie her up sometime, I could give you a hand," Kellen offered.

Owen's breath caught in his throat. "You mean it?"

Kellen nodded. "Yeah. I've been doing a lot of thinking. I need this last night to let her consume me. Seeing you with Caitlyn today made me realize that no one will ever take Sara's place, but maybe no one is supposed to. Maybe someone could find a different spot to fill inside me. I seem to be full of holes."

Caitlyn nearly melted at his admission. The man had a truly romantic soul. She wondered if he wrote lyrics. He seemed the poetic type.

"I have more holes than you do," Owen said, fingering the piercing in his brow and both ears. He didn't have to remind anyone about that extra hole down below.

Caitlyn chuckled. Trust Owen to take everything at face value.

"That's not what I meant," Kellen said. "I meant—"

"I know what you meant," Owen said. "You're making me look shallow in front of my chick, coming in here all deep and philosophical while I spout off incoherently about how hot she looks in a dress."

"I need that," Caitlyn admitted. "*That* fills a hole in me."

"I'd like to fill a hole in you right about now," Owen said.

Kellen chuckled and headed for the exit. "I'll leave you two alone," he said. "So Owen can fill some holes."

"Could you do me a favor?" Owen asked him.

"Name it."

"Go buy Caitlyn a Sole Regret T-shirt. I can't have her looking fuck hot in front of the crew."

Kellen appeared to be less than thrilled to be used as an errand boy, but he asked, "Anything else?"

"Give me twenty minutes of privacy and then bring me a sandwich."

"Pastrami?" Kellen asked.

"You guessed it."

Caitlyn gasped when Owen lifted her skirt by sliding his hands up her thighs. "Mmm," he murmured. "I am definitely going to need a pastrami sandwich when I'm done with you."

Now that sounded promising.

CHAPTER TWELVE

After the show, Owen threw a couple of guitar picks into the audience, kissed his fingertips, and tossed the sentiment to the crowd. He then jogged down the steps to the floor beside the stage.

"Oh my God." Caitlyn squealed and launched herself into his arms. His bass guitar made a low grinding sound as her belly rubbed against the strings. "I thought you were hot before, but now I'd have to say you're on fire. Molten. Nuclear."

He chuckled at her enthusiasm, but her deep, seeking kiss cut off all sound but the groan in the back of his throat. His arms moved around her body to pull her closer. The familiar stirring in his lower belly announced that he wasn't finished with her. Not by a long shot. He couldn't remember the last time a woman had consumed him so completely, so quickly.

She broke away and caught his face between her hands. Her brown eyes shone with admiration and, dare he hope, unquenchable lust. He was more than ready to see if he could satisfy it. At least temporarily.

"Wow," she said. "Just wow."

"So you like our music?"

She shook her head. "Not at all. I think my ears are bleeding. But I like you, so I'm willing to suffer to watch you on stage. You have an amazing presence." She leaned close and whispered in his ear. "My cow panties are drenched."

He laughed, not the least bit offended that she didn't like Sole Regret's music. He had a feeling it would grow on her, but if it didn't, that didn't matter. Not having everything in common actually made getting to know her a challenge. He hadn't been aware that that's what had been missing from his love life. His time with Caitlyn hadn't started with a challenge—getting her in bed had been easy—but he had a feeling that keeping her attention outside of the bedroom would hold his interest for a long time.

He traced the Sole Regret logo across her chest. "So you aren't wearing this kick-ass T-shirt because you're a fan?"

"I'm definitely a fan, honey. I just don't like your music."

"Hey," Kelly said from beside Owen. "I'm heading out."

"Are you sure you want to go?" Owen said, instantly concerned for Kelly. It couldn't be good for him to sit in that house by himself all night. "I can come with you if you think you'll be lonely."

"I need to be lonely for a few hours, get my head on straight. So don't try calling to check on me; I'm going to turn off my phone."

Owen nodded, even though he didn't understand what had Kelly's head so crooked all of a sudden.

"It was nice meeting you, Caitlyn," Kelly said, extending a hand toward her.

She ignored his hand and gave him a hug, seemingly oblivious to the sweat glistening on his bare chest. "Likewise. If you need Owen, call him. He'll come."

Kelly met Owen's eyes over Caitlyn's shoulder. His gaze was so intense that Owen's heart skipped a beat. Then Kellen grinned. "I'm sure he will, if he's between your legs."

Caitlyn slapped him in the chest. "Behave."

"Don't listen to her," Owen advised. "Get into a little trouble. You're starting to bore me."

Kelly chuckled and lifted his knuckles to share a bro-tap before walking away. Owen watched him until he disappeared through an open door and then turned to Caitlyn, who was scrutinizing him.

"You need to have a long talk with him," she said. "Sort through your feelings."

Owen rolled his eyes. You call out a guy's name once while enjoying an explosive orgasm as a woman fucks you in the ass, and she just won't let it rest.

"Come on," he said. "Let's go get naked on the bus."

He removed his bass, handed it off to a technician, and wrapped an arm around Caitlyn's shoulders. She turned her face toward his chest and inhaled deeply.

"Mmm, you smell so good."

As sweaty as he was, he surely smelled like a dirty jockstrap, but he never turned down a compliment.

"And you look good enough to eat," he said into her ear. "One guess what I'm thinking about eating right now."

"Pastrami on rye?" she asked, her eyes sparking with mischief as she gazed up at him.

"I'm sure before the night is over I'll be craving pastrami, but right now I want pie."

"Cream pie?"

"If it's not creamy yet, it will be when I get my mouth on it."

She sucked in a scandalized breath and then laughed. "Why are you the guy my mother always warned me about? She should have shoved me in your direction. Who knew bad boys were so much fun?"

"I told you I'll be bad if it turns you on."

"Everything you do turns me on. And seeing you on stage..." She took a deep breath and relaxed into a full-body shudder. "I had no idea how incredibly sexy I'd find that."

"That's the first thing that attracts most women."

"I find that very hard to believe, blue eyes."

He directed her behind the stadium where the buses were parked. One of their security team followed, keeping enough distance from them to not invade their privacy.

"So what are you doing tomorrow?" Owen asked.

"Returning to San Antonio to spend the day with Jenna," she said. One part of her still felt terrible for running off with Owen. It was supposed to be their BFF week and here she was tagging along after a guy. "I already ditched her once."

"And what do I have to do to convince you to come with me to Beaumont?"

"Call Jenna and explain why I'm being such a wretched friend."

"Done. I'll even take all the blame upon myself."

"I don't know if my body can take two consecutive nights with you. I'm not as young as I used to be."

"We don't have to have sex," he said. "I just like spending time with you."

She stopped in midstride and looked up at him, her eyes blinking. "Well, that might be enough for you, but my hormones are raging like a river thanks to you, and you better believe that you're going to do something about the state you put me in, Mr. Owen Pierced-Cock Mitchell."

He rubbed her lower back. "Maybe we'll try it without the piercing this time."

She winked at him. "Maybe."

"So will you accompany me to our next gig?"

"Depends," she said.

"On?"

"If you let me buy you dinner tonight."

"I think the tour bus is leaving in the next ten minutes."

"Oh."

"But you can buy me dinner tomorrow night."

"And the night after that?"

He grinned. "Probably."

Owen caught movement out of the corner of his eye a split second before one of their security team tackled someone to the ground right next to them. Caitlyn stumbled sideways as Owen instinctively shoved her behind him. She clung to his waist, her face buried in his back. Expecting to see an army of Samurai, he was surprised to peer down at a completely non-threatening individual.

"Oh God," the security guard said. "I'm so sorry." He couldn't seem to figure out where to put his hands. He brushed off the girl's pink-and-white-striped T-shirt. Then he lamely patted her head. "I saw you running toward Tags and I just reacted. Are you okay?"

The slender girl ran her hands over her distended abdomen, her golden blond hair obscuring her face. "I think so," she said breathlessly. "Luckily I landed on my butt."

Owen's muscles stiffened. Her voice was familiar, and he had a sinking suspicion as to her identity. *Please, let me be wrong.* This was the last thing he needed when he was trying to convince Caitlyn that he wasn't a man whore. He reached down to help the young woman to her feet, and she lifted her face. He cringed. There was no mistaking those big blue eyes as she searched his face. Her bottom lip quivered.

Oh no, no, no. No crying.

"I've been looking for you," she said, rubbing her hands over her pregnant belly. "I have something I need to tell you."

CHAPTER THIRTEEN

Owen's chest constricted until he feared he'd suffocate. "Lindsey?" he croaked.

"Oh, you remember my name," Lindsey said, and she struggled to her feet. "I'm surprised."

The security guard began brushing off her butt with both hands. She gave him a look of disbelief, which halted the man's attempts to undo the damage he'd caused. What the fuck was he thinking? Tackling a pregnant woman to the ground? What an incompetent asshole.

There were a lot of women Owen had slept with whose names he'd admittedly forgotten, but Lindsey wasn't one of them. She'd been the last woman he and Kelly had pleasured together. He sometimes thought she'd somehow wrecked Kelly. It was either something Lindsey had done or that wrist cuff Owen had given him for Christmas. That's when Kelly had started pushing Owen away, so no, Owen wasn't likely to forget her, even if it had been six months since he'd last seen her.

"How do you know her?" Caitlyn asked, her arms crossed over her chest.

Uh...

Now would be a good time for a meteor to strike him dead.

"Um, well, there was snow," he said, as if that explained anything.

Lindsey looked at Caitlyn and scowled. "Excuse me, lady. I'm trying to tell Owen that I'm pregnant with his child. You need to go away. This is a private matter."

"What?" Caitlyn spat.

"What?" Owen bellowed.

"What?" the security guard sputtered.

An unseen man in the parking lot yelled, "What!" and his companions laughed at his cleverness.

"I'm pregnant," Lindsey said.

"I can see that," Owen said, his gaze glued to her abdomen. Dear God, there was no denying she was pregnant. "What the fuck does that have to do with me?"

"Is this your wife, Owen?" Caitlyn asked as she took several steps backward, shaking her head and pushing her hands uselessly out in front of her.

"No, she's not my wife."

"Yet," Lindsey said.

"She's not even my girlfriend," Owen said.

"I see." Caitlyn said with a nod. "She's just a toy that you used to get your rocks off. Kind of like me."

Owen shook his head. "No. It was different with you. I *like* you."

"You don't like *me?*" Lindsey wailed. Then she broke into gut-wrenching sobs.

Owen squeezed his eyes shut. He'd made a pregnant woman cry. A pregnant woman who might or might not be carrying *his* child. He needed to sit down. Or lie down. Or drown himself in a toilet.

"I'm out of here," Caitlyn said.

He watched her march up the bus steps and then emerge thirty seconds later with her purse and overnight bag. It was as if his feet had taken root and his mouth had been sewn shut. When Caitlyn brushed past him, he caught her arm.

"Don't go," he said. His biggest fear slammed him in the chest. Not fatherhood, though he hadn't quite processed that yet, but rejection. She was flat out rejecting him, and he couldn't fucking stand it.

Her eyes narrowed, and she gave him a look that ripped his heart out of his chest and left a gaping chasm in its place. All the warmth had left her gaze when she looked at him. "You don't really expect me to stay, do you? What are you going to do with her?"

Owen glanced over at Lindsey, who blew her nose on a tissue offered by the concerned security guard. The guy glared at Owen, his mouth tight, his expression disapproving.

Oh yeah, I'm the bad guy here.

"I'll figure something out," Owen said to Caitlyn. "It's probably not even my baby. She slept with the entire band that night. No telling who else she spread her legs for."

Caitlyn rolled her eyes and jerked her arm out of his grasp.

"Right. Men! All a bunch of fucking liars. And you're the king of them, aren't you?"

"I asked you not to call me a liar, Caitlyn," he said, his own ire rising. What did she expect him to do? He wanted her to stay, but if she trusted the word of a sobbing, pregnant, twenty-year-old groupie over his, then maybe it was best if she said goodbye now.

"Goodbye, Owen."

He flinched. Nope. It wasn't for the best at all. "I'll call you," he said, glad they'd exchanged numbers at dinner, *before* his life had exploded into chaos. "Once I get this straightened out."

She tossed a hand up over her head as she stormed away. Did that mean not to bother or that she'd talk to him later or what? He watched her retreating figure for a moment before he started after her. "Wait, Caitlyn. I'll have the limo take you home."

"Don't talk to me right now, Owen; I'll figure out how to get home on my own. I don't need your help. The weepy, pregnant girl needs your help. Go take care of her."

But he didn't want her. He wanted Caitlyn.

"Fuck my life," he said under his breath and spun on his heel so he didn't have to watch Caitlyn walk away. He was sure she'd find a way home. She was an independent, resourceful, intelligent woman. Those were the qualities he admired most in her. Didn't she realize that he didn't want a girl? He wanted a woman. And not just any woman. He wanted Caitlyn.

"Thanks for getting rid of her," Lindsey said. "She was making me feel awkward."

If she'd been a dude, he would have decked her. "I didn't get rid of her. *You* got rid of her. Now, what are you doing here and why do you think I'm the father of your baby? We used protection."

"It isn't one hundred percent foolproof. And I know you're the father because I hadn't had sex with anyone for weeks before I was with you and I haven't been with anyone since."

"What about Shade? Adam? Tex? Gabe? Ringing any bells? I wasn't the only one who had sex with you that night."

The security guard no longer looked concerned. He looked slightly scandalized and very intrigued.

Tears flooded her eyes. "But I want it to be yours."

"Shit, that doesn't make it so. Are you here by yourself? You're a long way from Idaho."

"I lost my job and my parents disowned me. The entire town

turned its back on me. I didn't have anywhere else to go."

"What about your friend, the one who was with you on the tour bus? What was her name?"

"Vanessa?"

"Yeah. I'm sure she'd help you out."

Lindsey shook her head. "She joined the army to get away from that place. She's in boot camp in South Carolina right now. Don't you think it was hard for me to come here? I wasn't even going to tell you. I was going to raise him on my own, but I don't have any money so I... I... I can't."

She burst into tears again.

Owen wrapped his arms around her and drew her into a comforting embrace. He stroked her hair and murmured, "Don't cry. We'll get this sorted out. Don't worry."

So he held the woman who might or might not be pregnant with his child, a woman he had no interest in on an emotional level, while the woman he really wanted had left, perhaps forever. Why did he have to be so fucking weak to a woman's tears?

"I know it's your baby, Owen. When I feel him move inside me, I know he's your son." Lindsey's sobs increased without provocation. "Oh God, I love our baby so much."

Every hair on Owen's body stood on end. *No.* Just no. He was in no way ready to be a father and certainly didn't want to have a baby with a woman he didn't love. "You can't know that it's mine," he said. "You slept with every guy in the band that night. What makes you so sure I'm the father?"

Her sob fest made him wish he hadn't said anything.

"You hate me, don't you? I should just kill—"

He took her by both arms and shook her. "Don't finish that sentence. Even if it isn't my baby, I'm not going to toss you out in the street. Come inside while I figure out what to do with you." He really wished Kelly's calming presence was here. Kelly would help Owen figure out what to do. As it was, Owen couldn't think. What he really wanted was to push Lindsey aside and go after Caitlyn. Not that he expected Caitlyn to ever speak to him again after what she'd just witnessed. He rubbed the center of his chest, took Lindsey by the elbow, and helped her ascend the steep steps of the tour bus. Adam, Shade, and Gabe's round of laughter died as their eyes settled on Owen with Lindsey in tow.

"What happened to your other chick?" Shade asked.

"She, uh, had to go. We have a little situation here," Owen said.

"I remember you," Gabe said to Lindsey, a smile of recognition on his lean face. "Christmas Eve. We all…" His eyes widened as they settled on her distended abdomen.

"Is she…?" Adam's dark eyebrows rose to comical peaks.

Lindsey avoided their eyes but straightened her shoulders. "I'm having Owen's baby."

"You can't be sure that it's mine," Owen insisted. "Is there anyone on this bus you didn't fuck that night?"

Her big blue eyes flooded with tears. "I know it's yours, Owen. I just know."

"Did you do her without protection?" Shade asked.

"No, I wore a condom. Did you forget?" Owen asked Shade.

"Of course I didn't forget. I might be dumb, but I'm not stupid."

"I wore a condom *and* I'm getting a vasectomy, so it's definitely not my kid," Adam said.

"You have to actually have the procedure done *before* you have unprotected sex," Shade reminded him.

Adam turned green. "Shit! That's right. But still, it's not mine."

"Well, it sure as hell isn't mine," Shade said. "I already have one!"

"That doesn't matter. Having one does not decrease your odds of having another," Gabe said.

Owen looked at Gabe. His last hope.

"I only came in her mouth," Gabe said. "Adam and Tex were taking turns and she was sucking me and… Wait… I was drunk. Don't remember everything I did. But I always wear protection. Always." Gabe blinked hard and turned his green-eyed gaze to the floor. "It's not mine."

"Was Tex wearing a condom?"

"Yes, we all used protection, Owen," Shade said, "so it must be yours. Or Kellen's."

"Kellen didn't even penetrate her. And I know I was protected. I didn't even drink that night, so I clearly remember everything I did."

"This is the worst episode of Jerry Springer ever," Adam said.

Owen laughed so he wouldn't start crying.

"You were all careful," Lindsey said. "Condoms are not one hundred percent fail proof, you know."

"Seriously?" Owen asked. She must have poked holes in their

condoms hoping to get pregnant and make herself some bank off a group of idiotic rock stars just having a good time one Christmas Eve. They'd joked about it how many times? And now it had come to fruition.

"You don't think I wanted to get pregnant, do you?" Lindsey said, emotions going from distress to anger like a switch had been flipped. "I had plans for my life! Now I'm knocked up, homeless, and considered a whore by my entire family. I wouldn't have even come to ask for help if I had a choice."

Owen looked imploringly at each member of the band and realized that even if the baby wasn't his, he was going to be the one who took care of this. Why? Because he was a sucker. Or nice. Or something.

"She's not coming on tour with us," Shade said. "Put her in a hotel until after our show tomorrow night and then we'll figure out something more permanent."

Their driver, Tex, announced his arrival on the bus with a loud belch. "Y'all ready to hit the road? Where's Kellen?"

"Kellen will meet us in Beaumont tomorrow night," Owen said. "And no, we're not quite ready to go. We have a bit of a problem."

Owen shifted his position so he wasn't blocking Lindsey from Tex's view. Tex smiled when he recognized her. "Oh hey, honey, back for some more Texas-sized lovin'?" He wriggled his eyebrows and adjusted himself in the crotch of his pants.

Lindsey burst into tears again.

"What?" Tex said. "Hey, now, you didn't complain the last time. Begged for more."

Owen cringed and shook his head, hoping to get Tex to shut his big mouth.

"Did you remember to use protection that night, Tex?" Shade asked.

"What? 'Course I did. Don't know where these loose groupie girls have been, you know? Gotta protect Big Hoss. Wouldn't want him to catch nuthin'."

Lindsey swayed sideways, and Owen grabbed her before she collapsed. "You okay?" he asked.

She leaned heavily on him, clinging to his arm for balance. "I think so. I feel a little dizzy."

And who could blame her? He felt a little dizzy too.

"What's this all about?" Tex asked. "Y'all are acting kinda

strange."

"You're going to be a father, Tex," Adam said. "Well, one of you are. It isn't mine."

"We'll figure out who the father is when the time comes," Gabe said. "Just shut up about it for now. You shouldn't get a pregnant woman emotionally upset. It can harm the baby. Owen, help her sit down."

But if she sat down, that meant she'd be staying.

"What?" Tex said. "She's pregnant?"

"Just over six months pregnant," Owen said. "Which correlates to—"

"The Christmas Eve fuck-fest!" Tex interrupted. His eyes widened as one and one made three. "I swear it isn't mine."

Lindsey flinched as if someone had slapped her. Now that his initial shock had receded a bit, Owen started to imagine what it must feel like to be her. To become pregnant while having a bit of sexy fun—which he did all the time, so he couldn't judge her for it—and not know who had fathered the child. How would it feel to be ostracized by your family for making a mistake and have no one to turn to? He wouldn't want to be in her shoes. But he could help her. Even if the baby wasn't his. And he prayed to God it wasn't his. He didn't want to be a father but at the same time, he didn't want harm to come to the child. It wasn't the baby's fault that no one wanted him.

"Just so everyone shuts the fuck up," Owen said, "I'll claim the child until we find out otherwise, okay?" Under his breath he added, "Someone around here needs to take responsibility for the places he sticks his dick."

Owen eased Lindsey onto the sofa. She immediately covered her abdomen with both arms and gazed up at him with wide eyes. She had the face of an angel with the exception of the dark circles under her eyes. Physically, she was so Kelly's type it was ridiculous. Kelly couldn't resist a woman with big blue eyes and a look of innocence about her. But Lindsey wasn't Owen's type. *Caitlyn* was Owen's type. Why did this have to happen just when he was finally ready to consider a serious relationship again? Another snafu—situation normal, all fucked up.

"You okay?" Owen asked her.

Lindsey nodded and wiped her tears on the pink-striped T-shirt at her shoulder. As much as he didn't want to be involved in this mess, Owen couldn't stand anyone to look so upset. So desperate. So alone. "Do you want something to drink? Are you hungry?"

She hesitated and then nodded again. "I haven't eaten since yesterday."

"That's not good for you or the baby," Shade said. He opened the refrigerator and peered inside. "Neither is beer and leftover sushi." He closed the refrigerator door with his foot.

Adam rattled the single remaining peanut at the bottom of the can. "Have a peanut."

Shade slapped the can out of his hand. "Get the woman some real food. She's pregnant. Have you ever dealt with a hungry pregnant woman?"

"No."

"Well, I have and it ain't pretty."

"I didn't mean to get pregnant," Lindsey whispered, gazing up at Owen imploringly, as if she'd been declared guilty and he was her executioner with a readied ax slung over one shoulder.

Owen smiled at her and smoothed her check with one finger. Her eyes drifted closed, and large tears dripped from beneath her lids. He wished she'd stop doing that already. Did she have any idea what a sucker he was? Actually, that was probably why she'd approached him first.

"I believe you," he said. "Now don't cry any more. We'll take care of you."

"Let's go get something to eat before we hit the road," Shade said. "Then we can ditch her at a hotel until after the next show. We have a few days' break before our two shows in New Orleans; we'll get this mess straightened out then."

Lindsey ducked her head, but she didn't argue. Owen wondered how she could stand being talked about as if she were a problem, not a person.

"She can come with us to Beaumont," he said. "It isn't far. And she's probably afraid to be by herself in a strange city."

She looked at him as if he were her personal savior. A warm feeling spread through his chest. He liked helping people, and he was glad they'd found a temporary solution to the situation. Now if he could figure out what he could possibly say to make things up to Caitlyn. He missed her already.

If she'd have him, he wanted her for more than one night. A lot more.

He'd probably have to do something spectacular to regain her trust, but he had no reservations about giving his all to rock her world.

"Tex," Shade said, "drive out of the city, but stop at a restaurant in some small town."

Tex was staring at Lindsey as if she had a forked tongue and horns.

"Tex!"

He jerked and forced his attention to Shade.

"Did you hear me?"

"Restaurant. Small town. Got it." He rushed to the front of the bus and disappeared into the walled compartment that obscured the driver from the rest of the vehicle.

"Thanks for being nice to me," Lindsey said. She offered Shade a small smile.

"Do you need to stop somewhere and pick up your belongings?" Gabe asked, settling onto the sofa beside her, his long legs extending for miles in front of him.

"My car broke down in Oklahoma. Everything I own that's not in this bag is there abandoned on the side of the road."

She lifted her blue-and-white-striped bag, which was about the size of a sofa cushion, onto her lap and hugged it against her.

Gabe patted her shoulder. "How did you get to Houston?"

"A nice truck driver gave me a ride. If you guys had refused to help me, I don't know what I would have done."

"Five suckers form a band..." Adam said.

Owen's phone beeped, alerting him to the arrival of a text. He pulled his phone from his pocket and smiled to see Caitlyn's name at the top of his new message.

Call me in three days, the message said, *but not before.*

There was a short pause before her next message popped on the screen. *I need to pretend to be pissed at you for at least that long.*

"Yes!" he said aloud.

I'll try not to call you before then, he texted back, *but no promises. I have a huge crush on you, beautiful lady.*

I won't answer, she typed back.

He somehow doubted that. She'd texted him less than thirty minutes after being confronted by a pretty, young groupie claiming to be pregnant with his child. Owen pressed *Call* and lifted his phone to his ear.

OLIVIA CUNNING

Caitlyn answered on the first ring. "Owen! I said not to call me yet."

"I thought you weren't going to answer."

"I didn't." He could hear the smile in her voice and the relief in his.

"Are you free Saturday? I seem to have a rare night off."

"That's only two days away, and I'm determined to completely reject you for three."

"Okay, I'll give you time to consider my offer. I'll call back in an hour."

He grinned and hung up. He glanced at Lindsey, who jerked her gaze from him when she realized he was looking at her. And what in the world was he going to do with her while he romanced his new lover? Lindsey wasn't going to move in with him, if that was her plan. There was no way in hell Caitlyn would understand that arrangement.

He seemed to have one too many women in his life at the moment and if he was forced to choose, he knew who'd be on the first Greyhound bus back to Idaho.

He didn't care what it cost him. It couldn't possibly cost him more than his heart.

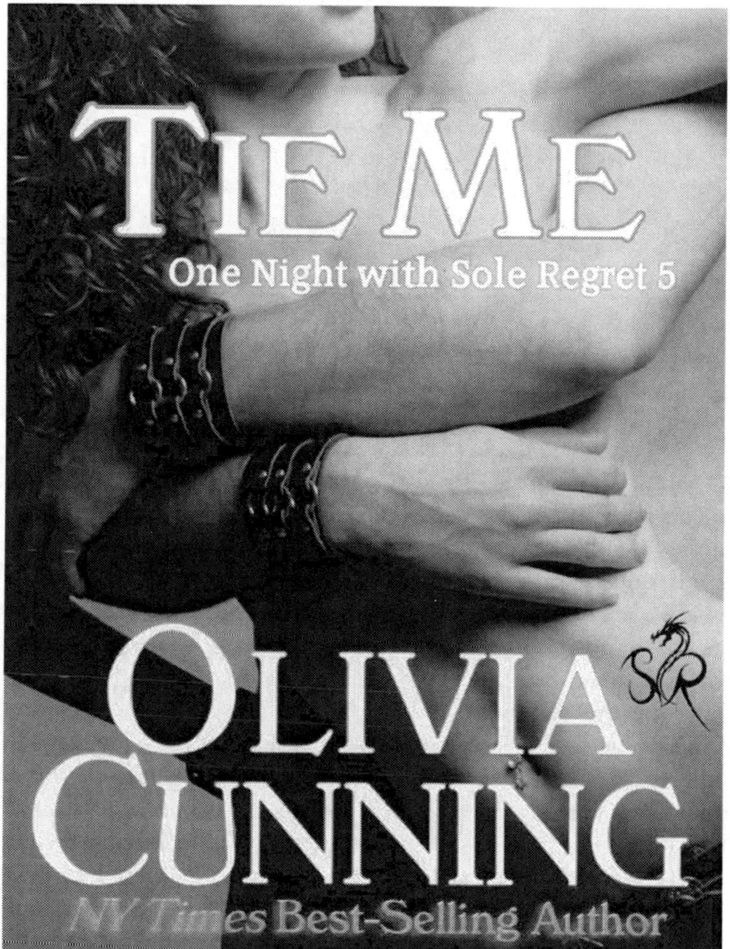
Tie Me
One Night with Sole Regret 5
Olivia Cunning
NY Times Best-Selling Author

Tie Me
One Night with Sole Regret #5

CHAPTER ONE

The night washed over Kellen, wrapping him in a cocoon of nothingness. The occasional flashes of yellow in the distant clouds would soon be overhead, and he'd have to go inside. Although a powerful storm brewed over the Gulf of Mexico, he wasn't ready to face that empty house. He'd just stay on the beach until resolve proved stronger than dread.

As the flickers above the horizon intensified, the wind picked up, whipping his long hair around his neck and face. He stared out at the endless water, fighting shivers as the damp bite of the salty sea air drew warmth from his body. His skin had become numb. He wished the Gulf breeze could numb the raw ache deep in his chest. Would the feeling that part of him was missing ever leave or was he destined to feel empty for the rest of his life? Sara's loss was still as tangible to him as it had been five years ago when he'd stared at that fucking heart rate monitor, holding his breath, waiting for just one more blip. Just one more.

Just one more, Sara. I'll do anything.

It had never come.

All the hope in the world—all the love he had to give—hadn't amounted to anything in the end.

Beneath the angry clouds, the water looked like shifting

obsidian—shiny, black glass with peaks and valleys. Random curves of white froth approached the damp sand at Kellen's feet and then receded, a ceaseless pattern of surge and withdrawal. The surf toyed with him—slowly retreating as the tide went out. Waves churned beneath the power of the storm, sometimes washing over his bare feet and drawing the sand from beneath his soles, but those waves never claimed him. Never pulled him under. Kellen stepped forward, following the slowly ebbing water, knowing eventually the sea would push him back toward the shore as the tide returned. There was little a man could count on in life, but he could count on the tides. And Kellen could count on memories of Sara haunting him.

He glanced over his shoulder at the dark house behind him. It was painted a sunny yellow, but at night it looked gray. Cheerless. Not like the happy place he'd shared with her before she'd gotten sick.

Oh, look at this house, Kellen, Sara's cheerful voice echoed through his memory. *Wouldn't it be fun to rent it for a week and pretend it's ours? I've never seen the ocean. I want to see it for the first time with you.*

Kellen had peered at the computer screen over Sara's shoulder. She'd flipped through pictures of an enormous, sunny yellow vacation rental with open, airy rooms, inviting furnishings, and sprawling decks with beach views.

You want to go see the ocean, honey. We go, he'd said. *How much is it?*

She'd clicked on a reservation link and both their jaws had dropped when the weekly rental rate had been displayed. She'd closed the laptop and looked up at him, her big blue eyes drawing him in. Like a riptide, they'd always pulled him under.

I don't need that, she'd said. *I have you.* And she'd kissed him the way only Sara could kiss. A kiss that stirred his body into a heated frenzy. A kiss that touched his heart and soul. Her kiss had always turned him inside out. That's what love did to him. That's why Kellen needed it and at the same time never wanted to find it again.

So Kellen had done what any fool in love with his perfect girl would do. He'd hocked his most prized possession—his late grandfather's vintage Les Paul guitar—and surprised Sara with a week in her dream house. She hadn't made him feel bad about giving up his guitar. She turned the sacrifice of his most cherished belonging into a week of his most cherished memories. The delight on her face as she'd stood in front of that obnoxiously large vacation rental with her hands clutched before her chest had been worth any cost.

I love you more than all the water in the ocean. All the grains of sand on the beaches. All the stars in the sky, she'd said as she'd flung herself into his waiting arms.

That's a lot of love, he'd said, burying his nose in her sweet-smelling hair and taking a moment to just feel her. She was his everything. She would be his forever. He didn't doubt it for an instant.

I love you more than that, Kellen. So much more.

Me too, honey.

Kellen swallowed hard and closed his eyes against the echoes of the past.

Memories of Sara continually tormented Kellen. They ripped his fucking heart out. Regardless, he sought things that reminded him of her. Losing her body and soul had been difficult enough. Losing those memories? He couldn't take that too. He needed reminders of her. Constant reminders. That's why, even though she was gone, he'd bought that huge fucking house on the Galveston shore as soon as he could afford it. Money had become a non-issue after Sole Regret's second album had gone platinum and they sold out concert after concert on their first headlining tour. What would Sara think of his success? Would she be proud? Jealous? She'd never understood his need to make music.

He'd have given up every penny, every cheer, every fan for one more moment with her.

That empty house was why he was here, standing on the beach. He had no business being here. He should be on the tour bus with his band and on his way to Beaumont for their show tomorrow, but he hadn't been able to stay away. Not when the band played in Houston. Not when he was so close to the place that had made Sara happy for a week in her short life. He wanted those joyous memories close. They were right on the other side of the sand dune behind him. In that house. That dark, empty dream house that had become another nightmare.

Now that he'd arrived, he couldn't force himself to go inside. He couldn't stand sipping a beer on the deck without her beside him. He couldn't stand knowing that when he climbed into bed, her pillow would be empty. He couldn't touch her, couldn't listen to her breathe. He could only lie there, staring up at the whirling ceiling fan trying to remember what they'd had for breakfast that first morning and the way the sun had danced through the golden highlights in her hair as she'd watched the sandpipers skitter through the surf. He could almost hear her laughing. Almost see her spinning in the warm breeze with her arms extended. Almost feel the water splatter against his legs as she kicked at the waves. She'd been so alive that day. So fucking *alive*. In his memory, she would always be alive.

And that was something he would never give up.

Owen had tried to convince him not to visit the house tonight. Owen's reasoning had been right—being here didn't help. It hurt. But Kellen couldn't stay away. And even though he knew it would be for the best, he just couldn't let Sara go.

It had been five years since Sara had slipped away from him. Five long years that Kellen should have been healing and learning to move on. Five fucking years of misery.

He'd hit rock bottom the day she'd been buried, and he'd thought that would be the worst of it. But he was below that now. *What's below rock bottom?*

"Hell," he whispered to the wind.

Why did you die on me, Sara? I need you beside me. Didn't I fucking tell you that enough?

Kellen wrapped his hand around the leather cuff on his left wrist. To him, it signified a lasting connection with the woman he still loved. The one time Kellen had thought he might let Sara go and move forward, Owen had given him this cuff, a Christmas gift. Its significance hadn't been a huge deal, but it was a sign—one that had insisted Kellen must remain attached to Sara for a while longer. His feelings hadn't ended when her life had. That wasn't how love worked. People who hadn't lost the love of their life didn't understand that. Owen, God love him, didn't understand that. He thought a man was supposed to move on when his soulmate died. Find some sort of replacement. Kellen didn't want to move on. He didn't want a replacement. He just wanted Sara back.

He wanted the impossible.

And he wanted Owen to stop staring at his cherished bracelet as if it were possessed with evil. Kellen wished Owen would just let him wallow in grief and stop pressuring him to move forward. But maybe if Kellen pretended, the recent tension between him and his best friend might lessen. His determination to remove Sara's cuff tonight wasn't for his own sake. It was for Owen's. He could do this for Owen. The widening rift between them was tearing Kellen apart. That woman Owen had met the night before—*Caitlyn*—had opened Kellen's eyes to a brutal reality. Kellen's weird head space—his inability to forge new intimate connections—was pushing Owen away from him. And he couldn't lose Owen too. He had no one else, no one that he'd allowed close to him. No one else he trusted. No one else who'd put up with all the weird shit he'd been going through.

Kellen took a deep breath and tugged one of the cuff's straps free of its buckle fastening.

I won't forget you, Sara. I meant it when I said forever. I'm so sorry, honey. I just can't... I can't center my life around you anymore. But I won't forget. I'll never forget.

He swallowed the lump in his throat and unfastened the second strap. The cuff fell into his right hand. His bare wrist felt foreign. Exposed. Inside he felt empty. So empty. Before he changed his mind, he flung the cuff into the sea.

You shouldn't litter, asshole. Kellen snorted as the first words Sara had ever said to him rang through his memory. He hadn't been paying attention when he'd thrown his empty water bottle on the ground instead of into the recycling bin at which he'd been aiming. She'd picked up the offending piece of trash, marched up to him, and jabbed the end of the bottle into his chest. He'd stared at her, his mouth hanging open, at a complete loss for words. He'd known in that moment that he'd found his everything. Before those eternal seconds that marked their first meeting, he hadn't believed in love, and certainly not in love at first sight, but he knew the instant his gaze touched upon Sara's innocent face that they were meant to be. She was of a different opinion. There was no love in her eyes when she'd asked, *Just how many planets do you think we have?*

Millions, he'd said. *Trillions.*

The corner of her mouth had twitched, just a little, and a bit of the fire had receded from her big blue eyes. For a second, he'd thought she found him funny.

Well, feel free to go live on one of them. I happen to be partial to the one I'm standing on.

Her long, light brown ponytail had slapped him in the arm when she'd whirled around and stomped to the recycling bin. She'd slammed the bottle into the big blue container and gone to rejoin her friends in the environment club. They'd embraced her as if she'd singlehandedly saved the planet by telling off the cool guy who'd missed the recycling bin.

Didn't matter. Kellen was hooked. He'd signed up to join her little tree-hugging group the next day, and he hadn't even been enrolled in her college. He hadn't let trivialities like rules stand in his way when he wanted something. And he'd wanted her. He still wanted her.

"I think leather is biodegradable," he said now, knowing she wouldn't approve of him throwing junk into the water. It just felt like a fitting burial for the thing, giving Sara to the sea she'd loved so briefly. He knew she'd wanted to spend more time there before she'd passed. Knew he was responsible for not fulfilling that want because he'd been terrified of letting her leave the hospital. He hoped there was an ocean in the afterlife and that she was always dancing in the waves.

Kellen rubbed his bare wrist, trying to work the feel of the confining leather from his skin. As with her memory, he couldn't seem to lessen its effect by simple effort. After a moment of kneading his wrist, something bumped into his bare foot. He looked down and caught the reflection of two metal buckles in the sand.

"Back so soon?" he said and released a sigh. He bent and retrieved the bracelet, stuffing it into the front pocket of his jeans. A circle of wetness blossomed over his hip. He'd carry the cuff a while longer, but he silently swore that he wouldn't put it back on his wrist. That wasn't going back on his promise that he would remove it tonight. Not exactly. He *had* removed it. Yet while it wasn't on his wrist, he was still very conscious of its presence in his wet pocket.

The soft tinkle of piano music competed with the roaring waves. Kellen glanced behind him, seeking the source of the sound. Most of the houses along the deserted Gulf beach were dark, but a soft yellow glow lit an open window in the house next to his. The southwestern end of Galveston Island was far removed from the tourist attractions of the city. Down here, late at night, one could pretend to be the only person for miles. Yet he didn't mind the intrusion of the poignant melody. In fact, he was pretty sure he needed something unexpected to draw him back to the present.

A strong gust of wind slapped his hair against his face. Thunder rumbled overhead.

The piano melody built—an inspiring crescendo—soaring

higher. Higher. Drawing him out of the darkness. Clearing his thoughts. Freeing his heart. Washing him with elation. If only for a few seconds.

The string of notes ceased suddenly. A loud *blam* on the keys ended the piece.

A moment later, an angry rendition of "Chopsticks" drifted from the open window and drew a smile to Kellen's lips.

A bolt of lightning split the darkness, followed by a loud crash of thunder. Kellen squinted as the rain began to fall in fat droplets. He was instantly soaked, water coursing over his face and bare chest. His hair stuck to his neck in thick chunks, but he didn't run for shelter. The melody had started again. He didn't realize he'd approached the neighboring house until he found himself standing beneath the open window, which was shielded from the deluge by a wide, overhead deck. Again the melody built. He held his breath, waiting for the next note. One more beyond the first time he'd heard the amazing piece of music. Just one more note. One more.

Blam!

"Argh!" he heard a woman's frustrated cry right before another bolt of lightning flashed and a rumble of thunder snapped him back to his senses. He turned his gaze to his beach house next door, trying to muster the courage to go inside and out of the rain. Without Sara.

"Nice night for a walk," a voice called down to him. The woman's words were muffled by the downpour and the churning surf. He looked up and saw her standing against the deck railing. He couldn't make out her features, as the light was at her back, but he could make out her curves when the wind blew her flowing white dress against her body.

A familiar and unwelcome heat stirred low in his belly.

It had been a long time since he'd been with a woman. Too damned long. And it was going to be a damned while longer if Sara's memory had a say in the matter.

CHAPTER TWO

The last thing Dawn had expected to see on the beach behind her rented vacation house was a soaking wet, shirtless hunk. She was too surprised to feel threatened by his presence. Had Neptune—lord of the sea—washed up on the shore? With that hard body and water dripping from every inch of his taut skin, the tall, muscular man sure resembled an immortal god.

"Are you lost?" she yelled.

Really, Dawn? The sea gifts you with this gorgeous, tail-less merman and you ask him if he's lost? Of course he was lost. Why else would he be standing half-naked on the beach during a thunderstorm? She doubted he was rescuing sea turtles.

He shook his head. "No," he shouted up at her. "I live next door. I was just enjoying the"—with an outstretched hand, he indicated the churning sea behind him—"view."

"Normally, I'd believe you, but the view is a little *violent* at the moment," she yelled back.

Thunder crashed overhead, and the wind blew cold rain against her. She stepped back from the railing. The storms here didn't mess around. Palm fronds slapped against tree trunks, rattling like a nest of angry snakes. The surf slammed into the beach with increasing retaliation as the storm advanced ashore.

The man cupped his hands around his mouth and yelled, "Was that you pla—"

Lightning broke the darkness, announcing another rumble of thunder. Dawn could see the man's lips were still moving, but the wind robbed her ears of his words.

"What?" she yelled.

"That melody I hear—"

She shook her head and pointed to her ear. "I can't hear what you're saying!"

He scowled and glanced around before turning and running for the wooden walkway that had been built over the sand dunes. Soon she couldn't see him at all and wondered if she'd imagined him. At least he'd found the sense to get out of the rain, even if it was rude for him to dash off without so much as a *see ya*.

Dawn shrugged and went back in the house. Perhaps that little interruption would wake up her muse. The lazy twit wasn't cooperating with her at all tonight, and Dawn had a deadline to meet. She had to find the rest of this song by morning or she was in deep, professional trouble.

She flexed her aching fingers and had just sat down at the piano when the doorbell rang.

Had Neptune come calling? Her heart rate kicked up. She was here in this strange house by herself, and she was pretty sure the nearest cop was ten miles away. What if that soaking wet hottie was a psycho? He had to be a little crazy to be standing out in a storm in the middle of the night, didn't he? That was the curse of having an overactive imagination. It served her well in her song writing, but damned if it wasn't a burden whenever something a little out of the norm came her way.

She hesitated for just a moment and then went to the door, drawing the shade up so she could look through the glass pane. The shadow of a broad-shouldered figure loomed outside. She switched on the porch light. Yep, there standing on her deck, dripping water and looking sexier than any drowned beast had a right to look, was her Neptune.

"Can I help you?" she yelled through the door. She wasn't about to unlock it. She'd seen a lot of horror movies in her day, and she knew what happened to women alone on dark, stormy nights who were stupid enough to open doors to strangers. Real killers didn't warn you of their intentions by wearing frightening masks and revving a chainsaw on your doorstep as they asked for entry.

"I'm sorry," the man said, his voice muffled by the glass door. "I hope I didn't scare you. I just wanted to know the name of the song you were playing when the storm hit. I won't trouble you further."

"The song I was playing?"

"Yeah. It really spoke to me. I was hoping you could tell me what it's called so I can look it up." A particularly loud crash of thunder caused him to flinch. "This is stupid. I'll go. Sorry for bothering you."

He took a step back, his gaze trained on the staircase that led to the ground. Like all houses along the shore, the rental was perched high on thick wooden stilts to keep it above the flood zone. Dawn reached for the lock. She no longer cared that he might be a little crazy. He'd complimented one of her songs at a time when she was feeling pretty down about her talent. She tore open the door and stepped out on the damp deck. Her feet found a puddle Neptune had left behind, and she curled her toes to avoid the cold.

"I'd tell you what the song's called, but I haven't named it yet," she said.

He paused at the top of the steps and turned. He'd been gorgeous at a distance in the dark, but up close and in the light, he stole her breath. Strong, rugged features—so masculine, it should be a crime—surrounded captivating dark eyes that captured her gaze and refused to allow her to look away.

"You haven't named it?" His voice was deep and as smooth as silk. It played on her nerve endings like a bow drawing magic from a violin.

"I haven't named it because I haven't finished it. Do you really like it?" she asked. "I was about to scrap it and start over."

"Don't do that," he said. "It's amazing. You composed it?"

"I'm trying to. It just isn't cooperating with me."

The lights flickered as another bolt of lightning snaked from the clouds to the ground. Dawn glanced at the open front door with longing. Neptune might not mind being caught in the storm, but she wasn't so hardy. The skirt of her dress whipped around her legs in the gusting wind. She hugged her arms around her body for warmth and started to creep back toward the threshold.

"Sorry for taking up your time," he said. "I'll just go… home."

Something about the way he said *home* made her heart twist.

"Do you want to come in for a cup of coffee?" she asked accidentally. Sometimes her impulsive mouth said stuff she immediately regretted. She wasn't sure if she regretted this particular outburst or not. Maybe if he accepted, she'd wish she'd gone mute. But if he refused, she knew she'd be bummed.

He bit his lip and stared at her with the darkest eyes she'd ever seen. She could drown in those eyes and wouldn't even fight sure death.

"Are you sure?" he asked.

She hesitated as they stared each other down. "Turn around first."

He lifted a slim, black eyebrow at her, but turned slowly, arms extended at his sides, to show her his back (and perfect ass). An amazing tattoo covered the left side of his back and shoulder. The black-and-gray-toned rearing stallion looked so realistic, she half expected it to kick her with one of its flailing hooves. Even the feathers braided into the horse's mane seemed to be dancing on the breeze.

When he'd completed a three-sixty and his eyes met hers again, she said, "I was just making sure you aren't hiding a giant ax back there." She didn't mention she'd enjoyed his gorgeous ass, muscular back, and the magnificent tattoo decorating the expanse of smooth, bronze skin while checking for deadly weapons. She might be a lot of things, but tacky wasn't one of them.

"I assure you," he said, "I'm not an ax murderer. Or any kind of violent criminal."

"Yeah? That's what *all* the soaking wet, ax-wielding, violent criminals say."

A corner of his sensual mouth turned up, and he traced one eyebrow with a fingertip. "I can only imagine what you must think of me, standing outside your house in a storm. I swear it was your pretty song that drew me to your window." His smile widened, softening his strong features, and every shred of Dawn's apprehension vanished. "What kind of soaking wet, ax-wielding, violent criminal would admit to that?"

She offered him a return smile and stepped into the house. "Come in. You must be freezing."

"Thank you for your concern, but I'm okay. The cold doesn't bother me."

"Then you must not be from around here," she said. She'd only been in Texas for a few months and had already acclimated to the warm climate. Sixty degrees felt cold to her these days.

"Not from Galveston, no. I'm from just outside Austin—born and raised."

"Then you must be naturally hot-blooded."

Her Neptune chuckled. "Maybe a little."

He entered the house and stepped to the side while she closed the door. Water dripped from his body and left quite a puddle on the tile floor.

"Stay there," she said. "I'll grab a towel."

"I don't usually make such an ass of myself," he said, and then chuckled. "I leave that to Owen."

"Owen?" she called as she hurried toward the hall closet, which held a stock of beach towels.

"Friend of mine."

"Is he a god too?"

"A god?"

"You're Neptune, right?" she asked. "Lord of the sea who washed up on the beach during the storm? Do you perform miracles? Because I could use a couple of them tonight."

He laughed again and took a towel from her to dry his straight, black hair. It was a bit longer than shoulder length and dripping water down the hard contours of his chest and belly. Dawn dropped a second towel on the floor to collect his puddle and forced herself not to gawk at his body.

"Sorry to disappoint you—I'm not a god. Just a man who sometimes loses his way."

"I'm trying to get you to reveal your name without asking directly," she said to his thighs as she squatted to collect more water.

"I seem to have misplaced my manners," he said, drying his chest and arms. "I'm Kellen Jamison. And you are?"

"Dawn O'Reilly." She slowly rose to stand straight and found that even though at almost six feet she towered over many guys, Kellen still had a couple inches on her.

"Your name sounds familiar." Gnawing on his fingertip, he examined her face thoroughly.

"I'm sure there are plenty of people who share my name."

His eyes lit up and he snapped his fingers. "But not any other Grammy-winning composers. You wrote the music that won for best movie theme song last year. Am I right?"

She flushed. He knew who she was? No one knew who she was. Well, a few people knew who she was, but composers didn't have fans. Pop stars had fans.

"It was actually the award for Best Instrumental Composition, but yeah, one of my works happens to accompany the rolling credits of a certain blockbuster movie. How do you know who I am?" Her suspicions were coming to a head again. Maybe he was one of those creepy stalkers who saw someone on TV and trailed them to the ends of the earth. Except no one knew she was here but her family, closest friends, and her agent. It wasn't public knowledge that she'd rented this beach house for a couple of months, hoping to spark her creativity. After her Grammy, several producers had contacted her to write music for them and like the star-struck novice that she was, she'd accepted every job that had come her way. Big mistake. Huge! Apparently her creativity was completely quashed by any sort of pressure or expectation.

"I saw you accept your award," Kellen said. "I don't remember your speech, but I remember your beautiful hair."

She touched a hand to her waist-length red curls. They were all sorts of frizzy due to the humidity in the air, but on Grammy night, the hairdresser had managed to make the loose curls smooth and elegant. "You saw me on TV?" She was pretty sure everyone in America had taken a bathroom break when she'd started thanking every person she'd ever met and even a few she hadn't.

He laughed. "I was in the audience."

She took a step backward. This was too freaky. "Are you stalking me?"

He paused and draped the towel around his shoulders, dropping his arms to his sides in a non-threatening stance. "Am I frightening you again? Dawn, you really don't have anything to worry about from me. I was there because my band was nominated for Best New Artist."

His band? Well, with all those tattoos and the leather cuff on his right wrist, he did look the part. "Did you win?"

"Nope. Some rapper won—Jizzy Wizzy Def Jam Grill Face." He made a fake gang sign and grinned wide to show off his grill—a set of straight, white teeth. "Or something like that."

She laughed, her defenses dropping again. "Wow, small world. What a bizarre coincidence to meet like this."

"I don't believe in coincidences," he said.

His intensity caused her heart to falter and butterflies to flitter through her stomach. "What do you believe in, Kellen?"

His dark brown gaze held hers for several poignant seconds. "Destiny."

The charge in the air between them had nothing to do with the electrical storm raging outside. She covered her pounding heart with her fist, wondering why she felt suddenly awake. She'd tossed open a window for air so she didn't fall asleep as she prepared for another unproductive all-nighter. When that hadn't perked her up enough to get the music flowing, she'd stepped out on the deck. Then she'd seen Kellen looking all wet and wild, and there was no way she'd be nodding off over the keys for the rest of the night. In his presence, she felt that she could run marathons and wrestle sharks. And maybe write a song.

"Can I hear your composition?" he asked. "Well, what you have written so far."

She glanced at the baby grand piano in the family room to her right. Sheets of score paper littered the floor and the piano bench. Unfortunately, most of the paper was blank or had only a few music notes scattered across the top few staffs. Crumpled wads of paper overflowed from her wastepaper basket. False start after false start. It frustrated her that music didn't come easily to her these days. Before her Grammy, piano compositions poured from her like the rain gushing from the angry clouds outside the window. Now? Writing music was like trying to wring water from a dry sponge.

She was so afraid to fail that it suffocated her.

"I…" She licked her lips, suddenly nervous. It was one thing for a complete novice to want to hear her unpublished work and a completely different animal that a Grammy-nominated musician wanted to hear it. It was true that as soon as she created a piece of music, it was copyrighted by law, but ownership was hard to prove.

"Let's have a cup of coffee first," she said. "I need a little break."

His features tightened with disappointment, but he nodded.

"Decaf?" she asked and turned toward the kitchen, which was beyond the large family room. The house's open floor plan made it easy for the piano to mock her if she let it sit silent too long. Maybe that's why she spent so much time walking the beaches. "It's pretty late for caffeine."

"I probably won't sleep tonight anyway," he said.

"Is that why you were standing out on the beach when the storm hit? Insomnia?"

"Something like that," he said.

She wondered if he was being mysterious on purpose or if it came naturally to him. She opened a cabinet and pulled out a canister of coffee. "If I'm up all night on a caffeine high, you have to stay and keep me company."

He shoulders sagged with relief. "I can do that."

"And since you're a musician, maybe you can help me with my writer's block."

He smiled, and the temperature in the room must have increased twenty degrees because even though she kept the thermostat at a cool seventy-two, Dawn was suddenly sweltering.

"I'd be happy to help," he said in that low, smooth voice that did distracting things to her girly bits. "Or try to. Were you B.O.I?"

"B-O-I?"

"Born on Island? I guess not, if you don't know the meaning."

She shook her head. "Just renting for the summer. I came here to get away from the chaos of the city and to seek inspiration." Or hide. She was totally trying to hide from impending failure. Unfortunately, it had followed her to Galveston.

"You find inspiration on the shore?"

"The voice of the sea speaks to the soul," she said, trying not to be obvious about checking out his flexing biceps as he dried his face and she filled the coffee carafe in the sink. "Chopin said that." When he didn't respond, she added, "The wildly talented nineteenth-century Polish composer and pianist."

"Yes, I know who Chopin is. I might be a metal guitarist, but that doesn't mean I don't respect the classics."

A metal guitarist? She and Kellen were about as far apart on the musical spectrum as possible. There was no way in hell he'd be able to help her with her writer's block. She wrote classical compositions, not wailing noise. "Oh," she said. "Well, I'm a huge fan. Of Chopin's. His nocturnes." She shuddered in bliss at the thought of his stirring piano pieces.

Kellen chuckled. "So you're not impressed by my fiddling with guitar strings, I take it?"

"I'm sure I'd be very impressed, but I do sort of have a *thing* for the piano."

Once Dawn had the coffee percolating, she turned toward Kellen. He looked incredibly uncomfortable in those sopping wet jeans.

"You should get out of those clothes," she said.

A crooked grin graced his handsome features. "Are you coming on to me, Miss O'Reilly? It is *Miss* O'Reilly, isn't it?"

"Yes, it's *Miss* O'Reilly, but no, I wasn't coming on to you." Though she probably should have been. "You just look wet. I can find you something to wear."

His gaze settled on the flowing white skirt of her loose dress, and he chuckled. "I suppose the jokes I make about wearing skirts have finally caught up with me."

"You wear skirts?" It went against the laws of nature for a man as unquestionably virile as Kellen Jamison to wear a skirt. A kilt was an entirely different matter, of course. She could see him in a kilt. She had Scottish blood in her heritage but Kellen appeared to be of Native American ancestry, and she'd much rather see him in a pair of buckskin breeches. Or skintight leather. Leather would work.

"Not really. It's a lame joke I share with one of my bandmates when we're on stage."

"Owen?"

His jaw dropped. "How did you know?"

"It's the only name you've mentioned."

"Right."

"I have some boxer shorts you can borrow." She couldn't take her eyes off his wet jeans. His crotch specifically. What was wrong with her? She was offending herself with her lewd behavior. Maybe getting him out of those wet clothes would get her mind out of his pants.

"Are they yours?"

She nodded, still staring south. "I usually sleep in them."

"You wear men's underwear and you criticize me for wearing skirts?"

She glanced up to meet his eyes. "In case you haven't been paying attention, there is a bit of a double standard in this country."

"And sometimes there's a good reason for that. I'd look like a complete tool in a skirt, but you'd look sexy in men's clothes. A pair of boxers and nothing else." His gaze rested on her chest, and she resisted the urge to cross her arms over her breasts. "Or in a man's long-sleeve dress shirt and… nothing else." His stare shifted to her legs, which were completely covered by her maxi skirt, but felt hopelessly bare. And suddenly hot. Why were her *legs* hot? Feeling foolish, she fanned them with her skirt.

"Are you picturing me naked?" she asked.

He shook his head. "Only half-naked."

She nibbled on her lip and allowed herself to gawk at him without pretending she wasn't. "I don't have to picture you half-naked. You already are."

"Sorry to spoil your fun." His gaze flicked up to meet hers, and her breath caught. "You could always picture the other half of me naked."

She grinned, her gaze dropping to his jeans. "I already am." It felt good to flirt. She'd had little time for men recently but looming deadline or not, she was willing to make a little time for this one.

Kellen cleared his throat and stared at the floor. "I will take you up on those boxers," he said. "I'm a bit chilled and dealing with some shrinkage issues down below. I wouldn't want to disappoint your imagination."

"My imagination is definitely not disappointed." If he lost those jeans, she was certain her reality wouldn't be disappointed either.

She fanned her face with one hand. Damn, what was wrong with the air conditioning in this house?

"I'll be right back," she said and dashed upstairs to the master bedroom to find him a pair of shorts. She riffled through a drawer and took out the manliest-looking pair of plaid boxers she owned— she did have an unusual fondness for plaid—and returned to the kitchen to find Kellen gazing into space. His knockout smile had vanished, replaced with a forlorn daze. He was fiddling with something in the front pocket of his jeans, and she was pretty sure he wasn't trying to remedy his shrinkage issues.

"I hope they fit," she said. Actually, she hoped they were skintight and aided her imagination.

He jerked his head and settled his gaze on her. His smile returned.

"Thanks," he said, accepting the thin pair of shorts she held in his direction.

"There are towels in the cabinet over the toilet," she said and nodded toward the half bathroom next to the stairs.

"Thanks," he said again and hurried to the bathroom. Her appreciative gaze settled on his muscular back as he walked away. She did have a thing for a sexy male back and they didn't get much sexier than Kellen's. Would he let her caress the lines of that tattoo? Maybe he would *if* she found the courage to make a move on him instead of staring after him as he disappeared into the bathroom.

That was a big if.

"You're too much of a chicken to make the first move," she chastised herself under her breath. But she hoped he wasn't.

CHAPTER THREE

Kellen entered the bathroom and closed the door behind him. What the fuck was he doing flirting with a woman he'd just met, promising his libido something he had no intension of delivering? He'd let his guard down with this one. He couldn't let it happen again.

He caught his reflection in the mirror over the sink and winced. Lord, no wonder Dawn had thought he was up to no good when she'd seen him on the beach. He looked like some pirate who jumped ship and swam ashore to avoid punishment for stealing the booty.

He had no plans to take any booty tonight, even if Dawn placed hers directly into his hands. And if he kept coming on to her the way he had been since she invited him into the house, he was pretty sure she would be prepared to do exactly that.

He struggled out of his wet jeans, leaving another puddle on Dawn's floor, and found a towel to dry his hair, legs, and the rest of his body, taking note of a certain stiffness he was not prepared to deal with. Apparently he'd been lying about his shrinkage issue. How was he going to pull off a pair of thin boxer shorts with a semi?

He tugged the boxers up his thighs and hips, then peered down at his crotch and groaned at the spectacle he was making of himself.

"Down, boy," he said and tucked his far too sensitive cock down the leg of the shorts. "I know she's hot, but you can't have her."

He pressed on the obvious bulge in his shorts. *Her* shorts, he reminded himself. Did she wear panties under them or had these recently been against her bare flesh? What did the hidden treasure between her thighs smell like? Taste like? His mouth watered, and he swallowed before giving himself a mental shake.

Snap out of it, stupid.

Great. Now his bulge was a full-blown, burgundy-and-blue-plaid tent.

Shit.

Maybe he should put his jeans back on and tell her the boxers were too small. They were definitely form-fitting, and his condition made them downright uncomfortable. Or maybe he should jerk one out real quick so he could think about something other than fucking a sensual redhead into a coma. Or maybe he should wrap Sara's wrist cuff around his misbehaving cock as a reminder that when he'd committed to her, he'd promised to never have sex with another woman. Ever. Or maybe his big head should remind his smaller head who was in charge here.

Who *was* in charge here?

Kellen settled for imagining the pair of drunk girls who'd been trying to get him into bed the night before. It took a minute, but his remembered disinterest did the trick on his libido. Mostly. It was only after he had his wayward cock somewhat under control that he realized the borrowed shorts didn't have a pocket to hold his recently removed wrist cuff.

Double shit.

He retrieved the leather band from his jeans and stared down at it. The urge to return it to his wrist overwhelmed him. He still had a cuff on his other wrist, but it wasn't a reminder of Sara, so it didn't count. He'd bought that one at the mall when he was sixteen and thought it made him cool. It held no emotional significance, was just an ordinary scrap of leather. But the one he'd removed earlier possessed the ability to yank his head out of the clouds and return his feet firmly to the ground.

He hoped.

Perhaps the best thing to do was leave Dawn's house as soon as possible. Why'd he come here anyway?

Dawn's song. The melody played through his head, and he smiled. That song possessed a power all its own.

He wanted to hear it again. Wanted to watch her play it for him. For as jumbled and confused as Kellen's thoughts were now, her song had given him a moment of peace and clarity. Even if it was a temporary condition, he wanted those feelings again. He needed them. Even more than he needed Sara's reminder on his wrist.

"Coffee's ready," Dawn called. "How do you take it?"

Jeez, the bathroom door was thin.

Triple shit.

Had she heard him talking to himself about her hotness?

"Black!" he called, glad he'd decided against jerking one out. What if she'd heard him gasping and moaning through the door? She already suspected him of being a dangerous criminal. If she'd discovered him masturbating in her spotlessly clean bathroom, she'd have pegged him as a depraved pervert as well.

Kellen tugged a brush through his hair until it lay flat, resting against his shoulders. He hoped she didn't mind sharing such a personal item as a hairbrush with him. Maybe it wasn't hers and had come with the house. Kellen checked to make sure he wasn't sporting wood again, shoved the wrist cuff into his jeans pocket, and retrieved his wet towel from the floor. He gave the cuff one last squeeze, took a deep, calming breath, and then opened the door.

The bathroom faced the kitchen, so there was no missing her. Dawn stood leaning back against the counter, sipping from a cream-colored coffee cup. There was something intensely erotic about the way she encircled the cup with both hands and brought it to her mouth as she watched him over the rim. Those hypnotic hazel eyes. All that thick red hair. That loose, white dress. Her bare feet with ten perfectly manicured hot-pink toenails peeking from beneath the hem of her long skirt. Everything about her was erotic, and she wasn't even trying. His cock throbbed in appreciation of her femininity.

Should have jerked one out after all.

Walking awkwardly, Kellen clutched his laundry to his waist, hoping to hide what was going on in his shorts.

Her shorts.

Fuck! Stop thinking like that, moron. You're going to rip her shorts in half if you get any harder. How are you going to explain that to her?

Excuse me, Dawn. I seem to have damaged your shorts with my raging hard-on. Do you have something a bit hardier I could wear? Perhaps something made of thick leather or stainless steel.

"Do you want me to throw your jeans in the dryer?" she asked.

"No thanks." He didn't want her to discover the wrist cuff hidden in his pocket, and he needed the jeans to shield his arousal.

Dawn turned and lifted a red cup from the counter. She walked toward him and offered him the coffee. Squashing his jeans and towel against his belly with one hand, Kellen extended his free hand to accept the cup.

"Thanks," he said. Damn, his voice sounded all gruff and slightly breathless. Was she aware of the not-so-little problem going on behind a pair of wadded-up jeans and a damp towel? Did she have any idea how much he wanted to lift her up on the counter and fuck her until he couldn't think straight enough to feel guilty about breaking his vow to Sara?

Dawn stared into his eyes and brushed her fingers over his in a slow, sensual caress as she handed off the cup. She wasn't making his devotion to abstinence easy, that was for sure.

A spattering of freckles graced the bridge of her nose, and thick, dark eyelashes made the green flecks in her hazel eyes stand out. He tried not to look at her pouty lips and wonder what she tasted like. Did she enjoy soft, gentle kisses or did she prefer the deep, plundering assault on her mouth that he craved? He wanted to sink his hands into all those thick, red curls, tilt her head back and... and...

Small talk! He needed to make small talk.

"So where are you from?" he asked.

She blinked and took a startled breath. Was she thinking along the same lines he was? He really needed her to be a frigid bitch at the moment, but doubted she was the type. The vibe she gave off was warm and inviting. He couldn't remember the last timed he'd wanted to be invited into a woman's warmth, all slick and hot and snug. His cock throbbed with interest.

Oh, for fuck's sake, woman. Say something. I can't be thinking like this.

"Originally or lately?" she asked.

"Both." *Please stop looking at me like that with those exotic cat-like eyes.* Kellen was used to women showing their interest in him. What he was not used to was losing control of his convictions and feeling anything in reciprocation.

"I was born in Pennsylvania, just outside Philadelphia. I've been in Los Angeles for several years now."

"Do you like it there?"

She shrugged and took another sip of her coffee. "It's not as humid as it is here. And then there is Hollywood."

"Ah, so that's why you moved out there."

"The job market for classical music composers is fairly small."

He swallowed a gulp of coffee. "Did you always want to write music for movies?"

She grinned at him. "In my rebellious years, I wrote music for video games."

"You had rebellious years?"

She lifted her eyebrows at him, which had him picturing all sorts of naughty activities she probably had not been involved in during her rebellious years, but damn if he didn't want to rebel with her now.

"Don't we all?" she asked. "At least until we grow up."

"Wait. Do you mean we're supposed to outgrow that?"

"Are you still rebelling, Kellen?"

He chuckled. "Some would like to think that, but no, I don't have anything to rebel against these days." He took another drink of his coffee and then nodded toward his cup. "This is really good," he said.

"If you think that's good, you should try my French toast."

His stomach growled in agreement. He'd had dinner before the show with the rest of the band—and in a bizarre twist of fate, with Owen's new love interest, Caitlyn—but that had been many hours and whole lot of physical activity and emotional turmoil ago. Kellen covered his noisy belly and managed to drop his fabric cock shield in the process. Luckily, their inane conversation had reduced his tent to a slightly enthusiastic bulge.

Dawn's gaze slid down his torso, and he tensed, trying to think of more small talk, but he'd pretty much lost his mental capacities.

When she drew her gaze up his body to meet his eyes again, she smiled and said, "Sounds as if your stomach is in agreement."

Had she noticed he was filling out her shorts more than he should have been?

She headed for the fridge, which meant he wouldn't be hearing her song again anytime soon. It also meant that they would be spending more time in each other's company, which, as far as his quickly failing defenses were concerned, was a bad idea.

"You don't have to do that," he said. "I can make myself a sandwich when I go home." Which was an outright lie because there wasn't a scrap of food in Sara's house. He'd be lucky if he found a year-old granola bar in the pantry.

"I want to cook for you," she said. "I'm trying to dazzle you with my impressive skills."

Done.

So he drank coffee at the breakfast bar while she whipped up a batch of French toast.

"Tell me about your band," she said as she used a whisk to beat an egg, milk, and vanilla in a bowl.

"Where should I start?"

"At the beginning."

"It's a long story," he warned.

"Good, because that caffeine high I warned you about is starting to kick in."

"So you want my long, boring band story to lull you to sleep?" he teased, feeling a bit more relaxed now that there was a wide counter between them. He was horny as hell, but he didn't think his cock would be able to hammer its way through several inches of wood and granite. When Dawn added butter to the warming pan and licked a stray smear from her finger, he decided he shouldn't bet on that certainty.

"No, I want you to entertain me." Her completely innocent comment had Kellen imagining not-so-innocent ways of entertaining her.

What the hell? He hadn't reacted this way to a pretty girl since his lust-fueled teenage years. Was this what it felt like to be Owen? No wonder he was always begging to try out Tony's newest sex club. This perpetual state of arousal was downright distracting.

"Um." What had they been talking about? *His band. Right.* "We've been together as a unit for about seven years now."

"What do you call yourselves?"

"Sole Regret."

Her eyes lit up, and a broad smile spread across her face. "That sounds familiar," she said. "Maybe I do remember the announcement of your nomination at the Grammy's."

"Was it accompanied by a really long air-horn blast?"

She laughed. "That was you?"

Kellen shook his head. "Owen. He isn't into proper etiquette at award shows. He also yelled, 'You suck!' during the winner's acceptance speech."

Dawn laughed. "I remember that. Didn't they ask him to leave?"

"We all had to leave. Owen's a bit loud and outspoken when he's been drinking, and we'd started celebrating our sure-win the night before."

"Oh," she said, her lips in a beguiling pout. "He must have been terribly disappointed."

She sliced a piece of bread from a loaf, soaked it in the egg mixture, and then carefully laid it in the sizzling butter.

"You wouldn't know what that was like," Kellen said.

She glanced up. "Why do you think that?

"Well, because you *won* your Grammy."

"But I didn't win the World International or the Peabody Mason Piano Competitions, did I?"

"Never heard of either of those."

"I also didn't win—"

"Dawn, you have a fucking Grammy. I've heard of that one. Celebrate your victories."

She gaped at him, her spatula gripped tightly in one fist. For a second, he thought she was going to smack him with it.

"I don't like to lose," she said.

Fire sparked in her voice, in her face. The rapid rise of her passion caused certain body parts in the room to rise. Again.

"Name one person who likes to lose," he said.

She sucked in a little gasp and blinked at him. He suspected that no one dared to call her out on anything, which inspired the urge to find all her buttons and push them repeatedly, see just how brightly her fire could burn.

"But I *really* don't like to lose. It's almost pathological."

He appraised her closely for a moment, looking beyond the sexual creature that had his full attention to the tense, slightly uptight, a-bit-too-proper woman he'd overlooked until now, what with the hormones swirling through his body. She seemed to cling to control a bit too tightly. He'd love to bind her and see how she responded to giving up complete control. To him.

"There's only one way to ensure you never lose," he said.

She flipped over a perfectly browned piece of French toast with her spatula. "What's that?"

"Don't compete."

"Well, that's not going to happen. I have a competitive streak a mile wide. I have to know if…"

She met his eyes, and the fire in them surged. Would rendering her defenseless with ropes cause that fire to burn brighter, dampen it, or extinguish it completely? He predicted she'd ignite under his meticulous attention as he included her body in one of his creations—where bondage became art. And he doubted she'd be the only one to ignite if he played with that particular fire. He took a deep breath. He needed to find focus, which was entirely impossible with her looking all defiant and tense. He wanted to draw both the defiance and the tension from her body and teach her how to relax.

"You have to know if you're the best," he completed her sentence.

She used her spatula to eject a perfect piece of French toast from the skillet onto a plate and then added a raw slice to the pan. It sizzled and hissed. Kellen inhaled the scent of vanilla and warmed bread. His mouth watered.

"I don't need to be the best at everything," she said, her attention on her task. "Just at what I'm most passionate about."

"Would that be composing or playing piano?"

"Both," she said.

"And does it make you happy to pursue perfection?"

Her gaze darted upward to find his.

He hid a grin. Another of her buttons found and pressed.

"That's a very personal question," she said, her voice a bit louder than necessary. "And how did we end up talking about me? I asked you about your band."

"We're talking about you because you're more interesting than I am," he said.

"I guarantee that I'm not."

"We'll see." He chuckled. "I started playing guitar when my grandfather caught me fooling around with the vintage Les Paul that he'd won in a bet. I snapped one of the strings and thought he was going to skin me alive, but instead he punished me by forcing me to take lessons from a friend of his who played in a local band. I was thirteen. That's the same year I met Sole Regret's bassist, Owen. He wasn't into music much. He liked to follow me to my lessons and watch, but he didn't want to learn to play himself. Not until a couple years later when the girls started hanging around me because I was *cool*. So Owen learned to play in an attempt to attract girls. He's very shallow that way." Kellen winked at her.

"So you didn't learn to play in order to attract girls?"

"Music is my escape," he said. "I quickly became addicted to producing sound. It's like a drug I can't get enough of."

He met her eyes and they gazed at each other. "I feel the same way about the piano," she said. "I just would have called it a compulsion instead of an addiction."

Sara had never understood this part of him. She'd thought of music as something that took him away from her. She seemed to think she was competing against music for his affection, not that it

TIE ME – One Night with Sole Regret #5

helped make him the man she loved. It was nice to meet a woman who understood how vital music could be to a person.

Dawn flipped a second piece of French toast onto a plate before adding a third to the pan. While it cooked, she set a tub of butter, a bottle of maple syrup, and his plate before him. He inhaled deeply.

"This smells heavenly."

"My grandmother's recipe."

Kellen's first bite had his eyes rolling into the back of his head in delight. "This is amazing. What's the secret?"

"Vanilla," she said. "And day-old, fresh-baked bread."

"Lucky I happened along the day after your trip to the bakery."

Her cheeks went pink, and she paid extra close attention to the toast sizzling in the pan.

Had he discovered another button? He wasn't sure where to push. "Is there a bakery nearby?"

She shook her head. "I baked it," she said. "Baking is a huge stress reliever for me."

"Lucky me," he said. "What are you stressed out about?"

She hesitated for a long moment and then let out a sigh. "Can you keep a secret?"

"Yeah."

"I'm supposed to turn in a completed composition tomorrow," she said. "I was commissioned for a piece to be used as the main theme in some feel-good summer blockbuster. I've been working on it for months and no matter how hard I try, I can't get it right."

"Maybe that's your problem," he said, trying to remember his manners and not talk with his mouth full, but the French toast was so delicious that he couldn't stop shoveling it in.

"My *problem*?"

Oh, another button? Poke. Poke. Poke.

"One of many, I'm sure," he said.

She leveled him with a heated glare, and he warmed from the inside out. He hadn't even realized he'd been cold.

"Maybe you're just trying too hard," he said. "Sometimes the best inspiration hits when you aren't paying attention. Let your subconscious write the music. It's purer that way."

"And what would you know about writing music?" she said, flipping her piece of French toast to an empty plate. She turned off the burner and reached for the tub of butter. He couldn't resist moving it out of her reach.

She closed her eyes and took a deep breath. Why did he get the impression that she was counting backward from a hundred so she didn't slap the shit out of him with her spatula?

"I've written a few songs," he said. "The band's lead guitarist, Adam, is our main composer, but he allows the rest of us to come up with a note or two."

"What do you know about writing *piano* music?"

"Absolutely nothing," he admitted.

She collected her plate and moved around the counter to sit beside him.

"I'm sorry I'm so testy tonight," she said. "I'm under a lot of pressure. I just... I don't want to fail at my own dream."

"You're not failing," he said. "You're just a little stuck. It happens to everyone."

She shook her head as she slathered butter on her French toast. "It doesn't happen to me. I can't permit it to happen to me."

"Reality check, Dawn. It already has."

"I can still finish the composition tonight," she said.

"And if you can't?"

Her lower lip trembled and she refused to meet his eyes, even though he was staring her down like a panther watching a tender young deer wander unknowingly beneath his tree.

"I'm not allowed to fail," she said. "Absolutely not allowed."

Allowed? Why would she say it that way? He placed a comforting hand at the base of her spine and she jerked so hard, she nearly launched herself straight off the stool.

"I can't promise you anything, but I will help, if I can," he said. "Relax, okay?"

"Easy for you to say," she mumbled under her breath.

He removed his hand from her back, cursing himself for touching her as he could still feel the tension in her muscles against his palm. She picked at her French toast and after a moment of appearing defeated, straightened her shoulders and turned slightly to look at him.

"So you and your friend Owen became guitarists to seduce naive young women. What about the rest of your band? Did they also suffer from an inability to pick up girls based on their looks and personality alone?"

He sighed at her obvious subject change. "Owen didn't really like guitar, so he switched to bass, which is the rock-band position least likely to get you laid." Owen, however, had stopped having that problem soon after they graduated high school. "We're not as shallow as I make us out to be."

"Why didn't Owen like guitar?"

"I'm not sure he was being completely truthful. I think he claimed that he didn't like the guitar so he wouldn't steal my thunder. He's actually a good guitarist, but he has this way of putting everyone before himself. Especially me."

"So he didn't want to beat you at your own game."

"Something like that."

"How many are in your band?"

"Five. Jacob is the lead singer, and Adam plays lead guitar. They've been friends since they were young. They're a couple years older than Owen and me. They'd started up a band with a drummer named Quint and were looking for a bassist to make up the fourth member of the group, which was called Desperation Normal. When Owen answered their ad on a bulletin board at a bar in Austin and agreed to join as their bassist, they had no intention of including me; they weren't looking for a second guitarist. But Owen has a way of getting what he wants, and he refused to be a part of anything that didn't include me, so they let me play along. Turns out two guitarists can be better than one. I couldn't outplay Adam Taylor as a soloist, so I switched to rhythm guitar and let him have the limelight."

"Are you satisfied playing rhythm guitar?"

"Yeah. I guess. I'm satisfied being a part of Sole Regret." He never really thought much about why Adam played lead and he continued playing rhythm. It just worked best that way. "And then Quint met a girl, got married, and left the band. And Jacob recruited our current drummer, Gabe. Well, more like kidnapped him." Kellen chuckled at those early weeks with Gabe and his constant whining about not having enough time to study for his quantum physics midterm. Perhaps the world had missed out on a fantastic engineer when Gabriel Banner had eventually dropped out of school after struggling to do everything for a semester—school, work, the band, and his girlfriend at the time. Missed out on an engineer, but gained one of the most skilled drummers to ever pound the skins. "We changed our name to Sole Regret a couple of weeks after the band was fully formed."

"Why do you regret your souls?" she asked.

"Huh?" He looked up from his plate, which had somehow

become empty while he'd been running off at the mouth.

"Your band's name is Soul Regret. Why do you regret your soul?"

"*Sole* Regret. Sole meaning one or single."

"Oh, *one* regret." Dawn speared the final bite of her French toast. "You only have one?"

"Well, at the time. I was young." He smiled sadly. He had dozens of regrets now, all centering around the things he should have done with Sara. He even regretted that he'd respected her too much to grope her early in their relationship. Maybe if he'd given in to those urges, he might have found the lump in her breast in time. Maybe her treatments would have been more effective. Maybe they could have saved her. Was it strange to regret not being after only one thing with the love of your life? Maybe, but he couldn't help it.

"Kellen?" Dawn said after she'd swallowed her final bite.

"Yeah."

"Why don't you want to go home?"

He hesitated. How had she managed to pick up on that? "What do you mean?"

"Earlier when you said you would leave me alone and go home, you didn't sound like you wanted to go."

He shrugged. "There's nothing there for me anymore."

"But there's something for you here?"

He dabbed his finger into a puddle of syrup and brought it to his tongue. "Yeah," he said. "There's you."

Her eyes widened. "Oh."

"And your song," he added, before she got the wrong idea. "Are you going to play for me now? You've already spoiled my hungry belly with your fantastic French toast; why not treat my ears to something just as sweet?"

He winked at her and after a moment, she nodded.

"I think I'm ready," she said. "Just don't expect a miracle."

"I won't." Kellen had given up on miracles five years ago.

CHAPTER FOUR

Dawn placed her hands on the keys and closed her eyes. The first notes of the piece came easily, and her fingers found them in natural succession. Music poured from every particle of her being as she gave herself over to the melody.

As the first crescendo built, her muscles began to tense tighter and tighter until she reached the dam beyond which she could not create. She froze. Her hands stilled. Her eyelids clenched tight. Anxiety churned in the pit of her stomach.

The piano began to play of its own accord. The notes that sounded weren't the correct ones—Dawn instinctively knew when the notes were right—but it wasn't silence. Thank God, it wasn't silence. Her eyes popped open, and she watched the long-fingered masculine hands move across the black and ivory keys. They went still suddenly, and she looked up at Kellen, wondering why he'd stopped.

"Well, that sounded better in my head than in reality," he said with a wince. "Did I offend you by messing with your song?"

She supposed gawking at him like an idiot might make him think that she was offended, but she wasn't. Surprised, yes. Grateful the sea had seen fit to wash him into her life, yes. Offended? Never.

"That wasn't quite right," she said.

"It was horrendous," he said. "I follow your masterpiece with that load of crap? You must think I'm a talentless hack."

She shook her head and touched the back of his hand with her fingertips. Sparks danced along her nerve endings, and her belly fluttered with nerves or excitement or just plain silliness. When he drew his hand away and rested it on his thigh beneath the keyboard, she could have cried.

It sucked to be attracted to a man who held no reciprocating interest.

"Play it again," he said. "I won't interrupt this time, I promise."

"You didn't interrupt. I always freeze at that exact spot. I'm afraid I'll never get past it."

"So instead of stopping, just play something—any crap that comes out—until the right notes finally find you."

She laughed. "I don't know how to play crap."

"Lucky you," he said, his white smile flashing in his strong, handsome face. She wanted to prop her chin up on her hand and stare at him dreamily. She needed to get a grip.

"Ninety percent of my work is crap," he continued. "Another nine percent is mediocre, and then there are those rare gems that are actually useable."

"It's not that I can't play crap. I'm just afraid to." She diverted her gaze to the keyboard. "I'm sort of a perfectionist." And it wasn't a trait she'd been born with. Her mother had ensured she'd paid for every mistake until the thought of making one crippled her. "What you played wasn't bad," she said.

"Liar," he said, still grinning, "but it was a little better than—"

Blam! His hands slammed on the keyboard as hers had so many times over the past week.

"Just a little better than—" She hit the keys with her fist. *Blam!*

"Shit, even your"—*Blam!*—"sounds better than mine does."

"Maybe you should just give up on music writing."

"Ouch! My ego isn't made of steel, you know?"

"I'm just teasing." Couldn't he tell? If not, she was sorry to have damaged his pride. "Let's try it again. Maybe something that comes out of you will complement something inside of me."

He groaned. "Don't say things like that. I've been abstinent so long, I'm likely to take it the wrong way."

Why would he ever so selfishly resort to abstinence? Dawn wondered if he'd like to break that dry spell, because she had her own abstinence thing going on, not that she'd planned it that way, and maybe they could end the drought together. Of course, for a gorgeous, virile man like Kellen, perhaps a week was a long stint of abstinence.

"Sorry," he said. "I shouldn't have brought that up. Please, continue."

But he had brought it up, so she had to ask. "Why have you been abstinent? Surely you have hundreds of women standing in line to get you into bed." Having just met him, she might be at the end of the line, but she was definitely in it.

"But not the one who matters."

She caught the anguish in his expression before he turned his face away and began to play a completely disjointed string of notes.

She covered his hand with hers to stop his playing.

"Are you being intentionally mysterious? Or does driving me insane with curiosity come naturally to you?"

"It comes naturally."

They shared a laugh, and Kellen reached for one of her score sheets. He propped it on the stand above the fall board. Reading the notes scattered along the staff, he played them slowly, but correctly. She fought the urge to play over him, to get the tempo up to where it belonged. She didn't know why, but it bothered her beyond reason when anyone took liberties with her music and didn't play it exactly as she envisioned it.

When the song shifted to a lower register, his arm brushed hers and his fingers went still.

She glanced at him to find him sitting with his eyes closed.

"I should go," he said.

"Why? I don't want you to go."

"Because I'm incredibly attracted to you, and I don't think I'm quite ready to act on it."

Well, in that case, there was no way she was letting him leave.

CHAPTER FIVE

He wasn't sure why Dawn had him in knots. She hadn't been overly flirtatious. She looked nothing like Sara. Dawn had gorgeous, deep red hair, hazel eyes flecked with green, and adorable freckles on her long, straight nose. Her lips were thinner than Sara's had been. She was tall, long limbed and fine boned. She didn't smell like Sara or sound like her or say things that reminded him of phrases Sara used to say. Dawn was nothing like Sara. Kellen couldn't remember the last time he'd looked at any woman and not been reminded of Sara at all. He couldn't remember, because it had never happened. He didn't know if he should feel relieved or guilty or sad. What he mostly felt was aroused.

"You're attracted to me?" Dawn asked, her expressive hazel eyes wide. "Because you're doing a good job of hiding it. Why do you draw away when I touch you? You make me feel like I have cooties."

"I don't want to be attracted to you."

"Are you married? Engaged?"

"I wish I were." He might as well just tell her what she was up against. "Are you attracted to me too?" He thought she was, but before he started saying things to scare her away and remind himself of the emptiness inside, he needed to make sure the revelation was worth the pain.

"Yeah, I am definitely attracted to you," she said. "I can't imagine there's a woman on the planet who wouldn't be."

He rolled his eyes. He didn't need her flattery. He just needed her to shoot straight with him.

"The woman I planned to marry died, so technically I'm not attached. But spiritually and emotionally I'm in a relationship that doesn't exist."

She stared at him, her eyes searching his until he had to look away. "Well, that sucks," she said. "Kind of hard for me to compete with someone who can do no wrong."

Not the empathy and sympathy to which he was accustomed. Dawn's eyes were dry and she wasn't doing that annoying pat his hand and avoid his gaze thing that so many people did when he told them about Sara.

"Okay," she said, turning back to her keyboard. "I'm going to start the song again and when I get to my stuck spot, I'd like you to play whatever occurs to you."

That was it? She wasn't going to hound him with questions and overwhelm him with so many memories of Sara that he was forced to retreat inside himself again? She wasn't going to give him a reason to push her away? He didn't know how to respond.

She started playing her unfinished composition and as before, the collection of notes lifted his spirit, made him yearn for the song to never end. With each successive note he felt happier, more alive, more connected to something than he had in years. When Dawn reached her final note, Kellen prepared to take over, but three additional notes poured from her fingers. She straightened on the bench beside him and played the three notes again. And again. Then she sang them in the most beautiful falsetto he had ever heard and played them yet again.

She released a long breath, the tension draining from her body. "Three is better than none."

"And better than crap."

She beamed and gave him a hasty hug. "I think my muse is intimidated by your crap, Kellen."

He fought the urge to wrap his arms around her and hold her close. He still wasn't sure how he felt about his attraction to her. It felt different than when he got sexually excited when a woman made unwanted advances toward him. Yeah, his cock got hard when women came on to him, but he felt so guilty about his body's reaction that he couldn't bring himself to give in to his sexual needs.

Sitting next to Dawn, he felt stirrings of lust, but the place she touched him was deeper than his baser needs. She touched him where his music resided. Sara had never touched that part of him. When they'd been together, he'd almost given up music. Sole Regret's first album hadn't been the success they'd hoped. With Sara in college and Kellen holding down odd jobs to pay the bills, they'd been hopelessly broke. Once Sara's medical bills started to pile up, it seemed the only thing to do was leave the band and find a decent job. He'd wanted to provide for her. Only Owen's insistence that Kellen stay had kept him from giving up the band entirely. Owen had believed in Sole Regret when Kellen had completely lost hope on their dream. Owen ever the optimist. Owen who always put other's needs before his own. Owen onboard for anything at any time. Owen...

God, what was he going to do about Owen? Kellen had made a complete mess of their friendship and just when he thought he finally had their relationship back on its proper track, he did something completely stupid. Like tie Owen to a pommel and show a woman how to give him a proper hand job by demonstration. What in the fuck had he been thinking last night?

Dawn abruptly stopped playing. "You're not listening," she said. "Are you bored?"

"No. I just have a lot on my mind," he said. "Don't stop. This song is like a break in the clouds during a storm."

"The eye of your hurricane."

He chuckled. His life was definitely in a whirlwind. "Exactly."

"If you want to talk about her, I'll listen," she said, playing softly again.

"Do you want me to talk about her?"

Dawn shook her head. "Not particularly. I'm sure if you loved her, she was wonderful."

"Sometimes I hate her for what she's done to me." Kellen tensed. Had he really just admitted that aloud? He'd never even admitted that to himself. *I didn't mean it, Sara. I could never hate you.*

"I can understand that," Dawn said.

He somehow doubted it.

"Have you ever been in love?" he asked.

Dawn hesitated, and then she nodded. "But he didn't love me in return. He thought I was a silly little girl and in retrospect, I was. I was sixteen and he was in his thirties. He'd been my piano teacher for years before my hormones kicked into high gear and I made a complete idiot of myself by throwing myself at him."

"I'm sure if you hadn't been jailbait, he would have caught you. What was his name?"

"Pierre," she said, releasing a dreamy sigh.

"*Pierre?*" Kellen chuckled. "You're kidding, right?"

"He's French," she said stiffly.

"*Vous êtes plus belle que les étoiles, mon amour,*" he whispered close to her ear.

She swayed against him, and he wrapped an arm around her back to keep her from tumbling from the piano bench.

"You speak French?" she said.

"Just that one sentence," he said. He didn't even remember exactly what it meant. Something about the stars being beautiful.

"So if I said, *je suis très excitée par vous*, you wouldn't know what I meant?"

"Sounds kinky," he teased.

"It could be."

She tilted her head to look up at him. There were mere inches between their lips. Would she taste as decadent as she looked? The green flecks in her eyes caught Kellen's attention. So exotic. His heart thudded faster and faster as he leaned closer. He hadn't kissed a woman since Sara. Hadn't wanted to. He sure the fuck wanted to now.

Dawn pressed a fingertip against his lips. "Hold that thought," she said and shifted away to pound on her keyboard with renewed vigor.

Kellen stifled a groan. He felt torn between his yearning to devour this woman's sensual mouth and his desire to be a part of the soaring composition she was creating right beside him. Dawn played with her eyes closed, her fingers moving swiftly over the keys. The loose bodice of her dress fell open as she rocked forward to press the foot pedals, and Kellen caught a glimpse of the soft swell of one breast and an expanse of pale freckles decorating the smooth alabaster skin of her chest. Would he find freckles elsewhere? In places hidden from his view? On her belly? Her thighs? His cock twitched as he thought about kissing every freckle he discovered until she spread her legs for him. Would she allow him to sample her fluids with his tongue? Permit him to breathe the musk of her arousal while he treated her pussy to the same deep, plundering kisses he craved from her mouth? He wanted to hear his name gasped, moaned, screamed as she came over and over again at the insistence of his tongue, his lips, his teeth.

When he noticed the pair of thin boxer shorts she'd loaned him were tented with his obvious arousal, he was glad she had her eyes closed. He shifted so that his belly was against the piano and his erection was hidden from view. He tried not to imagine fucking Dawn on the lid of her grand piano, with her dress bunched up around her waist and her bare breasts spilling from her bodice. Tried but failed. He could almost feel her heels digging into his ass, her heat gripping him. He wiped at sweat that formed at the base of his throat.

This was what he got for denying his needs for so long. And it didn't help that the song she was composing held the cadence of the sea—the repetition of surge and withdrawal, peak and valley—that was suddenly a lot more sexual to him than it should have been.

The storm raged outside, producing a clap of thunder so loud the windows rattled. Dawn jumped and pressed a hand to the center of her chest. "Oh," she said, "that startled me. Sometimes I get lost in my music and forget there's a world beyond my own sound."

"I get the same way on stage sometimes," he said.

She gnawed on her lips while she considered him closely. "You look a bit tense," she said. "Is the song not working for you? You can be honest."

The song was working for him in ways he was sure she hadn't intended. He couldn't very well tell her that it turned him on. Of course in his current state of sexual frustration, just about everything turned him on. He'd even gotten turned on while tying Owen last night.

He'd bound Owen so a woman could have her way with him, but seeing him like that... Kellen hadn't been able to keep his hands off him and had ultimately fled the room with a stiff cock. How fucked up was that?

Habitual masturbation helped ease Kellen's frustration, but it just wasn't the same as touching another, as being touched by someone he loved and trusted. He'd touched Owen—and had once allowed Owen to touch him—because in whatever alternate universe his morals were now living, *that* was not cheating on Sara. Even though he'd convinced himself of that, how in the hell did he explain any of that shit to Owen? Owen who was down for anything as long as it felt good. Owen who loved everyone unconditionally. Kellen had taken advantage of Owen's nature, and he felt terrible about it. Not terrible enough to have an honest conversation with him. Too *awkward*. What could he possibly say to make things right?

"Earth to Kellen," Dawn said. "Are you feeling this song at all?"

"If I was honest about what this song does to me," Kellen said, "you'd toss me back into the storm. Which actually might be for the best."

"What does it do to you?" she asked.

He leaned back from the keyboard and glanced down at his lap. She followed his gaze and gasped at the very noticeable bulge in his shorts. "Oh!"

He rubbed at his eyebrow. She must think he only had one thing on his mind, which wasn't far from the truth. "I'll go."

She grabbed his thigh before he could climb from the bench. "This song does similar things to me," she whispered. "I can't stop thinking about sex." She stared at him, all beautiful and beguiling, and his cock jerked. "I can't stop thinking about sex with *you*."

His mouth went dry.

"I've never gotten aroused while composing a song," she said, "so it must be the company."

Her hand slipped up his thigh, and his belly clenched. If she touched him there, he was going to explode.

"Don't leave. I need to see where this takes me and I'm afraid if you go, I'll never finish."

When she removed her hand and placed it over the keys, he groaned.

"I'm sorry to be selfish," she said, "but I have to keep going. I'm consumed by the melody now and I don't want to stop until I'm finished. I hope you understand."

Kellen understood perfectly. He never stopped until his partner was finished. At least, when he'd actually allowed himself to have partners, it had been that way.

Her fingers flew across the keys, drawing so many positive emotions from Kellen that he could have kissed her in gratitude. The song was a celebration of sensuality, and it had been far too long since he'd celebrated. The enraptured expression on Dawn's face as she worked through the composition over and over again made him want to drag her to the floor and claim her. Lose himself in her body. He'd already lost himself to her passion.

A flash of lightning illuminated Dawn's lovely face. An instant later, they were bathed in darkness. The storm seemed to grow louder as the humming appliances and the air conditioning system fell silent.

"I'll try to find candles," Dawn said. "I think there are some in the kitchen."

Kellen reached out to touch her and found the warm skin of her hand resting on her thigh.

"We don't need light to hear the music," he said, "or to feel it. Don't bother." Plus, he really didn't mind sitting with her in the dark while the heavens battled outside. He could get as aroused as he liked, and she wouldn't be able to see it. Too bad the lights hadn't gone out before he'd revealed his not-so-little secret. Before he'd been so absorbed in the sight of her and the music she created that he'd lost his mind and drawn attention to his painfully hard dick.

Lightning flashed, giving him a quick glimpse of her contemplative expression.

The rain lashed against the windows and wind howled through the rafters. The entire house swayed slightly on its sturdy stilts. Even so, Kellen was so fixated on the woman beside him that the most pronounced sound for him was her breathing.

Dawn turned her hand, still resting on her thigh, until her palm met his and held his hand in a loose grip.

"You're right," she whispered. "We don't need light. Just sound."

And touch.

Kellen's thumb stroked her skin. Why did holding her hand feel so intimate? Why did it feel so right?

"Kellen?" she said.

"Yeah?"

"What was her name?"

His heart twisted, and he tugged his hand free of hers. He focused on the rivulets of rainwater flowing down the windowpanes against a background of distant flickers. "Sara," he said around the lump in his throat. "Her name was Sara."

"Sorry," Dawn said. "I shouldn't have brought her up. It's just…" She took a deep breath. "If I had a man who loved me even half as much as you obviously still love her, I'd consider myself blessed."

"I don't feel blessed." Damned. That's how he felt. Damned.

Dawn leaned against his arm, and her free hand slid along his lower back. Kellen held his breath, not wanting to be comforted by her simple gesture, but he was. It felt wonderful to relax against her and allow himself that small bit of feminine contact.

"So why are you single, Dawn O'Reilly?" he asked. "A beautiful, sexy, talented, intelligent, successful woman such as yourself should be taken."

Her arm tightened around his back, which pulled her closer to his side. She was so warm. Smelled so sweet. He was glad of the darkness so he could experience her on an entirely new level. He'd been overwhelmed with the sight of her before; now his other senses had the opportunity to be dazzled. He leaned closer and detected a hint of honeysuckle on her skin.

"Just busy I guess," she said. "I haven't been able to find the right man. Or maybe I was waiting for him to find me."

Kellen closed his eyes and swallowed. He wasn't ready to be the right man for her. How did he convey that without hurting her feelings? There was absolutely nothing standing in his way but himself, but he sure as hell wasn't prepared to clear the road ahead just because this woman had his hormones in an uproar.

"Dawn, I…"

She drew away, and he immediately missed the feel of her hand in his.

"You don't have to say it. I understand."

A random note sounded on the piano as her fingers found the keys.

He squeezed her knee.

"I didn't realize how alone I've felt," she whispered, "with nothing but my music to fill the days and nights. I thought it was enough."

He knew what that was like. With the exception of Owen, he hadn't allowed himself to care about anything but music since Sara had passed and if he hadn't known Owen before meeting her, Kellen wasn't sure he'd have ever let anyone close again.

"What about your friends?" he asked. "Your family? Don't you see them?"

"From time to time," she said. Her hand moved to cover his on her knee, as if she feared he'd move it away. "They have their own lives. I've never been a priority to anyone." She laughed, a dry empty sound. "When I was little, my mother spent a lot of time trying to wring a bit of talent out of me—ballet, gymnastics, art, if they had a class for it, I was in it. When she discovered I had a natural affinity for the piano, she handed me off to the best teachers my daddy's money could buy and made sure they pushed me. It was almost as if she was relieved that she didn't have to bother with me anymore. Daddy…" She inhaled a deep breath and pushed on.

"Daddy always made appearances at my recitals to show he was proud of my accomplishments, but there just wasn't any warmth in him. I never felt close to either of them, not the way I imagined other daughters felt about their parents. I thought that the only way I could make them love me was if I was perfect."

He heard the pain in her voice and wished he could see her face. He probably should have encouraged her to find those candles. "What about your siblings?" he asked.

"Only child," she said.

"Me too. Well, until I met Owen, and his family treated me like one of theirs." He laughed, because even thinking about the Mitchells brought him joy.

"Tell me about Owen," she said, her hand tightening on his. "I was homeschooled by the best tutors money could buy, so I never got to be around anyone my own age until I became an adult. Piano isn't a team sport. More than anything, I would have liked to have had a childhood friend."

"Your family must be very wealthy," he said quietly.

"I never wanted for anything as a child," she said. "Except affection."

Kellen hadn't had a surplus of either wealth or affection. His grandfather had been an important part of his youth, but he'd been old and age had done terrible things to his memory. He hadn't lived long after they'd put him in a nursing home for his safety. Grandfather simply hadn't thrived away from the brushy wilderness he loved to wander. It was as if taking him away from his land made him give up on life. It wasn't long after his grandfather had passed that Kellen had met Owen. It was as if destiny had known how much Kellen would need him in the coming years.

"Living in the middle of nowhere, I didn't have any close friends as a child either," Kellen said. "I met Owen on the first day of seventh grade. We'd gone to different elementary schools, but they bused us to the same junior high. I was hoping for a fresh start. New school. Only half the kids there would know where I came from. Even then, no one would sit next to the poor kid who'd done a really bad job of trying to cut his own hair the night before, and no one would let the pudgy kid in orange and white horizontal stripes sit next to them. So Owen had no choice but to sit next to me. He'd given my bad haircut one long look, but he never said anything. He never made fun of me like the other kids did. Owen sat next to me on the bus every day for a week and we didn't say a word to each other. We had the same lack of popularity at lunch and sat at the same table, both trying to be invisible, because when you're thirteen, invisible is better than being noticed for being different."

Dawn squeezed his hand. "Thirteen is an awful age. So I guess you two finally started talking to each other. Or do you still just sit in silence, trying to be invisible?"

Kellen chuckled. "We started talking after his mother stood up for me in the principal's office."

"Principal's office? Were you a troublemaker?"

"I only made trouble when I couldn't ignore it any more. And there's just something in Owen so pure and good that I wanted to preserve it. I hated that those assholes would walk up behind him in the cafeteria and squeal like pigs as they shoved him against the table. I hated how they treated *him* far more than I hated how they made fun of my clothes, my shoes, my haircut, and the trailer I lived in with my mother and her welfare check. Owen had never done a mean thing to anyone in his life. Where I came from didn't matter to him, and he wasn't upset that he was forced to sit next to me on the bus and at lunch. He seemed grateful.

"So a week after we started hanging out in silence, Owen's sitting there across the cafeteria table from me, minding his own business as usual, and this fucking asshole, Jasper Barnes, picks up Owen's chocolate pudding cup and smashes it into his chest. 'You still going to eat that shit?' he said. 'I bet you will, Piggie. Lick it off. Eat your own shit, Piggie.' And then he starts making those pig-squeal sounds."

"That's so mean."

"I was pissed, not going to deny it, but I probably would have just sat there and tried not to watch, grateful it wasn't me being targeted. Then Owen lifted his head and he looked at me. I saw the shame in his eyes. *Shame.* What the fuck did he have to be ashamed of? That fucking bully was the one who should have been ashamed. When Owen started to clean the pudding off his shirt with a napkin, I fucking lost it. I was a scrawny kid and didn't have a chance against a big jock like Jasper Barnes, so I went after him with my fork. I didn't even get the chance to stab him with it before the teachers pulled me off him. I got suspended for using a weapon at school and later got my ass kicked by that bully and half the defensive line of the football team, but it was worth it because Owen started talking to me after that. Actually, he hasn't shut up since."

Kellen smiled as he thought about Owen's ceaseless prattle. He was definitely a talker. And something about sitting in the dark with Dawn O'Reilly made Kellen a talker too.

"I'm glad you became friends. I can tell he means a lot to you."

"I'd die for him. I don't say that lightly. Owen's always saying how I saved him by protecting him from the bullying, but he saved me a thousand times over. No telling where I'd be today if it wasn't for him and his family. He didn't see the dirt-poor bastard that everyone else in town saw. He never judged me based on my mother's poor choices. Owen just saw me. It didn't bother him that his mom gave me his older brother's hand-me-downs. Owen said great things like, 'You have no idea how glad I am that I don't have to try to squeeze into Chad's old clothes anymore' and 'I can't believe my mom gave you socks and underwear for your birthday. The woman is so embarrassing.' The woman is a saint, is what she is. I hit my growth spurt in eighth grade and if it hadn't been for Joan, I'd have been wearing high-waters and ripping the seams out of my Spiderman T-shirt."

"Did Owen realize that his mom was helping you?"

"He never said anything, but he had to have known. Everyone knew that I'd never met my father and that my mom took a welfare check because it's hard for a drunk to hold down a job. She'd given up hope for a better life long before I was born. Our lack of money was what defined me. But not to the Mitchell family. I was Owen's friend, so I was their surrogate son. His mother is a true treasure. Best woman I've ever known."

"So there's another woman in your life that I'll never measure up to," Dawn said.

Kellen chuckled. "No other woman can measure up to you either, Dawn. You are the only woman who sexually excites me with a mere song."

She leaned in and whispered close to his ear, "I'll take what I can get."

It wasn't only her song that sexually excited him. The tickle of her breath against his skin drew a soft moan of longing from the back of his throat.

"Kellen?"

He loved the way his name sounded when she spoke it. "Dawn?"

"How long has it been since you last had sex?"

He sat stunned that she would ask him something so forward.

"Uh, why?" he said after a moment.

"I don't usually have sex with men I've just meet, but I want to with you."

He closed his eyes and swallowed. How could he turn down her offer? It wasn't that women never propositioned him. They did it all the time—rubbed up against him, shoved their hands down his pants, whispered suggestions into his ear—but he hadn't been interested. Sara's memory had given him the strength to say no. Hell, when he was alone with a woman, he found forwardness downright repulsive, but he was alone with Dawn and her words didn't have the usual effect on him. He wanted her. God, he fucking wanted her.

Promise you'll never make love to another woman, Kellen. Sara's words echoed through his head. They were like a slap to the face.

"It's been five years," he said.

"You haven't done anything in five years?"

"I didn't say I hadn't done *anything*. I just haven't been inside a woman in that long."

"Oh," she said.

He could hear the disappointment in her voice. This time he was glad it was dark so he didn't have to see it on her face.

"What kinds of things have you done?" she asked unexpectedly.

"Alone or with Owen?"

She gasped. "With *Owen?* Are you gay?"

"I'm not gay, Dawn. A bit confused maybe." He rubbed at his eyebrow with two fingertips while he gathered his thoughts. "Can I talk to you about something? Something I haven't even talked to Owen about? Something I need to tell him but am so worried about how he'll react that every time I try to bring it up, I can't form the words."

What was it about the darkness that allowed him to open up? Or maybe it wasn't the darkness at all. Maybe it was the kindred spirit within the woman beside him that made him feel he could tell Dawn anything.

"I'll listen," she said. "I probably won't say the right thing though."

He doubted there was a right thing to say. "Soon after Sara died, Owen started going to sex clubs and guilting me into going with him."

"What's a sex club? Is it like a whorehouse?"

He smiled and couldn't resist running a hand along the base of her spine. Oh the naughty things he could introduce her to, Miss Sweet and Vanilla.

"No, you pay for a certain service at a whorehouse and that's what you get. Sex clubs are where people of certain sexual tastes congregate and hook up." He turned his face to whisper in her ear, and the tickle of her hair against his nose set off nerve endings that sent waves of pleasure to his groin and triggered alarm bells in his head—alarm bells he chose to ignore. "What are your sexual tastes, Dawn? I can tell you where there's a club for it."

"I wouldn't be comfortable hooking up with some stranger in a club," she said. The muscles of her back were taut beneath his palm.

No matter how much he enjoyed it, he needed to stop touching her. This thing between them wasn't going to happen. "I wouldn't want you to hook up with a stranger," he said, which was the truth, but he had no business saying that to her. And he really did need to talk about what was going on with Owen. Maybe someone outside their relationship could make sense of it. "So one night while I was waiting for Owen to finish up spanking and screwing some chick he'd just met, I caught the eye of a man named Toshi."

Dawn shifted beside him, squirming slightly.

"I didn't have sex with Toshi," he said.

"It's none of my business if you did."

"Do you want me to not talk about this? I can tell it's making you uncomfortable."

"Yeah, uncomfortable," she whispered. "We'll go with that."

"Toshi is a master in the Japanese art of Shibari."

"Does that involve swords and disembowelment?"

"No, ropes and release. Toshi spoke of tying knots as if it were a high art form—the way an inspired painter or a poet or a musician talks of his work. I was intrigued. I guess I'm a sucker for an artist. I let him show me a few techniques on one arm. He taught me to tie a couple of knots and then when Owen came to collect me, Toshi told me to keep the rope and if I wanted to learn more, where I could find him."

"So I guess you found him."

"I did a lot of research about Shibari on the Internet, even read a few books, but ultimately I did seek him out, because nothing compares to being taught one-on-one by a master."

"That's true."

"He has a studio in San Francisco," Kellen said. "He binds people with ropes and then he photographs them. For the first year after Sara died, nothing excited me—emotionally or physically. But as I walked through his gallery, admiring his work—flesh against intricate designs in colored rope—I'm not going to lie, I was aroused. The guilt almost made me leave."

"Why did you feel guilty? It sounds erotic to me. Aren't we supposed to get excited by things we find erotic?"

He didn't want to go into that, so he pressed forward in his story. "Yeah, well, I asked Toshi to teach me to be an artist like him, to show me how to tie the ropes into designs that accentuated every line of the human form. He said in order to understand the art form, I first had to be a subject. He told me to strip off my clothes and allow him to bind me."

Dawn squirmed again. When her hand lightly touched his bare knee, he gasped. He should have skipped this part of the story, he realized too late. That first experience with bondage had been one of the most intense emotional and sexual experiences of his life.

"Did you go through with it?" she asked.

"Yeah. I was scared to death. With each knot Toshi tied, I became more tense, more afraid, more aroused. When he was finished, I was aware of every inch of my body. I was completely helpless. I thought he might force me to have sex—thought I'd be okay with it even though I'd promised Sara. But once he had me bound, he whispered, 'Now, you are free, my student,' and then he sat beside me with one hand between my shoulder blades while I fought the rope. Not physically. I couldn't move if I'd wanted to. But mentally I raged against my restraints for a really long time."

"What did he mean *you are free*?"

"I didn't understand until I stopped fighting against the bonds. Physically, emotionally, and spiritually I gave the ropes control, and *then* I understood what he meant. By giving up control, I became free."

"That doesn't make sense at all," she said.

"It won't unless you experience it for yourself."

"Do you do the rope thing now? What did you call it?"

"Shibari. I haven't been practicing much recently. For about three years, it was an outlet for me. I enjoyed tying women, but I only did it when Owen was with me. I'm not sure I trusted myself to be alone with a woman. They tend to beg for sex after I tie them, and I wasn't willing to take it that far. Owen had no problem with that aspect. He'd have sex with them if they wanted it and eventually he started helping with the bondage too."

"So you and Owen tied women up and then he had sex with them?"

"Not always. We left that decision to the woman."

"But *you* didn't do anything sexual with them?"

He took a deep breath. "I would usually..." He coughed. Wow, was he really going to tell her this? "...perform oral sex on them."

Her breath caught, and she squirmed again.

"But I never penetrated them, never allowed them to touch my cock in any way. No blow jobs. Nothing."

"You had to have been miserable."

"I would have been, but Owen helped me out." His stomach clenched. What must this woman think of him?

"How?" she asked.

"Hand jobs."

"Oh, but no sex?"

"Isn't it all sex?" he said. "That's why I'm so confused. Sara was gone before I was introduced to Shibari, so somehow I convinced myself that it was okay. She didn't like oral sex—"

"I like it," Dawn blurted.

A long silence hung awkwardly between them, and he prayed for a bolt of lightning to light her features so he could see her expression.

"I mean if the guy knows what he's doing," she said. "Maybe she didn't like it because you're not good at it."

Kellen chuckled. "Trust me, I'm good at it. She was a bit timid in bed." Kellen rubbed the back of his neck. "That kind of deep intimacy embarrassed her, so she didn't want me making out with her pussy for hours on end."

"Dear lord," Dawn whispered.

"So I convinced myself that oral sex didn't go against my oath to her."

"Thank God."

Kellen chuckled at Dawn's little asides. "And though I told her

I'd never let a woman touch my cock, I never said anything about a man touching it. So I used Owen to get me off because I felt comfortable enough with him to let him touch me. The thought of any other man anywhere near my cock makes me ill, but Owen is different for some reason, and *that's* the part I don't understand. Why am I okay with him touching me?"

"Do you love him?"

"He's my best friend."

"So, yeah, you love him."

It wasn't as simple as that. "But not romantically."

"Are you sexually attracted to him or not?" Neither judgmental nor accusatory, her tone was simply inquisitive.

Kellen tried to sort through the jumbled feelings he had for Owen. He was so glad that Dawn was letting him air his filthy laundry without judgment. He'd needed to talk to someone about this for years. He couldn't discuss it with Owen when he really didn't understand what was going on in his head, and he obviously didn't want the rest of the band to know what went on between him and Owen behind closed doors, so he couldn't talk to Jacob or Gabe or Adam either. Dawn couldn't possibly understand how much she was doing for him by just listening and forcing him to face reality.

"I don't look at him and think, *damn, I want to fuck him unconscious.* It's more like, *please, will someone touch me there?* I can't stand this anymore. So Owen's handy. Literally." Kellen's stomach sank as realization hit him. "Shit, I'm just using him, aren't I?" His elbows hit the piano keys as he dropped his face into his hands. "How could I do that to him? He must be as confused about this as I am."

"Do you look at *me* and think, *damn, I want to fuck her unconscious?*" Dawn said.

Kellen's back stiffened, drawing him away from the keyboard as he thought about the way she looked in that loose, shapeless white dress. How she smelled of honeysuckle and the sea. The sound of her voice and the music she so easily drew from the piano before him. He knew he was in trouble when he imagined how she'd taste—as delicious as her sweet, vanilla French toast—and how her supple flesh would feel beneath his hands. Warm. Soft. Smooth. He could almost feel her writhing beneath him as he claimed her with slow, deep thrusts. His cock throbbed and his balls ached with an unbearable fullness. What he wouldn't give to be able to bury himself inside her. But he couldn't.

He took a shaky breath and held it deep in his lungs, willing his lust to dissipate.

Torture. This was fucking torture.

"Yes," he groaned. "That's exactly what I think when I look at you." He clenched both fists and rested them on either knee to keep himself from reaching for her. "But I can't."

The storm seemed to grow louder as their conversation lulled. He'd never been more tempted to go back on his promises to Sara. He had to leave this house. His convictions were strong, but his flesh grew weaker each moment he was in Dawn's company.

"Could you tie me?" she asked quietly.

He tensed and scrambled from the bench, stubbing his toe on the piano leg. Pain shot up his foot and shin, and he welcomed the diversion. She was already a work of art. How beautiful would she look with knots and ropes drawing attention to her graceful lines and soft curves?

Kellen licked his lips and swallowed hard despite the sudden dryness in his mouth.

"I'm going to go," Kellen said.

Lightning flashed in quick succession. Thunder made the house shudder. The wind howled, slashing the torrential rain against the windows in sheets.

"You can't go out in that," Dawn said. So matter of fact. So Dawn.

A gentle ping sounded on the piano as she found the keys in the darkness and began to play his song. Funny how he thought of it as *his* song. He wished Dawn could be his too.

He pressed the hard ridge of his cock against his thigh with one hand and closed his eyes, completely giving himself to the melody, even if he wasn't quite ready to give himself over to the woman.

CHAPTER SIX

Dawn tried to get lost in her music. Tried, but failed. She was so aware of Kellen standing in the dark several feet behind her right shoulder that he might as well have been plastered to her back. She wanted to feel that enormous bulge in his shorts pressing into her spine as he stood behind her. She'd give anything for those strong, masculine hands to reach around her to cup her breasts. For his thumbs to rub the unbearable ache from her stiff nipples. She squirmed on the bench, trying to alleviate some of the matching ache in the swollen flesh between her thighs.

Now that she knew the pieces of the entire song, Dawn needed to write it down so she could scan it and fax it to her agent in the morning. Unfortunately, it was too dark to see score paper and if the lights came on, she feared Kellen would find a good excuse to leave. Even if he refused to give in to her lame attempts at seduction, she didn't want him to go. She found his company inspiring. His interactions with his friend Owen seemed a little odd, but the way he described Shibari—which she'd never heard of before—had her squirming on the bench again. She was squirming so often that Kellen probably thought she had to pee. But her urgency was caused by something else entirely.

As she progressed through the music, she reached the second stanza, the one that had taken on the cadence of the ocean. Of sex.

Kellen released a sensual sigh, and it took every shred of willpower she possessed not to tackle him to the ground, straddle him, and show him the rhythm of her body. She'd never been with a musician before. She'd lusted after Pierre and imagined him making love to her—taking her virginity—but nothing had ever come of that infatuation. Not one of her few lovers had possessed the soul of an artist. Was that why she was so uncharacteristically fast around Kellen? Was it the spiritual connection between the musical part of their beings that made her want him at any cost, or was it just because he was so damned easy on the eyes?

No, it had to be more than that. She *felt* him. Even in the dark, she was under his spell, so it couldn't be only his looks.

So how did she get him to move beyond the dead woman who'd been lucky enough to win his heart? She didn't care if Kellen broke his vow to what's-her-name; his fidelity ran so deep it was a liability. But she did care if her come-ons hurt him. She didn't want to hurt him. She wanted to get lost in him. She wanted him to show her his rope-tying art and how letting go of her control to him could be freeing. She wanted to know all of him—good and bad, spiritual and physical. She wanted him.

So if she had to squirm around on this bench unfulfilled all night, she'd do it. The worst he could do was leave her here alone.

When she reached the end of the piece, she allowed the last note to ring. This was her best work, she decided. Like the melody that had won the Grammy, this composition rang true, as if the notes had always been inside her and had just been looking for an outlet. Kellen had drawn them from her subconscious. She didn't know if he realized his influence.

"Thanks for helping me with the song," she said quietly.

"Is it finished?"

"Mostly." A bit of that old anxiety twisted in the pit of her stomach. Maybe it wasn't as good as she thought it was. "Does it sound incomplete?"

"It's perfect," he said breathlessly.

She breathed a sigh of relief. *Perfect.* That's what she'd been going for. "I don't think I could have done it without you. Do you want me to give you credit as cowriter?"

"No," he said. "I didn't do anything but listen."

And apparently that was exactly what she'd needed. His presence had helped. The undeniable sexual attraction she felt for him had reached deep inside her and unleashed a daring and incredibly sensual force within her—one she had never recognized existed, but welcomed.

"Dawn," Kellen whispered.

"Yeah?"

"Do you have any rope? Something soft that won't damage your skin."

The surge of moisture between her legs was accompanied by a soft moan. Was he really going to tie her?

"There's a decorative rope along the banister around the upstairs loft," she said. "It has seashells and little red starfish hanging from it, but they'll come off easily. Will that work?"

"It will have to."

Dawn stumbled as she rose from the piano bench. "I'll get some candles. You get the rope. My bedroom is at the top of the stairs on the right. I'll meet you there."

"Not on your bed," he said. "On the piano."

Dawn's womb clenched and her mouth dropped open. A piano didn't sound like the most comfortable place to be tied up or tied down—she still wasn't positive what tying entailed—but it sounded sexy as hell. She bit her lip and nodded, not sure if he could see the gesture in the dark, but if she spoke, she was certain any words would come out as one long moan of longing. Days spent imagining her piano teacher making love to her on the lid of her daddy's baby grand hadn't prepared her for the impact of those three words—*on the piano*—spoken from Kellen's lips. Like every woman, she'd lusted after men, but not like this. Not with body and mind. Not to this degree. This was completely new for her, and the strength of it made her quiver in places she didn't know could move on their own accord.

She bumped into him as she attempted to find the kitchen. He caught—and held—her loosely by both arms. She felt his body heat, but he didn't drag her against him the way she wished he would. He didn't kiss her. He didn't grab her ass to crush her mound against his erection. Oh God, why wasn't he doing any of those things? All of those things?

Oh, please, Kellen.

"Are you sure about this?" he said, close to her ear.

If he hadn't been holding her arms, she probably would have sunk to the floor.

"Does it hurt?" she heard herself ask. Did she care? Some part of her did, apparently, but the primal part of her that he'd awakened didn't give a fig if she felt discomfort.

"Not at all," he said. "Being bound is a physical experience, but it affects most people psychologically as well. Being helpless will probably push you out of your comfort zone. If you're not sure you want to do this, you need to say so now. If you back out once I get started, I'm not sure I'll survive. I need to see my work finished. This has become a spiritual ritual for me. It's… it's hard to explain.

I will stop if you make me, but I'd rather not start if you have reservations."

She wanted to understand his words by experiencing his spiritual ritual for herself. "I'm sure. I don't have reservations."

He drew her against him at long last and gave her a friendly hug. "Thank you," he whispered.

She melted against him, pressing her palms against his back to draw him closer. She wanted more than a friendly embrace. She wanted some heat. Passion. She sensed it in him. How did she unleash it? She turned her face into his neck and couldn't resist rubbing her lips against his flesh.

He dropped his arms and pulled away. "I'll go find that rope," he said. A brief flash of lightning showed his retreating back and then he was gone again.

Was she really throwing herself so willingly at this guy?

A side table scraped against the floor several feet away. "Damn it," Kellen cursed. "I'm not sure if my toes are going to make it through the night."

Yeah, she was totally throwing herself at this guy. She hoped to God that he planned to catch her.

She smiled and turned to shuffle carefully in the direction of the kitchen for those candles. Maybe they'd save Kellen's toes from utter destruction.

Dawn located several pillar candles and the lighter for the grill and hurried back to the family room. She set the candles on a nearby side table—probably the same one that Kellen's toe had become acquainted with—and lit all three candles. She placed the nearby lamp on the floor and glanced up at the banister that ran the periphery of the second floor loft. The whimsical rope garland that had charmed her the first time she'd glimpsed it now made her shudder with longing. The candles gave off just enough light for her to see Kellen's hands freeing the long lengths of blue and tan rope. He was none too gentle with the seashells that had hung from the ropes. Several of them rained down from above.

"Almost got it," he said after a moment.

She couldn't see him well, but she imagined he had a perfect view of her standing below the loft, gawking up at him. She was so anxious to get started that a cadence of *hurry, hurry, hurry* began to sound in her head. Not wanting to appear as desperate as she felt, she grabbed a sheet of score paper and sat at the piano to write down the notes of the now completed composition. Her current favorite because it so reminded her of Kellen and all the things she wished he would do to her. If not tonight, then sometime in the near future.

Using a pencil, she marked the notes quickly, the melody filtering through her head as surely as if she'd been playing it aloud. She'd make the piece look pretty before she sent it off, but she had to get it down. The familiar task calmed her and ate away the time that she'd have spent pacing while she waited for Kellen.

She didn't realize he was standing behind her until she heard a clink against the floor. She glanced over her shoulder. He was watching her with a look somewhere between fascination and terror.

She tossed her pencil aside and collected the score sheets into a haphazard pile. He seemed to be having second thoughts, but she wasn't going to let him change his mind. She should have gone up to help him with the rope so he didn't have time to think of that other woman—Sara.

"Sorry, I interrupted," he said. "If you need to work, I'll—"

"No." She cut him off before he could say *leave*. She knew that's what he was going to say, and she wouldn't let him. "I was just passing the time while I waited for you."

She stood from the piano bench and leaned over to remove the prop that held the baby grand's lid open. She carefully lowered the lid and slid her hands over the smooth surface. Her heart was thudding like a jackhammer, but she wasn't going to chicken out. She always worried about doing the wrong thing, about appearances, about disappointing someone, but tonight she was doing what she wanted to do. For once, she'd forget about the pressures of the outside world and allow this man to set her free by binding her body. She still wasn't sure what that meant, but she trusted that he was going to show her.

She again turned to him and found him clutching the long coils of rope in front of his crotch. She hoped that meant he was hiding another erection, though he couldn't possibly be as aroused by her as she was by him.

"Will those ropes work?" she asked, nodding toward his crotch.

"They're surprisingly soft and supple. Exactly the kind of rope I'd have selected for your first time. It's almost like…"

"Destiny," she said.

He smiled and leaned back against the piano for support.

"Except I would have chosen a green rope instead of blue, to match the pretty flecks in your hazel eyes."

He'd noticed her eye color? She loved that he'd been paying that much attention to detail. It meant he was interested. Didn't it?

"Blue for the ocean," she said. "Like our song." She stiffened suddenly. "That's it."

"That's what?"

"The name of our song. Blue. I'll call it Blue."

"Doesn't blue usually mean sad?" he said. "That song is joyous, not blue. It made me feel happier than I've felt in five years."

Her breath caught, and she felt a strange prickling behind her eyes. Her work had touched him that deeply? "It did?"

He nodded.

"What would you call it?" she asked him.

"Dawn."

"Yes?"

"No, that's what I'd call it. Dawn."

She grinned. "Kind of narcissistic to name a song after yourself, isn't it?"

"But it's like dawn. A beautiful departure from darkness. The end of the inky night sky. The awakening of light that turns the sky blue again. The beginning of a new day."

Though her tummy was a jumble of butterflies, she couldn't tear her gaze from his. She knew he wasn't just saying strings of pretty words to woo her—though they were quite effective in that regard—but that he really felt what he was saying. And she realized he felt that way about her. She was his dawn. The end of his darkness.

Or maybe she was just wishful thinking.

"Take off your dress," he said.

Her mouth dropped open in shock. So maybe he wasn't as romantic as she thought.

"I mean, if you're ready to begin," he said.

She was. She just had whiplash from the speed at which he changed gears.

Dawn unfastened the wide belt at her waist, letting the strap of leather fall to the floor.

She grabbed the skirt of the loose dress and took a deep breath before tugging the entire garment over her head. She tossed it aside, standing before him in her white lace bra and panties.

The heat of his gaze made her blush, and a powerful shame drew her hands to cover herself as much as possible.

"Don't hide," he said. "You're beautiful."

She didn't feel beautiful. She felt awkward. She'd always hated that she was so tall, that her hips were too narrow, her breasts too small, her shoulders too wide.

"Beautiful," he said again. "I've never bound a woman as tall and slender as you," he said.

She stared at her dress on the floor, willing it to rise up from its puddle and cover her again. She was certain he'd much rather use a more feminine form for his bondage sculpture. Why had she agreed to this?

His legs entered her line of sight, and the rope he'd been holding landed in a tangle on the floor. She choked back a sob when his hand cupped her shoulder and then slowly slid down the length of her arm. She was sorry she was a disappointment. That she wasn't an ideal specimen for his art. That she wasn't pretty enough. Wasn't perfect.

"Can I see your back?" he asked.

She spun around. Annoyed with him. Annoyed with herself. His fingertips traced eight slow paths down her back.

"Your lines are amazing," he said.

Yeah, her flat as a board, straight as a stick lines.

"So graceful. I don't think I've ever seen a more perfect body for this."

Her brow furrowed. Perfect? But didn't he prefer curves? "Do you think so?" She lowered her hands and looked down at her too white belly and those stupid freckles that decorated her chest.

"Can I start? I don't think I can wait any longer."

She nodded, feeling almost proud of her body. How weird was that?

"Just take off your bra and panties and sit up here on the piano for me?"

Whoa. Too fast. "I'd rather leave them on," she said.

His fingertip traced the top elastic of her panties along her lower back. "I guess I can work them into the design," he said. "If you're more comfortable with that."

She nodded and was surprised when he moved to the side table and blew out all three of the candles.

"What are you doing?"

"I want to do this by feel."

"By feel?" she squeaked.

"I don't want to get distracted by your beauty."

She chuckled. "Okay. That was just cheesy."

"Just stating facts."

"You already have me in my underwear and willing to be tied and at your mercy. You can lay off the pick-up lines."

She felt him move to stand just behind her. His palms slid over her rib cage and down her quivering belly toward her small scrap of lace modesty.

"I don't want you to be uncomfortable," he said. "It's probably a good idea to leave them on. Your exposed pussy would be far too tempting to resist."

He cupped her mound and gently squeezed. Her breath stalled as she involuntarily arched against his palm.

"I can feel your heat," he whispered into her ear. "This doesn't have to be a sexual experience, you know."

With Kellen in charge, yes, it did.

"I can't help it," she said. "Just being in the same room as you turns me on. How do you expect me to react when you touch me in the dark?"

"Just as long as you realize I'm not going to make love to you. Not because I don't want to or because you aren't the most beautiful woman I've ever touched, but because I made a promise I'll never break."

Dawn scowled. That fucking dead girl again.

"If you want, I will make you come, though," he whispered. "Give you more orgasms than you can stand."

So maybe his inability to break a promise wasn't really a burden after all.

"Do you want that, Dawn? Do you want to come?"

"Y-y-yes."

His hand slipped into her panties. When his middle finger slipped over her fully engorged clit, her legs buckled. He drew her back against him until his hard cock was prodding her in the ass. She squirmed against him, wanting that big thick shaft buried deep inside her already.

He bit her ear and eased her around the piano until she faced the keyboard.

"Play my song while I make you come for the first time," he

demanded quietly.

As if she could argue with that request.

She fumbled with the keys and didn't start at the beginning. She started with the second stanza. The one that rose and fell like the waves, like a lover possessing what was hot and achy and swollen and wet just for him.

Kellen stroked her clit with the cadence of the song, rocking slightly against her with each soft and sensual caress. He wasn't rubbing her to get her off—he was increasing her need to a feverish level. When she reached the final crescendo, he sent her flying. Song forgotten, she clung to the keyboard and cried out with release as her pussy clenched hard on the emptiness between her legs.

Needing more, much more, Dawn bent forward so that the stiff cock that had been scarcely rubbing against her ass was lodged firmly in her cleft. The only thing separating his hard flesh from her slick heat was a pair of lace panties and a thin pair of boxer shorts.

He jerked his hand out of her panties and stepped back, sending the piano bench tumbling backward with a crash.

In the silence that followed, she was only aware of her ragged breathing and his. The intense pleasure began to recede as she slowly regained her bearings. Her release had been fantastic, but hardly satisfying. She wanted more of him. All of him. *Inside* her.

"I knew I should have bound you before I touched you," he said. "Do you think I'm made of willpower? You can't rub up against me like that and expect me to keep my promise to Sara."

But she didn't want him to keep his promise to Sara. Dawn wanted to fuck Kellen until she could no longer feel her legs. But he didn't want her enough to give her what she craved. She should probably feel bad about pressuring him into doing something he wasn't prepared to do, but she just felt bitter toward a woman who no longer existed except in Kellen's heart.

"I got caught up in the moment," she said, which wasn't a lie. "I didn't intend to rub up against you. It was involuntary."

He was quiet for a long moment. She couldn't imagine what he was thinking. Probably deciding if he should locate his clothes before he fled the house or brave the storm wearing only her boxers. She pushed away from the piano and turned to look at the space where he stood in the darkness.

He sighed. "You're right. That was my fault."

Kellen lifted a hand and cupped her jaw in one hand. He traced her lips with his thumb. She could smell her sex on him. Dear lord.

"I'll make you come harder next time," he said. "You weren't quite finished when I pulled away."

She hadn't been? News to her. She was just relieved that he seemed to want to continue. Because she definitely wanted to continue, even if he wasn't willing to give her the deep penetration she craved. Maybe with time and patience he'd be able to make love to her. She was sure he'd be worth the wait.

She turned her face to inhale their commingled scents. "When do *you* get to finish?"

"I'll finish myself when I need to."

She imagined him touching himself, wishing he'd allow her to touch him there.

"Can I watch at least?"

"In the dark?"

"You could light the candles again," she said.

"I'll light them after I finish tying you," he said. "I'm going to want to see how beautiful you look." His fingertips slid lightly from her jaw, down her throat, stopping just shy of her breast. "And when I come on your skin, I'll want to see that too."

And she definitely wanted to see that. The sooner the better.

She hopped up on the closed lid of the piano and planted her feet on the keyboard to give herself a boost backward. Even though she should have been expecting the discordant sound, she jumped at the loud pang of the keys.

She heard the rope scrape across the floor as he bent to retrieve it. The storm had finally abated, and the silence in the house was unsettling. Or maybe she was just more sensitive to sound than usual.

"I shouldn't have snapped at you," he said.

"You didn't."

"I can't tell you how hard it was for me to step back instead of pulling your panties aside and burying myself deep inside you."

She crossed her legs and wriggled her hips uncomfortably. What would he feel like inside her? Did he make love to a woman gently or fuck her unconscious? Sad that she might never find out. "Kellen, don't say things like that unless you mean to back them up with action. You aren't the only one fighting for control here."

His hands slid up the outside of her thighs. "Open your legs."

Her legs uncrossed and popped open as if they had minds of

their own. He stepped forward to stand between her thighs. She knew he was close, though the only part of him touching her was his hands. He caressed her hips and then her back. When his chest brushed the hardened points of her nipples, she gasped.

He immediately retreated slightly, and she forced herself not to crush her breasts into his chest. His terms. This had to be on his terms. He'd better make it worth her while.

"Lie back," he whispered close to her ear. "I want to get to know your body."

She obeyed. The cool piano lid was hard against her back and buttocks, but that mild discomfort was soon forgotten.

Dawn sighed as his hands slid slowly over her skin, bumping over curves, valleys, crests and depressions. No one had ever paid so much attention to her form. She thought it might make her feel self-conscious to be so thoroughly inspected from head to toe, but his attention made her feel beautiful. Appreciated. Cherished.

"I thought I'd have to remind you to relax," Kellen said, his deep voice drawing a shudder of delight from her.

"Did you assume that I was always uptight?" she teased.

His hands slid up her calves and gently kneaded her muscles until they were like warm butter. Her thighs fell open in complete surrender. The only part of her that felt any tension was the emptiness between her thighs. Her pussy clenched against the building ache and even though he'd already warned her that this wouldn't proceed to him making love to her, she wanted it to.

Kellen massaged her ankles and the insteps of both feet. "You're not always uptight?"

"Most of the time, I am," she admitted, "but something about you allows me to let go of my inhibitions."

"That's exactly what you need to do to fully enjoy this. Let go."

Letting go was surprisingly easy to do with Kellen in control.

"I'll try," she said.

"This will be a bit different for me, doing this all by feel," he said. "I'll be careful, but if anything is rubbing your skin raw or pinching you, you have to promise to tell me where. Usually, I can see any hang-ups in my design, but I'm going in blind here."

Her heart thudded faster as she strained to hear the sounds of the rope running through his hands. When the first loop wrapped around her ankle, she tensed. He tightened it so that she could feel the soft cotton against her skin, but it didn't cut into her flesh.

"Dawn?" he said. "Are you sure you don't want to be naked? Once I get started there will be no way to remove your bra and panties."

But her panties were the only thing keeping her fluids from dripping onto the lid of the piano beneath her.

"Is it better with them off?"

"Do you want release or just pleasure?"

Yes! "Can I have both?"

"I'd like to involve every inch of your body in this." His hand slid up the inside of her thigh, and she nearly shot up off the piano. "I think you'd appreciate a series of knots between your thighs, rubbing against your bare clit, your opening, and your back entrance."

She tried to imagine how she could appreciate knots between her thighs, but came up blank. It sounded downright uncomfortable. "What do you mean, Kellen?"

"I'd rather show you," he said, "but they'll be placed in such a way that minimal squirming should allow you to get off."

It could? What a completely sheltered life she'd been leading.

"If I say yes, will you remove my panties for me?"

He didn't wait for her to say yes. His fingers slid beneath the elastic at her hips and tugged. He paused so she could lift her bottom and he could pull her panties down over her butt. The piano clanged a protest as her feet pressed into the keys, and he slipped her panties slowly downward. His breath warmed her mound as he breathed deeply.

"You smell amazing," he whispered, the little gusts of air from his words dancing over her highly sensitized skin.

Her eyes flipped open in surprise when the soft, wet tip of his tongue slipped down between her lips to flick over her clit.

"Mmm," he murmured.

His tongue traced her inner folds and swirled around her aching opening. Dawn's back arched off the piano and her hand dove into his hair—so long and silky and still damp from the rain. *God yes, kiss me there.* She forced his face closer, her legs wrapping around his back to urge him closer still.

He pulled away, almost dragging her off the slick surface of the piano as he untangled himself from her limbs.

"I need to hurry up and tie you so I can feast on that pussy for hours."

"Why wait? I wasn't stopping you." Encouraging him. That's what she'd been doing.

"It's too easy for me to lose control of myself when you're free."

"If you don't like me pulling at your hair and digging my feet into your back, I can stop."

"That's not the problem," he said.

"Then why did you move away?"

"Because I *do* like it. I like it too much. It makes me want to do more than lick this."

His fingers slid down her seam and slipped inside her.

"It makes me want to fuck it."

It clenched around his fingers eagerly. *Yes.*

"I think I've changed my mind about being tied," she said. If it was that easy to make him lose control, then she'd encourage the hell out of him.

"Then I'll have to leave."

Damn. That didn't work. He really was in control here. But she trusted that he would give her what she needed and more. She was still worried that he wouldn't get what *he* needed from the experience. Making love should be about give and take, not take and take and take, but if he was willing to give her that much, she supposed she shouldn't complain.

"I don't want you to leave," she said. "I want you to feast on that pussy for hours."

He emitted a nervous laugh.

"I'd like you to fuck it too, but if you're not willing to go that far, I'll try to make do."

She could hear him taking deep calming breaths through his nose and wondered if she should push him farther. She felt he was at a tipping point and that a little shove would send him falling in her direction. Or might send him away from her forever.

After a moment, he removed the rope from her ankle, pulled her panties free, and slipped the noose around her ankle again, drawing it tight. His hands slid up her leg—altering its angle slightly so that her back and butt were in a more comfortable position on the surface of the piano and her knee in a natural bend. She closed her eyes and concentrated on the sensation of the rope being run up the side of her calf, around the top of her knee and down the other side. The rope pressed into the sole of her foot, and her toes curled under. Why did that feel so good? She sighed in bliss. He leaned away slightly, working the rope—she could hear the fibers scraping against each other. A knot pressed into her instep. She sighed again. If she wriggled her toes slightly, that knot rubbed at a spot on the bottom of her foot that made her nipples pebble with excitement. She had no idea if he'd intentionally put the knot in exactly the right spot, but she was grateful for the stimulation. She'd expected him to tie her spreadeagle to the piano legs, but apparently there was more to this Shibari stuff than simply rendering her helpless.

His secured the rope at her ankle and then ran his hands up the length of her body. He cupped both breasts through her bra, his thumbs tracing the hardened tips.

"Perfect," he whispered.

"Take it off." She wanted to feel the pads of his thumbs against her bare nipples.

"Is it pinching you somewhere?" he asked and shifted his hands to her bound leg, carefully running his fingers over the rope and knots he'd fashioned.

"No. I didn't mean the rope. I meant my bra."

"Oh." He chuckled and a pulse of pleasure converged between her thighs. So now even his laugh turned her on? She was a goner.

"Let me bind your other leg first," he said, "then I'll have you sit up."

He left the free end of the rope dangle from her ankle and picked up another piece of rope to bind her other leg. She had some experience with his motions now, so instead of concentrating on where he was putting the rope and tying it and knotting it, she allowed herself to feel how it affected her body. She most enjoyed the knots between her soles and the piano keys where her feet rested, but the tightness of the ropes on her thighs directed her attention to the open and exposed flesh between them. She hoped he'd do something about that soon; she couldn't close her legs and squirm as she'd been doing since she'd sat beside him at the breakfast bar and then on the piano bench. Even though he'd taken the edge off with that sweet orgasm earlier, she was hopelessly excited again.

When he had her legs secured the way he wanted them, he ran his hands over the ropes as if checking for flaws in his design. "Does that feel okay?" he asked.

"Feels great," she murmured.

His lips pressed gently against the inside of her thigh. "Your scent is driving me wild. Will you be able to keep your hands to yourself if I steal a small taste?"

"Yes." She was lying. Even before his tongue slid sensually over her inner folds, her hands were reaching for his thick, glorious hair.

He moved away before she could latch onto his scalp. He slid a hand between her lower back and the piano and eased her into a sitting position.

"Why did you stop?" she asked, her pussy still quivering from the brief feel of his tongue against her flesh.

"I know if I really get into it, I won't be able to quit."

"I don't mind."

"Do you trust me to make it good for you?"

"Yes."

"Then let me do my thing. You still haven't given up control yet."

She was letting him tie her up on top of a piano. Just how much control did he expect her to relinquish?

He took the dangling rope ends from either knee and wrapped them around her waist, crossed them behind her back. When he pulled the ropes taut, the action pulled her thighs wide open.

"Ow." She protested the pull on her muscles. She was stretched to her limit.

"Relax," he said.

Easy for him to say. He wasn't sitting on the edge of a hard surface with his legs spread wide in a split.

After a moment, her muscles adjusted and she sighed in relief. Forced yoga. That's what she felt like she was doing. He tugged the ropes another inch, opening her wider still and then tied the two ropes together just under her navel to hold her in that position.

"I don't stretch that far," she protested.

"Yes, you do."

He slid two fingers over her mound, against her clit and to the exposed, dripping-wet opening farther down. "I was going to put knots between your thighs so you could get your pleasure from the rope." He massaged her entrance with two fingertips, and she tried to close her legs against the invasion, but her bonds prevented it. "I changed my mind," he said.

"You're going to leave me all worked up like this?" She would surely die if he did.

"No, *I'm* going to give you all the pleasure you can handle. A couple of ropes don't deserve that privilege."

She wished she could see his expression. Because it was dark, she felt comfortable in being so exposed, but she also felt she was missing out on all the cues he could be giving her.

He shifted and his chest brushed her breasts as he reached behind her to unfasten her bra. Soon her arms would be rendered as helpless as her legs, so she took the opportunity to embrace him. He stiffened but when she did nothing but hold him in her arms, he eventually began to relax. His arms tightened around her, and he just held her like that. His heart thudded hard in his chest, thumping in a rapid staccato against hers. His mouth moved against her hair.

"I shouldn't," he said, hugging her closer.

Her hands slid up his back, and she tilted her head, seeking his kiss. His breath warmed her lips. She parted them, her eyes closed, her body completely in tune with his.

"Kiss me," she whispered.

He released her so abruptly, she almost tumbled from the piano. Her arms shot behind her to help her regain her center of gravity.

He immediately grabbed her to keep her from falling. "Sorry," he said. "I can't expect you to trust me with your safety if I put you in harm's way like that."

"Fine," she said, glad it was dark so he couldn't see how watery her stupid eyes had become. "You don't have to kiss me if you don't want to."

"Maybe this isn't a good idea," he said. He found her face in the darkness and cupped it between his hands. "I haven't been alone with a woman since Sara. I didn't realize how much I needed Owen with me as a spotter."

The ache in Dawn's chest lifted, and she laughed. "A spotter? You're not bench-pressing me, Kellen," she said. "Just touching me."

"But there are things a woman expects that I won't deliver. Kissing, for example. Owen handled that part."

"I didn't know, or I wouldn't have asked."

"It's not fair to you. I can't expect you to abide by my weird little rules."

"Maybe you should tell me what those rules are, so I'm less likely to break them. I'm trying to understand you, Kellen."

"Why?"

"Because I like you."

"Fuck."

She stiffened, and her temper flared to life. "Sorry you find my affection so revolting."

"I don't. I find it wonderful. And tempting. And scary as hell. I like you too. More than anyone before Sara," he said. "Or since."

So she was in second place after a dead girl? She supposed it was a start. What would it take to climb to the top? She needed to be first. Maybe not tonight. Maybe not this week or this month. But someday. Someday she wanted to be Kellen's number one. She just needed to not mess this up before then. Unfortunately, her mouth often spontaneously said things she regretted.

"Do you think Sara would want you to give up love for the rest of your life?"

"Now that she's gone, I'm sure she wouldn't care if I got a dog," he said, "but she was incredibly jealous. She wanted me all to herself. She forced me to promise her all sorts of things and I did. And I meant every last one of those promises."

"But shouldn't they have ended when she died?"

"No," he said. "They should end when I stop loving her."

Which would be never.

"Now I'm going to have to remind you to relax," he said.

"Relax?" she sputtered. "How am I supposed to relax?"

He lifted the heavy mass of her hair from one shoulder and gently caressed the bare skin he exposed. "First, you should stop trying to compete with Sara. You're not her."

"I'm well aware of that. I'm sure *she* didn't have to make sense of your rules and worry that she was going to ask you to do something taboo like kiss."

"No, I had no rules for her. But she had plenty for me. Rule one: no biting," he said.

His teeth nipped Dawn's earlobe. She shuddered and gasped as pleasure licked down the side of her neck. His nose brushed her throat, and she felt the warm moisture of his breath against her skin just before he nipped the side of her neck, her collarbone, her ribcage, belly, mound.

"Another rule: *don't put your mouth there, Kellen.*" His tone was as feminine as his deep voice could produce. "*It feels weird.*"

God, it didn't feel weird to Dawn. It felt great. He might not have been willing to kiss Dawn on the mouth, but he did one hell of a job kissing her lips.

"*I only want to come when you're inside me, Kellen,*" he repeated more of Sara's words. "*Looking in my eyes. Promise you'll never come inside anyone but me, Kellen. Promise.*"

Wow, that woman had his head all sorts of messed up. Dawn supposed most men would have made those kinds of promises to make their woman happy, but doubted they would have taken them to heart the way that Kellen so obviously had.

"Kellen," Dawn said. "You don't have to promise me anything. I don't want you to."

His only response was to suck her clit into his mouth and stroke it rapidly with his tongue until she exploded with ecstasy against his face. She clung to his hair, rocking her hips involuntarily as she moaned in bliss. After a moment, he dislodged her fingers from his scalp and reached for the rope again. He didn't speak as he worked, first crisscrossing the rope across her torso and back, around her breasts and over her shoulders. He climbed to sit behind her as he bound her arms together behind her back, starting at the tops and working his way toward her wrists.

Kellen tied knot after knot, as if building an intricate rope ladder between her arms. He spent so much time on each knot that it seemed to take forever. She wished she could see what he was doing back there. What did it look like? She'd never been more conscious of her skin. Her breasts, pussy, and above her neck were the only parts of her body that were not in some way associated with lengths of rope or knots, so she became fixated on those parts, wanting stimulation for those areas too.

"I wish I had more rope," he said when he moved away at last. "I'd really like to showcase your talented hands." His teeth sank into a bare spot on the back of her shoulder, and her spine arched involuntarily. She found her movement severely limited by the ropes binding her. "Yet I suppose they're beautiful enough on their own."

She felt unbalanced when he slid to the floor and left her teetering, sitting on the edge of the piano lid, her feet and legs bound, but resting on the keys, and her arms tied securely behind her. She leaned back on her hands and felt slightly more balanced. It didn't help that the darkness was so disorienting.

She heard the strike of the lighter just before a flame broke the darkness as Kellen lit the candles she'd brought from the kitchen. He carried the candles to the far end of the piano, increasing the amount of light near her. He stared at her in the soft yellow glow until her face burned with embarrassment.

"Don't look at me so intensely," she said and squeezed her eyes shut.

"I can't help it. You look just as beautiful as you feel."

She peeked at him from beneath her lashes as he circled the piano, sometimes touching her skin as if to ensure himself that she was real and other times gazing at her for long patches of time as if she were fine art on display.

"I wish you could see the pattern down your arms," he said. "I'm not sure how I managed to space the knots so evenly."

Probably because he'd taken such meticulous care that she'd thought he'd never finish. There wasn't an inch of play in her arms. She tried to pull them away from her sides and found she was breathing hard for no good reason.

"Easy, baby," he whispered.

Kellen's hands were suddenly everywhere, gently caressing her skin until the ropes felt as if they were part of her.

She looked down at her naked body. The candlelight gave a soft glow to her skin. She couldn't believe how exposed she was. Her legs were wide open. She could feel that they were, but seeing them like that was quite a shock. So that's what her pussy looked like. She'd seen glimpses of it while grooming, but she'd never stared at it before. Was he staring at it too? She was too timid to find out. She forced her attention to less erotic visions, but discovered that he'd transformed every inch of her body into something visually appealing. Erotic.

Kellen had used the blue rope on her right leg and the tan on her left. The knots were not only used to hold her limbs in a certain orientation, but to decorate. At her waist, the two ropes came together. She wasn't sure how he'd manage to combine the two colors into a contrasting design of diamonds and small rings when he couldn't see what he was doing, but it was beautiful. The way the ropes supported her breasts made them jut forward, proud and bare. It was as if he'd showcased them with his rope work, drawing attention to the light pink tips. She turned her head to try to see the work he'd done on her arms, but those knots were out of her field of view. She'd never felt more sexy in her life. Or more trapped.

Her hands were free, so she repeatedly clenched them, and her toes were capable of curling under, but that only managed to remind her of the knot in the instep of her foot which kept her nipples hard for some inexplicable reason.

"You're shaking," he said, moving to stand before her. "Don't fight it."

"I'm not," she said breathlessly. She looked at him, strangely not embarrassed that he had an unfettered view of every private part of her body. She felt separate from herself. Like an observer of her own form.

"Not physically fighting it. Mentally."

"I don't know what you mean."

"How do you feel?"

"Trapped."

"Are you sure?" He held her gaze, his dark brown eyes intense and deep.

She couldn't look away. "Actually, it's more like someone else is trapped and I'm watching her with envy."

"Are you allowing yourself to feel the ropes, Dawn?"

"I don't know." She honestly wasn't sure what she feeling. She was new to this. What was she supposed to be doing? What was she missing? She tried thinking about the ropes pressed into her flesh, forcing her into a position she would never be able to hold on her own. Keeping her there. Holding her completely stationary. *Can't move. Can't move.* Suddenly, it was as if a fist reached into her chest, squeezed her heart, and robbed her lungs of air.

Kellen stepped between her thighs and held her gently so that her forehead was resting against his shoulder. His hands felt so soothing against her shoulders that she practically melted. "Don't panic," he whispered. "I've got you."

"I'm not sure I like this."

"Do you want me to release you?"

He'd worked so hard to tie her this way, and she felt a million times better now that he was near. "Not yet. Just hold me a while longer."

"I probably should have tied you on your bed your first time. You would have felt more secure. More stable. I just couldn't stop thinking about how sexy you'd look on the surface of your piano."

"I feel secure as long as you're close," she whispered. She angled her face and kissed his neck. He tensed slightly, but didn't move away. She prayed that this wasn't one of those triggers that sent him fleeing, because once she started, rubbing her lips against his throat, nibbling, licking, sucking and kissing, she couldn't stop. If her hands had been free, she'd be plunging them down his boxer shorts right about now. God, she wanted his cock in her hands, her mouth, her wide open pussy. She was suddenly thankful that he'd tied her, so she wouldn't attack him.

His ragged breathing stirred her hair. His hands went from holding her shoulders to provide comfort to massaging her breasts to provoke excitement. He kneaded them gently in his palms while she desperately sucked on his neck, his shoulder, his collarbone, wishing she could reach more of his flesh. She wanted so much more of him. When he began to rub her nipples between his thumbs and forefingers, desire ignited deep inside her. She moaned in torment.

"Find your balance," he said gently.

She had no idea what he meant until he started to slide down her body and she teetered forward. She leaned back slightly, catching herself on her hands.

Kneeling on the floor between her wide open thighs, Kellen looked up at her as he tied his hair back with a leather strap he'd tugged from beneath the cuff on his right wrist. There was no hesitation at all as he shifted forward and plunged his tongue into her quivering hole. He traced her opening repeatedly, drawing her fluids into his mouth with each swipe. She could see it. She could see everything. When he'd collected most of what she'd had waiting for him, he nibbled his way up one swollen lip and then latched onto her clit with a tight suction. His tongue worked the swollen bud as he sucked and sucked, drawing her higher, higher.

"Oh God," she cried.

Two long, thick fingers slid deep into her clenching pussy. A third pressed against her ass, but didn't enter. Her hips bucked involuntarily as she exploded in bliss. As soon as the pleasure began to recede, Kellen began to thrust his fingers and rotate them in wide arcs inside her. She moaned for mercy as he kept her pleasure heightened far longer than she'd even known was possible. When her legs began to tremble from overstimulation, he slipped his fingers free and released her clit so he could slide his fingers into his mouth.

She watched him suck her fluids from his fingers with her mouth hanging open. She'd thought the sight of him between her thighs had been sexy, but that... that made her pussy quake with the tease of another orgasm.

He pulled his fingers free, took a deep breath, and said, "So fucking good," before he leaned forward and licked desperately at her juices.

He rubbed her clit with two fingers while he sucked at her pussy. "Give me more, baby," he pleaded.

When she came a moment later, he moaned with satisfaction at the flood of fluids that met his probing tongue.

Fuck, he was good at this.

He stood abruptly, drawing a gasp of surprise from Dawn. He freed his massive cock from his shorts and began to stroke his length in rapid, hard tugs. She couldn't decide where to look. At his eyes squeezed shut in bliss? His mouth hanging open as he gasped for air? His heaving chest? Taut abs? His hand tugging his length in rapid, sure strokes? Oh God! Dawn's pussy clenched in time with his motion. She could almost feel him inside her as he pleasured himself between her thighs. She strained toward him. *Fill me. Fill me. Fill me*, she thought. He cried out as he erupted. His fluids spurted from his body onto her belly and one breast. A second shot splattered across her thigh. His hand went still.

He leaned against her, his forehead against her shoulder, his shaky breaths warming her chest. She wished her arms were free so she could hold him tight. She nuzzled her face against his neck, and he wrapped his arms around her and pulled his body against hers—chest to breasts, belly to belly, cock to seam. She didn't move, afraid he'd pull away. His hips began to grind, rubbing the length of his still hard cock against her opening. He moaned as if in agony and his cockhead slipped inside her. Yes, she thought. Please. But she stayed silent, her eyes squeezed shut in preparation for his rejection.

He shifted his hips downward, but instead of pulling away, he pressed up inside her, claiming another inch. She clung to the piano beneath her hands. God, how she wanted to hold him as he slowly entered her in a deepening pattern of retreat and conquer. Her body adjusted to his thickness, stretching to accommodate his girth. When his balls pressed against her and she knew she had all of him, a tear dripped from beneath her eyelid and streaked down her cheek.

He buried his hands in her hair and pressed his lips to her cheek. "Dawn?" he whispered brokenly. "What did I just do?"

She wanted to speak, to soothe him, to say *it's okay, Kellen, it's okay*, but emotion clogged her throat and she couldn't find the words.

He jerked abruptly away, pulling free of her body, away from her, and she couldn't cling to him, couldn't stop him from fleeing into the bathroom and slamming the door. And she couldn't stop the tears flowing down her cheeks unchecked.

CHAPTER SEVEN

Kellen leaned back against the inner surface of the bathroom door, trying to catch his breath. What had he done? Shit. What had he been thinking? He *hadn't* been thinking. He'd completely lost control.

It was Dawn's fault for being so beautiful, so sweet, so warm and wonderful and willing. So absolutely amazing and accepting and so... not Sara.

He slammed his fist into the wall, relishing the pain that snaked through his knuckles and up his arm.

He could still taste Dawn's juices, still smell the musk of her sex, still feel her warm, soft heat sheathing his cock.

How could have done that? Just entered her like that? Promises to Sara aside, he hadn't even been wearing a condom.

He approached the sink, fumbling in the dark until he found the faucet. He turned on the water and cupped his hand to draw several sips to his mouth.

His promise to Sara echoed through his head. *Never, honey. I promise I'll never come inside another woman. You're my one and only forever.*

Technically, he hadn't come inside Dawn. He'd entered her after he'd spent himself all over her.

He banged the wall again.

What in the fuck am I doing? Qualifying my actions so I can tolerate the guilt again? He called bullshit on himself. First he had convinced himself that Shibari was okay because he'd never tied Sara, then performing oral was acceptable because Sara didn't enjoy that particular act, then it was fine if Owen was the one touching him and making him come because Owen wasn't a woman, and now Kellen was trying to convince himself he could enter a woman, just as long as doing so wasn't his reason for ejaculating. *Hey, Sara, how's my promise to you looking now? I failed you again.*

He had to go back to Dawn. He couldn't leave her tied like that without supervision. She could easily lose her balance and take a fall from the piano. But how could he face her after using her body so selfishly and then hiding in the bathroom as if he wasn't utterly lost in her?

Dawn was so sweet. So perfect. He'd been completely absorbed in her—her taste, her scent, the sound of her sighs and moans, the texture of her skin, her warmth, her exquisite beauty. When he'd claimed her body, he'd been seeking something more than pleasure. He'd wanted to be closer to her. He'd wanted to be deep inside—not just physically, but emotionally. And he knew that was a far worse form of infidelity than a round of meaningless sex. His main problem was that he had a hard time ever having meaningless sex. He chose his partners carefully for that reason. He had to have a deeper connection than lust with a woman to make love to her. Fooling around was one thing, but being inside a woman was spiritual to him. It touched far more than his body.

After Sara, every woman he'd been attracted to had drawn him because she reminded him of his lost love in some way. He'd been looking to replace what he'd lost. He knew that. It was sick and twisted and wrong.

And now there was Dawn. Dawn who was nothing like Sara. Yet being with her felt right. Why?

He heard a thump outside the bathroom, and his heart leapt. He tore open the door and rushed to Dawn's side. He was completely unprepared for what he found.

Dawn wasn't in any harm, but she'd managed to lie across the piano on one side, her arms still tied securely behind her. She was weeping silently, tears streaming down her face to pool on the shiny black surface beneath her. Deep red strands of curls spread out over her nude body and trailed out behind her, draping her piano.

"Are you in pain?" he asked. "Where does it hurt, Dawn?"

"My heart," she sobbed.

Was she experiencing cardiac arrest? An extreme panic attack? He'd heard that sometimes a panic attack felt like a heart attack. Being the self-absorbed asshole that he was, he'd forgotten that she'd been freaked-out about being tied unless he was close. He had to get her free as soon as possible. There wasn't time for him to slowly untie each knot.

He grabbed a candle and hurried to the kitchen. He found a knife in a butcher block and returned to Dawn.

She gasped when she saw him standing over her with a huge knife. There he went scaring her again.

"I'm not going to stab you with it," he said.

He sawed through each knot holding her arms together, starting at her wrists and working his way upward toward her shoulder blades. When the last knot came free, she surprised him by knocking the blade aside and wrapping both arms around his neck. Her muscles were trembling with fatigue, but she held on to him with surprising strength.

"I hate her," she sobbed. "I hate her for taking so much of you. I hate her for meeting you first. I hate her fucking guts."

"Easy," he said, allowing himself to hold her gently. "I'm sorry I left you by yourself. You shouldn't have been left unsupervised." It was the first rule of bondage. "Something bad could have happened to you. I'm so glad you're not hurt. I would have never forgiven myself."

"But I do hurt, Kellen," she said. "I hurt so bad... for you."

He leaned back and brushed strands of hair from her tear-damp cheeks. He got lost in her very watery hazel eyes. "Is that why you're crying? For me?"

She nodded. "I wish your heart was free, Kellen. I wish that for me, but I wish it for you even more."

"I should have nev—"

She covered his lips with two fingertips. "Don't say you regret it, Kellen. I couldn't bare it. When you were inside me..." Several tears dripped down her smooth cheeks. "It was beautiful."

He didn't regret being inside her. He felt a crippling guilt, but strangely the guilt was worth the connection he couldn't deny he'd felt. That moment of emotional bonding might not be worth it when Dawn was no longer pressed against his body, holding him close, staring up at him with something he feared was adoration, but in this moment, the guilt was minor in comparison to the joy he felt in just holding this woman.

"I won't say it," he whispered. "I won't say it because it's not true. Being inside you felt... right."

She caught his face between her palms, her gaze trained on his mouth. "I'm going to kiss you now," she said. "And don't you dare think of her when I do it."

"Dawn." He meant to speak her name as a protest, but it was more of a plea.

"Shh. It's just a kiss."

Just a kiss.

Her lips brushed his gently, and she immediately shifted away to stare into his eyes again. He saw her concern for him and while it touched his heart, it wasn't necessary.

"That wasn't a kiss," he said.

Her brows drew together. "It wasn't?"

He claimed her mouth with his—seeking, rough, deep, passionate, oh so intimate kisses. When her lips parted and her timid tongue brushed his lip, he felt as if a dam burst inside him and a tidal wave he had no hope of fighting slammed him against Dawn's glory, melding them into one. Once he started kissing her, he couldn't stop. He didn't want to stop. He never wanted to stop. Lust stirred in his groin, but for once it wasn't accompanied by guilt, just need. He needed this, needed her—*Dawn*. He was certain he'd feel differently in the morning, but he didn't care about the aftermath or the fallout. He only cared about the here and now. He didn't want her tied to prevent her from touching him, from encouraging his lust, and fueling his desire. He wanted her completely free, so she could continue to help free his heart from the bonds of his past.

Reluctantly, he pulled away from her delightful mouth and stared down into her eyes. He tucked a finger under her chin and traced her full, lower lip with his thumb. "Would you be overly offended if I said I want to fuck you until dawn?"

She smiled, and he was glad to say goodbye to the emotional knot that had been squeezing his throat. He didn't want his time with her spoiled with all the baggage that dragged him down. He wanted the same joy her music had given him to accompany their joining, and her looking at him as if he was a charity case wasn't what he needed or wanted from her. He knew her light would chase away his darkness—maybe only for a single night, but he'd worry about that later.

"Offended?" she said. "I don't think that's the right word for what I'm feeling right now."

"What are you feeling?" He palmed her breast, his fingertips tracing the rope that still crisscrossed her chest.

"Inspired," she said.

His eyebrows shot up. "You want to write music? *Now?*"

She shook her head. "I'll show how inspired I am by *you*, if you'll let me."

"Allow me to untie you and you can show me anything you like."

Kellen unwound what was left of the ropes from Dawn's shoulders. He took his time, not because he didn't feel an urgency to possess her, but because he wanted this to last for as long as possible. As he removed the ropes, he massaged and kissed her pale skin, making sure each freckle was given proper attention.

Her fingertips clung to his shoulders as he slowly made his way down her chest. When his lips rubbed over her nipple, she sighed, and then she moaned when his tongue flicked out to trace the hardened bud. He suckled her, his hand gently kneading her soft flesh. It was as if her breasts had been molded specifically to fill his palms.

"Kellen."

He loosened more ropes and lavished her other breast with attention. Adoration.

Her hands began to explore his shoulders, roam his chest, thread through his hair. It felt so good to be touched. He fought the urge to hurry in untying her legs so she'd wrap them around him. Imagining her heels pressed into the backs of his thighs, her calves hugging his ass, had him fumbling with the ropes at her waist. He didn't give her belly half the attention it deserved as he hurriedly untied the knots surrounding her belly button. He made his way lower, lower, until her pussy was too close to resist. He devoured her, teasing her clit with rapid flicks of his tongue until she was moaning and dripping fluids. Damn, she tasted good as he dipped his tongue into her opening and swirled it around again and again to collect every drop of her arousal.

Her hands held the back of his head as he lost himself in her scent, her taste, but her legs were still tied wide open, and he wanted them around him, pulling him into her. He wanted her free when he took her, and his rigid cock was throbbing, demanding entry into her slick warmth.

Crouched between her thighs, he leaned back and peered up at her, waiting for her eyelids to flutter open before he spoke.

"Do you have any condoms?" He had some in his wallet—Owen's back-up stash of all things—which was out in the glovebox of his rental car, but he'd rather not have to go out there to find them if it wasn't necessary.

"In my purse," she said and then she chuckled. "They've been in there a while. They might be expired."

"Where's your purse?"

"Finish untying me and I'll get them," she said.

"But I'm not sure I can wait that long."

"Then cut the ropes. Not that I'm not enjoying all this attention. It's just the longer you take, the more inspired I feel."

He still wasn't sure what she meant by being inspired, but he knew in order to find out, he was going to have to free her legs. He hesitated only because he knew that once she was free, there was no turning back. He wouldn't be able to stop even if his conscience was calling him every kind of cheater. A lecher. A weak man without principles.

He found the knife on the floor and carefully used it to cut the ropes from her thighs, then at the knee, and finally each ankle. She stretched her legs out in front of her, and he rubbed her hips to help her regain full mobility.

"Okay?" he asked.

"Better than okay." She scooted forward and wrapped both arms and legs around him to hold him close. "Perfect."

She kissed his jaw, his neck. He fought the instinct to deny himself pleasure—he'd been denying it for so long that enjoying it, seeking pleasure, felt foreign. Foreign and wonderful.

"But I think we can improve on perfect," she whispered.

Her lips trailed over his collarbones, her hands roamed his back, and her legs tightened around his hips, forcing his cock against the heat between her thighs. He needed that condom like yesterday.

"Dawn?"

"Hmm?" she murmured, nibbling a delightful trail around one of his nipples.

"I could really use that condom right about now."

She looked far too devious for comfort when she lifted her gaze to his. "I'll go get them. You climb up here on the piano and wait for me."

"But—" But he'd wanted her on the piano while he stood between her thighs and plunged into her.

"I want to show you how you've inspired me."

And he did want to experience that, even if it meant he had to wait a while longer to possess her.

He helped her down from the piano, unable to keep his eyes off her gorgeous ass as she hurried toward the kitchen. She'd looked amazing all bound in ropes, but she looked even more beautiful without a single adornment impeding his view of her smooth, white skin. He completely forgot to climb up on the piano until she was headed back in his direction with something in her hand.

He put his back to the piano and was about to do a triceps curl to hoist himself up, when she waved one hand.

"Wait," she said. "I see a problem."

He glanced around in confusion. She approached him and hooked her fingers in his borrowed boxer shorts.

"You won't be needing these."

She tugged his shorts down and jerked back unexpectedly when his cock sprang free in her face. She chuckled. "Whoa, big guy. Are you trying to black my eye?"

"That wasn't its target, no."

She laughed and helped him remove his shorts entirely. Then she stood and patted the surface of the piano lid.

"Up here," she said.

Who was he to argue with her inspiration? He propelled himself upward to sit on the piano, and she nibbled on her lip as she stared at him.

"Open your legs."

He cocked an eyebrow at her. That's the kind of thing he was supposed to say to *her.*

"Do I have to tie you?" she asked.

He chuckled. "Not this time, but I'd love to show you a few knots."

He did as she instructed and watched her—completely intrigued and entranced—as she bent over him. The feel of her tongue tracing the crease between his balls made him jerk upright.

"Dawn?"

"Don't interrupt," she said. "It's your turn to be driven mad by someone's mouth."

He groaned in bliss as she suckled his sac.

He watched her kiss and lick and use her lips to massage his most sensitive skin until he couldn't handle the sight of her giving him so much pleasure. He squeezed his eyes shut and allowed himself to feel the heat and moisture of her mouth, the heaviness of his balls, the unbearable throb pulsing down the length of his cock. He shifted slightly so he could bury both hands in the thick lustrous mass of her hair. He coaxed her head toward his cock, slowly, as if she wouldn't notice. She nibbled, kissed, and suckled the flesh all around the base of his shaft, but no amount of tugging on her hair convinced her to take his tip into her mouth.

"Dawn," he pleaded when he couldn't stand the ache in his groin another moment. She gave his balls a thorough licking and then blew cooling breaths over the damp surface. He was trembling so hard he feared he'd collapse.

She paused in her exquisite torture, and he pried his eyes open to look down at her. She smiled reassuringly and reached for one of the candles burning nearby. His eyes widened when she blew out the flame and tipped the candle over his body until wax dribbled onto his belly. His abs contracted involuntarily as she drew a trail in wax from his belly button down, down toward his cock.

"Wait!" he cried. While a little molten heat on his belly was exciting, there were areas that he'd rather she didn't burn with wax.

"Shh," she said. "I trusted you completely. You owe me the same courtesy."

Yeah, but he'd known what he was doing. He'd never have hurt her in any way.

But she hadn't known that. She had placed her complete trust in him. He cringed, prepared to breathe through the pain as the hot, slow trickle of wax got closer and closer to his cock. Less than an inch shy of his throbbing shaft, she righted the candle and blew a soothing breath over the hardening wax. She started at his belly again and trickled another line of wax parallel to the first, again slowly moving toward his cock. He held his breath as the hot trail burned closer and closer to her target. Surely this time she'd... But no, she started another new trail on his belly. When she ran out of wax, she reached for a second candle. When her lips pursed to blow out the flame, he groaned. Dear lord, she was sensual. She smiled when her fourth trail of wax caused a bead of pre-cum to seep from the opening at the tip of his cock.

"Is this turning you on?" she asked, her voice low.

His answer was a groan of torment. If she didn't touch his dick soon, he was going to die. The fifth line of hot wax had him sucking air between his teeth and his cock jerking with over excitement. A bead of moisture dripped from the rim of his cock head, and she caught it with her tongue, looking at him with those incredible eyes as she rubbed the small drop of fluid against her upper lip.

"Do you want me?" she asked, reaching for one of two condom packages resting near his hip.

His stomach ached, he was so turned on, but he couldn't find the mental capacity to even nod. She tore the package open and removed the circle of cream-colored latex. He shuddered as her hand wrapped around his thick, hard-as-granite shaft. She directed his head into her mouth and the pleasure caused his arms to give out. The back of his head thumped against the piano lid, but he didn't care. All he could focus on was the bliss Dawn's mouth gifted him.

"Oh God, baby," he moaned.

He groaned in misery when he fell free of his mouth. She rolled the condom down his length and then stepped away. His eyes flipped open when the piano keys pinged discordantly. She climbed onto the lid of the piano with him and placed a hand on his hip to coax him toward the center of the piano. Lying on his back on her beloved instrument, he felt panic seize his heart. What was he doing?

She straddled his hips, staring into his eyes, her glorious red hair surrounding her shoulders like a shimmering cloak. She held his gaze as she reached between her legs, grasped his cock, and rubbed its tip against her opening.

He squeezed his eyes closed. His stomach was in knots. He could scarcely breathe.

"Look at me, Kellen," she said gently. "It'll be okay."

He opened his eyes, focused on Dawn's face, her eyes, and a bit of the panic receded. He slipped inside her, and she moved her hand so she could take him inch by glorious inch. When he was buried deep, her eyes drifted closed.

"I feel you, Kellen," she whispered. "Inside my body. Inside my soul. I feel you."

"Yes," he said breathlessly, not sure why his heart was thudding so hard or why his eyes were stinging with threatening tears.

She began to rise and fall over him, churning her hips to increase her stimulation and drive him deeper. He couldn't take his eyes off her as she gave his body unparalleled pleasure. He wasn't sure if it was because she'd gotten him so excited beforehand, but sex had never felt so good. Maybe his memory was just iffy because it had been so long, but he didn't think so. Dawn just felt good, felt right. Felt safe and warm, exciting and soothing, all at once.

He lifted his hands to massage her breasts as she made love to him. When she began to croon as her orgasm approached, he shifted the palm of his hand to her lower belly and massaged her soft mound with his thumb.

"Yes," she whispered. "Almost, Kellen."

Her motions became exaggerated as she sought orgasm. His thumb slipped into the cleft between her swollen lips and rubbed her clit. Her back arched and she cried out, her thighs trembling and her pussy clenching around him as she shattered.

He struggled into a seated position and ran both hands over her smooth back, bending to kiss her throat, her jaw, her lips. She rubbed her breasts against his chest as her arms went around him to hold him close. She dropped her head to his shoulder and took a deep breath.

"I knew you'd be perfect," she said. "Inside me. Perfect."

They clung to each other for a long moment. Kellen's cock began to protest the stillness between them.

He rolled her onto her back, maintaining the connection between their bodies. Her grip loosened just enough for him to thrust.

Ah God, she felt good. He couldn't get enough. He wanted to plunge into her tight pussy for hours.

He could hear himself chanting her name, feel the tightening in his balls as orgasm approached, but it was almost as if it was happening to someone else. He pumped his hips harder and faster. Taking her. Taking her. Harder and harder. Scooting her along the piano lid until the back of her head dropped off the far edge. She'd been making love to him, he'd felt her in every particle of his being, but he was fucking her and it was hardly as satisfying. He paused to catch his breath and find his bearings. He looked down to find her watching him. The single candle still burning made her eyes sparkle.

"Are you okay?" she asked, touching his cheek with one hand. "Why did you stop?"

He didn't think he could speak, so he kissed her gently. Every nerve ending in his body seemed to be on edge. Still kissing her, he cradled the back of her head in one hand and by inching downward and drawing her down to meet him, eased her into a less perilous position on the piano. Once he'd regained a little sense, he said, "Sorry I lost control like that. I'll take it slower."

"I don't mind it rough, if that's what you like."

But he didn't like it fast and rough as much as he liked it slow and tender. He knew he hadn't been fucking her as hard as possible because it felt good—he'd been hammering himself into Dawn because Sara never allowed him to fuck her hard like that and he was still struggling with the reality of what he was doing. Enjoying Dawn bothered him. Not enough to make him stop, but enough to get in the way of what he truly desired. He was finally making progress, but he was a long way from being free enough to give Dawn the care and affection she deserved. If she hadn't been so understanding and patient, he'd have probably already left out of guilt.

"What do you like?" he asked.

"Both. But right now I'd like it slow. It gives me more time to think about how good it feels," she said.

And that, he decided, was what he would concentrate on until he couldn't hold back for another instant. Making her feel good. For as long as possible.

With a new purpose, and strict concentration, he began to move his hips again, watching her face for signs that he was getting it right. He found a slow, deep, grinding rhythm that made her writhe beneath him and moan in bliss. It took him a few minutes to realize he was making love to her to the rhythm of the ocean waves, the rhythm of her song, and apparently the rhythm of their bodies.

He believed in fate and destiny, knew in his heart that people were drawn to each other for a reason. From the moment he'd heard Dawn struggling to compose that song, he'd felt her pull on him. He was supposed to be with her. Maybe not making love to her on a piano during a power outage, but he knew that there was something cosmic about their joining. A reason they'd met. A reason she was so wonderful and accepting and downright irresistible.

Dawn framed his face with both hands and stared deep into his eyes as his pleasure escalated, one thrust, one crest at a time, higher and higher until he felt as if he'd lost contact with the earth and spiraled into the heavens. His muscles tautened as spasms of intense release pulsated deep inside him. He gripped her shoulders to hold her still as he drove himself deep and let go. This was more than a physical release. Years of pain and turmoil seemed to pump out of him with an even greater intensity that his erupting fluids.

His lower lip began to tremble and he knew he was about to

completely lose it, so he lowered his body on Dawn's and buried his face in her neck. He hoped she thought all those ragged breaths bursting from his lungs were due to physical exertion. How terrible would she feel if he did something as mortifying as cry while he spent himself inside her?

He refused to find out. He reburied some of his anguish, shoving it back into a familiar place where he could save it to dwell upon another day. He just couldn't let go of it all at once. He probably should have taken it a little slower with Dawn—not jumped in the fire with both feet. But it was too late for misgivings now. He was completely engulfed in her flames and had no desire to escape, even if the ties of his past were wrenching him in the opposite direction.

CHAPTER EIGHT

Dawn stroked Kellen's back as he lay trembling on top of her. She knew he was having a difficult time with the emotional aspect of this. He seemed to be okay with the physical part. Her body thanked him for that. She'd never been with a man who could stare directly into her eyes while he made love to her. It was as if Kellen wasn't only making love to her body, but also to her soul. He'd touched her everywhere—inside and out.

"I just need a minute," he said, his voice shaking almost as much as his body was. It made her heart ache for him.

If he cried, she was going to bawl right along with him. A tight knot was already lodged firmly in her throat.

"Take as long as you need," she whispered. "I like the weight of you against me."

She was actually finding it difficult to draw air, and the top of this piano was almost as comfortable as a cement floor, but her minor discomfort couldn't possibly match what he was going through emotionally. She almost wished they'd waited before taking this step. What if he hadn't been ready? What if by diving headlong into the physical side of their attraction, she'd completely ruined those deeper connections that she wanted to explore with him? The sex had been phenomenal and she had no doubt that it would get better between them as he shed the restraints of his past, but she would be devastated if her successful seduction hurt him. He was hurting enough already. And she didn't have a clue what she should say to him. So she just lay there, holding him, until his trembling abated and he slowly withdrew from her body. She immediately missed the fullness of him inside her. She hadn't realized the physical connection was so important to her until it went missing.

Kellen rose up on his elbows and stared directly at her forehead. "I... uh... *thanks?*"

Thanks? And not a statement, but a question. Wow, when had

Mr. Deep and Sensitive vanished? Shit, was he one of those guys who pretended to be wounded to get in a woman's pants? It wouldn't be the first time she'd been duped into having sex.

And, okay, she *supposed* that thanks were appropriate, but for some reason she got tickled by the earnest look on his face and started to laugh.

"Uh... *you're welcome?*" she said in the same uncertain tone he'd used.

He grinned and then snorted as he tried to hold in a laugh. "That was pretty uninspired," he said. "Let me try again. Your body is like a river of warm pleasure washing over me like... uh..." His eyes darted to the side as inspirational words apparently escaped him.

"A river of warm pleasure?" She was really laughing now. "You should have stuck with thanks."

"Sorry for being lame. I have a hard time stringing coherent thoughts together after a really intense orgasm." He grinned. "So yeah. Thanks!"

She wrapped him in an affectionate embrace, a little surprised that he wasn't making excuses to leave.

"Do you want to go upstairs?" she asked, crossing her fingers behind his back.

Yes, sex had definitely happened too soon with this deep and tortured man. She wanted him to stick around, but maybe it would be better to convince him to stay with something other than another really intense orgasm. Not that she'd mind another one herself.

"What's upstairs?"

She couldn't tell if he was joking. "Uh, something more comfortable to cuddle on than this hard piano."

He winced as he shifted slightly. "Such as a porcupine?"

"Even more comfortable than that."

"I don't think I can spend the night in your bed, Dawn," he said. "Not because you aren't the most wonderful thing that's happened to me in a long, long time, but because..."

He didn't have to say the words; she could read them on his face. He felt guilty for having sex with her. He probably even felt guilty for being attracted to her and talking to her and eating her fucking French toast, not to mention her pussy. Even in the low light given off by the single candle, the guilt in his eyes brought his reality crashing down around her. She knew letting go of Sara was difficult for him, and she wasn't making it easy on him by jumping into this relationship at rocket speed, but someone had to shake him up. It might as well be her.

He glanced around the mostly dark room. "Would you settle for a sofa?"

"Anything's better than this piano," she said. "For resting on. Making love on it fulfilled a long-standing fantasy of mine, and the experience greatly exceeded my expectations. So... uh... *thanks*?"

He laughed and kissed the tip of her nose before scooting off the edge of the piano. Once standing, he stared down at her. "I never made love on a piano or even fantasized about it, but I will be from now on. You look absolutely stunning lying there."

She basked in his attention as his gaze touched upon every inch of her naked body. She liked looking at him too. Especially when he was dripping wet as he had been the first time she'd seen him. "Have you ever made love on the beach?"

"Yeah," he said, looking suddenly detached and forlorn.

Must have screwed Sara there, Dawn figured. She was starting to recognize that lost look as an indicator of *that* woman commandeering his thoughts. "And?"

"Sand everywhere," he said. "In places you don't want it. Making sandpaper out of body parts that have no business being abrasive."

"Ouch," she said breathlessly, a little curious to know what that would feel like, but she wouldn't admit that to him. Mostly because it would make him think of *her*.

Would Dawn have to spend every moment with him watching what she said so she didn't set off Sara triggers? Was he even worth that much effort?

Hell yeah, he was.

Kellen removed the condom and disposed of it among her waded-up attempts at musical scores in the wastepaper can. She pretended not to be affected by watching him do something so intimate. Every little thing he did fascinated her for some stupid reason. She'd probably weep at his masculine beauty if she watched him shave. Sheesh, she was glad the man could not read her thoughts. It was bad enough that he knew how quickly she'd become physically attached to him—if he had any idea that she was already making an emotional attachment, she wouldn't be able to gaze at him for long, because he'd be gone.

"Making love on the beach seems as if it would be romantic," she said.

"Romantic, yes, but also uncomfortable."

She chuckled as he approached the piano again. "Apparently, making love in uncomfortable locations turns me on."

He laughed and lifted her from the piano, cradling her head against his shoulder. Her arms automatically circled his neck. She expected him to set her on her feet, but he carried her to the sofa and sat with her on his lap.

"Tell me about your parents," she said.

"While I'm naked and holding you in my arms?"

"Yep."

"My mom had a drinking problem and I never met my dad. Tell me about yours."

"My mom has a stick up her ass and my dad makes sure she keeps it there. I see them twice a year."

"Christmas and Thanksgiving?"

"Lord, no. They spend the holidays on their private island in the Bahamas. No way am I marooning myself in their company when I'm supposed to be feeling good will toward man and thankful for my gifts. I see my father for a week in April. He reviews my financial situation with his tax attorney. It's great fun. And I also get the pleasure of their company at the family reunion each year in July. That's when they all get together and talk about which politician they're currently courting and who has the most expensive yacht."

"Can't even begin to relate to that."

She chuckled. "Me neither."

"Didn't you grow up in that environment?"

"Not really. I had a piano teacher and a variety of tutors, a housekeeper who made sure I was fed and clean, but mostly I had me."

"You must have been lonely. I can relate to that. My grandfather owns a piece of land outside Austin. He lived in one trailer, and my mom and I lived in another. I made sure Mom was fed and clean, and grandpa tried to teach me how to find peace through connecting with the earth. I learned a lot from him before he died. He was half-Comanche and had a unique way of seeing things. When he passed, he left everything to my mom, so she started buying top-shelf vodka. Then my senior year in high school, she met some guy and left me on my own. I was eighteen, and she decided I'd rather finish school in Austin than follow her and Henry to Florida."

"Did she ask you how you felt about that?"

"Nope, but she was right. I preferred to stay on my own. But her not giving me the choice made me feel unwelcome and unwanted."

She squeezed his arm reassuringly. She'd never felt wanted either. But she wanted him and hoped that he wanted her too.

"I've never admitted that to anyone," he said. "Not even Owen. When my mom moved out, he and I made it out like it was a huge party. I guess I needed that lie, that I was glad Mom left. Owen tends to dwell on the good and pretend the bad doesn't exist. He keeps me going most days."

"I think I'd like to meet him. It's hard to find a good optimist."

He laughed. "Yeah, Owen wears optimism like a shield."

"Do you know who your father is?"

"Yeah. I never met him though. He contacted me when I was sixteen. Sent cards and letters, but I didn't want to have anything to do with him. I was too angry at him for abandoning me."

"You've never met him? Not even once?"

"No. He got killed in a car wreck before I could allow myself to forgive him. And then it was too late. I didn't even find out about his death until a week after the funeral. I'm not sure if I would have gone had I known."

"I'm sorry."

"Before Sara was diagnosed, that was my sole regret in life," he said. "Not getting to know my father when I had the chance. When Sara got sick, my list of regrets grew exponentially."

"You don't regret knowing her, do you?"

"Never. I regret not making her last months more about living and less about dying. I regret letting her convince me that the lump I found in her breast was probably nothing. Did you know that when breast cancer is caught early, it has a near one hundred percent cure rate?"

Dawn hated that he carried that guilt. How was he supposed to know what was going on inside her body?

"They didn't catch it early, did they?"

He shook his head. "It had already metastasized into her lungs. Breast cancer doesn't even run in her family. She didn't smoke. She ate healthy and took care of her body. So why did it happen to her?"

"It was just chance," Dawn said.

"I don't believe in chance."

"You believe in destiny," she said.

He nodded slightly.

"So you think she was destined to die at... how old was she?"

"Twenty-four."

"Jesus," Dawn said, sudden tears springing to her eyes. No one should die that young. "Does it make it easier or more difficult thinking she died because it was her destiny?"

"I don't know," he said. "I just really can't bring myself to believe that she suffered like that for no reason. But even though I've tried rationalizing her death, I can't come up with any sound reason for her to be taken so young."

Dawn didn't believe in destiny or fate. She believed in chance. So it was hard for her to understand where he was coming from. In her mind, there was no reason for Sara to die other than her cells had become cancerous, due to some chance event that would never be identified, and she'd died. She knew Kellen wouldn't find that any more comforting than not having the sound reason he sought. And Dawn's beliefs weren't important here. She didn't want to convince him that she was right and he was wrong. All she wanted was for him to find that comfort he needed, even if she wasn't the one who gave it to him.

"Maybe you're not meant to know the reason she died so young," Dawn said.

"I'm sure I'm not supposed to understand it," he said, "but that doesn't stop me from trying."

They sat silently, and Dawn found herself missing the sound of the storm raging outside. She could use a distraction from her thoughts and was certain Kellen's thoughts were equally as turbulent.

"So how many men have you slept with?" he asked.

Or maybe he was thinking about her vagina.

"Why?" she asked.

"You seem a little inexperienced."

"I do?"

"You're great at what you do," he said. "That trick with the candle wax had me ready to explode."

"I made that up on the fly," she said.

"Nice."

She chuckled. "But to answer your question, four. Including you.

You count, right?"

"I'm hoping by the end of the night, I'll count double."

That sounded promising. Was he thinking of getting intimate with her again? Yes, please. She'd never known a guy to come twice in one night, so if Kellen managed it three times, she'd definitely count him double.

"How many woman have you slept with?" she asked. It was only fair that he share the same information. Then she remembered he was a rock star. She'd probably have a stroke when he spouted some astronomical figure.

"Actual sex or fooling around and foreplay?"

"Actual sex."

"Four," he said. "Including you."

She gaped at him for what felt like five minutes and then sputtered, "Liar!"

"I didn't call you a liar. Why do you think I'm one?"

"Because. Because you're a gorgeous rock star. You must have women hanging all over you."

"Yeah, but I don't have sex with them. I only have sex when I feel a connection with a woman, and that doesn't happen very often."

So was he saying he felt a connection with her?

"I have fooled around a lot," he said. "I'm not a saint."

"Then why did you tell me you've only been with three other women?"

"Because I place a certain emphasis on being inside a woman. It's important to me and I thought maybe it was important to you too. If it's not, that's okay. I just wanted to know what kind of woman destiny insists I feel a connection with."

There he went with that destiny stuff again. Couldn't they have just met by chance, had a few things in common—most notably music—found each other attractive and decided that a little pleasure would go well with their newfound compatibility?

"Tell me about your other lovers," he said. "I want to know what I'm up against."

Her eyes widened. This was like taboo stuff to talk about so early in a relationship. But wait—was this even a relationship yet? Hardly. But she found herself telling him anyway.

"I lost my virginity on prom night."

"Cliché," he said with a soft smile. "Was it good for you?"

"No. It was awkward and it hurt and I didn't even like the guy. I hadn't ever been on a date before. My dad somehow talked one of his colleague's sons into taking me to his prom, since I was homeschooled and would have missed out on all the *fun*. I didn't know anyone there. I was so socially awkward and apparently naive. He gave me my first kiss. First tongue kiss. First boob fondle. First touch down below. First penetration. All in the same night. I didn't know how to stop him. I wanted him to stop, but I was scared and confused, so I just let it happen. I never saw him again after that night, and I'm glad. I'd probably have thrown up if I ever had to be in the same room with him again." Just thinking about that night so many years ago made her feel queasy.

"What a scum-sucking son-of-a-bitch," he said. "You don't count that one, Dawn. That's called date rape."

She shook her head. "Except I never told him no. I just thought it. And thought it. And thought it. But I never *said* it."

"If you didn't want to do it, it was rape. I've had a lot of women who can't take no for an answer. It's never progressed to actual intercourse, but even being touched when you don't want to be touched doesn't feel right. It bothers me every time it happens."

Dawn's belly flipped over. "But I touched you when you didn't want to be touched. I'm sorry if it bothered you." She hadn't even thought that her coming on so strong to Kellen might have made him feel the way that Jonathan Kingsley had made her feel. How wretched of her.

He chuckled. "Are you kidding? The only kind of bothered you caused was hot and bothered. I wanted you to touch me so badly I thought I was going to rip those boxer shorts in half with my boner. There is a difference between reluctance and rejection. That asshole stole something from you that he had no right to take."

Not many people knew what had happened to her on prom night. It wasn't like she could have told her parents. She didn't have close friends until college, and they'd thought losing her virginity behind a Dairy Queen was funny, because she usually told it as a humorous story. She didn't know why she'd expressed her true feelings when she'd told Kellen about it. And Kellen's understanding about why it had been so mortifying made her feel better.

"You know, it wasn't your fault," he added, and gently rubbed his knuckles up and down her bare arm.

Kellen was right—it hadn't been her fault. But for a long time she'd blamed herself for not knowing what to do or how to make him stop. It had never occurred to her to blame Jonathan Kingsley.

"I hope the other two treated you right," Kellen said. "I don't want to hear about some other jerk hurting you."

"No. There was just the one jerk. My second lover was my only long-term boyfriend. We dated for months before we finally slept together. Michael was even less experienced than I was, but once we became intimate, we had a whole lot of fun figuring out what felt good. We broke up after college. He wanted to go to China and teach English. I told him to have fun without me."

"You didn't want to go with him?"

"Our relationship had grown stale. I'd fallen out of love with him, but he never did anything wrong, so I didn't know how to break up with him. How do you end a relationship just because it's boring? His going to China finally gave me the excuse I'd been waiting for."

"Aww, you didn't want to hurt his feelings, did you? I didn't realize you were so nice."

"Nice? I was a doormat. But those were the end of my doormat days. I dated several guys after college, but I was so wrapped up in my music that none of those relationships progressed and I ended up sleeping with only one of them. That was a couple of years ago."

"Well, that explains why we jumped into bed with each other so quickly. We were both hornier than a bucket of desert toads."

His sense of humor continually surprised her. He seemed so serious and deep, and then he let loose with something like that.

"I can tolerate horniness," she said. "I think I jumped into bed—or rather onto piano—with you because you're the sexiest man I've ever met. I'm usually expert at controlling my baser needs. I've been called an ice princess and a cold bitch more than once at the end of a third date, fourth date, and fifth date with no action."

"I'll have to take your word on it. I didn't experience any ice or cold."

"Just a princess and a bitch."

"Neither. If I had to describe you, I'd say you're hot, talented, sexy and... horny."

"You got at least one of those right."

She shifted so she was straddling his thighs. Did she notice that her wide-open, bare crotch was perfectly aligned with his cock? Of course she did. And she'd be doing something about that soon, but first...

"Your turn," she said. "Tell me about your other three lovers."

He was silent for a long moment. God, she hoped he wasn't thinking about *her* again. But of course he was. Dawn had point blank asked about her. *Dumb, Dawn. Real dumb.*

"First there was Jennifer, then Becca, and I've already told you about Sara," he said. "So did you major in music in college? What was that like? I had some guitar lessons, but never studied theory."

"What?" she sputtered. "That's not fair. But if you don't want to share, I'll just make stuff up in my head. So Jennifer was your sweetheart all through elementary school, but she moved away before you went through puberty. When she returned some years later, she'd grown boobs and—"

He covered her lips with one fingertip.

"Nothing as romantic as that. Jennifer was my first groupie. We were both in high school, but she was a year older than me. She used to come to every band practice. She watched and danced and cheered and dressed in next to nothing and fed my ego. So I screwed her. She fed my ego some more. And I screwed her again. And again and again and again. Like three times a day. She eventually decided she liked drummers better."

"She cheated on you?"

He nodded.

"Well, that sucks. Did you love her?"

"I liked her. A lot. What seventeen-year-old doesn't like to get fucked three times a day? I was young and horny and needed my ego fed. No long-term damage was done when she switched band members, though watching her make out with Snake was weird. Not as weird as William Pierce suddenly insisting that everyone call him Snake, but yeah, a bit weird."

"So that didn't end too badly. What about Becca?"

"If you ever meet Owen, you cannot let him know I slept with her."

"Why?"

"Because she was his one. Or at least he thought she was at the time."

"You slept with your best friend's girlfriend?"

"Oh no. She never dated him. He thought he loved her and she rejected him. She didn't reject me though. I'm not even sure why I slept with her. I wasn't really attracted to her. She came on to me and it just sort of happened."

Dawn snorted. Yeah, that sounded like a boy's reasoning. It just happened.

"Stop that." Kellen squeezed her until she giggled. "Sleeping with her wasn't worth the orgasm. For years, every time I looked at Owen, I thought about the time I slept with Becca and I was revolted by my actions. Having sex with her is what made me decide that I'd only sleep with women I felt a connection with. Sex for the sake of sex was never worth pursuing."

"But the only other woman you've slept with is Sara."

"Yeah. And you."

Dawn sat back on his thighs and tried to read his expression, but there just wasn't enough light on this side of the room to even guess how that made him feel. "I'm not sure I'm ready to hear that."

"So don't listen. I'm a little tired. I tend to talk a lot about things better left unsaid when I'm drunk or tired."

"Do you want to sleep?"

"No." He stroked her hair. "I want to spend more time with you."

"Great," she said, "I want to spend more time with you too, but can we talk about something more superficial? I'm feeling a bit… overwhelmed. This is a lot of heavy stuff for a first date."

He chuckled. "You're right. We should save some heavy stuff for our second date."

Second date? Yes!

"How about we leave all the talking for the second date and the rest of this one can be all about pleasing your pussy?"

She laughed, simply because his suggestion made her uncommonly happy. She'd love the rest of the night be all about pleasing her pussy.

"I think it should be about pleasing your cock too," she said.

"Ladies first."

She squealed in surprise when he grabbed her around the waist and started to lift her over his head.

"Put your legs over the back of the sofa," he instructed.

She could scarcely see the back of the sofa. "Why?"

"Because I don't think I can hold you to my mouth like this for more than twenty seconds." He tipped his head to trace her cleft with his tongue. "And I'm going to need at least twenty minutes."

Feeling completely off balance, she slid one leg over his shoulder and the back of the sofa and then the other, so that his head was between her legs.

"Now lean back."

She clung to his head like a treed kitten. "I'll fall."

"I've got you."

She still didn't feel secure, because she wasn't sure what to expect and the room was so dimly lit, but she did trust him, so she let go and cautiously leaned back. He helped support her with a hand on her belly and another under her back until she found herself virtually upside down with her head between his knees, hair trailing down over his shins and the floor. Good lord, her legs were draped over the back of the sofa, and Kellen was seated beneath her with his face between her thighs and his hands gripping her ass. What in the world had she gotten herself into? She felt like some sort of perverse acrobat.

"Perfect," he said. "Let me know if you get dizzy."

She was already dizzy, but as his mouth latched onto her clit and his strong hands dug into her ass to pull her to his face, she could only focus on the pleasure between her trembling thighs.

The rapid flicks of his tongue against her clit made her come far too quickly, and she was actually pouting when he slid her ass down his belly so she could right herself again.

"You're so good at that," she said. "I scarcely have time to figure out where your tongue is before I'm coming."

"I've had lots of practice."

But not on Sara, because Dawn remembered Kellen saying that Sara hadn't enjoyed oral. Dawn began questioning the girl's sanity.

"On who?" she asked, wishing she could suck the words back in as soon as they erupted from her mouth. She honestly didn't want to know how many women he'd draped upside down over his body so he could be comfortable while he licked them to orgasm.

"Women I tied up with Owen, mostly. We haven't done it for months though."

"Why not?" *Oh, shut up, Dawn. Just shut up.* Thinking about Kellen tying women and putting his mouth on them made her stomach ache when she had no business feeling jealous of women he'd been with before her.

"Owen gave me a thoughtful Christmas present. Perhaps a bit too thoughtful. It reminded me of Sara. Made me question what I was doing. So I stopped doing it."

"What did he give you?"

"A leather wrist cuff."

She touched the leather band around his right wrist.

"Not this one," he said, capturing her hand and circling it with a loose fist to hold it against the worn leather. "I've had this one since I started playing guitar. Sort of a good luck charm. Owen gave me a cuff for my other wrist. I was down on the beach trying to get rid of it when the storm hit."

"*Trying* to get rid of it?"

"Yeah, I said goodbye to Sara and tossed the cuff into the ocean. It washed back to me in a matter of minutes. Destiny at play again. I don't think she was ready for me to let her go yet. And then I heard your song and... I'm not sure what possessed me to come to your door. It was as if I couldn't stay away."

"Oh, that was definitely destiny," she said with a smile. Maybe it was wrong of her to progress her own agenda by using his beliefs to draw him in. Or maybe it *had* been destiny that had landed him on her doorstep. She didn't have all the answers. Sometimes she wondered if she had any.

"I'm sure it was," he said. "I'm just not sure what I'm supposed to do now. Being with you feels right, unless I think of Sara. And then it feels so very wrong."

Dawn shifted so she could face him. She straddled his thighs again and took his face in both hands. She could just see the sparkle of his dark eyes in the candlelight. "Then don't think of her," she said. "Think of me."

She kissed him deeply, pulling away when his hands tightened on her hips and his kiss turned desperate.

She yanked her mouth away. "Who's kissing you, Kellen?"

"You."

"Say my name."

"Dawn. Dawn's kissing me."

She lowered her head and kissed his neck, nibbling and sucking on the corded muscles of his throat. He moaned.

"Who's making you moan, Kellen?" she whispered in his ear.

"Dawn," he said breathlessly. "Dawn is also making my spine tingle and my belly quiver."

"Is Dawn making your dick hard?"

"Yes."

"Good." She kissed his chest and stroked his skin with both palms. She loved the excited hitch in his breathing as much as she loved the texture of his skin against her hands. "Who's touching you, Kellen?"

"Dawn."

She slid onto the floor between his thighs and felt around in the dark until she had his thick shaft captured between her hands. "Who's giving you head?"

"What?"

She directed his cock into her mouth and rubbed his rim with her lips stretched tight over her teeth.

"Dawn," he gasped.

She sucked as she began to bob her head, taking him deeper with each dip. She loved the way he was chanting her name under his breath. Unexpectedly, his fists clenched in her hair and stopped her motions. He fell free of her mouth, and she looked up at him in question, cursing the darkness because she couldn't see his face at all. Had she done something wrong?

"Where's your bedroom?" he asked.

"U-u-upstairs."

He helped her to her feet.

"Why did you stop me?" she asked. Was her inexperience showing again? He'd seemed to be enjoying it, but maybe she'd been reading him wrong.

"I was almost to the point of no return."

"That's what I was going for," she said.

"But I want this one to last. Did you change your mind about wanting me in your bed?"

"Are you staying the night?" Dawn asked. She would love to wake up beside Kellen and watch him sleep. She wanted to see his bronze skin bathed in morning sunlight. Not that he didn't look spectacular by candlelight, but he'd been drowning in darkness far too long and it was time for light to illuminate him once more.

"That depends," he said, stroking her bare arms with feather-light touches.

"On what?"

"If I'm capable of moving when I'm finished making love to you."

Heat flooded her body. She'd never had a man make her feel so desirable.

"And considering all the things I want to do to you and *with* you," he said, his face mostly concealed by shadows as he leaned closer, "I don't think I'll be able to leave afterwards unless you call in a stretcher."

He took her hand and led her to the piano to collect the other condom she retrieved from her purse and handed her the last burning candle. Using the limited light to find her way, Dawn shuffled to the staircase that led to her bedroom. Kellen climbed the stairs behind her. Occasionally his fingers would brush her back, her shoulder, or her buttocks. She knew his eyes were on her so as much as she wanted to race up the stairs and leap into bed, she took her time, luring him to follow her, increasing her anticipation and hopefully his. At the top of the steps, she turned the corner and walked along the railing that was no longer decorated with a whimsical garland of seashells dangling from blue and tan rope.

On the threshold of the bedroom, she paused and looked behind her to make sure Kellen was still following. He walked as silently as a cat and hadn't touched her since they'd reached the top of the stairs. He'd stopped several paces behind her and was staring. Had he changed his mind? She would try to be understanding if he had, but damn, she wanted him to lie beside her in that big comfortable bed.

"What are you doing?" she asked.

"Looking at you," he said as he hurried to catch up with her.

She allowed her gaze to travel up his long, muscular legs. The sexy vee of his hipbones drew attention to his cock, which stood rigid before him. He was so hard, she could see the tortuous ridges of veins beneath the surface of his darkened skin. She forced her attention upward. His washboard abs begged to be nibbled on. Her hand clenched at the thought of exploring the contours of his firm chest. Her gaze didn't make it higher than the two bumps at the base of his throat. She grabbed him by the wrist and tugged him toward the bed.

She'd stare tomorrow. For the rest of the night, she just wanted to feel him. She set the candle on the bedside table and gave her hands liberty to touch him. Everywhere.

He grew impatient quickly and lifted her onto the high king-sized bed, settling over her so he could trail soft kisses across her chest.

"Don't know what it is about these freckles that I find so sexy," he said, rubbing his lips and tongue over her speckled skin as if determined to collect the little spots in his mouth.

"I've always hated them," she admitted. She didn't tan. In the sun, she generated dots, dots, and more dots, but never enough to completely cover her in an even tone. She envied Kellen's darker skin color.

"They're beautiful," he said. "Every last one of them."

He discovered her breast as he kissed her freckles. His lips brushed soft butterfly kisses around her areola until her back arched in bliss, and he flicked his tongue over the hardened tip.

She moaned his name and her fingers stole into his long, silky hair. She freed the thick mass from the tie at his nape, and it tumbled around his face to caress her skin as he pleasured her breast. She'd never thought long hair on a man was especially attractive, but it worked for Kellen. And as he kissed his way down her ribcage, it tickled her skin and worked for her too. He nibbled around her navel and continued lower. Lower. Was he going to kiss her there again? It was as if he couldn't stay away.

He nuzzled her mound, his breath hot between her thighs, his glorious hair draped over her belly. She parted her legs for him, and he groaned.

"You smell so sexy," he murmured. His tongue worked its way into her cleft and brushed her swollen clit.

She gasped as pleasure shot down the insides of her thighs, up her spine, all through her pussy, and even deeper inside her.

"So sexy," he said. "And when I lick you here…" His tongue stroked her clit. "It just gets sexier."

"Feel free to make it as sexy as possible," she said.

He chuckled. "I'd hate to become boring because I'm so fixated on tasting you again and again and again."

"Oh, trust me. I'm not bored with that at all."

And she doubted she'd ever get bored with the way his mouth moved against her clit, her lips, her opening. She rocked her hips involuntarily as he rapidly brought her to the pinnacle of desire and pushed her over the edge. His fingers slid inside her as she came. Again. She'd lost track of how many times the man's mouth had sent her flying to nirvana. She clung to the bedspread beneath her as she shook with release.

By the time his lips moved from her clit to brush the inside of her thigh, she was trembling uncontrollably. Her legs had turned to jelly.

He kissed his way back up her body. His fingers, still buried deep, began to move inside her. She recognized the rhythmic rise and fall of his tempo as the cadence of the sea and her song. He suckled her nipple as his fingers drew her back toward her peak. She hadn't even fully recovered from her last orgasm by the time he had her writhing in ecstasy and begging for more. His thumb brushed her clit. She groaned in torment; her body didn't know how to find release again. That unbearable feeling of *almost* had her in its clutches and wouldn't let go.

Kellen shifted his mouth to her other breast, his fingers still plunging into her body in that same maddening rhythm. A finger brushed her back entrance, and she gasped in surprise. His thumb worked her clit again. She could hear how wet she was as he continued to pump his fingers into her body.

"I can't take much more," she said.

He bit her nipple, and her hips lifted from the bed.

"You might as well stop fighting it then, because I'm not going to stop until you come."

"I can't," she cried.

"You will."

He sucked her nipple so hard she felt the pull in her womb, and then his devious mouth worked its way down her torso again. He peppered her mound with tiny nips. It drove her insane, but it was nowhere near as maddening or exciting as the unwavering rhythm of his fingers plunging and withdrawing, plunging and withdrawing. She strained against his hand, needing to come so badly, wanting to, but she just couldn't. She teetered on the edge for an eternity.

"I should have known you'd be stubborn," Kellen said.

"I'm trying."

"That's the problem, baby. You're trying. Just feel me, Dawn. Feel my rhythm. Our rhythm. Do you hear it?"

She heard the sounds of flesh moving inside slick flesh. The creak of the bed. Her breathing and his. The pounding of the surf outside her window. She could even hear the pulse throbbing in her ears if she concentrated hard enough.

He placed his lips against her mound and hummed her melody. She exploded like a supernova. Her core tightened as waves of ecstasy ripped through her body. Fluids gushed from her clenching pussy. Stunned, she lifted her head to gape at Kellen, but the pleasure was too intense, so her head dropped back on the bed and she squeezed her eyes shut as she continued to ride the waves of bliss shattering her.

"Fuck, yes," Kellen said in a sexy growl. His fingers slipped free of her body so he could lick her freely flowing cum like a starving man.

She wasn't sure when he stopped making out with her pussy or when he turned her onto her belly. She was still recovering from whatever the hell had just happened when she became aware of his strong hands massaging the globes of her ass. Each time he tugged her cheeks apart, her rear opening ached, until she was rubbing her mound against the mattress beneath her, wanting more of him. More. How could she possibly want more?

He shifted so he was suspended over her back. He rubbed the head of his cock up and down the length of her seam. She strained against him. Wanting him inside her.

"Do you like it in your ass, Dawn?" he whispered.

Her heart kicked with the thrill of anxiety mixed with excitement. She'd never done that before. "I don't know."

"We'll have to find out sometime," he said, taking her from behind, filled her aching pussy with ten inches of rock-hard cock.

"Oh God," she cried.

He gripped her hipbones and lifted her lower belly slightly off the bed. Her legs were too far apart for her to rise to her knees and when she tried, he pressed her chest back down with a palm in the center of her back.

"Stay where I put you," he said.

A bit of her temper flared, but it was extinguished when he began to move. He fucked her so hard, she had no choice but to fuck him back. She relished the fullness, the friction, the hint of pain, the explosion of pleasure. God, he was deep. So deep.

"Do you like to be fucked face down, Dawn?" he said.

"Yes. Yes! I'm gonna come again. Kellen."

She wasn't just saying that to spur him on. As another astonishingly hard orgasm gripped her, she clung to the bedspread, her mouth wide open since she couldn't get enough air no matter how hard she panted.

His strokes slowed abruptly. She thought he must have found release too, but she soon realized he was just changing his rhythm.

He trailed his fingers through the sweat that had pooled on her lower back.

"I need to look in your eyes now," he said. His lips brushed her back, and he pulled out.

She gasped for air, still not able to find her breath. She didn't have the strength to assist him as he rolled her over.

"You okay?"

"Just... need... to catch... my breath."

"I like you breathless."

"I'm gonna pass out."

"Slow this time. I promise."

He was inside her again. Taking her slowly. Deeply. Churning his hips to press deeper still. It felt so good. So right.

Yes, Kellen.

Just like that.

Perfect.

He stared into her eyes the entire time; until the candle sputtered out and they were bathed in darkness and he finally allowed himself to let go.

CHAPTER NINE

Kellen rolled over, cursing the sunlight streaming directly into his face. He reached for a pillow to bury his head under, but his hand found a warm body beside him instead. He smiled and allowed his fingertips the pleasure of stroking the smooth skin along Dawn's shoulders. If she was aware of his touch, he couldn't tell. Her soft snores never lost their rhythm, and she didn't stir even when he scooted closer and placed a kiss on her slender arm. Her body was completely slack, her expression oblivious.

I wore her ass out, he thought proudly. She wouldn't be forgetting him anytime soon.

He watched her sleep, wondering how the rest of the day would play out. He would have to leave soon so he could make it to Beaumont in time for Sole Regret's show that evening. Maybe Dawn would like to come with him. He knew she had to finish writing down the song she'd composed the night before so she could meet her deadline, but he hoped she had time to make it to his show. If not, he had another show in New Orleans tomorrow night, and then they had a rare couple of days off before a second show in New Orleans. Surely they could find time to spend together before he had to head to the Northeast for the next leg of the tour.

Now that he'd found her, he didn't want to spend a moment apart from her. He wasn't sure she'd feel the same way, but he had to give this a go, see what came of it. He hadn't felt this way about a woman since... well, never. And he wasn't going to compare Dawn to Sara anymore. It wasn't fair to either of them.

Kellen sat up, scrubbing the sleep from his eyes and combing his fingers through his tangled hair. He rolled out of bed and stretched his back, which was a bit sore from making love to Dawn for hours, but he felt more relaxed, more at ease, than he'd felt in years.

He leaned across the bed to place a grateful kiss at the corner of Dawn's mouth. When she didn't so much as flutter an eyelid, he decided to grab a quick shower. Once he was clean and alert, he found himself drawn to Dawn's bedside again. He'd never known anyone to sleep so soundly. He hated to disturb her, but he wanted her awake. He wanted to see the spark of mischief in her hazel eyes and bask in the warmth of her smile. He also wouldn't mind getting lost in her arms for a couple of hours before he had to leave.

"Dawn," he whispered close to her ear. "It's morning."

She moaned softly, grabbed a pillow, and smashed it over her head in protest.

"Are you going to get up soon?"

"Coffee," he thought she mumbled beneath the pillow. Or maybe she was just growling at him.

So she wasn't a morning person. Only unnaturally happy people, like Owen, were morning people. Kellen wondered what Owen would have to say about Kellen's reawakening. Owen would probably only enthuse about the getting laid part of Kellen's night. Which had been important, he couldn't deny it. But there were more important things going on than his departure from abstinence. And he had Dawn to thank for all of it. He had to think something had drawn them together. Some higher power or outside force. How else could he have found exactly who he needed at exactly the right time and exactly the right place? Or maybe he was reading too much into this.

In nothing but a towel, Kellen padded downstairs to fix Dawn a cup of coffee. Maybe he could coax her out of bed with caffeine. While she was beautiful in sleep, he loved to watch her in motion. Or maybe he'd save her a cup of java for later and wake her with tender kisses between her thighs. She seemed to enjoy being on the receiving end as much as he enjoyed delivering. That woman could take a permanent seat on his face and he'd die a happy man. He grinned wickedly at the remembrance of her sweet, addictive flavor. *That* was the true breakfast of champions.

He opened a cabinet, searching for a mug. He found an entire cupboard full of fresh-baked bread—Dawn's stress outlet. Sheesh. She must have really been having a hard time dealing with her writer's block. There was enough bread to feed a stadium. Kellen opened another cabinet and found what he was looking for. Mug in hand, he hummed Dawn's sensual melody under his breath. Amazed by how serene the weather had turned now that the storm was long gone, he glanced out the window. The mug dropped in the sink, shattering on impact.

Next door, Sara's yellow beach house glowed in the early morning sunshine. Kellen snapped his eyes shut and reared back. *Just don't look at it,* he told himself. He pivoted away. God, he was shaking. He opened his eyes and the first thing he saw was the crumpled heap of his jeans on the breakfast bar. Sara's bracelet was no longer in the pocket. It had tumbled out to rest in plain view. Oh God, what had he done?

Kellen's stomach plummeted, and his heart rate kicked up. "I'm sorry," he whispered, staring at the leather cuff as if it were accusing him of a crime he knew he'd committed. The walls started closing in. He had to leave. Had to beg for Sara's forgiveness. Had to repent for his sins against his memory of her.

Had to give up Dawn.

She didn't deserve to be entangled with someone like him—a man who couldn't get through a single day without being crippled by guilt and paralyzed by the past. Dawn deserved to be first. And he would never be able to give her that.

He hopped into his jeans, which were still slightly damp and cold against his skin. He jammed the cuff back into his pocket, wishing he could just throw the damned thing in the garbage, but knowing if he did that, he'd be digging through coffee grounds and banana peels to get it back. He needed this, this *torture*, for some inexplicable reason. Why couldn't he let himself be happy for more than one night?

Kellen knew he couldn't just dart out the door without any explanation. Dawn might think something had happened to him other than him being too fucked up in the head to take what she so generously offered.

He'd leave her a note. Something short and to the point. No sense in drawing out necessary goodbyes.

He went to the piano, where he knew he'd find paper and a pencil. He also found a discarded dress, bits of rope, and the remnants of candles. He didn't allow himself to think about the night before. Not the way Dawn had looked when he'd lit that first candle and he'd seen her bound and beautiful. Not the way she'd felt surrounding him when he'd been buried inside her that first time. He didn't even allow himself to touch the piano keys that had produced a melody capable of freeing him for a few short hours. He went straight for a blank piece of score paper and scrawled a hasty note on the back.

> Dear Dawn,
>
> Thank you for an entertaining evening. I had to leave early. I wish you well with your new song. I see an Academy Award in your future. Sorry things couldn't work out between us. Take care of yourself.
>
> Kelly

He frowned at his signature and covered up the *y* with *e-n*. He didn't go by Kelly anymore. It was too frivolous a name for a broken, melancholy man.

Kellen propped the note on the music stand over her keyboard, where she'd be sure to see it, bent to collect a short piece of blue rope from the remnants on the floor, and fled the house. He wished he had a way to lock the door behind him; he didn't like the thought of leaving her there alone with the door unlocked. Maybe he should have woken her before he fled like a coward, but he didn't think he'd have been able to do the right thing and leave if she'd offered him so much as a smile. A kiss. An embrace.

Fucking stop!

He avoided looking at Sara's house as he hurried to the rental car parked in its short driveway. He felt that the house was staring at him and its disapproval weighed heavily on the base of his neck.

He fished the keys out of the center console where he'd hidden them the night before and started the engine. He wished he was driving his faithful Firebird instead of this run-of-the-mill sedan, but at least he had a means of escape.

Colorful houses on stilts separated brief glimpses of the ocean as he sped toward the city of Galveston. Quaint housing developments blurred by one after another until he hit a stop light and slammed on his breaks to skid to halt. He had no idea how fast he'd been going, but he was sure the flashing blue lights behind him weren't a good sign. The officer squawked his siren, and Kellen cringed before taking a right turn at the light to get out of the flow of traffic so he could get his ass chewed properly. He retrieved his wallet and rental car agreement out of the glovebox while he waited for the cop to mosey his way to the car. Kellen rolled down the window, and a blast of warm humidity hit him in the face.

"Where's the fire, son?" the officer said in greeting.

Kellen forced himself not to roll his eyes. Police officers didn't seem to like it when he did that.

"How fast was I going?"

"Eighty in a thirty-five."

He couldn't even plead the "I forgot to slow down in the town speed zone" argument, as eighty miles per hour would have been speeding even outside of town.

"Sorry about that, I was..." Fleeing an anguished memory and the potential for a bright future. "...distracted."

"License and proof of insurance."

"The car's a rental," Kellen said, but handed over his driver's license and the folded-up insurance proof he kept in his wallet.

"Hold tight, Mr. Jamison," the officer said as he looked over Kellen's license. "I'll be back with your citation."

Kellen wouldn't argue. He deserved a ticket.

The officer went back to his patrol SUV, while Kellen sat and stewed.

Eventually, the weight of the cuff in his pocket became unbearable. He tugged it out, stared at it for a long moment, and then secured it to his wrist. He wouldn't be taking it off again. When he took it off, he forgot his promises, made mistakes, potentially hurt people besides himself. He felt his resolve strengthen as soon as the cuff was in place. Wearing it didn't keep his thoughts from returning to Dawn, but the reminder would keep him from turning this fucking car around and returning to her.

"I'm surprised this is your first ticket," the officer said from outside Kellen's window.

Why? Because he was barefoot and shirtless, tattooed and long-haired, or because Toyota Corollas were notoriously fast cars?

"Usually folks who go as fast as you were going make a habit of it."

"I don't speed. I just have a lot on my mind this morning."

"If you hadn't been going so fast, I'd have let you off with a warning—"

Kellen tugged the ticket and his identification from the officer's hand. He didn't feel like shooting the breeze, thanks.

"I understand. Have a nice day," Kellen said, rolling up his window.

"Watch your speed," he heard the officer call.

Kellen nodded and shifted the car into drive.

He kept his attention on the road and his speed. It was a lot easier to concentrate on his driving with Sara's wrist cuff in his peripheral view, reminding him to play by the rules, not take chances, and to love her forever.

He drove the length of Seawall Boulevard on his way to the ferry that would take him to Bolivar Peninsula and bypass the traffic nightmare that often surrounded Houston. It was still rather early, so there were only a few people out on the beaches that bordered the wide roadway. He sat at stop lights, watching pedestrians walk their dogs, parents lug beach gear while attempting to corral their children away from the road, and tourists snap pictures of ordinary seagulls. They all seemed to know where they belonged and what they were doing. Must be nice.

He passed hotel after hotel, restaurant after restaurant, and even a small amusement park that was built on a pier extending over the ocean. The Pleasure Pier. He couldn't even find enough of a sense of humor to develop a joke about that one. He bet Owen would like to go to a place called The Pleasure Pier, but Owen's preference wouldn't be family friendly. A tiny smile felt foreign on his Kellen's face. He needed to get back to Owen. Owen was the one person who only made him happy and never gave him grief. Kellen was lucky to have someone like Owen in his life, and he desperately needed someone to confide in at the moment.

Kellen followed the road signs to the ferry dock and was glad the line was short. He had no idea how long he'd be stuck on the boat with nothing to occupy his mind while it crossed the wide bay bustling with barge traffic. Maybe he'd have time to call Owen. Just a few minutes' conversation with him was sure to put Kellen in a better frame of mind. He was about to crawl out of his skin.

He waited until the ferry launched from the dock before removing his seatbelt and leaving the car with cellphone in hand to stand along the railing. He turned on his phone and found he had multiple messages in voicemail. All of them were from Owen. Kellen had told him that he was turning his phone off. He wondered if he'd missed out on anything important the night before or if Owen was just bored because he had no one better to bug when Kellen wasn't on the bus.

Kellen didn't bother listening to the voicemails, noting that his phone's battery was low, and dialed Owen's number.

Owen answered on the second ring. "There you are. I was starting to think you'd been eaten by sharks."

"Didn't encounter any sharks. A pig this morning, but no

sharks."

"A pig?"

"I got a speeding ticket."

"Are you sure?" Owen said. "Wait, is this really Kelly? Adam, did you steal Kelly's phone again? This has to be a joke."

Kellen smiled, feeling better already. "I had a lot on my mind when I, uh, *left*... the woman I... sort of slept with last night."

There was dead silence on the other end. Kellen tugged the phone from his ear and stared at the screen to make sure the call hadn't dropped. Still connected.

"Owen? Are you there?"

"You slept with a woman last night. You? Kellen Soaring Eagle Jamison slept with a woman? Were you conscious?"

Kellen chuckled. "Yes, I was a willing participant. But this morning, I sort of just... left. Should I go back? I shouldn't, should I? Better to cut all ties now, right?"

"I don't know. Do you like her or was it just a crazy, I-haven't-been-properly-laid-in-five-years, lust-type thing?"

Kellen blew out his cheeks. "A bit of both, I think. I do like her, but I don't think I would have slept with her if you'd been there to keep me in check."

"Fuck," Owen said. "Do you mean to tell me the only thing I had to do to get you to sleep with a chick was disappear?"

"No," Kellen said, shaking his head. "There was something special between me and her. I just got freaked out about cheating on Sara and left before she woke up."

"Then, yes, you should turn around immediately and go back to her, you fucking idiot. You haven't felt so much as a tickle in your cock for a woman in over five years, much less anything deeper. The thing with Lindsey can wait."

"Lindsey?" Kellen said, his eyebrows drawing together. "Who's Lindsey? Her name is Dawn."

"Didn't you get my voicemails? All seven of them?"

"My battery is low, so I haven't listened to them yet."

Owen laughed. "Well, dude, we all got a bit of shocking news last night. Lindsey, that pretty little groupie you tied up on Christmas Eve, she showed up after the concert and, you are not going to believe this bro, she's..."

Kellen waited for him to finish, knowing Owen liked to fuck with him by creating long, pregnant pauses. "She's what?" No answer. "Owen?"

He looked at his phone and found the screen blank. Dead battery. Damn it. With a huff of frustration, Kellen shoved the phone into his pocket, tugging a bit of blue rope free when he jerked his hand back out.

He clutched the piece of rope in his fist. "Dawn," he whispered and looked back toward the island. Missing her. Wishing he hadn't left without saying goodbye.

A large gray body, slick and sleek, crested above the water. His breath caught. He'd never seen a wild dolphin before. Sara would have been over the moon with excitement.

"Sara," he said under his breath.

Kellen sighed and clutched his forehead in one had.

Dawn. Sara. Lindsey. Women would be the death of him. He tried to avoid them, but his actions didn't do any good.

The ferry began to slow as it approached the dock at the tip of Bolivar Peninsula. Kellen climbed back in the rental car and contemplated his options. He couldn't go back to Dawn; she was sure to read something into that. And he was exceedingly curious to find out what was going on with that Lindsey woman. All he remembered about her was that she held a shocking resemblance to Sara, had a pussy that tasted sweeter than honey, and was really good at sharing. Had she come back to the bus for another orgy? Kellen was not interested. He'd find a hotel to hole up in for the night if that was the case. Besides, the guys were more involved with relationships than they had been six months ago. Surely they didn't plan to compromise something important for a piece of hot and willing tail.

Kellen decided he'd go straight to the bus. Maybe after he got his head on straight, he'd head back to Galveston to apologize to Dawn for being a cowardly bastard. But that wouldn't happen tonight. He could only stand so much confusion and heartache in one twenty-four-hour period.

The drive to Beaumont was uneventful. His churning thoughts kept him company. He thought about Dawn. And he thought about Sara. But mostly he cursed himself for not bringing his cellphone charger. He spends one night away from the band, and Owen sees fit to call him seven times to talk about some groupie. Kellen knew he wouldn't do that unless it was something important. Had she given them all some incurable disease? Kellen hadn't slept with her, but he had eaten her out.

Kellen parked near the venue where the band and crew were getting ready for the concert and headed toward the bus, prepared for the worst. But nothing could have prepared him for what he saw standing at the top of the bus steps.

Her hair was swept back from her lovely face in a loose ponytail. Her brilliant blue eyes sparked with recognition as a smile spread across her soft, sensual lips. She rested a hand on her obviously distended belly and offered him a small wave.

She was pregnant and beautiful and very much alive.

"Sara?" he whispered, clutching the doorframe so he didn't collapse into a heap on the asphalt.

CHAPTER TEN

Dawn shoved the pillow off her head and blinked in the bright sunshine streaming through the open blinds of her bedroom. It had to be close to noon. Why was she still so exhausted? She smiled as memories of the night she'd shared with Kellen filtered through her thoughts. She couldn't wait to add to her pleasant experiences today. She was a bit disappointed to find his side of the bed empty, but she vaguely recalled him murmuring her name to awaken her and her foolishly demanding coffee. Who needed coffee with that man as her wake-up call? She'd just been a bit groggy and obviously out of her mind. She was wide awake now. Still naked, she slipped out of bed and padded down the hall to the stairs.

"Kellen," she called down into the foyer below. "I changed my mind. I don't need coffee. I just need you."

When he didn't answer, she continued down the stairs. "Kellen, come out, come out, wherever you are."

She entered the kitchen and noticed a full carafe of coffee sitting untouched in the coffee maker. The power was obviously back on. It had been sweet of him to make coffee for her, but why hadn't he rejoined her in bed once he'd finished making it?

"Kellen, are you down here?" she called, peeking over the breakfast bar into the family room, where the piano sat as silent as a stone. Bits of rope littered the piano's lid and the floor. Dawn smiled. She would always remember the feel of it pressing into her skin and opening her eyes to truths she hadn't recognized about herself. It was a shame that the rope had been cut and was now unusable. She wondered if there was any spare rope in the garage beneath the house. If not, she was all about making a trip to the nearest hardware store for supplies.

She wasn't sure where Kellen had wandered off to. Maybe he was in the bathroom, or maybe he'd taken a walk on the beach. She always found the most interesting goodies washed up on the shore after a storm. She completely understood the draw of the water. She turned back to the kitchen. When she opened a cabinet, she noticed the broken mug in the sink. She picked up a large shard of ceramic and caught sight of the big yellow house next door. Kellen's house, she realized with a smile. She looked again at the broken mug, at the full coffee carafe. At Kellen's house. Her smile faded. *Sara's* house, she corrected herself.

Shit. He'd left, hadn't he? Saw that gorgeous, empty house across the way, started thinking about *her* again—*Sara*—and ran away.

Even after all they'd shared the night before, he still hadn't given up that other woman. What a jerk! If all he'd wanted from Dawn was sex, he could have just been straight with her. He didn't have to pretend to be so wonderful. She was a big girl. And even though her heart was aching so badly she could scarcely breathe and her lower lip was trembling uncontrollably, Dawn was *not* going to cry over this. She refused to let a single tear fall. She kicked a lower cabinet as hard as she could and winced when her toe exploded with pain.

"Damn him," she muttered. "He could have at least had the decency to tell me to my face that he wasn't interested."

Determined to have a great day despite the dark cloud that was suddenly obscuring her sunshine from the inside out, Dawn poured herself a cup of coffee and went to sulk—contemplate life—at her piano. She righted the piano bench, which had been overturned during all those wonderfully sensual activities she refused to dwell upon, and plopped down. She dribbled coffee down her bare front when she noticed Kellen's handwritten note.

She snatched it from the music stand and read it three times before crumpling it into a ball and tossing it on the floor.

"*Entertaining evening*," she muttered under her breath. "Was that what it was to you? Because it was magical to me, you ass!" She didn't know why she was yelling at her piano, but it felt right. "You're sorry it didn't work out between us. How could it work out? You didn't even give it a chance. I hope you choke on your guitar." She wasn't sure why he'd have his guitar in his mouth, but she wasn't thinking clearly enough to come up with better ill wishes.

She turned sideways on the bench and pulled her legs up against her body, hugging both shins and burying her face against her bent knees. She was not going to cry over him. Not going to cry. Those hot, wet droplets coming from her eyes and running down her thighs were not tears. Nope. Not crying for a guy who'd love another woman until the day he died. Not crying over a man who had taken a chance with her but decided he'd rather return to a dead girl. She sniffed. She really wished she could hate him for that, but it just broke her heart.

When she decided she'd wallowed in misery long enough, she turned to her piano and practiced her new song. Kellen's song. She would always think of it as Kellen's song, even if she did name it "Dawn." She began to feel better almost at once. The joyful melody lifted her spirits until her tears were forgotten and she was smiling to herself. She had to call her agent. He *had* to hear this song.

She dialed his number and had his secretary patch her through. As soon as she had him on the line, she interrupted his usual, "Any luck?" As if luck had anything to do with composing.

"Listen," she said and put him on speaker phone so he could hear her. She played the piece from beginning to end. When the last note rang out, she stared at the phone, her heart hammering with excitement. The song was wonderful. Perfect. She knew it was. But she had to hear it from someone who would give it to her straight. "Well?"

There was a long pause. "I... I'm speechless," he said.

What? Speechless? What did that mean? "Thanks for sharing. But is the song any good?"

"It's phenomenal. I almost hate to hand it over. It's too good to be closing credit music for some movie."

"But it will be heard, Wes. Well, by those who stay for the credits, at least. I'm just glad I finally wrote something worth listening to."

"You're too hard on yourself, Dawn. Everything you write is inspired."

She rolled her eyes. He thought that because he only ever heard her finished pieces. He'd never heard her bang out angry renditions of "Chopsticks" because it sounded better than the crap she was coming up with.

"So do you think you could get me an extra few days on my deadline? It's finished, but I haven't exactly written it down yet."

"So write it down now."

"I have something important that I need to do today," she said and before her impetuous mouth had even completed the sentence, she knew it was true.

"More important than keeping a movie studio happy?"

"Yeah. Much more important than that. Have you ever heard of the band Sole Regret?"

"The metal band out of Austin who were nominated for a best new artist Grammy last year?"

She knew Wes would have heard of them. "That's them."

"I don't know them, but I do have business connections with their manager. Why?"

Wes knew *everyone* in the music business either directly or by some outside contact. He loved to drop names. "I need to be on the VIP list for their show in Beaumont, Texas tonight. Can you make it happen?"

"Can you fax me a rough draft of your masterpiece in the next hour so I can get this producer off my back?"

She sighed loudly. "Yes, I'll fax you a rough draft."

"I'll make your groupie wishes a reality then."

"I'm not a groupie," she said testily.

"Oh. Are you writing music for them now?"

"No, I'm not writing their music. They're kind of out of my genre, don't you think?"

"Groupie," he teased in a high-pitched voice.

"Watch it, Wes. I know where you live."

"As soon as I have that rough draft in my hand, I'll get you on the list."

She grinned because she knew he'd deliver for her. "Slave driver," she muttered.

"Virtuoso," he countered.

"You really suck at insults, Bloodsucking Agent."

"And you really suck at lying, Groupie."

"Expect a fax in an hour," she said, already scribbling down notes as fast as her hand could move.

"I'll pull all the right strings in the meantime. Great work, doll. I think there's an Academy Award in your future."

Dawn paused to glare at the crumpled note on the floor. "Yeah, you aren't the first to make that prediction today. I'm just glad the song is finally done."

"And I'm glad you're a groupie." He laughed, and she could picture his overly white teeth gleaming in his overly tanned face. "We'll talk soon."

He hung up before she could reach into the phone and choke

him. Groupie? How could she be a groupie if she'd never even heard Sole Regret's music? She just needed closure or an opening— one or the other and preferably the latter. She wasn't sure if Kellen would even talk to her, but she had to try. She had to find out why he'd left and if he had any interest in her beyond one amazing night.

But first she had to get their song on paper and then she should probably consider putting on some clothes. While she was pretty sure Kellen would understand her need to be naked today, the public probably wouldn't be so understanding.

CHAPTER ELEVEN

"Are you okay?" Sara said as she trotted down the steps, stopping on the bottom one so that it was impossible not to notice her belly. She patted Kellen's shoulder. "You look like you've seen a ghost."

Not Sara, he told himself. Lindsey. The girl Owen had been talking about on the phone before they'd been disconnected. *She's not Sara.* Yeah, tell that to all the hairs on the back of his neck, which were standing on end.

He took a deep breath and clenched his shaking hands into fists.

"Where's Owen?" Kellen asked, staring at her pregnant abdomen and doing mental math. Could it be... Was this what Owen had been trying to tell him about? No. Not possible.

"I think he's talking to *her* again," Lindsey-not-Sara said. He glanced up in time to catch her rolling her pretty blue eyes. "It was good seeing you." She kissed his cheek and stepped off the final step. "If anyone is looking for me, I'm going to buy some food. I swear, how do you guys live like this?"

Still dumbfounded, he watched her walk over to Jordan, who was taking one of his hundreds of daily breaks, and with a few bats of her eyelashes and rubs of her belly, Jordan was on his feet and escorting her to the rental car he was responsible for returning. Completely transfixed, Kellen watched her get into the car. Lindsey really was a beauty. She definitely rivaled Sara, but was no comparison to Dawn.

Shit. He couldn't let himself think about Dawn right now.

Kellen climbed the bus steps and spotted Owen sitting at the dining table and staring intently at his iPad. He looked up when Kellen slid into the booth across from him. He smiled.

"So you're back. Have you given up on blue balls permanently or was it a temporary thing?"

"Had to be temporary."

"Had to be?"

Kellen nodded curtly. He didn't want Dawn to have to deal with his baggage. He had to forget her so she would forget him. "So Lindsey..."

"She's around her somewhere." Owen flicked his wrist at the expansive bus cabin.

"Yeah, I saw her. Is she..." Kellen's eyebrows lifted.

"Pregnant?" Owen nodded and went slightly pale. "Yeah. She thinks it's mine."

"Yours? But you wore a condom when you did her; how could it be yours?"

"Well, it's someone's from that night, assuming she isn't lying about not screwing some other dude after she finished with her Sole Regret band and crew orgy. When I left you alone to untie her, you didn't do anything with her, did you?"

"No." He hadn't been inside a woman for five years. Until Dawn.

Shit. He couldn't let himself think about Dawn right now.

"I didn't think so. Just making sure."

But Kellen had come on Lindsey's belly, so he supposed it was possible that in all the groping and fondling and fucking, some mighty Kellen sperm had somehow gotten inside of her. Possible, but not likely. Still, he felt he was going to throw up. What if it *was* his? What would he do? He could never bring himself to hook up with some girl he didn't feel a connection with just because she was the mother of his child, but he wouldn't be like his asshole of a father. He wouldn't leave the mother to fend for herself and ignore the existence of his own child until seeing his flesh and blood served his own purpose or agenda or whatever the fuck had made his father reach out to him after sixteen years of no contact. More than never meeting the fucktard, Kellen regretted not telling him what a worthless piece of shit he was when he'd had the chance. He didn't want Lindsey's unborn baby to ever have to feel that level of rejection.

"I figured you'd be smiling more," Owen said.

Kellen looked at Owen as if he was doing the Chicken Dance. *Again*. Why would he be smiling? This situation had the potential to fuck up someone's life in a pretty major way.

"About Lindsey being pregnant?" Kellen asked.

"About getting laid. Tell me about her. I can't wait to meet her.

I'm assuming she has blond hair and blue eyes." Owen rolled his eyes at Kellen's presumed predictability.

Kellen shook his head. "Redhead. That deep, dark red shade. Almost burgundy. And her eyes are hazel, with pretty flecks the color of spring leaves."

Owen snorted and burst out laughing. "I forgot how corny you get."

"Corny? What do you mean?"

"When you like a girl. You become the reincarnation of John Keats or some shit. So is she gorgeous? She must be to get your dick out of your pants."

"Stunning. And you've seen her before," Kellen said.

Owen went another shade paler. "I didn't fuck her, did I?"

"No. Believe it or not, there are still women out there who haven't taken a bareback ride on your lap."

Owen winked. "Are you sure?"

Kellen nodded. "A few."

"So if I didn't fuck her, where did I see her?"

"At the Grammy's last year."

"Oh God, did I say something stupid to her?" Now Owen looked like he needed a tanning session. "I was *so* wasted that night."

And he probably didn't remember the elegant beauty who'd graced the stage to accept an award for best instrumental composition.

"She won a Grammy for one of her compositions. She plays piano. And she had no idea who we are, but she remembered us getting thrown out for your air-horn incident and heckling the rapper who got our award."

Owen cringed. "Yeah, that was pretty obnoxious. I apparently thought I was attending a hockey game. Why'd you guys let me drink so much?"

Kellen chuckled. "We all drank that much. You're the only one who couldn't hold his liquor."

Owen raised fingers one at a time as he said, "So gorgeous redhead. Grammy. Gives Kellen a boner." Tapping his ring finger, he screwed up his forehead in concentration as he went over his clues.

"Her name is Dawn O'Reilly," Kellen said. He didn't want the guy to blow any overtaxed synapses.

Kellen had forgotten Owen had his iPad right in front of him. He immediately did a web search.

When Dawn's picture came up on screen, Kellen's heart froze in his chest until a rush of tangled emotions thawed it again. Standing before the awards' ceremony backdrop, she looked radiant in a floor-length green gown, holding her Grammy clutched in both hands at her waist. *Dawn.* He could almost hear her voice whispering to him in the darkness. Making him feel that everything would be okay. Was he really going to push her away? Give her up? Go back to feeling so alone that he shut out everyone in his life except Owen?

Kellen closed his eyes and swallowed. Yes. He was going to do exactly that. He'd been weak for one night, but would never give in to that weakness again.

"Wow," Owen said. "She's hot. I'd tap that."

Kellen's eyes flipped open as a surge of panic flooded his chest. Owen could seduce anyone if he put his mind to it. Probably even Dawn. "What about Caitlyn? I thought you really liked her."

"I do," Owen said. "I wouldn't tap that *now*, but a couple days ago, before I met Caitlyn, I would have totally tapped that. She's stunning. And she plays piano. Musicians are hot."

Kellen chuckled when Owen pointed at himself, pursed his lips, and offered a suggestive toss of his head.

Turning to his iPad again, Owen tapped a few screens and stirring piano music began to play from the device.

"She more than plays piano," Kellen said. "It's as if her soul comes pouring out of the instrument."

Owen looked up at him and then snorted before bursting into laughter. "Oh God, man, you have got it bad for this chick."

Kellen shook his head. "It was just a one-night hook-up."

"*Riiight.* Keep telling yourself that until you believe it. So I'm ordering flowers for Caitlyn. You should get some for Dawn O'Reilly."

He would not be sending Dawn flowers. She might think he was still interested, which he was, but he didn't want her to think that.

"Flowers already?" Kellen asked. "Didn't take you long to mess up."

"It wasn't my fault. When Lindsey showed up, Caitlyn flipped out and left. Not that I blame I her. I mean"—he made explosion sounds and opened his hands in bursts around his head—"mind blown."

"And no one is claiming this kid besides you? You weren't the only one who had sex with the girl that night."

"A paternity test will straighten it all out in a few months, but she's under enough stress, you know. It doesn't hurt to be nice to her and treat her like a human being."

Kellen wouldn't expect anything less from his friend, but his kindness might just come back to bite him in the ass. If Lindsey got too attached to him, he might be stuck with her for life, even if he wasn't the baby's father. But maybe Owen wanted that. He liked people to depend on him. Which was good, because Kellen depended on him in a big way.

Owen pointed at images of flowers on his tablet. "So should I send her roses or a mixed bouquet? And chocolates too, right? Too soon for jewelry?"

"Owen, I'm not sure…"

"You're right. She's not the kind of woman who wears much jewelry. What do you think she would like? Perfume? Or… I could send her chicken panties. Yeah, that's perfect. She'd get a kick out of that."

Chicken panties? Kellen was afraid to ask why she'd think chicken panties were the perfect gift.

"Some women feel uncomfortable when you buy them gifts," he said. "Especially early in a relationship." And Kellen took Caitlyn for that type of woman.

"I just want to keep her thinking about me," Owen said. "And let her know I'm thinking about her."

"Did you call her?"

"Yeah, like five times. She keeps joking that she has to get something done besides talking to me all day."

"So she knows you're thinking about her."

Owen smiled as he purchased whatever silly pair of panties had caught his eye. "Should I send them to her office?"

"Panties? Uh, no. I don't think she'd appreciate that."

"Then I need her home address." He started texting on his phone.

Kellen slapped himself in the forehead. So much for Owen following any advice. But he was smiling as he read Caitlyn's reply. Owen looked so fucking happy that Kellen hated to put a damper on things, but he really needed to talk to him about the elephant that was always in the room these days.

"Owen," Kellen said, "we need to talk about..." He took a deep breath and blew out his cheeks. Jeez, this was going to be even harder than he imagined. "...about all that kinky shit we did together."

Owen read from his phone and typed Caitlyn's address into his tablet. "Which kinky shit?"

"You know what I'm talking about."

He looked totally disconnected from the conversation, and Kellen really needed him to be serious. "Do you mean me assisting you with tying women up so you could eat them out because you were afraid they might touch you?"

"No. I mean the other stuff." He lowered his voice to a barely audible whisper. "The touching each other stuff. That we did. To each other."

"It was good for me. Was it good for you?" He laughed, and Kellen should have known Owen would try to make light of it. Getting him to confront anything serious was near impossible. So Kellen would just have to plow ahead and hope Owen took his words to heart.

"I want to apologize to you."

"For what? Making me come really hard? I honestly didn't mind."

"I only touched you because I wanted someone to touch me back."

"And there's always a girl waiting to do just that." Owen lifted his gaze from his cellphone before he'd finish sending his latest text. "So is this the conversation where you tell me you're gay?"

"But I'm not gay."

"And neither am I, so let's forget about it and move on."

"I'm not finished apologizing to you."

"You don't need to apologize." Owen's voice rose, as if he were angry that Kellen was even bringing this up. "I don't want your fucking apology. I just want to drop it, so drop it."

"But I used you, Owen."

"I use women all the time. It's not a big deal."

"It *is* a big deal. You're my best friend, and I made you do something you wouldn't normally do."

"You didn't *make* me do anything. I know you've been suffering, and I'd rather give you the occasional hand job than watch you mope around like your life is over. Your life isn't fucking over, Kellen. Sara's life ended, not yours."

His words were like a slap across the face.

"Do you think you need to tell me that?" Kellen yelled. "I live with that every fucking day of my life."

"Well someone has to remind you; you're apparently too stupid to see it on your own. And now you find some beautiful woman who might have a fighting chance of putting Sara in her grave where she belongs, and you can't even find the balls to tell her you're leaving."

Kellen was too stunned to reply. Owen had never gone off on him like that. Ever. He'd always been so understanding and careful to spare Kellen's feelings.

"Well..." Kellen sputtered. "Maybe I'll see her again and maybe I won't. It's none of your business."

"You won't," Owen said. "I know you won't."

"How do you know?"

"Because you're still wearing Sara's cuff."

Kellen looked down at his wrist and yep, there it was, right where he'd promised himself he'd never put it again.

Owen dove across the table and grabbed Kellen's left forearm in both hands. "Give me that fucking thing. If you won't get rid of it, I will."

Owen shoved his back against Kellen's chest to keep him pinned in the booth while he jerked on the buckles holding the cuff in place. Kellen didn't know why he was fighting Owen. He'd love for someone to remove Sara's burden from his wrist, but by the time Jacob wandered onto the bus and pulled them apart, they were both bruised and disheveled. Owen had the cuff in his hand, and Kellen had a scrap of Owen's T-shirt clutched in his fist.

"What the fuck?" Jacob said, holding Owen in a headlock. "Never thought I'd see the day when you two came to blows."

"Give me my fucking cuff back, asshole," Kellen said, yanking his wrist free from Jacob's steely grip.

"You took his cuff?" Jacob asked.

"He doesn't need it anymore," Owen yelled.

"I agree," Jacob said, "but don't you think he should get rid of it willingly? It just symbolizes Sara; it's *not* Sara. Getting rid of the cuff isn't going to change how he feels."

Kellen wasn't so sure. He'd had a whole lot of fun and shared a whole lot of intimacy with Dawn when the cuff had been off his arm the night before. He didn't know why he had such an emotional connection to a piece of jewelry. It was stupid. Like a little kid who wouldn't give up his security blanket because he was convinced the boogie man lived under his bed.

"Then he won't care if I burn it," Owen said.

"Don't!" Kellen's voice cracked. Already his wrist felt exposed without the cuff in place. "I tried to throw it away last night, but it came back to me."

"You did?" Owen asked, his stance shifting to one that was still guarded, but not threatening.

Kellen nodded. "I threw it in the ocean and it immediately washed back ashore."

"Try throwing it into a volcano and see if it comes back to you then," Owen said.

Kellen glared at him.

Jacob released Owen and pointed at the dining table. "Both of you sit down and talk this out. There's no sense in letting misunderstandings and petty arguments come between friends when everything can be solved with a simple conversation."

"Oh, hey, kettle, I'm pot and wow, you're black," Owen said.

Yeah, that was some pretty hypocritical advice coming from Jacob.

"What?" Jacob said.

"Uh, you've been holding a grudge against Adam for how many years now?" Owen said. "And for why?"

"But you and Kellen never fight. Adam and I have always had differences."

Owen looked at Kellen and held the cuff in his direction. "Here," he said. "Put it back on if it makes you feel better."

Kellen's hand felt like a leaden weight. His breathing became shallow. His lips trembled. He could feel the pressure of tears behind his eyes as his throat tightened until he thought he'd suffocate. For what? For a stupid strap of leather? It wasn't Sara. Wearing it didn't really keep her close. It wasn't even a tribute to his memories of her. It just made him miserable.

"Get rid of it," he said breathlessly.

Owen drew his clenched fist to his chest, holding the bracelet against him as if to comfort it. Kellen couldn't take his eyes off the black strap. He was tracking it like a cat preparing to pounce.

"Are you sure?" Owen said. "You know I can't stand you to be mad at me."

"I'm sure. Do it quick before I change my mind."

Owen brushed past him and hurried down the bus steps. Jacob caught Kellen's arm when after a few very long seconds, he turned to follow Owen.

"Stick to your guns, man."

Kellen nodded and sank onto a sofa. He stared down at his bare wrist. It looked as foreign as it felt. The skin was a shade paler than that of his hand and forearm. So even though the cuff was gone, the evidence was still there. He closed his eyes and massaged his arm with his free hand.

"You know what you need?" Jacob said, taking a seat beside him.

"A bottle of whiskey?"

"A wristwatch." Jacob unfastened the analog watch he sometimes wore before a concert—he was paranoid about being late and had a hard time reading digital clocks correctly. He handed the watch to Kellen. Kellen appreciated the gesture, but he didn't think it would help. He put it on anyway and while it wasn't the same as wearing a cuff—the watch band was cold metal, a bit looser, and about half the thickness of his bracelet—it did make his wrist feel less exposed and he wasn't compelled to massage it, as if he had cuff obsessive-compulsive disorder.

"Thanks."

Jacob slapped him on the back and then rose from the sofa. "Now you just have to make sure I get to the show on time."

Ah, so there was a catch.

Kellen reached for the clasp on the back of the watch's silver band. "I don't need—"

Jacob's hand circled Kellen's wrist. "Wear it until you get your head out of your ass."

Kellen laughed. "So you're not expecting this back anytime soon?"

"However long it takes."

Owen returned to the bus a short while later. Kellen had a bit of blue rope in one hand and was rubbing it with his thumbs, remembering how it had looked against Dawn's pale skin.

"So you traded a cuff for a watch and a piece of rope?"

Kellen didn't respond. He didn't want to talk to Owen at the moment. He didn't want to talk to anyone, but he did crave the feel of Dawn's arms around him and the feel of her soft breasts pressing into his chest. He missed her. Her smile. Her laugh. The way her eyes sparked when she was perturbed. The sound of her voice. The way her fingers moved across her piano keys. Across his skin. *Her.* He missed *her.*

Shit. He couldn't allow himself to think about Dawn right now.

He poked the piece of rope under the cuff on his right wrist.

Owen went back to buying Caitlyn gifts on the Internet and chuckling at various text messages that binged onto his phone every thirty seconds or so. Jacob had disappeared into the bathroom. Kellen wondered where Gabe and Adam were. The bus felt really empty. He had an uncharacteristic need to be surrounded by people and, as a loner, it felt strange to admit that to himself.

"What did you do with it?" Kellen asked in one of the pauses between Owen's text message alerts.

"I buried it," Owen said.

"Someplace nice?"

"Yeah."

Kellen nodded, grateful that Owen hadn't tossed Sara's cuff in a dumpster or flushed it down the toilet. Kellen stood, deciding he'd go watch the crew set up the stage. Something to keep him busy so that his thoughts didn't stray to his missing cuff or the continual turbulence in his soul. Or to the woman who had calmed that turmoil by creating the most beautiful melody he'd ever heard and held nothing back when she'd held him in her arms.

Kellen was halfway to the door when Lindsey climbed the stairs. Their band's twenty-two-year-old lackey, Jordan, was right behind her, carrying several sacks of groceries and chattering about NASCAR. Kellen retreated toward the back of the bus so he didn't have to brush against them on his way through the narrow corridor. Lindsey took the sacks from Jordan one at a time and set them on a counter in the kitchenette. She looked so much like Sara it was actually painful to look at her, but pain didn't stop Kellen from staring. Would Sara have looked that beautiful pregnant? With his child growing in her womb? They'd talked about having kids before she'd gotten sick. At the time, he had been a bit hesitant about all the responsibility a child entailed, but if she'd had a baby, a bit of her would have been left behind. Part of her, mixed inseparably with part of him, would have lived on.

Kellen started when someone bumped into his back. Jacob grasped Kellen's shoulders from behind and squeezed. "There's just something sexy about a pregnant woman," he said. "When Tina was pregnant with Julie, I couldn't keep my hands off her."

Uh... Was Jacob lusting after Lindsey? Weird. Especially since the baby was some other man's. Maybe. At least Jacob liked kids. What if the kid was Adam's? Adam detested kids. And what would Gabe do if it turned out to be his? A dude could go crazy wondering about such things. It was no wonder that Lindsey had insisted it was Owen's. Not knowing whose child you were carrying had to be a serious mind-fuck. And what would it be like to give birth to a child created out of lust, not love?

"She's cute," Kellen agreed, so that Jacob would stop squeezing his shoulders.

"You know who would look fuck hot pregnant?" Jacob asked, still watching Lindsey like some predator.

Don't say it. Don't say it. Don't say it.

"Amanda."

Fuck, he said it.

"Don't you think you should date a woman for more than a week before you start trying to knock her up?" Kellen asked.

Jacob slapped him on the back of the head. "I'm not going to knock her up. I just think she would look hot pregnant."

"I don't think you should tell her that."

Jacob chuckled. "You're probably right."

"Thank you, Jordan," Lindsey said loudly, cutting him off in the middle of a description of his favorite driver's car. She'd been patiently listening to him prattle for several long minutes. Jordan was very good at prattling and bad at recognizing shut-up-now cues. "I think they need your help outside."

"They do?" Jordan glanced toward the open bus door. "I was going to help you make sandwiches for the guys."

"I've got a handle on it," she said. "Go on now."

"If you need anything," he said, "anything at all, just ask."

"I will. Thanks for giving me a ride to the store."

Jordan stood there for another long minute, raking a hand through his dirty-blond hair, before finally turning to leave.

Lindsey released a relieved-sounding breath and began to remove fresh-baked sandwich rolls and deli meat and cheese from her grocery sacks. "Owen, what do you want on your sandwich?"

"Pastrami and rye?" Kellen teased him with a wink.

"Do I look like I got laid today?"

"Huh?" Lindsey said, turning to look at him.

"Nothing," Owen said, "Turkey and cheddar is fine if you've got it."

"Shade?" Lindsey asked.

"What?" Jacob answered.

"What do you want on your sandwich?"

"You don't have to make me a sandwich," he said. "Go sit down and put your feet up. You look a little tired."

"I'm fine," she insisted. "I can't just sit here all day and consume your oxygen. I want to do something."

"You're incubating a baby," Jacob said. "That's plenty."

"But it's not. I didn't come here to be a pain in the ass," she said.

"You didn't?" Owen teased. "You were sure making a go of it when you first arrived."

"I know I had a major meltdown last night," she said. "I'm sorry you all had to see that. You try riding next to a grizzly bear of a truck driver who insists on calling you sweet-tits. We'll see how rational you are after fourteen hours of thinking you're going to be raped, murdered, and fed to the load of hogs in the back of his semi."

"Yeah, I don't think I'd like anyone to call me sweet-tits for fourteen hours," Owen said.

Lindsey giggled.

"You hitchhiked here?" Kellen asked.

"Stupid, I know, but I was desperate. What do you want on your sandwich, Cuff?"

Kellen didn't care. "Roast beef?"

"Shade?" she asked Jacob again.

"Yeah, roast beef sounds good. I still think you should sit down and let us make our own damned sandwiches."

"Don't worry," she said. "I'm not going to force myself into your lives." She peeked at Owen over her shoulder, but he was back to texting on his cellphone, so he didn't notice. "I just need a little help until I can get on my feet. I'm not a mooch."

"You shouldn't be on your feet at all," Jacob insisted. He moved to stand beside her and placed a hand on her lower back. "You should be resting."

"No, I shouldn't be resting; I should be working. Making money.

I have a baby to support. I held onto my apartment for as long as possible while I looked for a job after Mrs. Weston fired me. That ate up my savings quickly, and I ended up completely broke. Hopefully I can find a job in Austin real soon and set up a little house for me and the baby so his father can come visit him as much as he can." She rubbed her belly and gazed longingly at Owen again.

Kellen wasn't sure if Owen was intentionally ignoring her or just oblivious that he was the main topic of her conversation. She obviously thought her baby was Owen's. Or she wanted it to be. Kellen didn't want it to be. He wanted his friend to have kids with someone he was in love with.

Also watching someone who looked so much like Sara pine for his best friend was a total mind fuck. Kellen would buy Lindsey a twenty-bedroom mansion in Hawaii if it meant he didn't have to see her looking all pregnant and beautiful and alive. But since he was waiting on a sandwich, he might as well sit down for now.

Kellen slid into the booth next to Owen. Owen glanced up to meet Kellen's eyes, his expression a mixture of fear, disgust, and desperation. He might be pretending that this thing with Lindsey wasn't affecting him, but Kellen saw through the pretense. He wanted to get Owen out of this jam, but he didn't know how. This wasn't just some overzealous groupie who could be dissuaded; there was a baby involved. A baby who needed a father. Any father—even a reluctant one—was better than no father at all.

"So what kind of work will you be looking for?" Kellen asked Lindsey.

"Something in banking," she said. She set a plate in front of Owen. "Assuming I can get a decent recommendation from my last employer." She brushed her bangs out of her face and held them back with one hand as she stared into nothingness. "We didn't exactly part on good terms. I sort of called her a frigid bitch."

"Thanks for the sandwich," Owen said quietly, not looking at her.

Yes, Owen, ignore the problem. That fixes everything.

While Lindsey was distracted with failing to gain Owen's attention, Jacob took her place at the counter to slap together more sandwiches.

As soon as Lindsey saw what he was doing, she grabbed him by one arm and shoved him into the booth across from Kellen and Owen. "Please, Shade, just give me this. Okay? I know it doesn't make up for much, but I have to contribute *something*."

"Will you just let the girl make you a sandwich?" Kellen said.

Owen hadn't touched his food yet and was texting faster than ever. Kellen snatched the phone out of his hand. "Your text can wait until you're done eating."

"Yes, Mommy," Owen said.

Owen glanced at Lindsey's back, turned a shade paler, and then reached for his sandwich. He took a small bite, as if worried she'd dosed it with a love potion. Owen really needed to talk about this. Kellen felt bad for having his phone off the night before and for keeping the topics of their earlier conversations all about himself.

"Hey, Lindsey," Kellen said, "could I get that sandwich to go? I forgot that Owen and I have somewhere we need to be in ten minutes."

"Sure," she said, offering Owen a disappointed glance.

"Where?" Jacob asked.

Kellen kicked him under the table. "You know. That *thing* we always do eight hours before a concert?"

"Masturbate?" Jacob said in all seriousness.

Kellen touched his fingertips to his forehead and shook his head in disbelief. Owen sniggered, then chuckled, and then burst into laughter as if Jacob had just delivered the greatest punch line of all time. Yeah, Kellen definitely needed to let the man vent. He was about to explode.

Lindsey opened a drawer in the tiny kitchen area and rummaged through the contents. "Are there any baggies around here?"

"Not since Adam went straight," Jacob said.

Owen laughed so hard, he was in danger of splitting both sides. Kellen slipped out of the booth and dragged Owen out behind him by the torn front of his shirt.

"Don't worry about wrapping it up," Kellen said, collecting his sandwich from Lindsey's hand. "I'll just carry it like this." He took a huge bite and smiled at her. "Thanks," he said with a full mouth. "I'm starving."

He made sure that Owen was carrying his sandwich before he shoved him toward the door. Kellen wasn't sure where he was taking Owen, but the bus was apparently the worst place for him at the moment.

"Do you need a ride to the hotel?" a man dressed in a black suit and tie asked as soon as they stepped off the bus.

"Yes," Kellen said. "We need to take our bags to our rooms."

"Is that the *thing* we always do eight hours before a concert?" Owen asked.

"No, we masturbate. Remember?"

Owen smiled and snapped his fingers. "Oh yeah. In the back of the limo. Hope you have some tissues in the back seat," he said to the limo driver, patting him hard on the shoulder.

Owen took a big bite of his sandwich and headed to the door that hid a baggage compartment under the bus.

"Don't worry," Kellen said to the stunned driver who visibly relaxed at Kellen's placation. "I'm sure he has his own supply of tissues in his bag."

"If not, I'll just use your shirt." Owen looked at Kellen and jerked, as if taken aback by his lack of shirt. "Where's your shirt, bro?"

"Where do you think, Jizz-o-matic Plus?"

"Sorry about that. We really need to stock up on more tissues."

When the driver was busy digging around in the trunk of the limo—probably for tissues—Owen and Kellen performed their secret victory handshake. Fucking with people was great fun. Owen had relaxed twenty-fold since they'd left Lindsey's company. So how exactly did he plan to put up with the chick for the next three months—and if the baby *did* turn out to be his, put up with her forever?

Owen yanked Kellen's overnight bag from the luggage compartment and handed it to him while he rummaged around for his own bag. By the time their baggage was in the limo's trunk, the driver was in a panic.

"It seems I'm out of tissues," he said.

"And I'm out of shirts," Kellen said.

"That's okay," Owen said to the driver. "I'll just use your sock. Hand it over."

Kellen knew it would give up their juvenile gig, but he couldn't help but laugh when the driver winced and then bent to remove his shoe.

"Dude!" Owen said, pounding the driver on the shoulder. "We're just fucking with you. I don't need your sock or a tissue."

The driver's shoulders sagged with relief.

"Kelly swallows."

Kellen slugged Owen half-heartedly and took another bite of his sandwich before sliding through the open back door of the limo.

"That was a joke too," he heard Owen say outside. "Lighten up a little, man."

"I apologize, sir," the driver said stiffly. "My regular passengers don't usually joke about such things."

"What do they joke about?"

"Uh, the stock market mostly, sir."

"Hmm, I'm afraid I'm not sophisticated enough to joke about the stock market, but I do know a joke about a donkey, three potatoes, and a sailor."

"Owen, get in the car," Kellen said. He was glad Owen was more himself now that they were out of Lindsey's presence, but he still wanted to have a serious conversation with him. If Owen ended up in an anus-and-fart-joke frame of mind, there was no way Kellen would be able to get him to have an adult discussion. He'd be too busy trying to make Kellen laugh.

Owen entered the car and sat next to Kellen. "Good sandwich," he said and took another bite. "Anything to drink in the minibar?"

Kellen opened the small fridge to his left and fished out a pair of beers. "Are you comfy?" Kellen asked him as he handed him a cold bottle.

Owen squirmed around in his seat. "Yep."

"Good. Start talking."

"About what?"

"What happened after I left last night?" Kellen opened the twist top on his beer and took a long drag.

Owen told him about Lindsey showing up unannounced and Caitlyn beating a trail out of there as fast as she could go.

"She was really upset," Owen said

"Because she likes you and she probably wonders how it can possibly work out between the two of you now that you have a baby on the way."

"I don't think it's mine," Owen said.

"Then why are you the one taking responsibility for it?"

"Because no one else would."

"So you had to stick your neck out and be the nice guy? Owen, sometimes you have to put yourself first."

"If you saw the look on Lindsey's face, you'd have done the same thing. She's better today. Last night, she had a complete emotional meltdown and everyone was treating her like she's toxic."

"And you're treating her like that today."

Owen winced. "I am? I'm not trying to. I just really don't want this to mess up things with Caitlyn. I should have gone after her last night, not let her walk away. I was just completely stunned that she took it so hard."

"Didn't her husband have an affair with a younger woman?"

Owen nodded. "Yeah, so? What does that have to do with anything?"

"Lindsey is younger. And hot. And very pregnant. Maybe Caitlyn felt threatened."

"She shouldn't. I haven't been able to think of anything but her all day. And I can't seem to stop texting her and calling her. She's going to think I'm a desperate loser."

"Because you are."

Owen's response was to slug Kellen in the arm.

"So how are you going to be with Caitlyn when Lindsey's around?" Kellen asked.

"I can be just friends with Lindsey."

"*You* can be just friends with a hot woman who wants you?"

"Yeah."

"Owen, if you really want to be with Caitlyn, you need to stay away from Lindsey as much as possible. She's vulnerable and interested and you're easy."

"I'm not easy."

Kellen lifted an eyebrow at him.

"Okay, I'm totally easy. But I don't have to be."

"So what are you going to do with Lindsey?"

"We'll get her a place to stay. Help her with medical bills and stuff. It's not like we can't afford it."

"Are we sure she's not just making up this whole thing so she can have a free place to stay?"

"You sound like Adam."

"He does have a lot of experience with mooches. His father, for instance."

"So what do you think we should do with her? We can't just toss her out in the street. And there is no way she's going on tour with us."

Kellen sighed. There really was no easy solution to the problem. "We can set her up in a place in her hometown."

"I mentioned that to her last night—tried to convince her that she'd be better off around her family and friends back home—and she cried for over an hour. Apparently her family has disowned her."

"Oh."

"I thought maybe my mom could keep an eye on her while we're on tour. You know what Mom's like. She loves these little charity cases."

Kellen knew exactly what Owen's mom was like. He'd been one of her charity cases, after all.

"Besides," Owen continued, "Mom's been bugging Chad for grandchildren ever since he proposed to Josie. Maybe this will get her off his case."

"Because she already has a grandchild on the way?"

"It's not mine. You were there. Was I wearing a condom?"

"Yeah."

"End of story."

Not necessarily, but Kellen figured it wouldn't do any good to argue about the baby's possible parentage. They'd just have to wait until this thing played out.

"So I guess you have this all figured out. You didn't need to talk to me about it after all."

"I always need to talk to you, Kelly. Seems I wasn't the only one who had an adventurous time last night. How'd you do at the house?"

Kellen shook his head. "I never went inside. I was out on the beach, trying to throw away that damned cuff you gave me, when I heard a piano melody that lifted me out of the depression that's been holding me under for five years."

"A song? Is that how you met Dawn? I wondered how you hooked up with her."

"She's renting the house next to mine while she works; she says the sea inspires her compositions. I knocked on her door so I could hear the song she was working on."

"And then you got busy with her." Owen slugged him in the thigh. "You stud."

"It was more than that. We talked and she shared her music with me and then…" Kellen winked at Owen. "*Then* I got busy with her."

"When are you going to see her again?" Owen asked.

"Never." It made his heart hurt to say it, but it had to be that way. There wasn't a woman alive who deserved to make do with what was left of his heart. And someone like Dawn deserved a man who could give her the moon and stars. Devote every piece of himself to her happiness. He just didn't have that much to give her. He'd already given it all to Sara.

"You're an idiot," Owen said.

"And *you're* the relationship master?"

"I don't deny that I suck at relationships," Owen said, "but at least I'm trying."

The limo pulled to a stop outside of the hotel. Kellen tossed his half-eaten sandwich into the seat and climbed out. He *had* tried. He'd opened himself up to Dawn faster than he'd let his guard down with anyone. Even Sara. Even Owen. But it just wouldn't work. And if he fell in love with another woman and she left him— on purpose or through no fault of her own—then Kellen didn't think he'd survive. How much of a heart did a man require to maintain a pulse? He was sure it was more than he had left to spare.

CHAPTER TWELVE

Kellen pretended to watch *I Love Lucy* reruns while he hid in a hotel room with most of his band. Adam was sketching realistic-looking boobs as he used the hotel phone to schedule some debauchery with his woman in New Orleans. Gabe was tinkering with the mechanisms of some crazy invention that had Kellen cocking his head in confusion—what in the hell *was* that thing? Owen fiddled with his cellphone the entire evening to prove once and for all that he was a desperate loser. Jacob had never made it to the hotel. Kellen could only guess what he and Lindsey were up to back on the bus. Probably picking out baby names.

By the time they were sitting in the limo and headed back to the stadium, Kellen was ready to climb out of his skin. Why had he told Owen to dispose of Sara's cuff? He had been fine without it when Dawn had been available to distract him, but now that he was alone with his thoughts, he found himself back in his ugly place. His very dark and oppressing ugly place. Should he call Dawn? He didn't have her number. Should he drive back to Galveston after their show in New Orleans? No, he was sure she never wanted to see him again. And in his note to her, he'd made it clear that he wasn't interested.

Except he *was* interested.

And he hated himself for the weakness.

"I'm going to punch you if you don't get out of your funk," Owen said. "I thought all your doom and gloom was caused by your lack of sex, but you got laid last night, so what gives?"

"You got laid last night?" Adam's dark eyebrows shot up toward his hairline.

"Yeah, by an elegant, classy, redheaded babe," Owen said.

"Were you there?" Adam asked.

Owen shook his head. "I Googled her."

Kellen sighed in exasperation. "I've told you a million times that my *funk*, as you call it, has little to do with sex."

"Then you must be doing it wrong," Gabe said and ran a hand along the row of red-tipped hair spiked down the middle of his head.

"Probably," Kellen said.

"If you need some inspiration, I could hook you up with some gadgets I… uh… *bought*," Gabe said.

"He doesn't need any gadgets." Owen said. "He's not seeing her again."

If Kellen hadn't been used to Owen spewing everyone's business all the time, he probably would have hit him. He was in that bad a mood.

"Nothing wrong with getting your rocks off and splitting as soon as you can get away," Adam said. "Before Madison, that was the only way I rolled."

Kellen didn't bother telling them that it wasn't like that. He hadn't actually wanted to leave Dawn. He'd felt that he'd had to, but his friends would probably take his denial as admittance. He'd rather not talk about last night or this morning and just forget about the whole thing. As if that were possible.

But he could *pretend* things were the same as they'd been for the past five years. They'd just think he was being moody.

At the stadium, several security guards escorted them inside. The backstage area was packed. The band was supposed to be entertaining a large group of VIPs. Luckily, most of them wanted to hang around with their lead singer, Jacob, who had no problem keeping two dozen women enthralled. The dudes in the crowd immediately surrounded either Adam—their guitar hero—or Gabe—the man behind the skins. Kellen was grateful that he went relatively unnoticed as he snuck past the crowd on his way to the dressing room. He had his eyes trained on the sign that said "Band members only. No guests."

"Kellen!" someone yelled from the crowd behind him.

He froze. He knew that voice.

"Wait!"

Some kind of bizarre reverse psychology had him jogging toward the dressing room. Just before he stepped over the threshold into the safe zone, a hand caught his arm.

He took a deep breath and turned slowly to face her. Best get this over with.

He searched Dawn's face for clues. What was she doing here? He backed into the dressing room. And guest or not, she followed him inside and closed the door behind her.

Dawn pressed a crumpled wad of paper into Kellen's chest. Her eyes were alight with passion and fire.

She was the most beautiful thing he'd ever seen.

"A Dear *Dawn* letter?" she spat at him. "We share the most amazing night of my life, and you leave me with nothing but a Dear Dawn letter?"

He was at a loss. Didn't she understand that leaving that way had been the kindest thing he could have done for her?

"Take it back," she demanded, shoving the paper harder into his chest. "Take it back, Kellen!"

He took the wad of paper from her hand, basking in the heat of her fury, blooming in her light. She was his fire. His Dawn.

"Did last night mean nothing to you?"

"It meant everything to me," he said. And now that she was here, in all her radiant glory, he couldn't deny it. He couldn't deny her. He couldn't deny himself.

"Then why did you leave? Why, Kellen?" Her voice cracked, and she might as well have taken a hammer and chisel to his heart.

"Because," he said breathlessly. "Because I'll never have enough to give. I'll never be enough. You deserve more than me, Dawn. *Better* than me. You deserve someone who can love you with everything he is, was, or will become. And I... I already gave that to someone else."

"You don't get to decide that, Kellen Jamison," she said, her eyes narrowed dangerously.

He fought the urge to drag her into his arms and kiss her silent.

"Who I deserve is up to me, not you. I say you're enough for me—you're more than enough—so you are. If you don't feel anything for me, that's different; I'll let you go if you want to go. But if you do feel something and the only reason you left is for *my* sake, I won't stand for it. Do you understand? Walking away from me does not save me heartache, Kellen. It causes it."

He looked away, wanting to believe they could be together or at least give it a Herculean effort, but he knew in his heart that he couldn't make her happy. And more than anything, he wanted her to be happy. He never wanted to dampen her light or extinguish her fire. He couldn't stomach the thought of doing that to her.

Her fingertips pressed over his pounding heart, and he wanted to push her hand away, wanted to turn his back on her, wanted to flee, but his fucking legs had forgotten how to move.

"Look me in the eye, Kellen, and tell me you don't want to be with me, and I'll leave."

He forced himself to meet her phenomenal hazel eyes and opened his mouth to tell her to get lost for her own damned good, but his tongue was in total disagreement with his common sense.

"Nothing would make me happier than to be with you, Dawn O'Reilly."

Her eyes lit up with hope. "Nothing?"

It was a loaded question, and he took a moment to contemplate it. Was there anything or anyone—living or dead—that made him happier than he was in this woman's arms? The answer was surprisingly easy. He didn't have to compare his time with Dawn to anything in his past, he just had to let himself enjoy her in the here and now. That was what was important. There was nothing wrong with loving Sara forever as long as he made a little room for someone new in his heart. With time, that little room might accommodate more, until he could let Dawn be his everything. But for now, at least they had someplace to start. Kellen's emotional doom clouds scattered before Dawn's radiance, his defenses crumbled, and he smiled at her. Really smiled. So wide it made his face hurt.

"Nothing," he said in all sincerity.

"Good," she said, "because I'm not above tying you to my bed until you come to your senses, Kellen Jamison."

Lord, how he admired the fire in her.

He laughed, and it didn't feel forced. It felt good.

"I could teach you a thing or two about tying a person to your bed," he teased.

"I don't want a person tied to my bed," she said, stepping close, so that only inches separated their bodies. "Just you. And I'd rather not have to resort to restraining you. I prefer you free."

He preferred that as well. Even if it proved a very slow process to free him of the bonds that held him back, he was ready to be untied.

Kellen wrapped his arms around Dawn and drew her against him, claiming her mouth in a slow, deep kiss. A part of him still struggled with finding intimacy with a woman who wasn't Sara.

Another part of him was shouting that kissing Dawn O'Reilly, *adoring* her, was wrong. But the best part of him told those other two parts to fuck off.

When they separated, he cupped her lovely face in both hands and just stared. He was so glad she'd had the courage to fight for this because he'd needed that little push to help see what was right in front of him.

"Say, Rockstar," she asked, "what are you doing after the show?"

"Hopefully just one thing."

"What's that?"

"You."

She nodded. "Yeah, I could go for that. And what are you doing tomorrow?"

"Going to New Orleans."

"Are you planning to run away from me again?"

"No. I thought maybe you'd like to come with me."

She smiled and kissed his lips gently. "Yeah, I could go for that too, Kellen."

"You can call me Kelly."

She tilted her head and stared straight into his soul, which always seemed to warm under her attention. "Yeah, you do look like a Kelly."

Good, because he felt like one.

ABOUT THE AUTHOR

Combining her love for romantic fiction and rock 'n roll, Olivia Cunning writes erotic romance centered around rock musicians. Raised on hard rock music from the cradle, she attended her first Styx concert at age six and fell instantly in love with live music. She's been known to travel over a thousand miles just to see a favorite band in concert. As a teen, she discovered her second love, romantic fiction -- first, voraciously reading steamy romance novels and then penning her own. Growing up as the daughter of a career soldier, she's lived all over the country and overseas. She currently lives in Galveston, Texas. To learn more about Olivia and her books, please visit www.oliviacunning.com.

CPSIA information can be obtained at www.ICGtesting.com
Printed in the USA
LVOW12s1753240614

391480LV00018B/468/P

9 781939 276100